Praise

Adventures on the Wine Route

"One of the pleasantest and truest books about wine I've ever read."
—M. F. K. Fisher

"Kermit Lynch's colorful portraits of some idiosyncratic vintners, and his commentaries on their wines, make for some of the finest reading since Joseph Wechsberg ate and drank his way through France in his book *Blue Trout and Black Truffles*." —Robert M. Parker, Jr.,
The Wine Advocate

"I am simply thrilled by it. I am bowled over by his blend of poetry and candor. What heaven-sent common sense." —Hugh Johnson

"Quirky, opinionated, maddening, hilarious . . . riveting, illuminating, totally original . . . Strongly recommended." —Clive Coates

"In Kermit Lynch's small, true, delightful book there is more understanding about what wine really is than in everything else I have read."
—Victor Hazan

"A great overview and tour through French wines . . . [Lynch] has helped push my thinking a little about what wines to buy . . . Fascinating."
—Otis Chandler, cofounder of Goodreads

"Kermit's book changed my thinking about wine. Colorful encounters with larger-than-life personalities, the primacy of the land and authenticity, plus a good dose of humorous anecdotes to keep you entertained. This book deserves to stay in print forever!"
—Alice Waters

"*Adventures on the Wine Route* is the best book I've ever read about wine. Kermit Lynch is as brilliant a writer as he is a taster, and his quest for authentic wine is more relevant than ever."

—Jay McInerney

"When one enters a bookstore nowadays and goes to the section reserved for books about wine, one is overwhelmed by how immensely it has grown. In this jungle where obsolescence is rampant, only a very few will become classics. *Adventures on the Wine Route* is surely one of them—a quarter of a century old and not one wrinkle! The author's prose, his lyrical descriptions, his enthusiasm—not to mention his unique experiences along 'his' wine route—awill delight, instruct, and cast an indelible spell on readers for years to come."

—Aubert and Pamela de Villaine

"One of the finest American books on wine."   —Eric Asimov, *The New York Times*

"Lynch's quest to find talented French winemakers made him one of the best-known wine importers in the country and the progenitor of an entire genre of books . . . *Adventures on the Wine Route* remains the gold standard of the genre for a very good reason."   —Lettie Teague, *The Wall Street Journal*

22 October 2025

To Mary,
Happy birthday and
here's to many more adventures
in Provence & elsewhere!,
Marguerite xxx

AT
POUPON'S
TABLE

AT POUPON'S TABLE

A NOVEL

KERMIT LYNCH

Podium

Cover design by Elizabeth Yaffe

ISBN: 979-8-89539-832-6

Published in 2025 by Podium Publishing
www.podiumentertainment.com

Podium

This work of fiction is dedicated to the memory of Lulu Peyraud from Bandol's Domaine Tempier where, in 1977, I showed up speaking little French. Lulu enveloped me into her world—her gigantic hospitality, unforgettable culinary skills, rollicking sense of humor, a capacity for fine wines, and an appetite for good old-fashioned fun. (After Lulu, Kermit weren't a hermit no more.)

But with all that, Lulu was quite bookish and early on presented me with *Ma Provence en Cuisine*, authored by Charles Blavette, one of Marcel Pagnol's band of Provencal actors. My French wasn't up to it then, but decades later I noticed it on a shelf and was swept away, dazzled by how it depicted everyday life in Provence back in the day. It inspired me to write this novel.

Of course it is dedicated to Lulu. She's not in it, but it wouldn't exist without her.

AT
POUPON'S
TABLE

CHAPTER ONE

On the first Monday of April 2006, Kendrick Thomas was preparing to leave his home outside Le Caniveau in Provence for a flight to Alsace, in what is nowadays the northeastern corner of France instead of the southwestern corner of Germany. In other words, from France's Mediterranean bottom to its Teutonic top. He would be on the same day's late flight back, so there was not much to prepare, other than himself. A morning cup of coffee in hand, with the other he parted strands of his cork mosquito curtain and stepped out from the kitchen onto the terrace. As the sun rose in the east, a vast, profusely blue sky deepened overhead, cloudless, unless you counted the three vapor trails from planes evidently heading south to Africa. During his many departures—business trips mostly—there was always at least a glimmer of anticipation and adventure edged with some regret at leaving his country home and hearth. He had no inkling of the trap set for this outing.

In fact, he was thinking about Alsace's heroic gastronomic concoction, *choucroute garnie*, which to Kendrick's way of thinking is to cuisine what Beethoven's Fifth Symphony is to music. Storm the barricades, shake your fist at indigestion, let loose thunderous timpani and stentorian brass. What other meal delivered such culinary bombast? Well, cassoulet? *Peut être.*

Choucroute is French for "sauerkraut," originally a German word, but if you were born Alsatian, you had a third language and a third word for it: *sürkrüt*. Kendrick could only guess at its pronunciation—those four floating dots stumped him and mangled his tongue. Two umlauts in one short word? He told himself to remember to ask about it during his tasting with Martin Dreissen, a native Alsatian vintner, simply for curiosity's sake.

Unless he was victim of a traffic jam, Kendrick's French home was an hour's drive from the Marseille-Provence airport, and from there what might look like a short hop to Alsace on Air France. But no, there was more to it than that. Kendrick was used to the ever-present airport parking mess, the security lines five years after the fall of the Twin Towers, then he would have a one hour fifteen-minute flight to the Mulhouse-Basel airport (one foot in Switzerland, the other in France), rent a car, then a forty-minute drive to his destination just outside Bergheim.

He'd reserved a window seat on an early morning flight, fourth row, and as he scooted into it, he wondered when was the last time the fake leather upholstery had enjoyed a good cleaning. Tattered in one spot, blotchy . . . Someone had stuck tape on a tear to act as a bandage. He hoped the aircraft's maintenance crew was more diligent than the cabin cleaners.

Oh well. His mind returned to contemplating the sumptuous *choucroute garnie*, one of France's favorite gastronomic triumphs. *Choucroute garnie* equals garnished sauerkraut. Once upon a time, cabbage was fermented in order to render it more digestible, less acidic, its flavors deeper and more delicious. It was adorned with multiple kinds of sausages and cuts of pork, like smoked ham. He'd once dated an Alsatian medical student and had asked her if her family might have their own recipe for the traditional *choucroute garnie*. She showed up with eleven single-spaced typewritten pages that detailed instructions for making four kinds of sausage from scratch, and three cuts of pork, all of which garnished the fermented cabbage. Nowadays it has become almost impossible to find such a traditional *choucroute carnie*. Even in the heart of Alsace, the dish is often nothing more than *Boiled Weenie on Canned Cabbage*, and such a naked example of culinary collapse pained Kendrick. The story was, however, no different from the story of *bouillabaisse* in Provence, which in today's Marseille can mean nothing more than a hunk of thawed-out fish floating in canned fish stock. He mourned when he read that 80 percent of restaurants in France no longer even cook: They simply defrost, microwave, or open a can. Why did it matter so much? Because more than anything, Kendrick valued beauty, and during his lifetime so far, he feared the world contained less and less of it.

On his earliest wine buying trip to Alsace, he had tasted in the ancient wine cellars of Jean-Luc Meyer in Eguisheim, near Colmar. Meyer was a middle-aged man with admirable posture. He wore a tasteful gray suit and forest green tie. Office wear. Not what vignerons wear outdoors working their vines. His calm eyes never left Kendrick's, which was not at all unnerving. He poured tastes of over thirty different wines, then afterward, instead of sending the young American novice away with a price list and a handshake, Meyer asked if he had plans for lunch. "Today we are celebrating my family's two hundred and fiftieth year in the wine business," he said. "There will be plenty of *choucroute garnie* for lunch in our next-door cellar, and one chair has turned up empty, if you care to fill it." Kendrick thanked his lucky tastevin and accepted. The extravagant lunch was prepared by a chef from the nearby three-star restaurant, l'Auberge de Lille, and when Kendrick stepped inside, he recognized that he would be at a table—a massive, dark, carved wooden table—with a roster of food and wine royalty. He noticed the tallest man first and for a moment thought he was dining with Charles de Gaulle, then realized it was Paul Bocuse without his white chef's toque. Then his eyes landed on Alain Chapel and André Pic. He counted twenty-nine at table, so he was the thirtieth. After foie gras on toast with Champagne, Meyer invited everyone to take their seats, clapped his hands three times, and all turned to watch as arched double doors—broad enough to accommodate the giant Alsatian wine casks as they entered or left the cellar—swung wide open. First to enter, two grinning, rosy-cheeked, pigtailed young blonde girls walking side by side and dressed in bridesmaid white, then two teenage boys wearing lederhosen and T-shirts emblazoned with the number two hundred fifty. The youngsters' task was to drag into the dining room an antique wooden wagon heaped high with an immense tangle of steaming sauerkraut that appeared to be writhing in ecstasy, adorned with glistening roasted sausages, pink hunks of ham, and various other cuts of pork. A sensational gastronomic entrance. Then came green bowls of boiled potatoes and blue bowls of creamy yellow mustard. The aromatic complex included juniper berry and clove.

With such a feast, Kendrick had expected a famous old vintage to be served, probably a Riesling from a notable vineyard, and he wondered how dry or sweet a wine Meyer would select to best accompany the monumental wagonload of *choucroute*. He was amazed when pitchers of a young, light yellowish white wine appeared.

Once everyone had a glass of it at hand, Jean Meyer raised his. "We have an American wine merchant with us," he announced, "who might never before have encountered an Alsatian Edelzwicker." He looked at Kendrick. "Monsieur Thomas, *edel* in German means 'noble' in English, and *zwicker* means 'blend.' Yesterday I blended this from noble grape varieties specifically to accompany this *choucroute garnie* on this very special occasion. Here's to my predecessors, to my branch of the Meyer family tree, two and one half centuries in the vineyards and in this very same cellar." With that, all raised their glasses toward the huge-beamed ceiling before downing a sip.

How noble was it of Monsieur Meyer extending an invitation to a green young wine merchant far from home whose French was perhaps a trifle ignoble? No problem. Kendrick found himself seated between a handsomely attired and groomed member of the Krug family from Champagne and a casually dressed, bearded *tonnelier* who produced wine casks—both spoke English.

Now, many visits to Alsace later, he periodically put his *Herald Tribune* aside to look down at the landscape and try to figure out where he was. Much of his flight followed the vast, methodical Rhône River. He recognized Arles, and north of Arles the vineyards of Tavel, where only rosé wines are produced. Then came the stony plateau where the grapes of Châteauneuf-du-Pape produced bold reds with a chewy texture. He recognized the rocky serrations of the Dentelles de Montmirail near Gigondas, where the grenache grape thrives. A few minutes later the large, boring city of Valence came into view, followed by the vine-covered massif known as l'Hermitage—Kendrick could not help but think of those down below who toiled to care for the vines (all Syrah grapes for the reds, by the way) and transform the grapes into wine. Might there be a winemaker as yet undiscovered who had the savvy to realize the site's legendary potential? Bottles of Hermitage are hard to come by—there are only 345 acres of vines producing wines there. Finding great bottles of it, well, that fit Kendrick's job description, because he was an importer of fine, artisanal wines.

If you happened to be on the same aircraft, in row three directly in front of him, you might have scarcely been aware of Kendrick's foot against the bottom of your seat, tapping to music only he could hear. It was nothing obnoxious, merely a musical tic. And Kendrick himself was not conscious of it, but he was tapping time to an ancient song that went back centuries titled "Banks of the Ohio" in its contemporary version. He had listened to it the previous evening, comparing different renditions recorded by various artists, and in his head he was reliving one beautiful collaboration sung by Doc Watson accompanied by the great Bill Monroe on mandolin. And if you'd turned in your seat and looked for the source of the gentle 4/4 rhythm, you'd have seen Kendrick Thomas on his way to work. While in his earliest youth, Kendrick's hair was considered blonde; by the age of five it had turned sandy; and by the time of this flight north, entering his late forties, Mother Nature had blended some salt and pepper into the sand. His beard was similarly colored but also showed a subtle reddish tint in the sunlight.

As a rule, Kendrick dressed casual. All the time. No matter what. His leanings had been solidified years before when he met the celebrated French restaurateur Jean Dugras in Paris one day. *Time* magazine had invited the two of them to lunch at Le Taillevent for an interview about the state of the French wine market while the dollar was so weak. Kendrick unearthed his only suit—a blue suit—and purchased a burgundy-colored tie for the occasion, figuring such attire was the only way to get in the front door of the famed gastronomic palace. Jean Dugras, however, showed up in black leather pants and the classiest black leather motorcycle jacket Kendrick had ever seen— a tasteful amount of silver zippers and buttons. They were ushered to a prominent table without a word about Jean's lack of suit and tie, and Kendrick could not help noticing that several interesting-looking women kept their eyes on Dugras as he passed. After dinner, Kendrick left his tie on the back seat of his taxi and hadn't suffered another one since.

Later that year, he'd accepted an invitation to dine with Dugras at his family's own three-star restaurant somewhat south of Burgundy. The two of them ate in the kitchen surrounded by a handsome battery of professional chefs, all wearing their white toques. Jean himself prepared chunks of black truffle in eggs and butter. The eggs weren't scrambled—they were caressed with a wooden spoon as lovingly as humanly possible. To Kendrick, the recipe looked like one-third truffle, one-third eggs, one-third butter—generously salted. And to accompany his *brouillade*, Jean, with an elegant *whhht*, eased out the cork of a thirty-year-old bottle of Santenay Rouge. It all confirmed to Kendrick that the most ravishing cuisine need not be the most complicated, that suit-and-tie is not a sign of class, and reconfirmed that a great bottle does not always wear a famous label.

As for his current Alsatian visit, he had requested a ten a.m. appointment at Domaine Dreissen with the hope of being invited to dine (after he'd tasted through samples of the new vintage) on Grandma Dreissen's incomparable, old-fashioned Alsatian cooking. Kendrick had imported their wines for well over two decades. As for quality, no one in the picturesque region had a better reputation or enjoyed stronger sales in the good ol' USA. Standing in front of the Dreissen's massive, centuries-old wooden door, Kendrick wondered how many times over the years he had lifted the same weighty iron door knocker to announce his arrival. Above the door, engraved in stone: 1439, the building's birth date. He glanced at his watch. Ten minutes late. After two reverberating thumps on the door, it was opened not by Martin, the Dreissen currently in charge of the wine domaine, but by his wife, Madame Dreissen to Kendrick. Yes, the lovely Madame Dreissen, who was smiling her careful smile between two diamond-clustered earrings. Kendrick looked her over. Her blonde hair must have been coiffed minutes before he knocked. Her silvery brocade dress fit her shape so well it practically begged to be caressed. Her necklace, bracelet, wristwatch—rings too glittery to count—our Kendrick felt like he was in the presence of the Queen of Alsace, although she lacked and longed for a crown.

The ancient door led one to expect a dark, stonewalled, medieval interior, almost crypt-like, but it was far from that. There was no tribute to the Dreissen past, no sepia prints, nothing weighty. The salon was paved with pink-and-white checkerboard tiles made of what looked like raw-cut unpolished marble. *Pink* was, in fact, the only word for half the tiles, but this pink needed an adjective. Normally, it was not a color Kendrick would have chosen. Normally, he would have scoffed at the very idea, but in his lifetime, he'd never seen such a noble pink.

"Oh, Kendrick," she began, whispering fondly, "you're always so prompt. You can't imagine what we suffer with most of our clients. We wait and wait. Sometimes as much as an hour or two, and as often as not they arrive after a previous tasting, barely standing up straight. I'll bet you anything they don't even spit while they're tasting. When it's free of charge, they cannot bear *not* swallowing. Pitiful. If only we could charge by the swallow for our tastings. In fact, I'm going to look into that."

She liked speaking English whenever she could, and her English was impeccable. Unlike Kendrick, she spoke with an English accent. Educated, of course. None of the *Blimey, mate* for her.

"Martin is just looking after a problem in the cellar, the refrigeration unit or something like that, so let's have a chat."

A chat with Madame Dreissen. Kendrick wished he'd worn a suit of armor.

She began with her two children, how incredibly gifted they were proving to be after having started out terribly—practically brain-dead until she whipped them into shape—how the weather during the previous harvest was abominable and everyone in Alsace made lousy wines except . . . guess who? Also the backbreaking taxes and social charges in France that ate up any profit, and on top of all that, they'd had to fire a woman who had worked in their office for thirty years, and the nasty bitch had had the gall to sue them.

"You know, dear Kendrick, we are working to preserve the Dreissen tradition for the love of it and nothing more, because even at our prices—I know, I know, some say the highest in Alsace—we make no profit. None at all. It is all eaten up here and there until I don't know what we'll do. I worry about Martin. He's an artist, not a business-man. I have to take care of the books and finances, and I don't know if we'll still be here next year. We'd live like kings if we just closed our doors and sold our priceless vineyard holdings. Martin would have a collapse, though, I'm sure. How could he meet the gaze of his uncle and all those ancestors who slowly developed Domaine Dreissen until it stands head and shoulder—isn't that the phrase?—above all the rest? You know it better than anyone because you've spread the word and contributed ceaselessly. But, Kendrick"—she sniffed—"Kendrick, my god, we have to take action together, both you and me, so Martin can continue in the vineyard and cellar to produce his masterpieces. You do see what's at risk?"

"My god, I hope it's not as bad as all that," Kendrick said with emo-tion. "But things are rough on my end, too. When you put together the new prices you sent me, the dollar plunging against the euro, the possibility of an economic recession . . . It's not easy."

"Kendrick, if you don't step in, we'll go bankrupt!"

Kendrick almost said *Well, you could sell some of your jewelry*, but he cleared his throat instead before saying forcefully, "You should try to understand, Madame Dreissen, I'm not sure I *can* help. I started working with Martin's uncle, Frederic, and at the beginning he had only a handful of vineyards. With our success in the Ameri-can market, he began adding choice vineyard sites to your holdings, and Martin has continued the expansion and the construction of your fabulous new winery. I've sold millions of dollars' worth of Domaine Dreissen in the US, and not once have I been a day late with a payment. I expanded the market, it's true. No other Alsatian domaine has come close to the numbers we've done, but you know as well as I do, we had a lot of help from Robert Parker's enthusiastic wine reviews. He's the greatest salesman the wine world has ever known, but he's no longer writing about Alsace. And not once have you heard me quibble about the endless price increases . . . until now. The market is changing, and I don't know what more I can do to help except possibly buy and drink all your production myself, because the clientele is no longer clamoring for increasingly expensive wines."

"Are you through? I'll tell you what you can do," she said. "From now on you will ship your yearly allocation in one fell swoop—yes, all at once—one delivery per year. Ship it to New York, Los Angeles, wherever you please, and distribute throughout the US from there."

"But if I agree to that, the transportation costs will make the price of your wines even higher."

"We can no longer waste our time with these different shipments all over the map. You can't imagine the logistics of all that, the godawful clutter it causes."

"I don't have to imagine it. It's the same from my end."

"So, you see. We'll both save time."

Kendrick was shocked at the audacity of this proposition. She, however, spoke as calmly as if she were offering marmalade on toast.

"And," she concluded, "you're going to pay for everything in advance from now on, before the wines depart."

Kendrick nearly asked if she'd lost her mind, but just at that moment her husband, Martin, strode largely through the doorway as if he were entering a miniature house. He and Kendrick no longer talked business—throughout the years, the Queen of Alsace had taken over that role. Martin gripped Kendrick's suddenly minuscule hand within his vast paw, but somehow or another it turned out to be painless. A gentle giant, bubbling over with enthusiasm. Blue eyes glittering, he seemed glad to see Kendrick.

"Sorry to be late. There was a technological problem with the airconditioning down in the cellar. It's working now, but come, let's get my car. I've got something incredible to show you before lunch."

What Martin wanted to show Kendrick turned out to be two *grand cru* vineyard sites. *Grand cru* vines supposedly make the finest wines, and the land, when it trades hands, is expensive. They climbed out of Martin's comfy baby blue Mercedes station wagon and walked up a steep hillside through the vines.

"This parcel is planted in Riesling and Pinot Gris," Martin said. "All old vines. From them we'll be able to produce the finest dessert wines in Alsace. Every year the noble rot settles in here earlier than anywhere else. I promise you, Kendrick, we'll be the Château d'Yquem of Alsace. Next, I'll show you the other *grand cru*, which is planted in Gewurztraminer and Pinot Blanc. The soil promises wines of great charm, irresistible wines."

"Are you renting the two vineyards?"

"Can you believe it? Both came up for sale this year. Now they are ours."

"You bought them?"

"Isn't that great?"

"But, Martin, I thought you were having financial difficulties."

"Oh sure, but when land like this comes up for sale, you don't say no."

"But how will you pay for them?"

"Oh, I don't worry about that. They'll pay for themselves. But, Kendrick"—Martin focused his eyes and gazed intensely into Kendrick's—"I promise you one thing. I'll make wines so good, your customers won't be able to resist. You'll see."

Right, we'll see, Kendrick was thinking. *Or maybe not.* To pay for everything in advance, he would have to put up what he owned as collateral, borrow money when each vintage appeared, and pay interest on the loan. And Martin claiming that Kendrick's customers wouldn't be able to resist? They already were, in droves. Martin's uncle had always revealed a welcome streak of humility, grateful that his wines were appreciated, but Kendrick feared that for the current generation, success had gone to their heads. You succeed, you receive praise in the media, and you start believing you are a talent, an artist, a genius— which is never good for your wines, your business, or your friendships. You believe you inhabit a sphere above the rest of us run-of-the-mill mortals. When you develop a *grosse tête*, Kendrick was convinced, you can't see what's really going on, as if conceit has swollen your eyes shut.

Back at the domaine, they went directly to table. Gramma Dreissen's *baeckeoffe* was sensational, but Kendrick was still digesting the implications of everything that had transpired. The piping hot terrine dish had been sealed with what looked like pie dough. When the browned crust was cracked open, he could see chunks of pork, lamb, beef, and potatoes bubbling away in a creamy wine sauce. For

Kendrick, however, the aroma that escaped didn't even make his mouth water. He was too busy realizing that there had been no tasting through Dreissen's new wines, the 2005s, which was the only reason he'd flown up north in the first place. It had to be their way of telling him that there would be no doing business as usual until he agreed to their impossible new terms.

CHAPTER TWO

Long live Provence, where the sacred hour of the midday aperitif was approaching and thirst was almost tangible, sweeping across the landscape like the shadows of fast-moving clouds. Kendrick liked thirst and quenching it. In fact, that was his métier, his wildly aromatic métier.

After locking his doors, he walked down the elegantly curved stone stairway to a small gravel parking area in front of his house. Dressed in black shorts and an orange T-shirt that announced WINETASTERS DO IT TASTEFULLY, he strapped himself into his little black Renault Modus, a car that he'd once described as an automotive version of Soviet architecture. He had plans for lunch, which meant heading downhill from his vine-covered property. Its landscape of olive, cypress, and fig trees is so common thereabouts that the locals take it for granted. Not Kendrick. He did not know why, but the visuals created strong emotions in him, especially if a slice of the blue Mediterranean was included in the mix. In fact, the first time he visited the Bandol vineyards, looking for good wines, he'd remained a week longer than intended, and when he finally drove away, leaving behind the glorious landscape, it had such an emotional pull on him, he could not keep his eyes from tearing. The soundtrack in his head was playing the Beatles's tearjerker "Eleanor Rigby," complete with sawing cellos. On this bright summer day, however, there were no tears. He was on his way to have lunch with one of his favorite people and the weather was perfect, the sky a deeper blue than usual, and the sea off in the distance an even darker shade, creating a remarkable contrast.

Leaving Le Caniveau, Kendrick had to navigate not one, not two, but three of France's ever more plentiful traffic circles. He took the second exit of the third circle, crossed the bridge over the crowded six-lane autoroute, and drove uphill about two hundred yards past the local cooperative winery, its parking lot crowded with buyers on a budget. The road there was lined by plane trees, then by a row of olive trees, and finally grapevines filled in the rest of the space up to the first houses of the medieval village, l'Estournel d'Azur. Kendrick, however, turned left onto a narrow, paved road through even more vineyards. After about five hundred yards, he reached a sign engraved in stone: DOMAINE DU VIEUX LAURIER, HENRI POUPON.

Everyone called him Poupon. He was waiting for Kendrick under the cool shade of a leafy mulberry tree, feeding his fish in a swimming pool–sized rectangular stone basin in front of his house and winery. Four brown-and-white hunting dogs were sprawled out waiting with him. Kendrick remained in the car for a moment, looked Poupon over, and a question crossed his mind. Could anyone look more Provençal than Poupon? If filmmaker Marcel Pagnol had produced a boxing film, he could have cast Poupon as a Provençal Rocky Marciano. He looked bigger than he was—a husky chest, thick upper arms and shoulders, big hands with fingers like bananas. And what a mug—clay-colored, porous, meaty, with heavy eyebrows, a thick, flattened nose, and crinkled ears. Kendrick wondered, maybe Poupon really had been a boxer. The nose and ears said so. Poupon's gray eyes shone brightly, but they turned somber in a flash if something happened to displease him.

Kendrick climbed out of his car as Poupon greeted him. "*Bonjour, mon ami.* How's it going?"

"It's going well enough, but I'm thirsty." He glanced at his Swatch. "It's almost noon, and my stomach's already growling for attention."

Poupon took Kendrick in a half embrace and slapped him on the back a couple of times. "When things aren't going well, you don't feel hungry, right? But you can feel thirsty all the same. Well, how shall we get started? White or rosé?"

Such an innocent question, isn't it, to almost anyone else, but Kendrick was Poupon's importer *and* close friend, and the truth was, while he liked Poupon's rustic reds, the white and rosé bugged him. Enologically correct, lifeless, soulless rosé robots. You've tasted one, you've tasted them all. Sometimes he wondered if he should shut up, evolve with the times, but he questioned whether evolving was always progress. Modern enological wines left him cold and never touched what he called, for lack of a better word, one's soul. Therefore, trying to be polite, he answered Poupon's white or rosé offer by saying, "I know your white and rosé by heart, but don't you have a bunch of bottles—gifts from friends and clients? Maybe you even buy wine once in a while. Isn't there something there that might capture our interest?"

"We won't know until I pull the cork, right? You can't judge a wine by looking at its label, and anyone who doesn't know that hasn't been paying attention."

"Poupon, what an acute observation. You should write a song about it." Kendrick was thinking of the old Muddy Waters song "You Can't Judge a Book by Looking at Its Cover," but Poupon looked puzzled.

"Are you kidding? I don't even listen to music. Me, write a song? That's about as likely as me jumping into the sack with that cranky old witch up at the *tabac*."

"You're the one kidding me. And now you're trying to tell me you're picky about women? I'd have thought for a macho guy like you, any port in a storm." In his far-from-perfect French Kendrick had said, "*N'import quel port dans un horage.*"

This is a popular game in Provence—men and only men get a kick out of trying to out-insult each other. Women do not seem to be bitten by the same bug. Kendrick and Poupon were developing the game to a high art, or maybe it is more appropriate to call it a very low one. A successful sally forth has the victim laughing, too. Kendrick was not born to it, but he enjoyed the constant give-and-take with Poupon. A jab symbolically below the belt was considered great fun, and to denigrate the size of your close pal's weenie, well, it was all in the game.

"What are you talking about now?" Poupon asked. "What storm? Which port? Bandol?"

"Oh, you know what I mean, Poupon, you're out in a boat, a storm kicks up, and you've got to find a safe place—any safe place will do—to anchor and wait it out."

"Ah, *n'importe quel abri dans une tempête*. Is that it?"

"That's it exactly."

"But what does a boat have to do with that loony woman at the *tabac*?" Poupon asked. He looked Kendrick up and down and chuckled. "Hey, what gives here? Are you going to Saint-Tropez after lunch?"

"No. Why?"

"It looks like you're dressed for the Côte d'Azur." Poupon laughed at what he considered his joke—as if Kendrick were the type to head off to Saint-Tropez to mix with the in-crowd—then asked, "What's that say? There on your T-shirt?"

"Poupon, even in French, you'd never understand."

"Try me."

"It means *un goûteûr de vin fait l'amour avec du goût*."

Poupon thought about it. "If she screams with joy at the end, does that count as tasteful or distasteful? Oops, I see that you still look thirsty." He stood up, saying that someone had recently given him a bottle of Chablis, then sauntered off sockless in his dusty leather work boots to find it. A breeze fluttered the green and silver leaves of Poupon's nearby olive trees, but Kendrick, more than a little frustrated, gritted his pearly whites as Poupon disappeared inside his front door. The failure of his Muddy Waters and any-port-in-a-storm comments being understood in French bugged him. He felt like his success at repartee was limited by his lack of language skills. The fact that he dropped out of French A1 in college in order to read Hölderlin and Thomas Mann in their original German—that was one of his most consequential mistakes, but of course, how could he have known back then that his career would involve speaking French? In the meantime, his wine French was fine. He'd learned it, after all, in wine cellars, and wine has a way of loosening one's tongue.

A little later, the two of them stood at the stone barbecue where Poupon liked to cook. They swirled the white wine around in their glasses. Each sniffed, sort of grunted, took a sip, mulled that over, then downed a swallow.

Poupon's nose and forehead crinkled up like an accordion. "Ouch! My god, Kendrick, that stuff's so sharp you could shave with it."

"Not at all. It's normal for a Chablis to show some acidity. I'll bet if I served a glass of your white to a winemaker in Chablis, he'd say it lacks acidity."

"Well, then, his palate would be up his ass."

Poupon tossed the golden-green Chablis out onto the ground. "Lemme grab a bottle of the same vintage of my white. We'll taste them side by side. Compare them."

They discussed the two whites until the fire of vine trunks was ready—the acidity, the malolactic fermentation, sulfur dioxide, sterile filtration, enologists—Poupon faithful to his own Provençal white while Kendrick stuck with what he considered to be a mediocre Chablis.

Poupon threw various chunks of red meat onto the grill and went to his wine cellar again for a bottle of red. Kendrick considered Poupon a red wine kind of guy. Red is macho. White and rosé? Well, most Bandol domains seem to believe they have to have them, so they're the result of a marketing decision that does not quite coincide with Poupon's personality. When he returned, Poupon nodded at the grill and asked, "You know what we've got there?"

"What is it, rabbit?"

"No, it's hare. Once in a while, I'll draw a bead on one in the vineyard. They're rare nowadays. They have a wilder flavor than rabbit, and of course nothing to do with those white-meat bunnies you buy at a butcher's."

"I've never had hare grilled, only stewed in its own blood, *en civet*. I liked it, but a little goes a long way."

"Yeah, eat too much, and with all that blood in the sauce, it'll give you a *crise de foie*."

"A crisis of the liver? What's that, a French disease?"

"How would I know the translation? No speak English, remember?" Poupon was digging a speck of something from the corner of one eye. He shook his head and smiled. "You don't have a *crise de foie* unless you live it up, have too much fun, go a little bit too far, you know? Too far, you end up suffering for it." His smile broadened. "Maybe you Americans are too, you know, puritanical."

"Only in public. Not behind closed doors."

Once they'd sniffed and tasted Poupon's new red, surprisingly he asked not what Kendrick thought of his wine, but what he thought of Zarina Hassine.

"Oh, she's a beauty," Kendrick said. "I've known her for years." He took a sip of red and swallowed. Fond memories of Zarina floated through his mind. Oh yes, he knew her. There was the tryst in Monforte d'Alba, another in Florence largely spent in their luxurious suite above the Arno River, and three Arabian nights in Asilah where they changed roles and she was his guide through her Moroccan parents' hometown (Zarina herself was born French in Le Caniveau). And they'd had Paris. He'd flown in from New York, Zarina TGVed from Marseille to meet at the Hôtel Rive Gauche. When he walked into the lobby, he saw her through a doorway, standing in the reading room, dressed in white, and he remained unmoving, admiring her bearing, her perfect skin. She was beautiful, he thought, and for a weekend, his Moroccan princess. She turned and saw him, anticipation sparkling in her eyes—her first trip to Paris!

Poupon poked around in the fire and offered his highest praise. "Her ass deserves a medal."

"She's a prize," Kendrick said, "and not only for her looks."

"Yeah, but I don't know. On top, maybe she's not quite as, uh, successful."

"Spoken like a true jerk. And you, who do you think you are, Mister Perfection? Mister Perfect from top to bottom? Sorry, Poupon, but this new white of yours is nothing but a big, fat puddle!" Poupon criticizing Zarina bugged Kendrick—she was one of his favorite people. "Listen," he continued, "the most beautiful thing about Zarina is her attitude. Life for her doesn't seem to have a downside. Whatever happens, she greets with a smile. Look at her. She's a raving beauty with that thick black hair, and here she is stuck in a hick town taking care of babies in a nursery school for a shitty salary, yet you never hear a discouraging word from her. Hey, what brought this up? Don't tell me you're seeing her."

Poupon turned the pieces of hare on the grill, then emptied his red into a flowerpot. "Let's take a look at my 1995," he said. "You watch the coals—no flames, please." He trotted off to his cellar for the next bottle of red even though they'd barely put a dent in the first one.

Returning, he passed a rosemary bush and broke off a few branches. He threw them on the coals where they began smoking up, enveloping the meat. Then he uncorked the 1995 and poured some for them.

"I don't know what you'll think," he said, his flat, fleshy nose aimed into his wine glass. "Sometimes it seems like this old whore is finally opening up, other times she's shy as a virgin."

"It smells great next to all this meat and smoke."

"The grapes—I wish you'd seen them—they looked perfect in 1995. Exactly what a winemaker likes to see. Picture perfect, high sugars. But the wine has always had a stubborn streak."

Kendrick asked if it wouldn't help to decant it ahead of time.

"Ah, you know me. I never know what I'm going to uncork until it's time to pour it in the glass."

They each took a taste, swished the wine around a bit in their mouths before swallowing, then silently pondered what was happening in the aftertaste.

"It's not a lightweight," Kendrick said, "not even a middleweight. It's powerful. Almost too much so, but then that rustic tannin from the stems emerges and saves the day by supporting the wine's weight— without it, the wine might seem clunky."

"You think it's clunky?"

"Poupon, what did I just say?"

"Maybe you're just trying to be nice. How do I know?"

"If I couldn't tell you what I think, I wouldn't be here. Believe me, the tannin in there supports the weight, makes it easier on the swallow."

"I'll quick go and get the 1997. It's lighter in body. It's not my favorite, but . . ."

"What about lunch?"

"Ah, *merde*, I'd better get it off the grill."

Finally, they sat down at the wooden table in the shade of a plane tree with the fountain gurgling not far away. After the main course, Poupon brought out a little platter of goat cheeses. "About Zarina," he said, "yes, she's quick to smile, even though life hasn't always smiled back at her. What do you know about her husband?"

"I know that they never officially married because of his family. They didn't approve, probably because she's Moroccan and they're racist. A few months after they began living together, their baby girl was born. Three years later, he left her and moved back in with his mother. Then—it's incredible—a few years after that, he shows up at her door, they produce another baby girl, then the guy quits his job with Primagaz and buys a herd of sheep. So Zarina was supporting four people, including herself, and a herd of sheep on her tiny salary at the nursery. After another couple years, my god, he packs up and moves back in with his mother."

Poupon said, "I know him, of course. You grow up around here, you know everybody. Or at least you did before they built the autoroute and the TGV and so many people invaded the coast. Raymond's not a bad guy, but he's totally fucked up about religion and his family. I'll bet you anything the local priest got into his pants. When I was a kid, the holy bastard tried to unbutton mine, for Christ's sake."

"Why all this talk about Zarina all of a sudden?"

Poupon glanced down with a sly smile and feigned a little embarrassment. "Oh, I saw her last night. Did I ever plow her fields. *Mamma mia!*"

"Yeah, Poupon, I'd bet anything you're a real tractor in bed."

"Well, she seemed to like it. She stayed 'til the end, anyway, the fireworks. She loves life," he continued, "and I'd bet that right about now, she loves me, too."

CHAPTER THREE

Kendrick slid straight across onto the cheap seat of his Modus and left Poupon's winery the same way he'd arrived, but as he turned back downhill toward the bridge and the first traffic circle, an oncoming car blinked its headlights at him. On French roads, headlights can communicate a lot. When they flash from behind, they're telling you to get out of the way. Oncoming, they warn that there is either an accident or cops up ahead. To avoid the two *rondpoints* where the local gendarmes like to stop cars randomly in order to, for example, administer alcohol tests—obviously an occupational hazard for wine professionals—Kendrick exited into the cooperative winery's parking lot, made a U-turn, passed by Poupon's Vieux Laurier again, and drove home on a series of narrow, winding, badly paved backroads. Only about four miles as the crow flies, the drive home via the backroads took five times longer.

He turned onto his funky dirt road, wide enough for one car but meant for two-way traffic. For the time being, there were only five houses on the half-mile dead-end road, so other cars were rarely encountered. As usual, when he turned into his driveway, he gave the property a good look. It was so different from his city home in Seattle. *Milles Vents*, a Thousand Winds, as the lieu has been called for centuries, was just under five acres of hillside carved long ago into leveled terraces supported by dry-stone walls of various heights. The hillside swells pregnantly outward toward the west and the setting sun.

The original building had been the home of a vigneron who also grew almonds, olives, and apricots. From tools left behind, Kendrick knew that the hillside vineyard had been farmed with a horse. Built tucked up against a smaller hill facing north, the house's ground floor, cool and humid, was where the vigneron made and raised his wine. His habitat was on the second floor, which had very small rooms—a kitchen with a fireplace, two bedrooms, and a bathroom—nothing like the châteaux of Bordeaux and the palaces you can visit in Napa Valley today. Milles Vents had been the home of a dirt farmer eking out a living.

With only his own taste and pleasure in mind, Kendrick had slowly remodeled and enlarged the house (keeping the fireplace in the kitchen). There was no one to negotiate with, because he was long since divorced, and he and his wife had not wanted children. After the divorce, he halfway swore that he would never remarry, because he and his wife had been so much in love, yet no matter how much they loved each other, they could not make the marriage work. Kendrick put a lot of the blame on himself—maybe he'd taken the sexual revolution a little too seriously, and in certain moods he regretted his infidelities.

After a good nap, bells from the church down in Le Caniveau sounded—*bom ding, bom ding, bom bom ge-ding*—and footsteps crunched up the gravel driveway. Kendrick pulled on his shorts and T-shirt, then stepped out the door onto his terrace to find a neighbor walking up the steps two at a time. It was André Kintzler, a tall, angular, buzz-cut Alsatian, who, three years earlier, had purchased an unremarkable beige plaster house just down the hill toward the village. To help pay for the purchase, Kintzler divided the lot in two, built a little cottage with a miniscule swimming pool, and quickly sold it to a couple who commuted to Marseille five days a week and unfortunately owned a loudly barking, indefatigable German shepherd that ferociously tried to climb their chain-link fence at the merest hint of provocation. Monsieur Kintzler showed up for five-week summer vacations. Other than an occasional three- or four-day visit throughout the rest of the year, that's all anyone saw of him.

Kendrick invited him up. There were a couple of armchairs at the other end of the terrace where he liked to read, and in the center, a rectangular, stained oak dining table with two matching picnic-style wooden benches where, weather permitting, he enjoyed lunch and dinner. It was a large space with a grand view—to the east toward Toulon, up north to Aix-en-Provence, westward in the direction of Marseille. And if you positioned yourself just right, there was a glimpse of the Mediterranean and the Bay of La Ciotat, which provided endless colorful sunsets—an exceptionally vast view except for the terrace's northwest corner, where he had four large terra-cotta pots of mandevilla trained to climb up an iron trellis and block the sight of a recently built house down the hill that Kendrick wished would go away. He shook hands with Kintzler, pointed to a chair, and offered him a glass of wine.

Kintzler waved off the offer. "No, no, I know you're a wine importer, but it's way too early in the day for me."

They each took a bench and sat facing each other at the well-worn table. It was empty except for a vase of roses the color of faded iris. Kendrick noticed the way Kintzler was looking at the funky tabletop and wondered if in his eyes it might seem unhygienic. Maybe his neighbor from the north was a germaphobe? In fact, Kendrick kept it scrubbed pretty well. The table had been built by hand long before Kendrick bought Milles Vents and discovered it discarded there. It was weathered and blemished, and some of the round stains must have come from wine poured a century ago. Kendrick liked that. It mattered to him, sort of like his collection of old blues records—simple song structures, used, often abused, even scarred, but with stories to tell.

They talked some weather, international politics, the contrasting work ethics in Alsace and Provence, and about how Kintzler's widowed neighbor across the road would not allow him to hook up his sewer pipe to the one her husband had installed three decades ago before a lifetime of Gauloises Brunes finished him off.

"She's just a mean, pigheaded old cow," Kintzler said, speaking with precise, vehement gestures. Everything he said seemed underlined. "Really, Monsieur Thomas, what would it hurt if someone else's shit slides down the same pipe as hers? I assure you, at the bottom of the hill, hers connects to the village sewer lines and everybody else's sewage."

"Maybe she's sentimental about it," Kendrick said. "It is her husband's legacy, and it would dishonor him to share it with anyone. Something like that? He did have to dig a fairly long trench, after all."

Kintzler's eyebrows jumped up in unison, as though wondering if Kendrick was serious or not. He wasn't. Honoring a legacy of human waste—yes, Kendrick found it amusing.

"The real reason for my visit," Kintzler said, "is our Cro-Magnon neighbor, Alexandre Pageot. You know the one. He is proceeding with plans that will not only ruin our little paradise here on the hillside but also cost us a lot of money."

"I haven't a clue what you mean."

"Of course not. Nobody knows yet. The guy's like a thief in the night. He gets away with murder because his father works at city hall." He gestured down the hill below Kendrick's property and just to the south of his own place. "See how he had his house built around the old windmill? Well, that windmill is a historical site. It is registered, protected. No one can tear it down or change it. It is, quite simply, against the law, but he built his house encircling the walls of the windmill—in effect, burying it from view. All you can see anymore is the slanted, tiled roof that sticks up in the middle."

"Well, yes, I'm certainly aware of that because I have to look at it from here. The windmill used to stand in a glade of trees. It was quite lovely from here. And it explained why the hillside was named Milles Vents. The mill was built here because it is often windy."

"So, listen to this," Kintzler said. "He did all that without a building permit. It's scandalous. But I can't say anything—I'm not from here. And you can't protest either—you're not even French. From this point, however, the story is going to become even uglier. Do you hear me, Monsieur Thomas? Especially for two people very dear to you and me. Namely, you and me. Because this swine's property is right there in the foreground of both our gorgeous—and valuable—views. Views with the celebrated Massif de Sainte Baume in the background. Our neighbor is going to rent part of his property to the SFR for an antenna!"

"An antenna? Like for television?"

"No, no, no! Not at all. That would be nothing, wouldn't concern us at all. I'm talking about a large antenna for cell phones. Six meters high. And a dangerous antenna. The waves, you know?"

"Afraid I don't."

"If you think Chernobyl caused a lot of cancers, that was nothing by comparison. But first, there go our birds and bees. They flee the waves."

He offered a cigarette and looked at his watch. "Maybe I will have that drink," he said.

"White, red, or rosé?"

"Oh, I can't stand the local wines. Too rustic for me. I'm trying to learn to like pastis. Would you have that?"

Sure, he would. Very handy when a plumber, mason, electrician, or handyman finishes a job. In Provence, pastis and a cigarette seals the deal. Kendrick brought out the pastis, a pitcher of water, ice cubes, and put some of each into their water glasses.

"*Santé*," Kintzler said. Glasses clinked. "And the health problems, that's only the beginning. I've done my research. Here's a copy for you." He handed over a dossier about an inch thick. "When one of those damned antennas goes up, neighboring properties lose, on average, thirty percent of their value. That pirate is taking money right out of our pockets so he can collect rent from the phone company. They'll pay him well to poison our neighborhood. He doesn't want to work like the rest of us."

Kendrick almost asked, Apart from all that, do you two get along? But instead he asked what they might do about the situation.

"Some of the neighbors want to take a stand against it, form a collective, hire a lawyer. Others are afraid of angering Pageot, or they don't want to spend any money. It's shortsighted, because if the antenna goes up, they stand to lose a lot more in property values. Thirty percent! Do the math. It's not nothing. Let's say with all this land your property would sell for a million euros. Once the antenna goes up, you've lost three hundred thousand of it. How would you like that?"

Kendrick said he wouldn't like it at all, and that birds and bees leaving the neighborhood didn't please him, either. "I'll take more birds and bees, not less," he said, reaching for the dossier. "And thank you. I'll read your dossier with great attention."

CHAPTER FOUR

Poupon and Kendrick found excuses to get together fairly often, tasting through the new vintage from cask again and again—Poupon would love to taste and discuss his wines day and night—or it might be for coffee in the morning or to share a glass (or more) at the aperitif hour, meaning late morning or early evening, and, often enough, they might end up having lunch or dinner together.

The day after Kintzler's visit, Poupon phoned and officially invited Kendrick to dinner. "We'll be a dozen at table," he said. "I'm inviting Arnaud Obémy, my enologist, and his wife, who also happens to be an enologist, plus Edward Hattier from Domaine du Lapin Blessé, Benoit Auriol and his mistress from Domaine Velomorte—you've heard about that, right? Well, Benoit left his wife to live with a young woman, and he's totally in love with her. Has his tongue hanging out of his mouth. Anyway, we'll have my cousin, the plumber, and his nephew . . . Oh, and Gigi. You know, the guy who hangs around all the time and never says anything? You'll see, it'll be a great soirée."

"Shall I bring some wine?" Kendrick offered.

"Bring a starter, something to get things going."

"Champagne? Chablis?"

"Champagne! Perfect. That's class. We'll show them how to throw a party."

When Kendrick arrived a couple of nights later, no one was there except Poupon and a decisively blonde woman. The two of them were smoking at the long rectangular outdoor dining table under a trellis of grapevines. What a perfect evening—a vast, calm, cloudless sky and a postcard view of the vineyards up the slope in front of Poupon's home and winery. Perched atop a hill on each side of the autoroute were the two medieval villages, Sainte Anne de la Bastide and l'Estournel d'Azur. Originally, they were built on high so the citizenry could spot invading barbarians attacking from below. Very handy back then, but useless against marauding tourists today, one of Kendrick's pet peeves, if *peeve* could describe his ire. Tourism ruins everything—the food, the views, indeed, the originality of any beautiful site, and it pollutes reality for future generations.

Poupon introduced his date, "Babette d'Orsini, from Nice." From the giddy way he said it, he might have been introducing Grace Kelly, princess of Monaco.

Kendrick wondered how such a foreign object fit into Poupon's world. He was of peasant stock and proud of it, his Provençal character and accent thick as the gnarled trunk of an ancient olive tree. Babette was, at first glance, totally different. She was all spruced up, every hair in place—a blonde helmet that looked like it would remain unruffled even in the midst of a wailing mistral. When she said hello, her face did not—or could not—budge much either. Black lashes and fingernails seemed to add length to her—to her what? Kendrick could not come up with the word. The length of her falseness? Unnatural she might be, but she was definitely not unattractive, and Kendrick admitted to himself that if he saw her from a distance on a street somewhere, he might do a double take.

Kendrick's eyes brightened, and he held up his bottle. "Let's get this Champagne good and cold."

"Follow me into the kitchen," Poupon said. "I bought an ice bucket for tonight, and I've got something else to show you." Poupon was all revved up for his dinner party. He had a glow and a nervousness Kendrick had never seen. In the kitchen, Poupon threw a few ice cubes into his gleaming new ice bucket and placed the heavy magnum of Champagne on top.

"*Mon dieu*, Kendrick, it's got some age to it, your Champagne. Let's see, three minus seven makes, hmm, what is it, twenty-six years old?"

"Thirty-six. I've had it a long time, waiting for the right occasion."

"Won't it be tired by now?"

"We'll know when we pop the cork. But tell me, why do you only want to chill the bottom of the bottle?"

"What do you mean?"

"Well, you put the bottom of the bottle on the ice. How long do you think it'll take for the chill to get from there to the first glass you pour out of the top of the bottle?"

"No idea. What the hell, I never even thought about it. I bought an ice bucket, I put in some ice, then I put in the Champagne."

"Yes, and I've even seen it done like this in the best restaurants. But watch, see if this doesn't make more sense."

Kendrick removed the magnum and poured the ice out of the bucket. He centered the Champagne in the bottom of the bucket, which he filled up with ice from the ice cube maker, totally surrounding the bottle with it. He then added cold water up to the bottle's neck.

"Now, in just a few minutes it'll be cold enough to drink. You can do the same with whites or rosés when you need a quick chill."

"Whatever you say, my friend! Now, take a look at what we're eating tonight."

Poupon laughed with delight as he pulled open the huge oven door. He stepped back and gestured with a flourish. Kendrick bent down to look. Inside, there was an oversized roasting pan holding a massive hunk of meat surrounded by onions, carrots, garlic, and sprigs of thyme.

"What's that?"

"It's the leg from a boar I shot up above Signes last week." He stooped down, too, admiring his work. "Uh-oh. *Putain de merde!* It's not possible."

"What's wrong?"

"It's not roasting. It's not even hot. Don't tell me I forgot to turn on my brand-new oven."

They straightened up and turned toward the sound of two cars approaching Poupon's gravel parking area.

"Here they come. Oh, Kendrick, how dumb can I be?"

"What shall we do, call out for pizza?"

"There's only one solution." Chef Poupon turned on the oven. High! Which was sure to darken the outside but leave the interior uncooked. But Kendrick held his tongue and followed Poupon outside.

With all the guests having arrived and been seated at the long table with a yellow and blue Provençal tablecloth, Poupon was an eager host, dressed to kill with a garnet and cream-colored polka-dot shirt unbuttoned to his belly and a gold chain hanging down his hairy chest. He kept everyone's glasses topped up, and everything he said was intended to spread good cheer.

His date for the evening, Babette, acted as if she were the lady of the house. Her every movement and occasional comment were careful and studied.

Poupon followed her with his eyes and glanced at Kendrick, aiming his Champagne flute at her and raising his eyebrows as if to ask *Ain't she somethin'?*

Kendrick smiled. She was *something*, all right, but Kendrick suspected that he and Poupon did not share the same definition.

The enologist and his wife were both long-legged lean machines—of Lebanese origin, it turned out—and elegantly attired. More Paris or Beirut than l'Estournel or Bandol. Silk suit and finely knotted tie for him, while she was in an apricot-colored dress that seemed to be designed around her cleavage.

Of course they all talked wine, wine, and more wine. Everything the enologist uttered was spoken from on high. His expression remained lordly, his self-confidence supreme. At one point he tried to sound humble. "I am simply a doctor, but my patients are wines. I absolutely do not want my patients to fall ill, so I work hard to prevent diseases before they can take hold."

Kendrick was no fan of enologists. Since their arrival on the wine scene in the 1970s and 1980s, yes, there were fewer horribly stinky wines on the market, but in Kendrick's experience, there were many fewer great wines—more conformity, less originality—so he couldn't let the enologist's boast stand. "I've heard that French doctors are not legally allowed to own pharmacies," he said, "which must have been designed to prevent a few bad seeds from prescribing unnecessary drugs in order to line their own pockets. As I understand it, doctors cannot even own stocks in pharmaceuticals. But enologists, can't enologists, like yourself, prescribe products for treating wines? Prescribe products that you yourself sell?"

The enologist ignored the edge of sarcasm in Kendrick's voice. "For one thing," he began, "a doctor deals with human lives. Even wine professionals, like most of us collected here at table, would never claim that the life of a wine matters as much as the life of a human being."

That depends, Kendrick thought, *on which wine and which human being.*

"Secondly," Monsieur Obémy continued, "there are no wine pharmacies for winemaking products. So in this instance, it is nothing but a service, a convenience for the winemakers."

"A charitable, nonprofit service, I suppose?"

Poupon raised a hand to shush Kendrick and said, "Let Obémy finish."

"And my goodness, my friends, winemakers have enough to worry about. They don't need to waste their precious time running around the countryside looking for winemaking products. They already carry enough weight on their shoulders."

Serge Bavet, another producer whose wines Kendrick imported, spoke up. "Hey, Poupon, did you ever get your rosé fixed?"

"Fixed?" Poupon stopped in his tracks like he'd run into a strong jab to the heart. "What's there to fix?"

"Oh, you remember, I came by during that big rainstorm in February, and your rosé smelled like geranium leaves and blue cheese."

"*Merde alors*, that's a pretty tough thing to say. It was just going through a phase. Let's say it was under the weather. And hey, come on, time to eat!"

Out came the roast boar. Or, as it happened, the unroasted boar. Poupon, enthusiasm undiminished, sliced the leg into bloody hunks and passed around the plates. The meat was cooked about half an inch deep. When Kendrick took knife and fork to it, it was like cutting into a tire. His teeth bounced off the first bite. No one said a word, but there was a lot of arduous mastication going on. Kendrick was wondering if ever he could manage a second bite when he felt something brush firmly against his knee. It was not the enologist's lovely wife but the eager muzzle of one of Poupon's four hunting dogs. As inconspicuously as possible, Kendrick raised his hand to his mouth and pretended to cough lightly while he pushed the bite of boar into his hand and slipped it down under the table. *Slurp*—it disappeared immediately.

It seemed to take Kendrick forever to slowly carve his dinner into little pieces and discreetly pass each bite down one by one to man's best friend. When he'd finished it to the last stubborn bite, he exhaled a sigh of relief—he would not embarrass his pal Poupon by leaving his boar uneaten—then he stood up and proposed a toast with a glass of Poupon's Domaine du Vieux Laurier Bandol Rouge.

"Here's to Henri Poupon, everyone's favorite host. Long may he live, and his wines, too."

Everyone saluted Poupon with their glasses and each tossed back a healthy swallow.

Poupon appeared next to Kendrick. He gestured down at his empty plate with a beaming smile. "Ah, Kendrick, it gives me real joy that you—an American—enjoy wild boar. Not everyone, not even in France, has a real appreciation for it." And he flung down another raw slab for Kendrick's dining pleasure.

CHAPTER FIVE

Two days later, Kendrick received a call from Louis Cuisson in Chambolle-Musigny, raving about a Côtes-de-Provence rosé he'd tasted at the hotel-restaurant Chez Chantal in Vosne-Romanée. "It's right up your alley: indigenous yeasts, biodynamic farming, aged in casks, bottled unfiltered, and listen to this, all three colors—red, white, and rosé—complete their malolactic fermentation." It was exactly the kind of tip for which Kendrick hungered. Or better, thirsted. The very next morning, he hit the road toward Nice and the Italian border armed with six other leads from his files. Collecting addresses to wine domaines worthy of visiting was an important part of his work. An importer cannot simply show up and knock on every door of an appellation. In the Côtes-de-Provence region alone, Kendrick would have had about six hundred addresses to visit and sample. A year's work. It was a good idea, his three-day tour, because it included two sensational tastings.

The twelve-acre domaine mentioned by Cuisson was on the road from Nice to Grenoble, well removed geographically from the rest of the Côtes-de-Provence appellation. The landscape had attracted geology buffs for centuries, including Thomas Jefferson in 1787, and the neat bundle of prospects had Kendrick's tail wagging.

The vineyard was below Villars-sur-Var in the Alpes-Maritimes, where once upon a time, there'd been an inland sea. It disappeared some one hundred and fifty million years ago but left behind sedimentary layers of sea creature remains. Tectonic movement caused upheavals that churned up layers of strata—marl, for example. Exposed sedimentary layers had been squeezed upright to almost vertical by the various natural forces, and gazing at the dramatic landscape, it felt to Kendrick like those forces were still at work, alive and kicking. Here and there, rocky formations spilled out of the earth's surface like petrified innards. He imagined the grapevines' roots digging deeper and deeper into such a geological wonderland. He knew from experience that the quality of a wine is due to more than the grape varietal and the winemaker's savvy. A good deal of a great wine's interest starts underground. The unique geological complexity is drawn up into the roots and into the grapes, into the wine and the wine glass, to be swallowed, and finally to make an impression on us. Of course the wine goes to our stomachs and bladders, but it also goes to our heads in more ways than one. According to Kendrick, there is an aesthetic appreciation and an inebriation. Certain experiences led him to wonder if the word *vin* was not the root of the word *divine*. Over millions of years, billions of sea creatures left remains that, in the right hands, can influence the taste of a wine. He had a name for wines grown on such ancient slopes that provided such a deep and complex impression of the very earth itself: subterranean wines.

The other domaine he decided to import was across the Italian border in the mountains just above the coastal town of Bordighera, next to Vintimiglia. Kendrick had never tasted a Dolceacqua before, but tasting at one of the few remaining wineries, he was convinced he'd found a forgotten gem. The impossibly steep terraced slopes reminded him of his earliest view of Côte-Rôtie, one of France's most splendid, most picturesque vineyard sites.

During the drive back to Le Caniveau through Nice and Toulon three days later, the sky was a deep, dazzling blue worthy of van Gogh when he painted at Saint-Rémy-de-Provence. All it lacked were his brushstrokes. Navigating the dirt road up to his house might irritate some drivers, but the bumps, ruts, zigzags, and steep climbs kept people away, and once one arrives at Milles Vents, it felt quite peaceful.

As he drove past Alex Pageot's property, Kendrick noticed a cypress tree at the side of the road that hadn't been there before. When Pageot inherited the place and built his house around the old windmill, he cut down every tree on the property, even the olive trees, and since then had planted nothing—zero. There was something bizarre about Pageot's new cypress, the way the sun hit and reflected off its leaves. *My god*, Kendrick thought, *it's plastic! Pageot finally plants a tree, and it's plastic!*

He stopped the car to look more closely and noticed a short metal fence around a concrete slab. A plastic tree planted in concrete? Then he saw metal rods sticking out of some of the branches. "I'll be damned," he said out loud. "It's an antenna masquerading as a cypress tree."

Kendrick stood and gazed at the surrounding hillsides—vast areas with no homes, nothing but pine forest—and wondered why they didn't put their antennas up there. Wouldn't it be cheaper to rent a few square meters where no one would suffer their presence? He looked over the Pageot property. The fake cypress wasn't even the worst eyesore. The house won that contest. And the waves or rays? Maybe they weren't as dangerous as environmentalists proclaimed.

There were two phone messages waiting for him. One from Kintzler: "Urgent, contact me." And one from Serge Bavet: "Come down to the domaine when you have a chance. I want to know what you think of a new oak cask I recently purchased."

First things first. Kendrick put on his bathing suit and trudged about forty yards up a rocky path to his swimming pool. It was buried in the woods, very private. He rolled back the cover and dove in for a few casual laps. A couple of blue and gray pigeons landed in different oak trees, hoping to drink from the pool while it was uncovered. After he dried off, he called Poupon, who hardly ever answered his phone and was also not likely to fiddle with it, listening to voice messages. Kendrick left one anyway. "I'm back home now, and there's something I need your advice about. Why not come on over after six? We'll drink a glass of something to fire up the muscles inside that armored skull of yours. Call me to confirm if you get this message."

Poupon drove up in his white camionette at six forty-five, and when they were seated on the terrace, Kendrick uncorked a Meursault "Perrières" and poured a couple glasses.

Poupon sniffed. He read out loud the name of the wine and took a second sniff. "What's this? *Putain*, it smells woody."

"Normally, up in Burgundy—that's what this is, a white Burgundy—they ferment and age their whites in oak barrels," Kendrick said.

"If I did that to my white, you'd tell me it's too oaky."

"True, but your vines aren't Chardonnay, and they're not in Burgundy. Once I had the chance to taste a *grand cru*, Le Montrachet, vinified in a barrel made not of wood but of stainless steel. It was a winemaker's experiment, and we agreed that it tasted like a simple white wine, not at all like a *grand cru*. Without a little oak, a great white Burgundy tastes more like a Macon blanc."

"Montrachet? Macon? What's that got to do with it?"

"Listen, my friend, I'll explain to you when we have a bottle of each to taste. A little Burgundian show-and-tell. That's the only way to explain, right? Samples of wines in our glasses. But right now, take a look down at my neighbor's property."

"Oh yeah, the Pageot place, right?"

"Unfortunately, yes. Do you see anything weird?"

Poupon looked it over. "What, he's not even going to paint the walls?"

"Well, he built it five years ago and hasn't touched a thing since. No, I'm wrong. He added an outdoor hot tub."

"It looks like there's a big television screen on, right in there through those glass doors."

"It's always on, day and night. All they do is watch TV and scream at each other."

"Stop, you're reminding me of my first ex-wife."

"I can't imagine what happens to your brain if you watch television nonstop."

"You'd be better off drunk," Poupon said. He shook his head. "No, no, it's really ugly what he's done. There's no way to excuse it. No respect for anything or anybody. It used to be beautiful around the old mill. In a grove of pine trees, you remember?"

"And a nice picnic table for whoever needed one."

"I used to bring girls to the mill when I was a teenager," Poupon said. "It was private here."

"See the cypress?"

"Oh yeah," he said, "that one with nothing around it near the road?"

"See anything funny about it?"

"Not really. Do you? It looks like it was badly pruned or hacked up. It looks lonely."

"It's fake."

"How's that? What do you mean 'fake'?"

"It's plastic."

"A plastic cypress? Why would anyone do that?"

"In order to hide a cell phone antenna."

"Really? You're not joking?"

"Any great ideas what I can do about it?"

"Why? Do you have something against plastic trees?" Poupon burst out laughing as if he'd scored some points for his sharp wit.

"Oh, hell with it," Kendrick said, frustrated. "I need help, not your laughably bad sense of humor." He'd hoped Poupon might have a friend with some pull at city hall to help with the antenna, but at that moment, he could tell that Poupon was not going to understand, and Kendrick didn't have the patience necessary to try to make him.

"Now," Kendrick said, "why aren't you drinking your Meursault? Believe it or not, at auction I could have sold it for thousands of euros. If, of course, I hadn't uncorked it."

"What the hell?" said Poupon, sincerely mystified. "I must have a lame palate. But it's hot, and I'm thirsty. Honestly, I'd rather drink a cold beer. And besides, I don't want to get any splinters in my mouth."

As Poupon drove away, Kendrick was shaking his head. How could anyone be anything less than bonkers for a taste of that incredible Meursault? He did, however, appreciate Poupon's joke about the splinters in oaky wines. Finally, he telephoned his neighbor Kintzler, who was in a lather.

"Now that the antenna is a fait accompli," he ranted, "the lawyers won't get anywhere. The mayor won't do anything. In fact, the mayor admitted that because the antenna is on private property, he can't do anything even if he wanted to. Which he doesn't!"

"Maybe we'll get used to it," Kendrick said. "Although, for the moment I can't look down there without cringing."

"Oh, the fabulous view, that's the least of our worries. Remember, my gardener says it will drive away the birds, the bees. It will affect surrounding vegetation, your vines, your olive grove, your vegetable garden. And of course it will affect our health. It's a good thing my kids are grown. Those waves are known to cause brain tumors in children."

They hung up, and Kendrick gazed down the hill at the scene of the crime. He wondered why no one on America's ecologically-minded West Coast ever raised hell about cell phone towers? Those antennas must be all over the States, but he'd never heard a single discouraging word about them. He reminded himself to study Kintzler's dossier, but first he called Serge Bavet and made an appointment to check out the domaine's new oak cask the next morning.

CHAPTER SIX

Traffic permitting, Domaine Constanzo was only about five minutes downhill from Milles Vents. Many wine drinkers experienced an emotional reaction to the domaine's wines, including Kendrick. To a wine magazine early in his career, he described their red as a wine with soul, and that image seemed to resonate and stick: "It's like tasting a philosophy of life—the good life."

The founders, George and Georgina Constanzo—Papageno and Papagena—built the domaine's reputation from scratch. When they retired, their two children, a son and daughter, took over. Neither really caught the winemaking bug, so eventually they hired Serge Bavet away from another Bandol domaine to take over. A couple years later, they turned the day-to-day direction of the domaine over to Serge, too. It turned out to be a good move. The domaine's reputation still topped that of its competitors, although there was now a small group barking jealously at their heels.

Way back when, the winery occupied an idyllic site surrounded by grapevines, fruit trees, and rows of giant Tuscan cypresses, but with the arrival of the autoroute and TGV, the area suffered a population explosion, and the domaine became increasingly hemmed in by a vast supermarket, a Peugeot dealership, and several Soviet-style apartment blocks, all of course with their requisite asphalt parking lots. Kendrick left his Modus in the domaine's grassy parking area and was on his way to the winery building when Franck Constanzo turned the corner of the main house and walked right up to him. Franck, son of the domaine's founders, was coproprietor with his sister. He and Kendrick had been quite friendly before his parents retired. Diving for sea urchins with a baguette and a bottle of rosé on board Franck's Zodiac was one of their favorite pastimes. He was stocky, even barrel-chested. Hair seemed to sprout from every inch of him except his head, which was shaved. He looked strong but weather beaten from working outdoors in the vines all his life, usually on a tractor, well before goggles, ear mufflers, and face masks came along.

This time, Franck offered no enthusiastic handshake, no welcoming smile, not even a *bonjour*—he simply went straight to what was on his mind. "Poupon tells me you are importing so much Gros Laurier, he can't fill all the orders." The words careened from Franck's mouth almost faster than he could say them. This was not a Franck that Kendrick had ever encountered. In fact, they'd never discussed business before.

Kendrick replied, "Oh, you know how Provençal Poupon can be, so you should be used to him exaggerating. But it's true, his wines are well received in the States."

"We gave you the exclusivity for Domaine Constanzo, but now it seems that we should have demanded exclusivity from you, too."

Kendrick was puzzled and taken aback. "But why would you do that? For years, I've taken every bottle your family offered, and each and every vintage you tell me the same thing—that you can't increase my allocations because you have no more to sell."

"None of that matters. We can't sell to others in the US, but you can buy other Bandols."

"But if you have more for the United States, I'll take it. No problem. Believe me, when I tasted Poupon's wine, I knew there was no way it would interfere with my sales of yours. I've always done business that way. You couldn't, or wouldn't, increase my allocation, so when I found another good one, I decided to buy some, and you must admit, it hasn't hurt Domaine Constanzo's sales at all."

"It is a one-way exclusivity, that's what it is."

"You mean you want me to stop selling Poupon's—"

"I don't care what you do or don't do." He about-faced, and that was that. Kendrick shook his head as if waking from a bad dream.

What the hell was that? He had always liked Franck, admired him, considered him a pal. Now he was wondering if he would ever again be invited over to Franck's for his wife's showstopping octopus stew with a hand-turned aioli.

Serge, Constanzo's director, stood at the winery's cellar door saying goodbye to some clients who were speaking French with German accents. A couple of minutes later, Serge walked over to greet Kendrick. A tall, well-muscled fellow, he'd grown a little too middle-aged to actively pursue his passion for playing rugby. After the usual *Ça va?* and *How's Mother Nature treating the vines?*, Kendrick and Serge descended the stairway to the large cellar filled with oak casks, called *foudres*, in which the reds aged.

Kendrick was still in a state of shock. "What's up with Franck?" he asked.

"You saw Franck?"

"On my way in, yes."

"What happened?"

"Well, mainly unfriendliness. He seems totally bugged because I'm importing Poupon's wine."

"You do a great job for us, Kendrick, we all know that. Maybe he is jealous, you know, afraid your attention will be divided. Here, let's taste from this cask first. It's one of the old casks, like we're all used to tasting."

The cask had a brass faucet sticking out from its oval frontispiece. Bavet turned it a couple of spins, and the dark black cherry–colored wine splashed into his glass. He swirled it a couple of times, then poured the contents into Kendrick's glass, who swirled it and threw the contents into the spit bucket, because the first taste might have a faucet taint.

After serving Kendrick tastes of the same red from four different well-used, old casks, Bavet said, "Now let's taste the brand-new oak! You could say it is a virgin *foudre* and getting to know its first wine."

They swirled and sniffed.

Kendrick started by saying that he liked the way the vintage kept its energy and freshness. "Both nose and palate seem unusually alive this year."

"Yes, wild berries, especially raspberry, almost active in a way, as if the wine were still fermenting, which it's not, of course."

"But, Serge, back to Poupon. You know, don't you, that this is nothing new? It's how I've always worked. At one time, I imported four domaines from Châteauneuf-du-Pape, three from Gigondas, three Volnays, four growers of Chablis, and five in Meursault, and that's just for example. Limited to importing one wine in an appellation? I've never heard of that rule."

"Oh, ignore Franck," Serge said. "He's not aging well. He's growing into a cranky old fart. Sometimes he drives me crazy, too, always second-guessing my decisions. Old and mean, you know? It could happen to us someday."

Kendrick shrugged and again turned his attention to the wine in his glass, which bore little resemblance to the first one. "What can I say? Even in a large *foudre* like this, the brand-new oak makes its impression on the wine. It takes on almost a lumberyard smell. Strange, it's not at all like the oakiness you get from a small barrel, is it?"

Serge pondered Kendrick's question. "Hard to say. Even with barrels, each can be quite different, as you've experienced, and so can each *foudre*. It depends on the tree, of course, the preparation of the staves, the char, and so on."

"And yet, there is no way to taste a wine from the specific *foudre*, barrel—or whatever size it is—before you buy it? You know, in order to know how it will make your wine taste?"

"You do the best research you can. After that, it's just luck, the luck of the draw."

"Thank god marriage isn't handled like that." Kendrick leaned forward for another sniff, took another taste, and spit it out into the bucket at their feet. "Well, you can't say there's anything off. No technical flaws. But the aroma is half wine/half oak, and that tannin from the new wood cuts into the aftertaste and dries out the palate."

"We agree. Thank goodness this new one will be blended with the four older *foudres*, and every year afterward the woodiness will impact the wine less and less."

Kendrick said, "I remember old man Malfatto at Domaine Le Chant des Vignes. He told me that he would never, ever put his top cuvée, his old-vines Gigondas, into a new *foudre*. When he had to buy a new one, he'd begin by putting his cheap little *vin de table* in it to leach out the new oak flavors. He would always wait until a new *foudre* had been seasoned by five vintages of *vin de pays* before he raised his prized Gigondas *Vieilles Vignes* in it."

"Yeah, if you ask me, that would be perfect. Too bad we don't make a *vin de table* here. And just think, all those fans of new oak out there would fight to have some of our *vin de table*. We could sell it as a *Cuvée Speciale* more expensive than our Bandol!" Serge said in jest.

Kendrick appreciated the joke. "True," he said, "a lot of people adore an oaky flavor and are willing to pay for it."

"Personally, I like the smell of wine better than oak."

"Me too, but there are the exceptions to the rule. Bordeaux and Burgundy, for example—they love the kiss of new barrels."

"Here in the south, new oak acts more like a punch than a kiss. Here, Kendrick, I opened a bottle of our 1988 Cuvée Alphonse for the Berlin buyers—let's have a look." He poured a taste into Kendrick's glass.

"What a beauty," Kendrick said. "I've known the 1988 since it was born, and it's giving all of itself right now, isn't it?"

"Have you had a look at our new secretary? If she wanted to open up to me like this '88 does, I'd turn into a blithering idiot," Serge said with a big smile. "But back to Poupon. You know that I love the guy. I see him a lot, too. He's my buddy, and I want him to succeed. It took a lot of courage, what he did, starting a winery when his family had simply been selling their grapes. I wish I'd had such good luck. I give Poupon winemaking advice, of course, while he's finding his way. But it doesn't bother you, the inconsistent quality?"

"Oh, at first, sure, but if I didn't like a cuvée or a vintage, I didn't buy it. And now it's no longer an issue. Every vintage has been good recently."

"But sometimes it's so massive, lacking finesse. A brute, you know, sort of like Poupon himself when you really think about it. Not that I'm criticizing."

"Yes, but watch out, Serge. Poupon is a work in progress, and I think he's been listening about the lack of finesse in his earlier wines."

"Yes, of course," Serge said. He poured Kendrick another taste of the remarkable 1988. "But is anyone really capable of learning finesse? Don't you either have it or not?"

"Well, look at the winery and cellar Poupon designed and constructed himself. It's not a brute, not a mass of concrete—it might be the most beautiful winery in the Bandol appellation. And, as for the wine, most of my countrymen like wines that have *cojones*. Next to a lot of California wines—much more expensive—Poupon's doesn't really seem all that massive. And once in a while, when it's cold and wet outside, or when your blood needs strengthening, Poupon's big red can be just what the doctor ordered."

CHAPTER SEVEN

Poupon didn't wait long. The very next morning he called to ask if Kendrick was busy for lunch. "I found some mussels, and we can cook outdoors. How does that sound?"

"I'll bring along a bottle."

"If you like, but if you bring one of those oak bombs, you'll have to drink it all yourself."

"When should I arrive?"

"As soon as thirst starts clawing at your throat."

That occurred at a quarter to twelve, so Kendrick hopped into his Modus and popped over to Poupon's. Everything—the sea, the sky, the Eagle's Beak at La Ciotat—all seemed vividly in focus. There was just enough breeze to ruffle the leaves of the olive trees and reveal their two-tone allure. Kendrick's part of Provence is known for the wind they call the mistral, which originates in the north of France. It is almost a rule: when it is stormy up north, a fierce wind is channeled south along the Rhône Valley. After Montelimar, it fans out, and by the time it reaches Milles Vents, it seems to be blowing from the east. Day after day of mistral will alter a brain's circuitry. Some people turn into dazed, mumbling idiots. Others stay in bed with earplugs to block out the howl and roar. Outdoors, you must be en garde for flying pine branches. However, around Toulon, Bandol, Marseille, and north around Aix, Arles, and Avignon, a mistral sweeps away pollution, and, therefore, in its aftermath you can still enjoy the legendary crystalline light of Provence's sky.

When he drove through Poupon's open iron gateway and into his stone-paved parking area for visitors, there were no other cars. The front door of the house was wide open, but no one appeared when Kendrick knocked.

"Anybody here?" he called inside. Nothing. He turned back outside, made a bullhorn with his hands, and hollered again. "Anybody home?"

"Hey, around back. At the barbecue."

When Poupon built his winery, he designed an outdoor fireplace just for grilling, a beautiful piece of masonry with lovely curves and a background of tiles giving a Provençal sunburst effect. It had a motorized rotisserie built of forged iron for larger pieces of meat like legs of lamb and whole fowl. Poupon stood at the fireplace with his hunting dogs, Kendrick's fast friends since their wild boar feast. Poupon and Kendrick shook hands.

"Ça va?"

"Oui, et toi?"

"Ça va. I'm preparing the fire for the mussels."

"Barbecued mussels? I've never heard of that. Won't they fall through the grill into the fire?"

Poupon straightened up. He looked as though he'd just heard something beyond comprehension. "Kendrick, don't you have mussels in California?"

"Poupon, in the modern era, they have mussels everywhere in the world. Even Iowa or your Massif Central. Of course we have mussels in California, even growing right there on that little ocean right offshore. The Pacific? You have heard of it."

"Sure, but mussels? Falling into the fire? You weren't joking?"

Kendrick noticed Poupon's slightly bloodshot eyes. "Joking? What's so funny about barbecued mussels?"

"Who said anything about barbecued mussels? You'll see. My father used to make them cooked over smoky coals, but not barbecued. Maybe you won't like them. But look at this. Two clean, empty wine glasses. What shall we do with them? It would be a shame to waste them."

"I brought along a white. I'll go find a corkscrew."

"Look in the fridge while you're there. Bring out my white, too—the bottle from yesterday. Let's see what the overnight aeration did for it."

When Kendrick opened Poupon's fridge, three bloody, skinned rabbits were laid out on one rack—fresh game awaiting some future meal. He grabbed Poupon's white, a corkscrew, and headed back outdoors.

"Let's start with my white," Kendrick said.

"Whatever."

Both gazed at the yellowy green color and clinked glasses. "*Tchin-tchin.*"

"*Santé.*"

They proceeded to the swirling, then sniffing stage, and each took a sip.

Poupon put his nose back into his glass. "That smell, you know, the nose? I'm no expert—you're going to tell me I don't know anything—but it smells bizarre."

"Bizarre?"

"Yeah, bizarre, you know what I mean?"

"It doesn't seem bizarre to me. It's very typical."

"Typical of what? Not of wine, certainly."

"Typical of the kind of wine it is."

"Which is what, then? What kind of wine could possibly smell like this?"

"It's a Cheverny from Sologne. In the Loire Valley."

"Never heard of it."

"Well, you've heard of Sancerre, which is also made with Sauvignon Blanc. And Poupon—I made sure for your sake—no new oak taste at all. Zero. Vinified in stainless steel."

"True, true, but why did they harvest it so green? And, my god, it's sharp. My poor tongue, is it bleeding?" Poupon stuck out his tongue, which looked dreadfully white, took Kendrick's glass, and tossed out the wine from both glasses. Then he rinsed them with his white and filled both halfway to the top.

"Kendrick, *merde*, I know I'm no connoisseur, but really, people drink that stuff? You have clients for it? It smells like cat piss, if you ask me."

Kendrick stared at Poupon for a long moment. "First the Chablis—too much acid. Then the woody Meursault. And now my crisp
little Cheverny tastes like cat piss. You ought to get out of your own
cellar, see what a big world of wine there is out there. Wine is not like
marriage. You don't have to be faithful. You can enjoy diversity."

They were then interrupted by none other than Franck Constanzo,
who appeared from around the corner of Poupon's house. "Aha," he
said, "I thought I heard voices."

"Hey, Franck, *comment ça va?*" Poupon asked.

Franck did not approach near enough for a handshake. His eyes
gleamed demonically, as if he'd just found his wife in bed with the
plumber. "Well, Kendrick," he said, "is this your new home away from
home?" He then faked a smile, as if he'd told a joke. "Poupon, just
tell me quickly which house belongs to Monsieur Marino. He lives
around here, doesn't he?"

"Franck, please, sit down, let me get you a glass . . ."

"Merci, no. It's too early for me. Drink up with your best client
here. Is it true he's moving in with you? Never mind. Just tell me how
to find Marino's place."

"Third road to the left, second house after you turn. It's got a big
fir tree as you enter his driveway."

"I see you know how to keep a client happy. Yes, just keep their
glass filled."

"You mean Kendrick?" Poupon asked. "He's a client, sure, but he's
more than just that."

"Well, keep up the good work," Franck said. Then he turned back
the way he'd come and was gone.

Poupon and Kendrick looked at each other as if they'd seen a Mar-
tian. "Franck knows exactly where Perpigné lives," Poupon said. "That
was really curious."

"And I can tell you from experience," Kendrick said, "that noontime
has never, ever been too early for Franck to down a glass of wine. He
climbs out of bed in the morning, takes a leak, and drinks his espresso
while he looks for a corkscrew. He's obviously got a hair up his ass."

"Hey, that's pretty good. *Un poil dans son cul.* I've never heard that
one before. Anyway, what do you think of my white, after all?"

"Not bad, but I'm in the mood for some cat piss, so I'll go back to drinking the Cheverny."

On the table sat a platter with slices of toasted *levain*, a couple of raw garlic cloves, a few anchovy filets, and a bottle of Poupon's own olive oil. The idea was to scrape the toast with a clove of garlic, then put on as many anchovy filets as you please, and splash a little olive oil over it all.

Meanwhile, Poupon poured a bunch of raw mussels, still closed in their shells, into an immense iron skillet. He half mumbled as he worked, "I don't know how anyone could drink cat piss with anchovies."

"I'm simply in the mood for something light and crisp," Kendrick said. "Something to wake up my palate. It's as simple as that—a mood. Not an earthshaking gastronomic decision."

"I'm right, though, aren't I? If I'm not mistaken, there are no anchovies in the Loire River."

"You're right about that, Poupon." Kendrick was beginning to feel defensive because, he realized, Poupon was right, the Cheverny did not at all go with the flavor of an anchovy.

Poupon was not finished. "I don't know. *Merde.* It's like showing up at the beach in July wearing ski clothes. Or trying to fuck somebody in the ear."

"You have a knack for going too far. Has anyone ever enlightened you to that fact? Where did you learn to, not once, not twice, but always go too far?"

"Which went too far for you? The ski clothes or the ear? There is simply a logic to the universe, and anchovies don't swim up the Loire, even to lay eggs."

"Fine, fine, but, I mean, for Chrissake, Poupon, you could use a few lessons in self-control. What's in that white wine of yours?"

"Well, *mon ami*, there's a lot of sunshine in it, for one thing—a lot more than in that green cat piss in your glass, for example."

To the black iron skillet filled almost to the brim with mussels, Poupon added several whole cloves of garlic. Then he went to a nearby rosemary bush, broke off a few short branches, and threw them on top of it all.

"My father liked a lot of garlic," he said, "and a lot of rosemary."

"I've seen pictures of him, remember, and I'd say he liked to eat a lot of just about everything."

"He was a big man, true enough. But if a person doesn't like to eat—well, I don't know, but I'd be suspicious, you know, suspicious that something wasn't quite right."

He placed the skillet directly on top the fiery coals.

"Hey, you forgot the wine," Kendrick said.

"What wine?"

"In the skillet. With the mussels."

"Is that another idea from the Loire?"

"Isn't it like *moules marinières*? Don't you have to have some liquid if you're going to have any sauce with the mussels?"

"You'll see. Watch what happens."

"Or some people add pastis," Kendrick said.

"What? And screw up my father's recipe? Look, when you cook mussels, go ahead. You can add ice cream if you want, pour cat piss in the pot for all I care. And what's the story here? I didn't know you like pastis."

"I used to like it when I was a smoker. A glass of pastis outdoors in the summer with a good cigarette—not bad. But now that I don't smoke, I don't drink pastis. If I do, I want a cigarette. It's Pavlovian."

Incredible smells were rising from the huge, steaming skillet while Poupon constantly stirred up everything in it with a long wooden spoon.

"Take a look," he said.

The skillet was about a quarter of the way full of liquid. The smoke, the garlic and rosemary, the juice from the mussels—all magically combined. Kendrick's stomach responded with a gurgling pang of appetite.

"See my sauce now?" Poupon asked. "That's nothing but the juice from the mussels as they open. I'm not going to ruin it by adding wine or pastis or anything else. Here, dip in a piece of bread and give it a try. Good?" He spooned out a hot mussel and offered it. "Try it and tell me if it's done."

Kendrick took the mussel and placed it in his mouth, chewing thoughtfully. "No, not quite yet. It's still a little too tough. But that sauce—you could market it!"

Poupon handed Kendrick the spoon. "You keep stirring, and I'll get a red out of the fridge. We're due for some red by now, right?"

"I couldn't have said it better. A fresh, young red, I hope."

"An old red with mussels tastes like shoe leather."

When the mussels were cooked and the shells open for business, he showed Kendrick how to eat them. You tear off the empty half shell and toss it away. The half with the mussel in it is then employed to scoop up some of the sauce, and down the hatcht. As simple as that.

"It's a great recipe," Kendrick said, "and so easy, all you have to worry about is obtaining good mussels and cooking them just right— not too raw, not too cooked."

Poupon lifted his wine glass toward Kendrick, and they clinked glasses. Then he raised it toward the heavens. "Here's to my father," he said. "To my mother and father. They were peasants, you know, but I owe them for everything I have." He gestured in a big circle, including the house, the winery, the vines, and the olive trees.

"Listen, Kendrick, I know where to get good mussels. The guy shows up twice a week in his camionette, drives all the way from the Atlantic coast. He sells them up there, when you enter Bandol from the west, where there's the bakery and the épicerie. You like mussels, right?"

"Well, look, we've eaten everything but the shells."

"My dogs eat anything and everything." He threw down a shell, and the dogs jerked lazily into action trying to get to it first. The winner crunched the shell once, twice, three times and down the gullet it went, while the others looked up mournfully at their lord and master.

Kendrick looked at the poor beast, waiting for it to start howling in pain. Then he remembered Poupon after another meal throwing out a pail of chicken bones to his dogs. They'd survived.

Poupon simply ignored them, turning back to Kendrick. "The shellfish truck will be there Wednesday. I'll show you another way to prepare mussels if you want."

"Lunch or dinner?"

"Oh, let's do lunch. I like to cook outdoors when the weather's like this."

"Sold."

CHAPTER EIGHT

The next day at noon, Kendrick finished writing a short article about the progress he'd witnessed in wines from the Savoie region, poured himself a glass of cold Corsican rosé, and considered the possibilities for lunch. He had a good *saucisson* and three fresh eggs from the chicken coop. From the vegetable garden, he picked two handfuls of bright little red-and-white radishes. While he was deciding how to prepare the eggs, the phone rang. He debated for a moment whether to answer the damned thing. He was in a good mood and had a recent issue of the *New Yorker* to read at table. He didn't want anything to spoil it, but then decided, what the hell, and answered.

"It's about the antenna," the clearly enunciated voice of his Alsatian neighbor began. "I've organized a collective with a few neighbors. We're hoping you'll join us—a neighborhood united against the antenna. We've found a lawyer in Toulouse who has experience fighting the construction of antennas in populated areas."

"What does the lawyer think of our chances?"

"Frankly, she doesn't offer a lot of hope. But she'll do her best, and apart from blocking the construction crews with our bodies, there are no alternatives," Kintzler said.

"Wait. The antenna is already built. Isn't it too late?"

"Oh, I've been so busy with it all, I must have forgotten to inform you. My mistake, because we need everyone united. Alex Pageot has applied for permits to build two more cell phone antennas, both quite a bit taller than the plastic cypress. Our view will be fatally marred by them. We'll live in a metallic jungle."

Kendrick felt a self-protective nerve spring to life. For a moment, the conversation stalled while he took a sip of rosé. "I'll have to think about the collective. Remember, I'm American and not very informed about what the ramifications of all this might be. Has Madame Pardieu signed? Or the d'Ornanos?"

"No, not yet. I'm sure they're afraid to anger Pageot, afraid he might take some kind of revenge. You understand? I mean, who knows what he's capable of?" Kintzler continued, "The lawyer says the proximity of the school will be one of her strongest arguments. There is evidence that children are more susceptible than we would be."

"Yes," Kendrick said, "I read carefully the statistics about brain tumors in the dossier, but I would like to discuss the matter with a couple of friends who grew up around here. So, I'll get back to you."

He went back to cleaning the radishes, posed them on ice cubes in a small black bowl, and sliced some *saucisson*. The circles were nicely dotted with tiny morsels of black pepper. He decided to make his version of eggs sunny-side up, and broke three into another bowl before the phone started ringing again.

"No thanks, I'm busy," he said out loud. He let the phone keep ringing, and each ring bugged him. He reached for a small skillet, put in a few drops of olive oil and a dollop of butter, adjusted the flame as low as it would go—all the time enjoying the chilled rosé, the peppery *saucisson*, and the crisp, cold, freshly gathered radishes. "Ain't simplicity great?" he asked his empty house.

After carefully pouring the eggs into the skillet to avoid breaking any yolks, he salted and peppered them, then scattered dried thyme from his hillside over the gleaming raw eggs—eggs that he cooked ultra slowly with a glass lid on top. In his opinion, crispy edges are not desirable, so he checked continually on the progress, looking for barely cooked whites and a nearly raw yolk. The yolk with the dried thyme makes a heavenly sauce for the egg whites. Slid onto a heated plate, the eggs also make a lovely still life. He sliced and toasted some *levain* for scraping up what his fork couldn't. Then he enjoyed some bites of goat cheese with a glass of fruity, light-vintage Gigondas left over from the previous night. All was right with the universe. For a moment. Then he made the mistake of listening to the answering machine.

"Kendrick, it's Martin Dreissen, Domaine Adolf Dreissen. This is a very important message, one of the most important of your life. You really should come back to Alsace to talk business in person. You have some decisions to make. We have had no response from you about our terms. Call back before it's too late." *Click.*

Kendrick grabbed his *New Yorker* and went outside on the terrace to read, trying to ignore the distant cypress with metal spikes sticking out here and there in the plastic foliage. What a presence! He imagined the dangerous rays shooting out in all directions, driving away the birds and bees, stunting the growth in his garden, creating tumors in the brains of the local youth, and doing who knows what to his own body. His cat, Kali, jumped onto his lap and stared into his eyes with an expression that asked *Why aren't you protecting me from kitty cancer?*

He read a bit and went inside for a short nap on the sofa, leaving the doors open to a warm breeze. When he woke up, he wondered what to say to Martin Dreissen. He looked up Martin's private cell phone number and punched it in, thereby supporting the multiplication of antennas all over the poor, unprotected planet.

It rang five times before someone picked up, but it wasn't Martin's voice he heard.

"Kendrick, I know it's not easy for you, and you are avoiding the issue, but we have to have your answer." It was the Queen of Alsace, protecting her jewels.

"Martin called me. Is he there?"

"He's right beside me and we're on speakerphone, so go right ahead and say what you have to say."

"Well, I fear the repercussions if we change our terms. Under our current agreement, you have prospered, as have I . . ."

"Kendrick, we are nearly bankrupt!"

"Well, neither of us wants to go bankrupt," Kendrick said, "but if I have to pay for a year's worth of wine in advance, I won't be able to pay my other growers on time, and I've never been late yet, as you, Martin, and your uncle Adolf have seen for yourselves over the years."

"We are not being unreasonable. The Domaine de la Romanée Conti demands payment in advance, too."

The blood rushed to Kendrick's head. The gall, the nerve, the brazen . . . It was ridiculous comparing Domaine Dreissen to the crown jewel of Burgundy. Of course an importer could pay Domaine de la Romanée Conti in advance because it would be easy to presell every single bottle purchased. He tried to speak to her in his normal voice. "Madame, are you aware that Romanée Conti's reputation was centuries in the making? We've only been building yours for the past twenty-five years. And to change the terms and shipping conditions now, when the market is getting tighter and tighter—"

"Kendrick, we need a yes or no answer."

"After all these years of successful collaboration—certainly the most successful an Alsatian domaine has ever seen in the US—you're going to put everything we've built in jeopardy?"

"It's your decision."

"It should be *our* decision, taking into account the economy, the exchange rate, the demand, the changing taste I'm witnessing in the US."

"You know Martin is a genius in the cellar. Anybody who's read Robert Parker knows."

"I'm certainly not going to contradict Robert Parker, but he hasn't reviewed Alsatian wines in years, and that has made a difference in the market, too. When he likes a wine, his prose is so convincing, the phones start ringing in wine shops all over the world, but that's not happening like it used to."

"So, if I understand you, you are refusing our terms?"

"It is a big decision to make," Kendrick said, "for both of us. Let's each take a step back from the precipice and reflect on the possible consequences a little more. You two should think about the risks you are taking."

"What risks? What possible risk are we taking as long as we are paid fully, up front, every year?"

"Well, that's one of the things you might think about before we speak again. Someone might make promises, then pay in advance the first year, but what guarantee would you have . . ."

"Listen, I have to get to a hair appointment and can't keep going round and round with you all day. This is Monday, so as a favor to you, you can wait until Thursday to tell us. Thursday noon, at the latest! And Martin and I would both like to hear it from you here, in person!"

CHAPTER NINE

When the next Mussel Day at Vieux Laurier rolled around, Kendrick coasted in and slid to a full stop by setting the hand brake instead of using the brake pedal. He climbed out of his trusty Modus, stretched, and once again found his host around back at the barbecue. Poupon saw him coming and yelled, "Hola, Kendrick. *Comment ça va?*" He wore a dirty white T-shirt, khaki shorts, and mud-splashed heavy leather work boots. He'd already bearded and cleaned a big batch of mussels and with a well-aged wood-handled knife was removing the top shell from each one. He pointed to the fire with the knife. "Take a look at the platter there. You know what that is?" Chunks of tomato, red pepper, and slices of onion alternated with hunks of some kind of white meat on skewers.

"It looks like fish," Kendrick said. "Fish kebab?"

"We're eating from the sea. We'll start with our mussels, then I'll throw the skewers on the grill, and that's that."

"What kind of fish is it?"

"It's *congre*, shaped like an eel. It was fished during the night. A fisherman pal dropped one by early this morning when he came back early into port. What suits you? White? Rosé?"

"Here, I brought along a starter again, a Patrimonio blanc from Corsica."

"Great! Can't wait. You know, I have friends in Corsica. I go every year to hunt, but I don't have much experience with their wines."

"It was love at first sight for me," Kendrick said. "I've been going to Corsica for the past twenty years."

Once Kendrick had poured two glasses, Poupon put down his knife and sniffed the Patrimonio.

"*Merde, c'est bon ça.* And doesn't it smell like the sea?"

"Sea and stones and Vermentino."

They clinked glasses and took their first sips. Poupon kept smacking his lips emphatically while he thought about the wine.

"What sort of soil are we talking about? Corsica is granite, right?"

"Not at Patrimonio. There's a lot of chalk and decomposed oyster shells, much like you find at Chablis."

"Tasting it takes me right back to Corsica," Poupon said. "It makes me wish I were there."

"It's not far anymore. A forty-minute flight from Marseille. We could fly over in the morning, have a *figatellu* for lunch, and be back home for a nap."

"Maybe, but I'd rather stay a few days. Wouldn't you?"

"Corsica? I'll take whatever I can get. But listen, Poupon, that problem I mentioned when you were up at my place . . ."

"Oh yeah, that gorgeous cypress tree?"

"Very funny. It turns out Pageot has plans to install two more. One will be ten meters high."

"You're going to have an orchard of them before long. And Pageot will touch a pretty penny when he collects the rent for three of them. *Putain!*"

"And day and night I'll look out onto a plastic forest emitting death rays. Now that I have Milles Vents fixed up, moving elsewhere doesn't appeal to me."

"And if you moved away, I'd lose a good friend," Poupon said. "But his antenna, it's not against the law. And it's his property; he can do what he wants. The government isn't going to cross swords with the phone companies, either, no matter how deadly the rays might be. You can be sure of that."

"I was wondering, though. Can't the winemaker's syndicate here do something for me? Throw their weight around? Given my work putting the spotlight on the wines of the region, I'd think they would be happy to help. I know that Alex Pageot owns some vines, but I'm not sure what kind of surface he has."

Poupon thought a minute, then laughed. "Pageot may have a few vines left, but he's sold most of the land he inherited. He still sells some grapes to the *cave cooperative*. If the syndicate asked him to give up all that rent from the antennas, he'd laugh in their face and enjoy doing it. Do you know him?"

"Just in passing. He doesn't even say bonjour."

"Well, he's a case apart, a walking, talking asshole. If he heard about how upset you and your neighbors are, he'd crow with satisfaction."

Poupon began placing the mussels still on their half shells onto the grill, lining them up in neat rows. Then he carefully set the grill over the coals. After three or four minutes, the mussels released their juices into their shells and began to sizzle.

"I've never seen anything like that," Kendrick said.

"This is one of the simplest dishes you can make, although we won't need any dishes. The shells serve as spoons—just like the other day. Remember? No dirty dishes. Anyway, the only work is cleaning the mussels and removing the tops of the shells while the little beasts are still alive. They don't like that at all."

"I can imagine," Kendrick said. "They're probably thinking *Uh-oh, trouble brewing, and there goes half my armor.*"

Poupon raised his glass to the mussels. "Thanks to all of you for nourishing us with so much deliciousness. Amen. And look. Their liquid's evaporated, so it's time to add a little olive oil and a dusting of ground black pepper. Then, when they're cool enough to pick up with our fingers, we'll eat 'em. See how finely I ground the black pepper? If it's too chunky, believe me, it ruins the dish."

They downed the mussels as fast as they could reach for the next one.

"Now that," said Poupon, gesturing toward the empty iron grill where the mussels had been, "is what I'd call a simple dish. You find decent mussels, you prepare them, they cook in their own juice, olive oil, pepper . . ."

"And," Kendrick said, "you have a thing of beauty."

"Exactly. You don't need a battery of genius chefs or a fancy kitchen. And I'm not sure if the simplicity doesn't make it better. I don't read

books. I'm not a philosopher. In the old days, peasants cooked like
they did because they couldn't afford not to. And they created great
beauty with their simplicity. The coq au vin—it exists because they
needed a way to eat a tough old granddaddy rooster. If you cook a
normal chicken the same way, which is what everyone does nowadays,
it's insipid. They've taken the coq out of the coq au vin. One doesn't
have to look far for other examples. How they learned to cook veal
kidneys, you know, and turn the pissy kidney into a thing of beauty.
You see what I'm saying?"

"I'd say the same about wine. Don't muck it up; help it realize
itself."

"What I'm getting at isn't easy to say. At least not easy for me to
say. But I think if you can live your life in the same way I'm saying for
cooking, you'll be better off."

"You mean contemporary life is too complicated, too hurried?"

"Yes, but it sounds silly when you put it like that. Here, let's drink
a toast to the simple pleasures of life."

"Here's to a cool breeze on a hot summer day," Kendrick added,
raising his glass.

"And to a toss in the haystack with a happy, healthy *mamma mia*,"
Poupon added.

"And to the bottle of red you're serving with the *brochette de congre*."

The wine flowed down the hatch. Poupon threw the brochettes
onto the grill and lurched off purposefully to his cellar. "Take your
eyes off those brochettes, and it's into the fire with you," he shouted as
he started through the doorway and down the stairs.

Once back home again, Kendrick had enjoyed the luxury of a
deep, two-hour siesta, which was probably why, well after midnight,
he was wide awake, trying to clean up the clutter on his desk while
listening to a playlist he'd compiled twenty years earlier. Cleaning up
a desk or anything else, a quirk lodged deep within prevented him
from ever finishing it 100 percent. A woman he was once seeing had
pointed out to him what he'd never noticed about himself. She asked,
"Do you realize that when you washed the dishes after lunch, you left
the dirty silverware in the sink with one of the two coffee cups?" No,
he hadn't. "And you stopped eating with three string beans and half a

yam still on your plate. You always leave something, which isn't illegal but is a little weird."

"Maybe I don't like to come to the end," Kendrick said.

In his headphones, the overture to Mozart's *The Marriage of Figaro* came to its snappy conclusion. After ten seconds of silence, Charlie Watts tapped his snare drum one, two, three, and on the next beat he was joined by Bill Wyman's bass guitar, Keith Richards's rhythm guitar, and Brian Jones's totally cool marimba for the Rolling Stones's intro to "Under My Thumb." *Anyone hears that,* Kendrick thought, *and they are going to be led right into the song.* It also started him daydreaming (even though it was now the wee hours) about Denyse Boucard, one of the most important loves of his life.

He had met her at La Dernière Goutte near l'Odeon in Paris, where she sold wine and conducted educational tastings. They dated a couple of times, hit it off, and he invited her to accompany him on a buying trip to the Languedoc region in southern France. Suddenly, they were voraciously in love and seemed never to have enough of each other. A brunette with straight hair cut so it covered her ears but left her pretty neck bare, she possessed what Kendrick considered a smile a puritan would ban. Her lips remained closed, each side barely turned up. Maybe it was the smile in sync with her dark eyes. Once in a while, he'd check in the mirror, hoping to find his own eyes flashing. Nope. He asked if she did it on purpose, and she denied it. "I don't feel them flashing," she said, "except maybe when I want you closer." Closer was fine by him.

Both showed a passion for wine, food, music, and creating or finding good reasons to laugh as frequently as possible. Denyse even figured out what was funny about his jokes and plays on words. She soon changed to working part time in order to travel with him. On the road in the car one day after a picnic near Fleurie, Kendrick slid in a CD of oldies from the fifties. As they cruised through a forest of yellow-, orange , and maroon-colored leaves, some songs had them laughing—like the Coasters's "Poison Ivy" and its ocean of calamine lotion—and several inspired them to sing along. After the final song, Denyse started singing "Don't Be Cruel" a cappella with her French accent, and Kendrick joined in to handle the bop-bops. They followed Elvis with Fats Domino's "Blueberry Hill." When Denyse sang, "Though we're apart, you butter me still," Kendrick broke out laughing, and they both stopped singing.

"Did I do something?" she asked.

"That's not the line—although, yes, I agree, it sounds like Fats sings 'You butter me still.'"

He was surprised she knew so many American songs, while he could not name one of Johnny Holliday's.

For singing on the road, "Under My Thumb" became one of their favorites. When Kendrick mentioned that in the US the song riled up the fur on the backs of certain listeners, Denyse said the lyrics didn't bother her. "He sings that the girl in the song once dominated him, once had the singer down. But I'll bet nobody got bugged about that. The song's just a lark, an incident, stuff that could really happen, sure, but why pretend it's a philosophy of life? Just to be on the safe side, though, I'm going to change my part and sing, 'He's under my thumb.'"

"Yes, dear, but won't it sound weird to sing that the guy is a Siamese cat of a girl?"

"I'll say he's some kind of dog of a guy."

After a couple of months, Kendrick and Denyse were practically living together even though she kept paying for her apartment, which came in handy when they were in Paris. Kendrick liked time in Paris for the fine-wine-detection part of his job. Dining out or visiting the abundant wine bars, he encountered wines and producers that were new to him. As one, two, three, then four years had passed, little by little it turned out that Denyse considered herself more and more to be at the age to be married and starting a family. There was ample pressure on her as a woman in France—when the two of them visited wineries, Kendrick noticed the endless interrogations: "Are you married? Do you have any children?" Kendrick considered it nosy, a slight irritation, but he could see that the incessant questions were piling up and weighing heavily on his French lover.

Kendrick was convinced that he loved Denyse as much as he could love anyone, but the ugly failure of his first marriage still poisoned his system. Living happily ever after was not a sure thing, nor could he commit to creating children and how that might change his hit-the-road lifestyle. Kids? They might be the best thing that ever happened to him or chains that he forever resented. When he confessed to her that he could not do it, she broke it off tearfully but couldn't help returning again and again, and he was there for her with arms wide open.

One day she announced that she was dating someone else, which wounded Kendrick horribly. They continued to meet until she told him it was now or never—her boyfriend had proposed marriage. After she saw that even then Kendrick could not change, she successfully locked the gate, threw away the key, and they did not see each other again. She sent him a wedding invitation and one year later, a birth announcement. Through the years, he would find himself looking up into the wild blue yonder, remembering how it had felt, so often, over so many years—flying off to meet her and that surge of joy being together again.

It was now two a.m. He considered pulling the cork on something, but didn't. He contemplated writing to her. The urge was powerful, but what would he write? Why would he write? Would it satisfy him, simply to feel like he was communicating with her again? No. She was someone else now, he told himself.

After every one of his romances, he'd hoped at least a friendship would remain. Two or three had—Zarina's, for example. They broke off cleanly, and the romance had turned into something else. Something even more meaningful.

CHAPTER TEN

Early next evening while downing a glass of luxuriously deep, fleshy Champagne, Kendrick was whacked by a swoon-like urge to smoke a cigarette alongside his bubbly treat. He didn't keep any around the house, so he locked up and took off down the bumpy dirt road past Kintzler's house, past the fake cypress and the driveway to Pageot's property, joined the paved road and, all those familiar roundabouts later, slid loudly to a stop in Poupon's gravel driveway. Six minutes total. The tree branches were bending and waving around a bit, and he wondered if a mistral was loosening itself up for a big blow.

Poupon was sitting on the wall of his fishpond, checking out the paw of one of his hunting dogs. Kendrick put his bottle of Champagne on the edge of the pond, turned, and walked into the kitchen for a couple of wine glasses. Inside, he grabbed Poupon's tobacco and rolling papers off the dining room table.

When the two of them were finally Champagne in one hand, cigarette in the other, Poupon said, "Bonsoir, but *merde*, what's wrong with you? Judging by appearances, things must be going badly, or not at all?"

Kendrick took a puff, reflected for a moment, and said, "Yeah, everything's just great." He pushed the smoke out of his lungs slowly through his nostrils, then said, "Hunky-dory," which Poupon did not understand.

"Good for you, Kendrick, because for me, things aren't going well at all. Look at this," he said and pointed to a three-inch bloody gash in his dog's foreleg.

"Uh-oh. How'd that happen?"

"I took a shot at a good-sized male boar, wounded him, and the dog went on the attack. Before I knew what was happening, he'd taken a tusk in his leg. I just got it cleaned out at the vet's. He'll be all right. The boar's in the freezer, cooling off."

Silent smoking ensued. Kendrick refilled the two glasses. More silence. Poupon, for a change, seemed reflective, gnawing his lower lip, wiping a hand across his jaw, looking everywhere except at Kendrick. He tossed his butt into a clay ashtray.

"*Le vie est belle et la vie est de la merde*," Poupon proclaimed.

"Life is beautiful, life is the shits," Kendrick said. "No argument from me. In fact, let's drink to it."

"Let's drink a bucketful," Poupon said. In the early evening light, his skin looked terra-cotta.

"So, what's the story? Are you pissed off about something?"

"How can you not be? The good lord created everything, right? And now it's all fucked up. Why create it in the first place if you're going to let it get so fucked up?"

"For example?"

"Like here, when I was a kid. It was just a little farm, you know? Water in the well right there inside the kitchen. A good horse, a clunky tractor. A car was a luxury, so ours barely ran. You wouldn't set out on a trip with it, for example. And my parents shipped me by bus to La Crau, north of Toulon, to a Catholic boys' school. They meant well, but I wasn't meant for schooling. I was born to be outdoors. Anyway, I told you about the priest here, trying to get into all our pants. At La Crau, it was worse. There we were like prisoners. I came home for Christmas—couldn't wait to tell my mother and father the ugly truth. They'd save me from those holy monsters. Justice would be done. You'd think so anyway, right? I'm their son. I'm family. But no, the priest is their Father, shit on his grave. The priest's grave, not my real father's. But, in fact, my parents beat me when I tried to tell them. Can you imagine? They turned on their own son. 'Don't spread your dirty lies,' they said, and they put me on the bus and sent me back." Poupon's eyes were red, and a tear or two rolled down his bristly, unshaven cheek.

Finally, Kendrick broke the silence. "Catholics. Who would ever have imagined? A secret pedophile club. A pedophile club worldwide, and we're all supposed to give them ten percent of our earnings to keep the club going. To keep them in marble and jewels and good wine. Not a bad deal. For them."

"Ten percent and your son!" Poupon shouted. He grabbed the empty Champagne bottle and heaved it as far as he could into the vines across the driveway. "I'm getting us a red, an old red. Agreed? Because I'm not finished talking, drinking, or smoking."

Night was on its way as their two noses once again descended into their wine glasses. Kendrick was impressed by what he smelled. "My god, that smells like the essence of something—not sure what. Something primeval, sort of like entering a deep cave and finding traces of ashes and bones and cave paintings. Something vivid, but it's like music—you can't find words for it. Subterranean truth, maybe. Like what I feel when a passage in music stops me in my tracks."

Poupon took another sniff. "What music is that? It's not on my radio. And what have you been smoking? This is nothing but a red wine my father and I made in 1989, just to have something around the house. Back then we were selling almost all our harvest to other wineries. We were grape farmers, not winemakers."

Kendrick took a long, slow sniff. "Well, I'd put it on my top ten list—one of the ten best Bandols I've ever tasted, and I've tasted hundreds. Make your wine like this every year, and I'll buy every bottle you'll sell to me. But go on, tell me more about your Catholic school."

"No, that's enough of that. But here's another one for you to chew on. You might think you know someone, but you don't know a damned thing. Even your best friend, your brother, your mother, even the woman you marry. You sleep with her, make love to her, but you don't really know what makes her tick. And if you did know her, knew the deep-down truth about her, you might just turn and walk away and say to your lonesome self, 'That? No. That I cannot accept.'"

"Christ, Poupon, you're in a darker mood than I am."

"I'll tell you a true story that happened right here in l'Estournel, *centre ville*. A bunch of local guys were at the Café Centrale drinking pastis outside, you know, up there above city hall? The one with all those red tablecloths? And two of them start arguing about I forget what, but it really heats up, and one of them says, 'You know the truth about your mother, right? Well, when she still looked young, she'd sell her body for a fresh fish or a few grams of black truffles.' Like, tells him his mother was a whore, you see? And the other guy, Charles Lapierre was his name, he says, 'No, you're wrong. I'd call my mother wise. After all, she ate well and got laid a lot.' He picked up the bottle of pastis and swung it as hard as he could, right across the guy's face. Almost ripped his jaw off. Lapierre spent a year in prison at La Farlède, near Toulon. And the other guy? Ten years later, and he still can't talk right."

Kendrick was feeling no pain as they neared the end of the old Bandol, admiring some good-sized dark purple chunks of sediment at the bottom of his wine glass. "That's a helluva story," he said, although his last word sounded more like *shtory*. He stood up and looked up into a starry sky. "Thanks for everything, my friend."

CHAPTER ELEVEN

Kendrick made do with Poupon's leather-upholstered couch for the night, even though there were several empty bedrooms. He'd drunk himself into the mood for the quickest, closest flat surface available in order to achieve maximum horizontality before his lids slammed shut. Come morning, when he managed to open his left eye, albeit in extremely slow motion, there stood Poupon inside the kitchen doorway at his espresso machine as if he'd been waiting—not altogether patiently—for signs of life.

"Hey, you might be on vacation," he said, "but some of us have to work. Are you awake enough for some coffee?"

Kendrick raised a hand a couple of inches off the couch.

"Black?"

"Totally." Kendrick the lionhearted squirmed, twisted, and finally worked his body up into a sitting position. He cleaned the sleep out of his eyes and reached out for the coffee cup.

"It's a double," Poupon said. He waited until Kendrick had a swallow or two before continuing. "You try to drink your problems away once in a while, but when you wake up, there they are, the same problems, even bigger and brighter."

"Come on, Poupon. Why don't you spell it out? You still haven't explained what you're so blue about."

"Blue? No, not blue. More like bitter, you know? Because some-times life presents you with choices and none are completely the right choice, but you have to choose anyway."

"Go on. What choices? What's your problem?"

"Ah, good timing. Impeccable! You hear that?"

It was a car pulling up in the driveway. The car door slammed shut even though the engine was still running.

"I know that car," Poupon said, "Here's one of my problems, in the flesh, right . . . about . . . *now!*" And without knocking, in swept Babette, perfume and all. This time her hair was a dry, rusty orange, as solid as the hair on Michelangelo's *David*. She gave Poupon a quick kiss on the lips, saw Kendrick, and said, "What's this? Did you know you have an American on your couch?"

"Yes," Poupon said, "and the stories are true—Americans can't hold their liquor."

She bent over and almost reached each of Kendrick's cheeks with a kiss. "Don't bother to put on your pants," she said. "Your Calvin Kleins are *trés, trés chic.*"

Kendrick's head bobbled downward, and as his bleary eyes began to focus on his Calvins, he was perplexed to see a pale, chalky-pink member of his reproductive team peeking meekly out of his fly. *Chic* it was assuredly far from.

Babette downed an espresso, and *Sorry, had to run, appointment in downtown Aix-en-Provence, just had to stop by and give Poupon a kiss, so long, see you next time.*

Poupon stared at the door after she'd closed it. "*Merde!*"

"Why *merde?*" Kendrick asked.

"Why? You're lucky to be so uncomplicated. I mean, she's here, and then she's gone, but what does she do when she's not with me? When I called her apartment the other day, some guy with a foreign accent answered the phone. What the hell was that?"

"So? Why shouldn't another man answer?"

"Maybe I don't like the idea of her with another man."

"You don't like the idea of another mule kicking in your stall? If you are so in love with Babette, maybe you should consider marriage."

Poupon grimaced, then looked up toward the ceiling as if seeking divine guidance. "I'm cornered. You see? That's what I've been talking about. None of the choices open to me are the right choices. It's painful. My sciatic nerve is pulsating hot flashes. I wish I could shoot some novocaine into my left hip."

"Here's my prescription: Take two aspirin with a glass of strong red wine; see if that helps."

"Novocaine would be faster."

"You've got a cellar full of red wine, but how many dentists are going to agree to poke a needle into your rear end? Especially *your* rear end. Better you stick with aspirin and red wine. You still haven't answered: Why don't you ask Babette to marry you?"

"I like my liberty, for one thing. I like to go hunting whenever I want without being scolded. Stay out all night if I want, come home drunk, leave the toilet seat up. Married? Ha!

"So, you better marry a woman who accepts you for who you are, toilet seat and all. However, that's not sure to be Babette d'Orsini. I'll bet you want your Babette to be married to you—a chaste Babette—but you don't want to give up your precious freedoms. Have I got that right?"

"Yes, because I think I'm in love with Zarina, too. But in a different way."

"You're joking. Babette versus Zarina? Hey, I know. You should move to Utah, marry them both.

"Where's Utah?"

"So, let's try to put this in perspective. What is it you love about Babette?"

"What, are you crazy? You have eyes, don't you? You're not blind?"

"You mean she's good looking?"

"Is that all you see? You don't see class when you look at her? I mean, maybe it's different for you, but I'm just a farm boy, you know, uneducated, never taught manners or how to talk fancy. There's mud under my fingernails, shit on my boots. Take a longer look at Babette. Look at the way she acts, too. She could be a duchess or something, and yet she tells me, Henri Poupon, that she loves me."

Kendrick held his cup out for another coffee. "Poupon, don't forget, you own a lot of land not far from the Mediterranean, and you've created a prosperous wine domaine. So, in the eyes of a lot of people, you are a desirable bachelor—that's what I want you to realize. Don't put on your humble pose for me. And Babette, she *could* be a duchess, but is she?"

"Not that I know of, no."

"How does she make a living?"

"What the hell? How would I know?"

"Well, by talking to her. Don't you two talk?"

"Not when she's climbing up my leg, trying to get into my pants."

"Would you like to trade pants? Nobody ever tries to get into mine."

"Hey, I know, before you leave, I want you to taste something if you have a minute. It's the new rosé I haven't shown you yet."

Down into the cellar they trooped, armed with the tools of their trade—two wine glasses. Kendrick had his blue jeans on by then with a wrinkled blue-and-white-striped linen shirt hanging out untucked.

"Okay, go ahead," Poupon said, "you can talk about Babette while I make a blend of the new rosé cuvées."

They were subterranean now in Poupon's spacious winery, surrounded by large oak casks and several vats, some stainless steel, some concrete. An air conditioner whirred, keeping the wines cool.

Kendrick said, "Well, just tell me anything you can about her. What's the real color of her hair, where's she from originally, has she been married . . . ? Things like that."

Poupon went from *cuve* to *cuve*, taking a bit of rosé from each into his wine glass. "She's probably blondish, right? I mean, now that they all wax everywhere, how do you know anymore? Zarina dyes her hair, too. She says she'd be gray if she didn't, but down there she's still brunette. And Babette, I suppose she's French, but I never asked her where was born or grew up. She doesn't have a Provençale accent, that's for sure. She sounds kind of educated, don't you think?"

"Hard to say. I haven't heard her talk all that much."

"Okay," Poupon said. "Here, taste this. This will be my new rosé. Then we'll taste that kid's rosé from Tavel that you like so much. That way you can compare them."

Kendrick held his glass up to the light. "Thanks, Poupon. Well, first, I don't see much difference in color compared to past vintages." He swirled the wine around and lowered his nose into the glass. "Oh my god!" He shuddered, tossed a taste of rosé into his mouth, swished it around a little, and spit it out.

Poupon frowned. "You obviously don't like it. Am I right?"

"Are you out of your mind? It smells like pineapple and grapefruit with a little coconut mixed in. Horrid! It doesn't smell like it was made from grapes."

"Sorry to inform you, but that's exactly what it was made from. My grapes. I should know, right? I mean, I was here the whole time. We harvested the grapes nice and ripe, crushed the grapes, I added the yeasts, the juice fermented perfectly until dry—my grapes, my rosé."

"Well, it tastes like some concoction from another planet, but I wouldn't call it wine, because it doesn't *smell* like wine. You say you added yeasts. Why add yeasts? Haven't your wines always fermented without adding yeasts?"

"Oh, Kendrick. Here you go again. Yes, of course, but you know, it's always scary for a winemaker, waiting for the wine to ferment completely dry. When the fermentation gets stuck, *ai yi yi*, you've got problems."

"I buy from a domaine; their 1996 red took three years to finish fermenting."

"Oh *merde*, that's a catastrophe."

"Not at all. At the domaine, they consider it one of their three greatest vintages. Maybe it's different with rosé, but pineapple and coconut in a wine's perfume? Where are we, Hawaii? And anybody who wants to drink grapefruit juice—fine, buy a grapefruit and squeeze it. It's a lot cheaper than your rosé."

There was silence while Poupon tried to digest all that. Then, true to form, he said, "*Merde!*"

"Exactly," Kendrick said.

"But my enologist says if we don't add the yeasts, the rosés from the Côtes-de-Provence appellation are going to take over the Bandol market."

Kendrick took another sniff, his wine glass a safe distance from his nose. "True, this does, in fact, smell a lot like all of those technologically manufactured Côtes-de-Provence rosés. But try to explain to me why you always listen to and agree with your enologist. Where's his logic? Côtes-de-Provence taking over the Bandol market? Can't you see? He's tyring to scare you—in fact, *has* succeeded in scaring you into using yeasts. *Your baby will die if you don't do what I say.* I'll bet you anything he said something like that. But tell me, why would any winemaker want to copy the taste of a cheaper, less exalted rosé? Bandol is at the top of the rosé pyramid. Why copy a wannabe?"

"I don't know. *Merde.* It made more sense when he explained it. He says it has a bouquet of tropical fruit."

"More like tropical bullshit, if you ask me. And you *did* ask me. So, tell me something. Where does one go to buy such delicious yeasts?"

"Oh, no problem. He sells them."

Kendrick stared at him as seconds ticked by.

Poupon shrugged and mumbled, "What's wrong?"

"Who sells them?" Kendrick asked again.

"He sells . . . *Putain de merde!* Are you telling me . . . ? You really think . . . ? He wouldn't . . . Come on, a lot of people add yeasts now. It's the latest progress."

"Your grapes are already covered with yeasts. Zillions of them. Selling you yeast is like selling sand to an Arab. And listen to me. This is important. Different yeasts give different flavors. Surely you smell the difference in your rosé. You change the yeasts, you change the wine's flavor. You're fucking around with its *gout de terroir.* You're fucking around with god! Tell your enologist that your biggest client, me, is going to stop buying your rosé if it continues to taste like a Hawaiian fruit cocktail."

After the tasting, winding up the circular staircase and out to the car, Poupon poked Kendrick in the arm. "But hey, you have to admit, Babette is a choice hunk of woman, isn't she?"

Kendrick broke into a big smile. "I'm proud of you, my friend— two lovely women in your bed. Babette d'Orsini *de* Nice. Nobility. Have you noticed her white teeth? So white and perfectly straight, you feel like you could play a Chopin mazurka on them."

"Mallorca?"

"Oh, never mind," Kendrick said. "Don't pay me any mind. If you're not going to listen to me about your rosé, you're certainly not going to listen to me about your love life."

CHAPTER TWELVE

Cobwebs, moldy patches on the wall, wear-a-sweater cold, and lit by two naked, dim, yellow bulbs—most of Kendrick's morning was spent under his house in his funky wine cellar rearranging bins of bottles and putting away new arrivals. He had decided that whether he deserved it or not, something special might change his mood, so he brought up a 1972 Clos de la Roche from Jean-Marie Ponsot for lunch. Kendrick had been eleven years old when Monsieur Ponsot harvested the grapes to make the wine, and he now had a brief hesitation—a well-aged *grand cru* red Burgundy probably wasn't the most appropriate choice to serve with thyme-flavored tomato sauce on slices of fried polenta, but *What the hell?* he thought, that's what there was for lunch, and he wanted to drink that particular wine. Once in the kitchen, however, he remembered the mild, creamy *Gorgonzola dolce* he'd purchased in Bordighera. He put it on top of the hot polenta instead of tomato sauce and thought it went just fine with the miraculous old Ponsot, a true *grand cru* in every way.

Before air-conditioning, everyone in southern Europe enjoyed an after-lunch siesta. Kendrick had taken to the custom wholeheartedly. A nap, a jolt of espresso, and the day begins anew. For him, in fact, it was like turning one day into two—wake up in the morning, coffee, work or play, lunch, nap, coffee, work or play, dinner, off to bed for the night. He felt like he was doubling his days on earth.

He woke up just in time to brew a cup before walking down into Le Caniveau for a haircut appointment. The barbershop was *centre ville*, the oldest part of town, with its square, fountain, and several plane trees for summer shade—just like hundreds of other Mediterranean villages.

At the BNP, he withdrew some cash from the automatic teller. Population only seven thousand, Le Caniveau had seven other banks. As usual in overly medicated France, the village was also loaded with pharmacies. Kendrick was continually amazed that even with so many pharmacies, you usually had to wait in line to be served.

Cash successfully pocketed, he crossed the square to Chez Bobo, a stuffy one-chair barbershop, a relic that smelled of decades-old burnt hair. It was frequented by middle-aged and older local men who wouldn't be caught dead paying five times more for a "coiffure." To Kendrick, Bobo himself looked to be right around sixty years old. He was short, fit, and Kendrick marveled at his ostrich-like eyes, super-concentrated on whatever head of hair he had before him. As usual, there was no wait, and Bobo started clipping away with his scissors. No chitchat, either. A stooped old fellow limped in—he looked like age weighed on him like a sack of cement—and he and Bobo cheeked each other.

"Bobo, remember that chicken? You promised you'd tell me how to make it." The man glanced down at Kendrick and said, "Bonjour, monsieur." Then back to Bobo. "It's hot in here. If I had any money, I'd give you an electric fan for your birthday. Anyway, that was the best chicken I've ever eaten. I swear it's even better than my mother's chicken, and she raised her own."

Kendrick paid attention, always eager to add to his kitchen repertoire.

Bobo, however, asked how Veronique was doing, whoever that might be.

"Oh, it's too sad to talk about. She can't walk by herself anymore. She has to use a walker, which she calls her Mercedes. Remember how she used to outrun us boys?"

Except for the scrape of the razor on the back of Kendrick's neck, there was silence as Veronique's running was considered.

"For the chicken dinner, I'll have my cousin over. Hippolyte. Remember him?"

In the mirror, Kendrick saw Bobo nod yes.

"He and his wife, my nephew, Marcel, and his girlfriend, Claudine, with her two daughters, plus René Reboul, who just retired."

"René retired? So much the better for him," Bobo said. "It's too bad we can't retire when we're young and work when we get older."

"So, I have to have your recipe. What's the trick to it?"

Kendrick started to pay close attention again.

"Oh, you can't spoil this one if you do exactly as I say." Bobo stopped mid-clip because, after all, food is serious business to the French, and he wanted his old friend to get it right. "Go to Super U in Bandol. It's only ten minutes from here, more like seven if you get on the autoroute."

"But then I have to come up with one euro and sixty centimes at the tollbooth."

"That's up to you. Go to Super U, but not to the butcher's counter. Instead, you go to the frozen food section and get a bag of chicken legs. Much cheaper! Thaw them out the very morning you are going to serve them. Once that's done, pat them dry with a paper towel and sprinkle cumin powder on them. Don't be stingy. Oh, I forgot—don't forget to rub them first with cooking oil, because that way the cumin powder won't fall off. Salt them just like you do any chicken. Put them in a hot oven for fifty minutes. No more, no less. It's the best way to cook chicken. Especially with rice."

"Monsieur," the old fellow said, addressing Kendrick, "when Bobo served his chicken dish to me, I swear, I spoke of nothing else for days."

Bobo picked up his electric razor, circa 1932, and began applying the final touches of his handiwork. Then he stopped to proclaim, "We must preserve the old recipes, you know? It's up to us. Have you seen the mobs at McDonald's in La Seyne? You can't even find a parking place at lunchtime. No one takes time to cook anymore."

On the street, returning to his car, Kendrick looked enviously at the patrons seated outside at tables under the plane trees, enjoying coffee or a drink, most of them smoking guiltlessly, as far as he could tell.

"Fucking cigarettes," Kendrick said with a glance at the tempting *tabac* next to the café.

He spotted Maitre Jobard, Le Caniveau's mayor and *notaire*, walking toward him. Jobard was notable for his phony smile and swollen, pitted nose, which he tried to blot out with some sort of clay-colored paste, and his head of hair, which looked like he had a punk streak in him trying to get out against his will. His hair was spiky and electric, and somehow it looked like he suffered an itchy scalp to boot. When he saw Kendrick, he started to burst into a smile and raise his hand for shaking, but it apparently quickly registered in his mind that Kendrick was not French and, therefore, could not vote. In a flash, the friendly smile disappeared, and he returned to his conniving trains of thought.

Alas, there went one of Kendrick's anti-antenna plans—to personally seek out the mayor's help. When Kendrick purchased Milles Vents, the mayor as *notaire* pocketed a healthy commission. Kendrick now realized that without a vote or a way for the mayor to profit anew, he might as well try spitting into a mistral.

This was the afternoon of the day when Kendrick was supposed to show up at Dreissen's before noon, or at least call them, but so far, he hadn't done either. To call or not to call—the arguments pushed and pulled back and forth in his mind. Part of him urged himself to call and try to save the relationship. On the other hand, he was not about to agree to such monstrous terms. Plus, the insulting, cavalier treatment he received after all the years of collaboration and success left a bitter aftertaste. He passed a little jewelry shop and pictured Mme Dreissen inside trying on every piece of jewelry around her fingers, wrists, neck, ankles, and dangling from her ears until she collapsed under the weight of it all. *Never enough, never enough, never enough,* she would say until her voice gave out and there was nothing to be seen of her under a heap of glitter on the floor.

When Kendrick got back to the house, a new email from Martin Dreissen awaited him.

* * *

Mon cher Kendrick,

While I am disappointed not to have your visit, I understand why you would not want to face facts. Just know that you will always be welcomed as a friend at Domaine Dreissen.

We will soon be releasing exciting news: Our new importer is Ziggy Bakerman, the Chicago real estate tycoon. He is creating an import company called Only Z Best. He is talking to Romanée Conti, Yquem, Petrus, and so on to have all of the finest from France imported by one company, all paid in advance, all shipped in one fell swoop to the warehouse he's building. It will be almost as big as Bergheim. My wife and I are honored to be in such fine company. Bakerman is a man who truly understands business. Now the future of Domaine Dreissen is assured.

Many thanks for helping us get started, best regards, always your friend, Domaine Dreissen

P.S. There will always be a slice of my grandmother's tarte aux *quetches* if ever you drop by to say hello.

Kendrick wasn't in tears, but the whole thing hurt like a wallop, even though deep down he was also relieved to get out from under what had recently turned into a heavy load. Later, toward dark, but with little appetite for dinner, he went down into his wine cellar and pulled out a 1988 Riesling made by Martin's uncle. He drank it by candlelight outside on the terrace. Looking into his glass, he thought the golden depths of the old Riesling rivaled any color the great painters had created—nuanced gold with light and dark shades while green and silvery glints (thanks to the candle's flame) darted around inside. By today's standards, he thought the wine might be considered lightweight, but Kendrick saw perfect balance, an ethereal delicacy and finesse, a feathery touch on the palate as opposed to Martin's sledgehammer approach.

While munching on sliced sausage and a local goat cheese, Kendrick allowed some remembrances of things past to surface, reliving the excitement he had experienced when he discovered the Dreissen wines. Previously, the marvelous potential of the varied Alsatian terroirs had been wasted, the best cuvées from the best sites often blended with flatland grapes, and when he discovered Frederic Dreissen's wines, he knew he was witnessing a change that would rock the world of fine wine.

Kendrick was surprised when he reached to pour another glass and there was almost nothing left. He raised the last glass, dregs and all, to Frederic Dreissen—Martin's gifted uncle—and thanked him for the memory. He was one of Kendrick's wine heroes.

CHAPTER THIRTEEN

The next day, an unusual occasion at Milles Vents: company for lunch. Yes, somewhat of a rarity, because typically in the wine biz it is the buyer who is invited, not the seller, so in France, Kendrick was more often invited by winemakers, while in the States, he or his staff invited his customers. However, Mme Martignac, like Poupon, was a special favorite of Kendrick's, and they traded dining invitations at least two or three times per year.

Mme Martignac had been widowed seven years earlier when Kendrick had already been working with the family wine domaine for over two decades, so he'd known her husband well. Strangely enough, for years she acted like the gestapo guardian of the property. Dressed always in grays or black, she also wore a severe, judgmental expression, and when she spoke, it was usually to whip her husband and son into line. *Hey, everyone is drinking too much* could have been her tagline. Both men tended to be laid back, blessed with what-the-hell attitudes, and liked nothing better than to live it up at every occasion. They enjoyed their work and were known in the wine trade as a couple of happy-go-lucky bons vivants. One day, tragedy struck, and not out of a clear blue sky. Father and son were flying to a wine fair in Grenoble with another vigneron, who piloted his own plane. They ran into bad weather as they neared their destination, which is surrounded by sturdier-than-thou, almost flat-topped mountains, one of which did not yield an inch as their pilot blindly had flown right into it.

Lo and behold, however, there was another Madame Martignac inside the watchdog, and she did not wait very long to emerge after her widowhood when she no longer had to police the two men in her life. She loosened up, showed a wicked sense of humor, and, of all things, gave up drinking water. To replace water, she turned to red wine, especially lusty, deep-flavored reds.

She liked to ask people, "Do you know how many additives there are in your average tap water?"

Most would reply, "I have no idea. How many?"

"I don't know either," she'd say, "but my red wine doesn't have a one. Better dead-drunk than poisoned, right?" Kendrick imagined what an MD back in the USA would say. The medical establishment would probably commit her to a mental hospital even though she was as healthy as could be. "Water makes me rusty," she liked to say.

Previously, she and Kendrick had only tolerated each other. Then, spending time with her became a treat. When she drove up in her pale blue Alpha Romeo, two women got out. She'd asked if she could bring her niece, Valerie, with her, and Kendrick had said, "*Mais oui, bien-sur.*" Valerie was dressed for a Grateful Dead concert in Golden Gate Park. She had naturally smiling eyes, high cheekbones, and a dark complexion, maybe picked up by an ancestor in one of the French colonies.

Of all things, Kendrick was making hamburgers for lunch because the last time he and Mme Martignac had met, she'd lashed out with horror at McDonald's and fast food and American eating habits. Kendrick told her she was mistaken. "The hamburger is actually quite an intelligent creation. You don't judge French cheeses by the crap French pizzerias pile on their pizzas, do you? Well, don't judge the burger by a fast-food joint." He'd promised to make her a McKendrickburger.

They moved into the kitchen where a rosé from the Corbiéres region was waiting in an ice bucket. Kendrick explained that a good burger bun is hard to find even in the US, much less in a French boulangerie. A brioche roll might answer but is likely to be too soggy, so he was going to use slightly toasted slices of focaccia from an Italian bakery in Signes. "Mainly," he explained, "you should have something tender enough to chew with ease, so a crusty baguette won't work—you'd squeeze out all the filling biting into it. At the same time, the bun should be solid enough that it won't turn to mush when saturated with meat juices, the tomato's juice, and whatever dressing you use, like mayonnaise, mustard, or ketchup."

From his fridge, he took out three different cuts of beef and began slicing them into small hunks: a beef filet, meat from the neck, and *ris de veau*. Finally, he was mincing everything together until they were fine enough to press into three balls.

"Not too thick," he said, flattening each into a patty. "A lot of chefs err by making the meat so thick it won't fit into anybody's mouth. A burger should be *handy*. That's part of its beauty. And you want the fillings balanced, not all meat and bun. There's more to a burger than meat."

He de-salted some capers from Salina, sliced tomatoes from the garden, and whipped up an aioli in a marble mortar. When the french fries were almost done, he seasoned the meat patties with dried thyme, salt, ground black pepper, and he positioned them in a huge, black, searingly hot iron skillet.

"You want to seize them because a little crunch to the exterior of the patty adds a good flavor and texture. Let's eat."

The women enjoyed Kendrick's burgers, said they'd had no idea what a treat one could be, and wasn't it good with the nine-year-old Morgon from the Beaujolais? They ate on the terrace with its grand view of the Massif de Sainte Baume and a vibrant blue sky full of mile-long, tubular clouds, snow white.

After they finished their coffees, Madame Martignac told her niece to give her and Kendrick a few minutes alone because she had a joke for him about wine, and it had some words in it the niece shouldn't hear.

"Are you losing your mind?" Valerie asked, laughing with her eyebrows raised in disbelief. "Dear auntie, I'm thirty-six years old and could teach you some words that didn't exist back when you learned to talk."

"Oh, how dull of me. Stick around, then. So! I assume you've both heard the phrase *faire pisser les vignes*? You know, you prune your vines long and you irrigate in order to make a lot of diluted juice to increase quantity. Well, it does happen, and no region is more famous for it than the Beaujolais. However, one year in the village of Amplepuis, the grape juice they harvested was of such beauty, everyone was astonished. And when the juice finished fermenting and turned into wine, it was proclaimed one of the best ever—another 1947 or 1929! It had a splendid deep purplish color and was certainly the most delicious vintage of their lifetime.

"One night a bunch of winemakers got together. You know how they do—men only, and each one bringing samples of the fresh new vintage, and lots of it. They built a fire and started cooking and drinking. The wine was so tasty, they kept chugging it down and got drunker and drunker. They drank so much that when they had to piss, it started streaming out pure Beaujolais.

"The next morning, all the men in the village were slow getting out of bed. And one of the wives asked her husband how things went at the party. 'Oh, the wines this year are so delicious—I remember drinking it straight from the neck of the bottle.'"

Kendrick and Valerie sat waiting. But no, apparently the punch line had been delivered.

"It must be my French," he said, "because I don't get it."

The niece shrugged and turned her palms up. Neither did she.

"Oh damn, maybe I forgot a line or two," said Mme Martignac. "When I heard the joke the other day, everyone screamed with laughter. Don't you see? The winemakers drank so much and got drunk out of their minds. Everyone was pissing pure Beaujolais, and the guy thought he was drinking *du goulot*, right out of the neck of the bottle, but, in fact . . ."

"Oh, he was drinking . . ." Kendrick began.

"From someone's *zizi*," finished the niece.

"But damnation, when you have to explain a joke," said Mme Martignac, "it's not as funny. So listen to one more. You'll like it, and I'll try to tell it better. I heard it from my neighbor, Mme Laval. She's over ninety years old, but she loves risqué stories, god bless her."

"Hold on, hold on!" Kendrick jumped up and started through the cork fly curtain into the kitchen. "I have a half bottle of Sauternes on ice, and I'll bet a glass would go quite well with your next joke."

After the golden dessert wine was poured and some words about the miracle of noble rot were exchanged, Mme Martignac smoothed back her gray hair and began anew. "A woman in her late sixties loses her husband, and she was not at all happy about being left alone. The only eligible men were of an advanced age and looking mostly for a hot, young thing or live-in nursing care. More and more lonely, the poor thing couldn't figure out where she might meet eligible bachelors, so she decided to place an ad in the local newspaper. 'Recent widow seeks mate. Age unimportant. Warning! Do not apply if you are violent, chase after other women, or are not healthy enough to satisfy a woman.'

"For a few days, the ad did not elicit a single response. Then one fine morning, her doorbell rang. She peeked out the peephole but saw no one. The doorbell, however, sounded a second time. She pulled the door open, looked down, and there in a wheelchair sat a man with no arms or legs.

"'*Chère* madame, I am Hervé Etalon, and I'm here to answer your ad,' he said.

'Well, that's very fine, monsieur, but didn't you read my stipulations?'

'Indeed, I did. However, my dear woman, you have nothing to worry about. You specified the desire to avoid a man who chases after other women. Correct?'

'Yes, monsieur,' she said.

'Well, look at me. How can I chase anything? I have no legs. And how in the world do you think I could beat you or anyone else when I have no arms?'

'Yes, monsieur, I'm sure you have a lot of wonderful qualities, but I made it very clear that the man must be in perfect physical health, if you know what I mean.'

The fellow looked up at her with a seductive look in his eyes and a sly grin. 'Well, madame, how do you think I rang your doorbell?'"

Maybe it was that additional glass, the Sauternes, but they had no problem appreciating the second joke, and their laughter made Mme Martignac quite proud of herself.

Valerie pulled out her smokes, and Kendrick supplied the flame.

"That joke goes into my arsenal," Kendrick said.

"The older I get, the more I'll appreciate it, I'm sure," Valerie said.

"But please allow me to change the subject," Kendrick said. "Do either of you know the city of Nice very well?"

Both women nodded, exhaling.

"I used to visit it often," Mme Martignac answered. "Not so much nowadays. It's not the same. Now it's cluttered, full of riffraff, grown almost tacky, you know?"

"Nice, where the whores charge twice as much. That's sort of a saying I've heard," the niece added.

"Well, if I were young and sexy," said Mme Martignac, "and looking to marry into money, I'd go to Nice or Cannes. Were I really high class, Monaco or Monte Carlo. Nice has the silver, but Monte Carlo has the gold."

"And the gold diggers," Valerie said. "Isn't it the same everywhere? Women interested in marrying well, women considered sexy—they go where the money is. And where there's a beach. Beaches, where they can display their wares to full advantage."

"I remember when Biarritz was the same kind of destination," said Mme Martignac.

"Excuse me if I change the conversation again just a little bit," Kendrick said, "but do you have private detectives in France?"

Valerie laughed. "Sam Spade? Philip Marlowe? That sort of detective?"

"Exactly."

Madame Martignac's jaw dropped. "Oh my god, Kendrick. What have you done? Are you in some kind of trouble?" She signaled to Valerie for another smoke, just in case the situation justified one.

"No, no, it's for a friend of mine. Nothing to do with me."

Madame Martignac wagged her forefinger at Kendrick. "Well, watch out for detectives. Promise me that you will not hire anyone unless you have a recommendation from a friend. If you get some shady character, he might end up working against instead of for you. Let's say a wife suspects her husband of some infidelity. She hires a detective who spies on the husband and discovers that indeed, he has a lover, who also happens to be male. You follow me? So, the detective then blackmails his client. You know—if you don't give me so much money, I'll show these photos of you and your pal to your wife."

"You really think that could happen?"

"Absolutely. Think about it—things like that are too easy to pull off, so you know they happen."

CHAPTER FOURTEEN

When his two guests were tucked into the Alpha and heading down the hill, Kendrick sacked out on the living room couch hoping for some shut-eye, but his mind was too active to fall asleep. Fifteen minutes later a fly worked its way inside the cork curtain, and the chase around the room trying to swat it with a magazine shattered the peace and quiet for good. Once he had the fly splotched on the window, Kendrick stretched out again, but knew he'd missed the moment—his mind was too busy trying to figure out what to do about Poupon and Babette. He surprised himself—how much he really cared about the big lug and wanted to protect him. She was the fox, and mighty Poupon the hare. If one day Poupon was damaged by Babette, and Kendrick hadn't followed his instinct to intervene, he'd forever suffer a monstrous load of guilt. Poupon saw her as a classy duchess of somewhere or other, but something smelled off. In the wine trade, Kendrick had some experience dealing with barons, dukes, even one prince who owned vines at Vouvray. Nothing about Babette struck him as aristocratic—not that there was anything conclusive to be drawn from that.

Poupon's mind turned to jelly when he was around her. Evidently, she fit some kind of adolescent farm boy fantasy of his—the lady and the tramp? But was she on the up and up? Everything about her seemed false to Kendrick.

Poupon had mentioned that he'd telephoned her at her home in Nice and a man had answered. Big deal, right? It was probably nothing, or maybe it was a lead to follow. So Kendrick decided to pursue his idea to hire a private eye. At least he'd have done something. He'd be happy to pay for a few days' surveillance just to see what might turn up. If, however, word somehow got back to Poupon, it could ruin a beautiful friendship—not between Poupon and Babette, perhaps, but between Poupon and Kendrick.

He decided on a plan of action—first he needed Babette's full name, phone number, and address.

Next on his mind was Antenna Man himself, Alex Pageot. It occurred to Kendrick that with all the talk about it—the *collectif*, a lot of parents up in arms, the lawyer—he hadn't tried talking to Pageot himself, face-to-face, neighbor to neighbor. He stepped through the cork curtain out onto the terrace and looked down the hill. Pageot's silver pickup was there, as was the blue Smart car his wife drove.

First, Kendrick went down the inner staircase to his wine cellar. His eyes roamed the bins. In his experience, Provençals never understood wines from northern France, so a red Burgundy wouldn't do. He spotted a few classics from Bordeaux, but he wanted to be present when those corks were pulled. A bin of mixed vintages of Gigondas? He found no arguments against them and grabbed a 1995, probably *à point* at ten years of age. He hoped a neighborly gift might help. Off he strode to do battle, bottle in hand, down the hill.

He passed wild blackberry vines in flower, equally wild fennel and rosemary, then walked up Pageot's dirt driveway and around the new house, a house without corners, following the circular shape of the ancient windmill, a gray, plaster-walled house that the young man and his wife had never bothered to paint. As Kendrick rounded it, looking for a front door to knock on, suddenly there they were—Alex and his wife seated on chairs next to their plastic hot tub. The wife, notably, wore her hair pink and was topless. Kendrick's eyes raced to her breasts even as he began commanding them not to. His heart beat faster, speeding the blood flow. It occurred to him that Mother Nature's work is not always fine-tuned.

Alex leapt out of his chair and charged right up until his scowling face filled Kendrick's vision. His breath smelled of pastis, and his stance seemed to say *You are an invader, and your survival is questionable.* He wore a white T-shirt, slim black jeans, and work boots. His face was lean with flat, swept-back ears and short black hair. He showed a physical toughness that probably came from a history of barroom brawls over some soccer match or another, or jealousy, or just plain nastiness. He had a hardheaded look in his eye that told Kendrick whatever he wanted, he was *not* going to get.

His wife, however, spoke first. "Don't they teach you manners where you come from? Like to knock at the front door?"

"Sorry, I looked for the front door . . ."

"Well," she broke in, "you might start with the front of the house."

The front of a round house? The conversation was not going in the direction Kendrick had imagined, but at least she'd jerked a T-shirt over her head. It was bright red with an atomic bomb exploding over each of her breasts.

Kendrick said, "Bonjour. I've never introduced myself since you moved in. I know it's been three or four years, but still, better late than never, I wanted to welcome you." He held out the bottle of Gigondas.

Pageot never took his eyes off Kendrick's as he took the bottle, then reached behind him where his wife could take it out of his hand. It was like a cowboy movie, and the gunslinger can't look away in case the other guy goes for his gun.

"Yes, anything else?" Pageot asked.

"You have a *great* view." The sentence hung in the hot air until Kendrick followed it with a question. "Are these your vines?"

"Why do you want to know?"

"Just curious. I'm in the wine business. An importer. French wines to the USA."

Apparently, to the two Pageots, that was utterly unremarkable.

Inside the house, a child started to whimper and sob.

"Shut your ass!" Mama Pageot screamed, and Kendrick, now that her chest was covered, noticed that she had a black eye. With her pink hair, he wondered if the black eye was real or some new fashion statement.

Kendrick gave up trying to finesse the situation. "I see you've installed an antenna down there. I hate to be the one to tell you, but there is scientific evidence that such cell phone antennas are known to cause brain tumors in infants."

This time it was Madame's turn to leap from a chair. "We did it, and I don't care who you are or what you do. No one is going to stop us. This is our property, and we can do whatever we want!"

Alex Pageot was still waiting for Kendrick to draw first.

"Listen," Kendrick said, "how much does the phone company pay you? Maybe I could rent the same space instead of them and take down the antenna! Then you wouldn't have to look at it, either."

"We'll have two more up soon, producing around twenty-five thousand euros each. Per year."

Kendrick calculated that at the current exchange rate, the three antennas would earn them around one hundred grand per year. He found it hard to believe.

The excitable Madame Pageot was almost hysterical now. "That's our money, and you can't take it away from us!"

Kendrick upped the ante. "I have no idea what your property is worth, but tell me, how much it would take to tempt you to sell it?" He was serious. He would buy the place for more than it was worth in order to tear down the antenna and their house with it to protect his view.

Alex spoke up. "Once upon a time, my family—Pageot—owned all this hillside and all the hillside on the road to La Diguoa. Piece by piece, each generation sold off some land in order to survive. This is all they left for me—this lot and two acres of vines. It's not for sale and never will be. Thanks for the wine," he said, and that was that.

Kendrick walked back in a dismal mood. What kind of people were they—didn't care about exposing their baby to danger, didn't care about trees, didn't mind *plastic* trees? He had expected himself to be the experienced businessman—cool, calm, collected—making a reasonable proposal. He felt like he'd been thrown offtrack by the immediately hostile reception, and he hadn't handled the situation at all as he'd intended.

CHAPTER FIFTEEN

Even very early morning was hot, the air a bit heavy, but to Kendrick the sky proved to be one of Mother Nature's most sublime achievements. Were he ever to look upon a body of water the same color, he would have to dive right in. It was one of those summer days when all the slander northerners hurl at southerners is true, when any effort or serious thinking is useless, a day to rent a chaise longue on a beach, plant a parasol in the sand, and take some time to profit from existence, which, Kendrick realized, very few people really do. Even rich folk, who already have more than they can spend cannot stop trying to earn more, more, and even more instead of taking time to enjoy what they already have. Not Kendrick's idea of smart.

He had plans to go with Poupon to a restaurant between Arles and Saint-Rémy-de-Provence, about an hour and a half drive from Milles Vents, where they were to meet Eloi Roux, who had a wine domaine up in those gorgeous hills, the Alpilles, so they would probably piddle away the entire day eating, drinking, and talking wine. As he turned into Poupon's driveway, he saw a big flatbed truck loaded with large wire cages blocking his way. One cage had been lowered to the ground, and Poupon and a couple of guys were gathered around it. Poupon looked up.

"Hey, bonjour. Come take a look at these old tiles. I'm tearing out a wall so I can double the size of my bedroom. These tiles'll look great on the floor. I found them up near Apt."

One of the guys was a skinny kid who couldn't have been over sixteen. The other was a beefy fellow with a big-veined schnoz that dominated the unshaven landscape of a sunbaked face. He asked Poupon if they could unload the other cages—it looked like about a dozen altogether.

"We've got to get back to Apt before eleven," the guy said.

"Sure, put them over there on the cement in front of the big double doors. I'm going to take a few tiles inside to show to my friend."

Poupon and Kendrick looked down at the layer of rectangular clay tiles, each about a foot long and an inch thick, each a variation of earthy burnt terra-cotta, each obviously handmade. Kendrick admired them, thinking that as much as they try, variations from one tile to another cannot successfully be imitated by technology. One of Poupon's tiles even had a clearly visible paw print from a dog who'd stepped on the tile before it was dry, which to both of them was a plus.

Poupon started piling up tiles in Kendrick's arms. He called the kid over and started loading him up, too, so he could show a few of them laid out on the floor of his future master bedroom. When he had removed the top two layers and started grabbing a couple from the third, he stopped short. His enthusiasm turned to incomprehension, then amazement. He began grabbing out tiles and tossing them randomly on the ground. One or two shattered. "What the hell . . . How could they . . . Hey," he yelled to the driver, "get over here!"

The fellow lumbered over and calmly surveyed the tiles thrown down at his feet while Poupon pulled himself up onto the truck and started clearing off the top tiles of another full cage. With a ferocious snarl, he focused his gaze back on the driver.

"Are you the boss or just the driver?" Poupon asked. He jumped down and they stood almost nose to nose, barrel chest to barrel chest.

"I'm the driver, and I'll tell you god's truth—you are keeping me from doing my job, and my boss'll kill me if I don't get back and load up the next delivery before lunch."

"Get this cage loaded up again and you and your truck outta my sight before I kill you myself."

The driver turned his head and spit—not far from Kendrick's black espadrilles. Kendrick looked down and found the gross puddle remarkably colorful. He figured that whatever brand the guy smoked, it must be unfiltered and lethal.

"What's your gripe?" the driver asked Poupon.

"You're a bunch of thieves. That's the problem."

"You ordered the tiles; we delivered them. Simple as that. You signed the order. They're yours."

"There's no mason in the world who could lay these tiles, and you know it. Shit *de merde*! Look at this."

Kendrick studied more closely what was in the cages while Poupon raved on.

"Every tile on top is from the batch I ordered"—he tapped the driver thunkily on the chest—"and signed for. What I didn't sign for is a batch of totally random tiles—just an assortment of leftovers. Junk! Look at this—half as thick as the ones I ordered. And here's a few square ones. Mine are rectangular. How the hell could anyone fit them all together?"

"Listen good, big shot, you ordered them, they're yours. I'm unloading them, and then you do whatever you want with them."

"What do you take me for? An American? Oh, sorry Kendrick. I didn't mean you. I'll explain later."

"I'm not losing my job on your account," the driver said.

Poupon leaned against the fender of the truck, shaking his head. Finally he said, "I'll get my cell phone and tell your boss what he's going to do with these tiles. Maybe you'll listen to him."

He walked about ten paces to the kitchen door, went in and came out not with his cell phone but with one of his shotguns. The straggly kid hightailed it on foot as fast as he could, back out the way the truck had come in.

Poupon held the gun loosely so it pointed vaguely in the direction of the driver's private parts, which seemed to instantly take a hunk out of the guy's confidence supply.

"Your bullshit might work with some, but not with me. Now get this loaded and out of here before I blow out your windshield. You drive back to Apt without a windshield on a day like today, your face will be the color of bug juice for the rest of your life."

It took the driver about twenty minutes to get off the property. As soon as he did, Kendrick and Poupon hit the road. First Kendrick drove into Bandol so Poupon could deliver three cases of rosé to the Auberge du Port.

Leaving Bandol, there is a tollbooth, or *péage*, where drivers take a ticket before entering the autoroute. About ten minutes later, there's another at La Ciotat. Then, after another ten minutes, more to pay at Aubagne, and twenty minutes after that, another at Aix-en-Provence, plus the final payment when they exited at Sénas—altogether a mere hour's drive from Bandol.

For the fun of it, Kendrick added it all up and reported, "It amounts to five full tollbooth stops. Then, of course, waiting in line to pay. So, twelve euros in tolls and probably fifteen in gas consumption for one stinking hour on their lousy autoroute."

Poupon chimed in, "By the way, eight of the fifteen bucks go to pay gasoline taxes, and don't forget, we've still got to get back home this afternoon."

"It's a river of money your autoroutes are producing for somebody."

"Imagine being an old-timer," Poupon said. "You've paid all manner of taxes . . ."

"Yeah," Kendrick said, "even a French tax on watching television. I love that one. You pay the government for the luxury of watching commercials."

"Right, but listen, you're retired—not you, but a Frenchman—and you paid taxes and social security charges all your life, and you'll end up receiving about twelve hundred euros a month retirement. Once you pay your rent, it doesn't leave much for everything else—food, gas . . ."

Kendrick calculated in his head. "It would cost a retiree about four percent of his monthly income to drive two hours on the autoroute."

"I never did the math like that," Poupon said.

From Sénas, they drove west. The landscape was striking—short, rocky mountains, Les Alpilles, which look not at all like little Alps. There were often silvery green olive groves on their two-lane country road with hardly any houses or villages around. In the middle of the summer, everything had a dry, combustible look, especially the pine forests. At a hand-painted sign that indicated MAS DE L'EAU VIVE, Poupon took a right onto a dirt road. It was a well-kept dirt road, but they were lucky no one was ahead of them, because Poupon's own car was kicking up quite a bit of dust behind.

After about half a mile, the vegetation on the roadside turned greener and more abundant. It also began to look more like creek-bed vegetation, the earth darker and wetter until, looking out the passenger window, Kendrick began seeing little pools of standing water. Trees, including wild-growing fig and lilac, became larger until he and Poupon were enjoying their ride in the shade. The temperature dropped as if they'd run into a cool breeze.

There was more and more water flowing along outside the car window, and they soon passed the ruin of a deserted stone mill with its wooden paddle wheel still somewhat intact. By the time they reached the restaurant's parking lot, they were in a small forest of cedar and pine, although the dirt lot itself was bordered by and in the shade of several towering plane trees.

Almost immediately after they arrived, Eloi drove up in a dust-covered Deux Chevaux as old as he was—around fifty. To Kendrick, Eloi looked like a Hollywood actor from yesteryear. Put Gary Cooper and Robert Ryan together—that would be pretty close to Eloi—handsome in a rough-hewn sort of way. His father was a celebrated architect, so Eloi had it made—looks, personality, talent, surrounded by wealth, and raised in van Gogh's Provence. He could have been spoiled rotten, but wasn't. He believed he was every bit as capable of creating beauty in a wine bottle as his father had with his bridges and buildings.

Kendrick thought it would be fair if everyone had a chance to dine at least once at Mas de l'Eau Vive. Well, everyone except Alex Pageot and his lovely bride. First, because of the beautiful scenery. Once out of the car, they took a pathway through the woods alongside a good-sized creek or river, "depending on the season," according to Eloi, who continued to point out chestnut trees, green oaks, cypresses, linden trees, a deserted Gothic abbey from the thirteenth century, a Roman footbridge of stone—until they entered a clearing with olive and fruit trees and a thriving vegetable garden.

Eloi announced that he was going to treat Kendrick and Poupon to the best aperitif they'd ever tasted, and it wouldn't cost him one single centime. He did not, however, lead them into the restaurant, even though they were outside its screen door. They walked around to the left of it and out in back where they discovered the origin of all that water—a spring pouring out of a pile of rocks into a large cement *citerne*. All three dipped their cupped hands in and gulped down the delicious, icy, gravel-flavored water, which, Eloi explained, probably came from the Alps. Indeed, Eloi's aperitif was free of charge. "And just over that rise—you can't see it from here—the restaurant has a zoo. An edible zoo. They have chickens, ducks, rabbit, goats . . ."

"You can meet your victim before you eat him," Kendrick said.

The interior of the restaurant was wooden: walls, tables, chairs, and a long bar made of olive wood where a few people were wetting their whistles with pastis.

Madame Tropbeta, a tall, skinny, hawkeyed woman of indeterminate age—forty to sixty, roughly—greeted the trio. When she saw Eloi, she called out, "*Eh, Gabrieu, c'est Eloi.*" Out came the chef and proprietor of the Mas de l'Eau Vive—restaurant, bar, farm, and enchanted site. Kendrick smiled—talk about a ball of fur, Chef Gabrieu stood about five feet two. His big hippy mane was salt and pepper colored, his fluffy beard white as snow, and his unbuttoned shirt allowed a view of his chest, from which sprouted a wiry nest of white hairs.

"Eloi," he said, "*cher* Eloi, a visit from you is always a special occasion. How's the new vintage? But first, who are your friends? Welcome!"

"This is Henri Poupon, Domaine du Vieux Laurier, the very pinnacle of Provençal red wine, and Kendrick Thomas, our importer in the USA."

"Come on, the three of you, back into the kitchen with me. I don't want you out here on the floor with all the riffraff who can't talk about anything beyond Sunday's match—Marseille against Lyon. It's the biggest event since the Americans landed in 1944 and liberated us. So, thank you, Kendrick Thomas, for your country's help kicking out the Krauts. Whatever you eat and drink today will be on the house! We'll set up a table in the kitchen so I can keep an eye on you, and so your wine glasses will never be empty. For starters, you choose: pastis or a Champagne from yet another widow—this one called Veuve Fourny—or my own creation, a glass of rosemary-infused Muscat de Beaumes-de-Venise."

Kendrick, Eloi, and Poupon nodded at the last suggestion and quickly held cold glasses of it in hand. At a round table tucked out of the way of three working cooks, they toasted Gabrieu loudly and raised their glasses toward him.

"Okay," he said, "here are your choices today. First, a joke menu because everyone in France is complaining about all the frozen food in our restaurants."

"Today, you even find it in some two- and three-star Michelin joints," Eloi said.

Poupon joined in. "It's a disgrace. A crime against the *patrimoine*."

"So, for today I am offering a menu *Déjeuner, Surgeler, Rigoler*. You'll eat the joke, because each course has something frozen. Frozen but not hidden. Openly frozen with pride and humor. You eat, you taste, you judge, and you tell me if frozen food is a crime."

And with that, he picked a cigarette from the fuzz around his ears, ignited a match with his thumbnail, and torched it into life—the cigarette, not the fuzz.

Eloi told Gabrieu that he'd surpassed himself, that the idea was almost poetic, worth a place in the Restaurant Hall of Fame, and that we awaited the pleasure of downing his creations.

"But wait, my dear friends, there is the other menu to consider before each of you makes your choice."

"Go ahead," Poupon said. "It's always nice to have a choice."

"But what if I can't make up my mind?" Kendrick said. "I like it when the cook decides for me." He looked up at Gabrieu. "A chef knows what the day's best ingredients are, so I'd prefer you tell me what I'm going to eat while I look over the wine list."

Poupon took a sniff of the rosemary-infused aperitif and nodded his approval. "This smells as much like Provence as anything I've ever smelled."

"Haven't you ever pissed on wild thyme in the heat of the summer?" Eloi asked. "Maybe it's different where you live, but here in the Alpilles . . ."

"And has it ever occurred to you," Poupon asked, "that some of us might prefer the smell of Muscat to the smell of urine? But listen, Kendrick, what if you have just one choice, one menu, but you don't like what they're offering that day?"

"I'm lucky. No allergies, and I like everything. Well, coconut and grapefruit aren't my favorites, but you don't often run into them in the kind of restaurants I frequent. As long as the food is, you know, correct, which is to say made from good ingredients well prepared, I'm open to new tastes."

"Well, my American friend," Gabrieu said, "cover your ears while I announce the alternate menu. That way, you will not experience your dilemma of too much choice." Kendrick ignored the suggestion. "Lunch would start with the legendary *barigoule Provençal*—baby artichoke quarters with lots of thyme and garlic and a splash of dry white wine. Then the Provençal onion, olive, and anchovy tart we call the *pissaladière*, followed by one of our own chickens roasted to sublimity, accompanied by a potato gratin *à la Provençale*, which means no cream or cheese, lots of garlic and thyme."

"Too good to be true," Poupon said.

"Superb progression," said Eloi.

"I wish I had closed my big ears," Kendrick said. "I want to eat that menu yesterday, today, and tomorrow. Eloi, Poupon, think how good your wines would taste washing down a menu like that."

"But wait," Eloi said, raising his forefinger in the air.

"Wait for what?" Poupon asked. "Our glasses are already empty. Let's order so they bring us something to drink."

"But we haven't heard the frozen lunch menu yet," Eloi said.

Gabrieu took over. "It's true, you would have to choose without having all the details. So, here is the soon-to-be legendary . . ."

"Everything is legendary at l'Eau Vive," Eloi said.

"*Déjeuner, Surgeler, Rigoler!* Okay, the curtain rises, and the spotlight is on my octopus salad: morsels of smoky roasted octopus in a cold salad dressed with aioli, capers, shallots, chive, and parsley."

"Nothing but good stuff," Poupon said, "so it has to be good. But what's frozen?"

"In the old days, fishermen tenderized octopus by pounding the leggy beast against a rock. Today we are much more civilized. We freeze it overnight to achieve the same tenderness. Therefore, the octopus was frozen.

"Number two. One of the most delicious egg preparations is *brouillade aux truffes*, but this is not the season for truffles. Far from it. No, none are in the market fresh except those flavorless little balls they call summer truffles. No! Never. Not *chez moi!* But I've taught myself the best way to freeze black truffles. They're better in the months of December, January, even February, you might insist—and I would agree with you. But you'll see, you'll tell me what you think. Eggs and truffles are so good together—divine, in fact—that we shouldn't have to wait all year long to enjoy next winter's crop."

Eloi asked if Gabrieu was going to divulge his method.

"I wrap them tight as can be in aluminum foil and freeze them. Each one wrapped separately, of course. But when you are ready to cook them, the trick is to unwrap them, wait until just *before* the moment they are one hundred percent thawed out, chop them up, and use them immediately. So, chop them rapidly, throw them into the stirred eggs and then into a well-buttered double boiler. But wait, I see, unfortunately, that while your mouths are watering, your glasses are dry. That will never do."

Gabrieu looked around the kitchen, then stuck his head out the door into the dining room. "Jules," he shouted, "a bottle of the Patrimonio blanc, *s'il vous plaît. C'est urgent!*"

Kendrick was in seventh heaven, not saying much but still wearing a big smile. The chef was a showman, so much more entertaining than a printed menu. While the waiter filled their glasses, Gabrieu's show continued.

"You know that here on our farm, we raise animals, too. We serve lamb year-round. Nowhere is there better lamb than in Provence with all its wild herbs. The lambs are nourished by the extravagant perfume of the garrigue. However, even here, no lamb is better than spring lamb—from those sweet, succulent babies, slaughtered as gently as humanly possible toward the end of March or early April—well, it's so good, I always freeze a few for serving later in the year. To you to judge if I'm right: frozen baby lamb shanks are allowed to thaw out, then roasted in a slow oven with rosemary branches, whole garlic cloves, and a lot of them. With it, a very lean, young Gigondas. Young lamb, young Gigondas. It's not the only possibility, but it's not at all bad served cool on a hot summer day.

"To conclude, we'll combine the cheese and dessert courses: Parmesan ice cream sandwiches—a creation of Ferran Adrià." Gabrieu tapped Poupon's shirt pocket, which held a pack of Camels. "So, if you all go outside to smoke with Monsieur Poupon after lunch, I'll bring you each a glass of iced coffee. Therefore, something frozen for each course, even the wine, because the Patrimonio is in an ice bucket."

The three wine men looked at one another.

"*Déjeuner*," said Eloi.

"*Surgeler*," Kendrick piped up.

"*Rigoler*," Poupon said after a moment's hesitation, throwing off the beat.

All four of them raised glasses of Patrimonio.

"These Corsican whites," Eloi said, "I consider them some of the best in France these days."

"This one is really good. I'll bet it's from Baltazaru Vezzani," Kendrick said. "He's quite a guy, quite a personality."

Poupon spoke up. "Yes, I know Baltazaru, and Kendrick is right. He's someone I like a lot, personally."

"He makes everyone think they're his best buddy," Eloi said.

"That's a rare quality," Kendrick said. "I had an uncle like that. Some said he was a man's man, others that he was a lady's man. But he made everyone feel special. And since most of us like to feel special, everyone likes Baltazaru."

Almost in a whisper, Eloi said, "I don't know if you're aware, but if ever you need anything done in Corsica or have any problems, you know what I mean? You discuss it with Baltazaru. He is actually quite an influential man. He's not voted into office, but he can get things done. For example, the Corsicans don't like foreigners buying land and building there. Give it a try, Kendrick. Buy yourself an acre or two with a beautiful view. Start building your dream home. One evening the builders go home, and when they show up the next morning, there will be a big hole in the roof." He gestured like a bomb going off in his hands.

"It's true. I've seen it with my own eyes," Poupon said.

"No one will be injured. They'll do it when no one is around. Construction project never to be completed. But if you are in tight with Baltazaru, your home won't be touched."

The octopus salad arrived to a chorus of oohs and aahs. Kendrick was reminded of his gramma's potato salad, but this was full of smoky roasted octopus instead of hunks of potato.

Poupon spoke with his mouth full. "Yeah, Baltazaru helped me get access to some great hunting at the base of the Monte Grosso. If there really is a Corsican mafia, Baltazaru is certainly well placed in it."

"We should go together someday," Kendrick said, which inspired another round of clinking glasses.

Not too long after the octopus plates were removed, a cloud of heavenly perfume invaded the air around their table.

"Frozen truffles," Kendrick said. "Well, they smell good from here."

With the truffled eggs, Gabrieu brought up a well-aged bottle of Domaine de Trevallon blanc.

Between the eggs and the lamb course, Eloi raised his hand in the air. "There is something else very pleasant about this restaurant, and it has nothing to do with wine or food."

"The service?" Poupon ventured, but Eloi shook his head no. "The prices?" Another no. "*Merde*, what else is there? The forks?"

"I think I know," Kendrick said. "You can't see it right? Can't taste it or smell it."

"The toilets!" Poupon said.

"Poupon, what is it with you? Your nose isn't functioning? It can't smell a toilet?"

"Well, the hell with you. This is some kind of trick question."

Kendrick looked at Eloi. "It's not something that is, right? It's something that isn't."

"Correct."

"Spit it out," Poupon said. "Here comes more food."

"No music," Kendrick said. "They don't force us to listen to *their* music while *we* eat."

"And thank the good lord for it," Eloi said. "No music. And listen to the result—the clatter of the silverware, the ringing of the wine glasses, the chatter of the diners, the laughter—it's like an orchestra of pleasurable sounds and not some imposition played so loud you can't even think straight."

"Amen," Kendrick said, and the three had yet another reason to clink glasses and down another swallow of their delicious white wine, produced, in fact, not that far from the restaurant, at least not far as the crow flies.

CHAPTER SIXTEEN

Spirits were high as Kendrick and Poupon left the restaurant, shook hands with Eloi, and headed back south around five p.m. Rear bumper gazing in the commuter traffic around Aix-en-Provence made the return trip longer than the going. Once he'd dropped off Poupon at Vieux Laurier and was driving up the *route nationale* toward Milles Vents, Kendrick started to relax his attention on the road and his tight grip on the wheel. He felt a peaceful doze on the couch coming on, but when he passed the cypressed antenna, he couldn't help muttering a string of dirty words. He turned into his driveway, parked, got out, and stopped to stare down at Pageot's eyesore again. From a distant neighbor's property came the dentist-drill buzz of someone cutting wood with a chainsaw, and the noise pollution also began to annoy the hell out of him. He realized that Pageot's damned antenna was taking up too much space in his head, souring his frame of mind. And decidedly, not all pollutions are due to progress improving the quality of life on earth. Blow or rake, for example. Blowing leaves, you get less exercise while polluting ears, eyes, nose, throat, and lungs while you're at it. Where is the progress?

Once up the stairs to the terrace, Kendrick noticed a carton on his wooden picnic table. He pulled out a miniature red Swiss Army knife from his front pocket and slashed the carton open as if he were Don Quixote taking on the antenna. Inside were a dozen Alsatian samples from a Domaine Werner Süssmann. There was a letter in an attached envelope, and the handwriting was as easy to read as a typed version would have been.

Dear Mr. Thomas,

I have heard your name from acquaintances in the wine world who are satisfied with your work. I hear rumors that you are no longer associated with Domaine Dreissen, and as I begin my search for an American importer, I cannot help hoping that you will find my wines of interest.

All of my vines are at Robeswiller, including the *grand cru* Zauberberg, often mentioned as the greatest of the Alsatian *grand crus* along with Geisberg and Rangen. I have taken the liberty of sending you some samples of my craft.

Please accept the expression of my sincere respect,

Werner Süssmann

Tasting samples was part of Kendrick's job description, but this assortment inspired more curiosity than usual. Now that the Dreissen collaboration—which had meant so much to him in earlier days—was officially kaput, he looked forward to prospecting for a perfect replacement, if such a domaine existed. In his mind, he moved the Süssmann sample bottles into first place on his "to try" list. He was not, however, ready to take them on that evening. Tasting samples was usually a morning job, before coffee, when nose and palate are fresh, awake, receptive, and perceptive.

He opened the fridge and took out some lamb shanks he'd cooked earlier in the week. They weren't from spring lamb, but the recipe was almost the same as Gabrieu's at l'Eau Vive. All he'd done was throw them in a casserole with thyme branches, a full head of garlic cloves, covered the pot, and let them cook in their own juices for a couple of hours. He put the shanks in the oven for reheating, then poured himself a cold, crisp glass of Manzanilla before sitting down at his desk to look through his emails.

Jake Edwards was resigning from Kendrick's warehouse staff. Too bad. He was great with clients and would be hard to replace. Kendrick decided he should give him a call, see if there'd been some situation that might be repaired, change Jake's mind.

Domaine Veneau had five more cases of Monteé de Tonnerre for the US if he wanted them. *But of course!*

A wine merchant in the US was arrested for a wine scam—offering futures on rare wines, taking payment, then never delivering the goods. Somehow it had taken years for anyone to scream loud enough to be noticed and for the house of cards to collapse.

Meanwhile, the salty taste of the Manzanilla made Kendrick nostalgic for the funky, no-nonsense bars on the beach at Sanlúcar de Barremeda in Spain—the barmen working the bar, and a long grill fired up behind them. They served Manzanilla and grilled the catch right out of the water to go with it.

His accountant wanted to know whether to file for something and thereby defer something else, but Kendrick didn't understand what he was talking about. He understood French and Italian, but he did not speak accountant. "What is your advice and why?" he answered.

A travel agent in Chicago wanted to pay him 10 percent commission and offer "Kendrick Thomas Wine Tours of France and Italy." All the guy wanted was the use of Kendrick's name. Kendrick considered it and imagined a tidal wave of possible catastrophes wearing his name. He used about fifteen words to politely say *Thanks but no thanks.*

He sliced bread and a tomato, then went down in the cellar for a red fit to accompany a warm leftover lamb shank sandwich. Beaujolais sounded appropriate.

After he finished the meal and began clearing the table, his phone rang. It was Poupon.

"Poupon, you already? What's up? Did I leave something in your car?"

"Hello," Poupon said in his one word of English acceptable in polite company, but for a change there was no self-conscious chuckle in his greeting. Not even a smile. "Can you come back to my place?"

"When? Tomorrow?"

"No, I'd like you to see something right now."

That was unusual enough that Kendrick told Poupon he'd be right over, so off he went. Poupon was outside, waiting in the dark, his stocky silhouette visible before the open door. Grim faced, he also looked dazed. They were standing right about where the tile truck had been parked earlier in the day. Kendrick wondered if it had returned and the son of a bitch had unloaded all those cages of tiles while Poupon was gone. But no. Poupon simply said, "Follow me." They maneuvered through Poupon's cluttered office, down his beautifully curved wooden staircase and into the part of the cellar where the wine was made. Kendrick was puzzled—what the hell was going on? It couldn't be that Poupon wanted Kendrick's opinion of a wine at eleven o'clock at night. *Well*, Kendrick thought, *that could be the case*—Poupon was capable of such a thing, especially if he'd had a few too many glasses of wine with supper. Still, something would have to be terribly wrong with the wine to need Kendrick's opinion so urgently.

The lights were already on. At first glance, Kendrick noticed nothing abnormal. Poupon led him down the aisle between two rows of oak casks, each about ten feet high, containing sixty to seventy-five hectoliters of red wine. On each cask, the vintage was written in white chalk on a small blackboard. At the fourth, Poupon pointed at the faucet on the face of the *foudre*, which was drip, drip, dripping. Kendrick's eyes followed the bright scarlet drops down into a gutter in the cement floor, which led slightly downhill to a drain. The gutter was wet with wine.

"That asshole!" Poupon shouted.

"Which asshole?" Kendrick asked.

"The truck driver, of course."

"How much wine is left?"

Poupon tapped the *foudre*. It sounded seriously empty.

"That's about ten percent of my harvest," Poupon said. "That ten percent, after expenses and taxes, would have been my profit for the year's work. I should have shredded his balls to bits when I had my shotgun aimed at them."

"You think it was the truck driver's revenge?" Kendrick asked. He quickly looked around the cellar. "Sure, he's a likely suspect. But how would he have gotten in here?"

"You know how I am. I can't keep track of every door and window every time I take off somewhere. That could be fifty times a day. You understand? And Jean, my brother, he comes and goes all day long, too. His son, Gregoire, too. And Thomas, the Tunisian guy."

"Let's not quit thinking this through," Kendrick said. "When I picture the driver, I can see him wanting revenge and taking revenge. Oh yes, I wouldn't put it past him, but he'd have heaved some rocks through your windows or spit in your face or set fire to something. I cannot imagine him entering and merely twisting the faucet a turn or two. See what I mean? No, this took someone who is thoughtful. The driver would have broken the cask with an axe."

"It's obvious, Kendrick, you're not a winemaker. You don't understand. What could be more violent? I've lost a year's labor. The pruning, working the earth, the harvest, making the wine, raising the wine . . . All in vain. I feel like someone kicked me in the head, stomach, and balls all at the same time."

"Well, maybe I'm not a winemaker, but I'm a hell of a lot closer to being one than the truck driver is, and I'll tell you my opinion. Again. This was not violent, not brutal enough for him."

Poupon shrugged. Kendrick continued looking around. "Is anything else different in here?"

"I haven't really looked. I guess I should call the gendarmes. Not that they'll roll out of bed to rush over at this hour."

"They'll probably look for fingerprints on the faucet and footprints—wine-stained footprints," Kendrick said. "And here we are, standing right where whoever did it would have stood."

"Call the police? What a joke. They couldn't find the culprit if they did it themselves. They're that useless. They file a report and boom, case closed."

"Calm down. Think for a minute. Who has it in for you?"

"Calm down? I know where that truck driver works. I know how to find him. And I know that with a blow from my fist to his Adam's apple, his voice will change to soprano for the rest of his days. He'll never forget Henri Poupon."

"Okay, don't calm down. But think, who else might want to hurt you like this? Who might have something to gain? Like when Kennedy was assassinated in Texas, Lyndon Johnson took power, took over the government. Anybody in their right mind would first look to Johnson or his rich Texas backers, right?"

"I don't give a damn about politics. I want my wine back."

"We have the truck driver on our list. What about an employee or ex-employee? Someone who left angry and knows you leave doors unlocked."

Poupon mulled it over. He shrugged sheepishly. "All right, I can be a tough boss, but this is a business, not a site for making friends. If I want to put a good wine into bottle, sure, sometimes I have to crack the whip. Symbolically, you know?"

"Anybody you fired recently?" Kendrick asked.

"Oh, are you joking? In France you can't fire anybody. You have to pay them to go. Flo, my secretary, she and I tangle all the time, but I have to admit, she knows how to get the best of me. I'd be more likely to empty her cask than she would mine."

"What about Raymond, because of you and Zarina?"

"That little mouse. He pees his pants if I look at him cross-eyed."

"What about Franck?"

"Constanzo?"

"Well, he seemed beside himself since you told him I was selling a ton of your wines in the United States. And such a revenge, opening the faucet on a *foudre*, it implies some familiarity with the wine scene."

Poupon gazed off into the rafters. He shook his head no, no, then he looked intently into Kendrick's eyes. "*Merde*, you really think so?"

"Listen, at the least he has to go on our list. That was such a weird moment when he dropped by the other day. There might be a screw loose in there, you know? Now, find us a flashlight. Let's look outside the cellar door. Maybe we'll find some tracks or a cigarette butt or some kind of clue."

They found nothing incriminating, but when they reentered the cellar, Kendrick stopped Poupon with his arm. He closed his eyes and sniffed the air. "Do you smell something other than wine? I noticed a little something when I first got here, but I forgot it as soon as you showed me the dripping faucet."

Poupon sniffed and stared once again into the great oak rafters above. "You're right. I'm not used to that smell. It's not a cellar smell. What the hell is it?"

"It's perfume, and I'm almost sure I've smelled it before."

"Perfume? A woman's perfume?"

"Exactly. In the old days I used to give wine classes, and when people arrived, I made them go into the bathroom to wash off any perfume, and the men, too, if they'd used aftershave. No one can overcome those smells while trying to judge wines. And somewhere in my life I have encountered this same perfume in the context of tasting wine. I'm sure of it."

"So you think it was a woman?"

"Well, it's not aftershave, that's for sure. Right at this instant, I can't recall where I smelled it. But it is a strong perfume. Notice how long it's lingered in your cellar. We don't know when during the day the intruder was here, but the perfume persists."

"*Merde*! Try harder. The wine. A woman. The perfume. I'll make whoever did this pay for it and more."

"Fine. Meanwhile, it's been a long day. I'll see you tomorrow morning for coffee?"

"Not in the morning. I've got to meet the mayor early to dissuade him from approving a Hotel Ibis right there at the autoroute exit. Can you imagine? We live in paradise, and he wants to let them put up an eyesore in order to have a little more tax money."

"Politicians are the same worldwide. None of them care about quality of life."

"There, my friend, you're being naïve. They care a whole lot about the quality of their own lives."

"I'm really wasted," Kendrick said. "When are you free?"

"Lunch. Let's eat here. I'll see what I can find to eat while you search your memory for the guilty perfume."

CHAPTER SEVENTEEN

At eight o'clock the next morning, as much as the idea of a hot press pot of Sulawesi-Kalosi beckoned, Kendrick managed to forgo his usual cup of black coffee in order to attack his Alsatian samples. He began by selecting a single bottle to uncork. If something about it grabbed him, he would then spend the time to uncork and taste the eleven others in Süssmann's carton. If the first sample left him feeling blasé, then his gardener would have some free unopened wines to take home.

He chose what would probably be the simplest and cheapest of the bunch and poured a glass. It was labeled *Gentil d'Alsace*, which means nothing more than a nice wine from Alsace and is produced from a blend of grape varieties such as Pinot Blanc, Riesling, Sylvaner, and Muscat. Each domaine can come up with more or less their own recipe. The label showed a colorful bouquet of flowers to set the mood. As he lowered his practiced sniffer into the glass, an aromatic pleasure rose to meet him. Kendrick opened his eyes wide in astonishment. "One hell of a nose," he exclaimed, and in his ever-handy tasting notebook, he wrote *A perfume of simplicity, freshness, and immense charm*. The word *divertimento* occurred to him, as if he were listening to music. *Divertimento d'Alsace!* That's what Kendrick would have labeled it. There was something very classical about it, something harmonious and almost melodic on the palate. He nodded, imagining the excitement his customers would feel when they had a chance to taste it. *My god*, he thought, *deliciousness and charm, who could not like that combination?*

Kendrick pulled out the other eleven bottles and spent a minute or two putting them into some kind of logical sequence for tasting. There was Sylvaner, then a Pinot Blanc, a Muscat d'Alsace, two Pinot Gris, various Rieslings, and a Gewurztraminer. He tried to order them for tasting from the simplest to the grandest. Were one to taste a cheaper village Riesling after a *grand cru* Riesling, the cheaper wine might suffer by comparison, which would not be fair to it. And if the cheaper wine transcends the *grand cru*, a wine importer might conclude that the more costly *grand cru* is overpriced. To Kendrick, the order of the wines tasted was important, because when tasting a wine, one's palate is always influenced by whatever happens to precede it. Precede a Romanée Conti with a bite of artichoke—you might prefer a crisp little rosé four hundred times less costly even though the Romaneé Conti is by far the grander wine. Whenever asked "Which is best?" Kendrick invariably replied "The best for what?" With the Alsatian selections before him, he thought he had to finish with the Gewurztraminer, because Gewurztraminers are usually so flashy aromatically and on the palate—a hard act to follow, even though Rieslings are invariably finer wines.

He admired the charm, balance, and class all twelve wines showed. Also, very important, each aroma rose from the glass unobstructed to give all of itself. A trip back to Alsace looked certain, because Kendrick could not believe his good fortune—losing Dreissen's wines after so many good years, the ugliness of it all, and the next thing he knows, he's tasting samples that he prefers to Martin Dreissen's—even if they weren't as utterly fabulous as the ones Martin's uncle had produced. Kendrick could not wait to meet Monsieur Süssmann, the creator of such beauties. Flawless, classy—all twelve samples. That was rare, the sign of a master.

Finally, he brewed his coffee and sat petting Kali's thick tabby fur as he mulled over possible scenarios for the near future: a trip to Nice to see what he might learn about Babette, to Alsace, for sure, and why not a trip to Corsica for the fun of it with Poupon and Eloi—do some wining and dining with his Corsican producers, splash around in those comparatively virgin waters of the island's gorgeous beaches?

Kendrick headed out early to Poupon's for lunch because he wanted to first drive into downtown Bandol. He parked his Modus in the public lot next to the boat harbor. The sky featured puffy, low-flying white clouds that were racing overhead even though there was nothing more than a pleasant breeze at sea level. He took an alleyway off the main drag to a one-way stone street full of restaurants and boutiques, and at the Parfumerie l'Astrance, he entered to the *cling-cling* of a little bell above the door.

A rather well-groomed, well-dressed woman turned to greet him. She had light brown hair, very nicely held in place by a silver hair ornament. The shape and depth of her eyes made her look slightly astonished whether she was or not. She wore a light green blouse and skirt, quite refined for Bandol, and was close to Kendrick's height. He could imagine her on the cover of a fashion magazine. He said, "Bonjour, madame," and introduced himself. "I'm looking for a specific perfume, but I'm afraid I don't know the name of the brand."

"That's going to make it difficult," she said, "because I have over four hundred perfumes."

"I'll try to describe it, and we'll see if we speak the same language— I mean, my French comes out of wine cellars, while your vocabulary is from the perfume business. Both of us rely on our sense of smell, maybe our vocabularies have something in common. Anyway, sometime in the past, I was around a woman whose perfume impressed me. It persists in my memory, and if I find it, I'd like to buy some."

"Can you find a few words to describe the smell? Pretend you are describing the bouquet of a wine, if that helps. What would you say?"

"I'd start with vanilla bean. And what you might call a woodsy note. You're in a forest, not a lumberyard. Fresh raspberry and violets. And leather, new leather, like when you buy a new car."

The saleswoman pulled out a bottle and sprayed some perfume onto a thin strip of white cardboard, offering it to Kendrick to sniff.

He shook his head. "That smells more like normal perfume. It's not as unusual as the one I'm looking for."

"It's one of the most popular brands, so I thought you might have been more likely to encounter it."

After several more sniffs, rejections, and efforts to narrow it down, Kendrick stayed with one for a minute and began to nod, slowly at first, then with more and more confidence. "I can't be one hundred percent sure," he said, "but I also don't think we'll find anything closer than this last one."

"It is indeed an unusual perfume. Habanista is the name. It used to be more popular, but nowadays it is rarely requested."

"Do you have any customers who buy it regularly?"

"Yes, three of them, as a matter of fact. It was created back around 1920 but was not originally marketed as a woman's perfume. It was for perfuming cigarettes and cigars. That fad passed, but in its second life, it grew very popular with women. But, you know how tastes change."

"In the wine world, too. Fashion does play a role."

"Really? I would have thought wine is like it's always been."

"Oh no, they're always coming up with newfangled this-and-thats, always some new miracle way to 'improve' wine. But please, can you tell me who keeps buying Habanista?"

"I'd love to, but in the perfume business, that could get me into trouble. People like their privacy, especially if romance is involved."

Kendrick liked the way she carried herself. He saw a stack of her business cards on the glass counter between them and slipped one into his shirt pocket—someday he might call her when he needed to hire someone for his French office, or perhaps a dinner date. He purchased a bottle of Habanista, and off he went to his rendezvous with Poupon.

CHAPTER EIGHTEEN

Quarter past twelve p.m. and Kendrick was yet again standing outdoors at Poupon's gorgeous stone barbecue with four beige-and-white hunting dogs sacked out here and there on the ground, wherever they could find some shade. The clouds had drifted on, and the wind lessened. The sun directly overhead shone lavishly down upon them while Poupon explained his mother's Provençale mussels.

"If you feel like it, you can throw in whatever you like as long as it's Provençal. Whatever: pastis, fennel, rosemary, red peppers, thyme—but that's dressing it up more than it needs. That's the way I see it. My mother told me 'It's not really Provençale mussels without tomatoes and plenty of basil.'"

"No garlic?" Kendrick asked.

"Of course garlic, *mon dieu*, of course."

"Well, you didn't mention it."

"Who needs to mention garlic? Everyone knows that you put garlic into Provençale mussels."

"Well, there you go too far, yet again. Bet you anything an Eskimo wouldn't know."

"Kendrick, you're the one who goes too far. How do you get from Provençal mussels all the way to Alaska? And this wine you brought. I saw Cassis on the label. Is it Bobo's?"

"No, it's from François at Clos Sainte Magdeleine. What do you think?"

Poupon smiled, sniffed, and took a sip of the white. "I think it'll be good with the mussels and rougets."

Kendrick swirled his glass, sniffed, and downed a swallow. "I think it's his best ever, at least since I've known him. Ever since he quit filtering, all the fleshiness is still in the wine. By the way, how are you going to prepare the rougets?"

"Wrapped in grape leaves, grilled over coals. You can help me, unless you're too busy thinking important thoughts."

The red mullets, or rougets, were about five inches long. There were a dozen of them, and Kendrick offered to clean and gut them.

Poupon looked up to the sky and spread out his arms as he shrugged his thick shoulders. "Didn't your mother teach you anything? You don't gut rougets. Where'd you get such a loony idea? Kendrick, now listen to me. Here's a lesson in life. Don't forget what I tell you. Let's say you're in a restaurant, and on the menu you see that they offer *filets de rougets*. You stand up, walk out the door, and find another place to eat. Rougets are not rougets without the guts. *Merde*, everything today has to be sterile, pasteurized, castrated."

"But rouget guts are inedible. They taste like sewer."

"Kendrick, did I say anything about eating the guts? You cook the rouget whole with the guts still in them, but, *mon dieu*, of course you don't eat them. Nor do you leave them in the house in the garbage overnight. You'll stink up the place for days. But cooking them with the guts, that gives the flesh of the fish a little something. Without that something, the filet would be . . . What's the word I'm looking for?"

"Mundane?"

"Yeah, like that. Mundane."

After lunch, which ended with a glass of Corsican Muscat and a round little Provençale goat cheese wrapped in a chestnut leaf, the two of them got down to business.

"About that perfume in the winery," Kendrick said, "I decided to try to locate some of it, and, with the help of a professional in Bandol, I found what I think is the same fragrance." He handed the bottle over to Poupon. "Not only that, I purchased a bottle of it."

Poupon unscrewed the lid and put a few drops on the palm of his hand. "Whoa, that *is* strong. *Putain!* That's stronger than the cheese."

"I think it will come in handy, because just one big whiff of it reminded me where I originally encountered it. For three years in a row, I've been invited to Serge Bavet's house for dinner. He'd pull old bottles of Domaine Constanzo out of his cellar, but I couldn't appreciate them because his wife was at the table soaked in what I believe to be this same perfume. She considers herself to be a real fashion plate, you know—high heels around the house, always something overdressed about her."

"Serge's wife?" Poupon looked at Kendrick, then repeated himself. "Serge's wife?" Then came moments of silence while the ramifications bounced around inside his rather thick-looking skull. "When you said last night that Franck Constanzo might have had something to do with it, yeah, okay. He has been acting weird, so I could see the possibility. Especially after he came over the other day and you said he must have a hair up his ass—thanks for the expression, by the way, really useful. So, I would not say that his involvement is impossible, but Serge is Franck's winemaker, a hired hand. Plus, he's not the type. And I don't even know Serge's wife. What's she like?"

"I only know her from those three dinners. She looks solid—not fat, not massive, but someone hard to move. And I've never seen a sign of any sense of humor from her. What is most notable—she has a helmet of bright purple hair. More like raspberry. It is thick, falls straight down as if petrified, and anybody would know her from a kilometer away, because that head of hair is neon. And as a finishing touch, every moment I spend in her presence, I feel actively detested. I wonder what I ever did to her. Nothing. Zero."

"I think it's bizarre that you find her so sexy," Poupon said, trying to suppress a devilish grin.

"Ugh. On the contrary."

"Well, listen. Maybe she detests you because she knows how sexy you don't find her. Ever think of that? Women sense that kind of thing, you know."

"I've barely exchanged a bonjour or au revoir with her. I *have* sold a ton of her husband's wine. You'd think she'd like that."

"You've got to be wrong, Kendrick. Why would she drain one of my casks? Who gains?"

"We don't know that she was alone."

"That's all too crazy," Poupon said. "Just because you think you smell a perfume like hers, we leap to the conclusion that she or she and Serge did this horrid thing to me? Maybe we should take a deep breath and start again from the beginning."

"No, we've got to find out if it was her. Once she's eliminated from the likely suspects, we can start again from scratch. Let's go back to the cellar, see if there's maybe a bright raspberry-colored hair in there. You haven't cleaned it all up yet, have you?"

Poupon hadn't touched a thing, so they inspected the cellar thoroughly but gave up after about ten minutes.

"So, what's next?" Poupon asked.

"You're going to call Serge now and ask him to come over right away if he can. Just make something up, or, hey, tell him the truth, sort of. Tell him you have a serious problem with one of your casks of red wine. Can he come over and advise you?"

"And it's true," Poupon said, "Serge has always been a help to me ever since I got started—given me advice, introduced me to people like his cork producer. I tease him sometimes—tell him I'm going to pass him by, take over the number one spot. And you know, he can stick it to me, too, like when he criticizes one of my wines in front of you, my best customer. But, *merde*. I am one hundred percent sure that he is not capable of such a terrible sin. I mean, imagine, one winemaker pouring another winemaker's wine down the drain? It's like killing somebody's kid."

"Almost," Kendrick said.

"No, Serge isn't capable of that."

"I don't think so, either, but his wife is another matter altogether. Who knows what she's got fermenting under that raspberry hair of hers."

When Poupon phoned, Serge said no problem, he'd be right over, and ten minutes later they saw his black SUV pull up.

After greetings were exchanged and hands shaken, Kendrick told Serge that he had a gift for his wife. "If my memory serves me well— you know, I've forgotten your wife's first name, but I think she likes this brand." He handed Serge the bottle of Habanista.

"Oh, *mon dieu*, it's the only perfume she'll wear. Kendrick, you amaze me. What a memory."

Kendrick and Poupon looked at each other and shook their heads at the pitiful situation they were in. It was obvious to them that Serge had nothing to hide. In fact, he was happy to have been invited over, and even if there was a little rivalry between the two Bandol domaines, Serge considered himself among pals.

There was a silence in the cellar even an elephant could not have filled. Both Poupon and Kendrick were wondering which tack to take.

"Hey," Serge said, "anything wrong? You two act like your wine's turned to vinegar."

"I've got an idea!" Poupon blurted out, looking a little too happy given what he then proposed. "Let's have a cup of coffee."

"What about the problem cask?" Serge asked.

"We'll tell you all about it over a cup of Poupon's espresso," Kendrick said.

As they filed into the kitchen, Serge said, "Wait 'til you hear about the wines I had night before last. I went to Jonathan Pinard's place. He's a master sommelier, you know—lives in La Ciotat. He uncorked an old Baptiste-Pertois Champagne. The label had no vintage on it, but the winemaker has been dead for at least twenty years, so you know it was at least that old. Toss out all your big-name Champagnes. That Baptiste-Pertois was a marvel—a finesse, a presence, a purity you never see anymore. An artisan's wine, not a factory job."

Poupon set the three little cups on his kitchen table, offered around his pack of Camels, and everyone took one.

"Then he uncorked not one, but three vintages of Échezeaux from Henri Jayer. 1985, 1982, and 1978. Better than marvelous. And worth a fortune, especially 1978. We finished with a 1975 Château de Fargues, a Sauternes property owned by Alexandre de Lur Saluces of Château d'Yquem fame."

Poupon asked, with a foxy cunning written all over his big mug, "What time did you get home from the tasting?"

"Oh *merde*, it was late. I left La Ciotat at midnight. Why?"

"You didn't swing by here on your way home, did you?"

Serge's good humor took a hit. He managed a piercing little smile. "Why should I do that? Were you waiting for me in bed? I wasn't drunk enough to jump in the sack with you."

Poupon worked up a laugh. "Don't worry, you're not man enough for me."

Kendrick took over. He raised his hand between them and shook his head. "Listen, Serge, we've got a delicate problem here. Don't mind us if we're a little discombobulated."

"If you're what? Hey, don't pull out such long words with us. Poupon and me, don't ever forget, we're just a couple of peasants."

"And Poupon and I are just a little dazed. Last night, were you with your wife?"

"My wife? Well, first of all, as you should know, her name is Sandrine. And second, what business is it of yours whether I was with her or not? This is one weird conversation."

"Okay," Kendrick said, "listen, and you'll understand why we're acting so weird. Last night someone broke into Poupon's cellar and opened the faucet of one of his casks. All the wine—*poof*—down the drain."

Serge swore slowly, precisely. "*Putain de merde.* Down the drain."

"And whoever did it left a trail of Habanista perfume."

After Kendrick said it, he saw clearly that it rocked Serge, almost took his head off like an uppercut. Serge was not acting.

"It's not true, not possible, she wouldn't . . ."

His face cycled through a hall of mirrors' amount of contortions. Surprise, fear, anger . . . The idea that his Sandrine was capable of doing such a thing announced a huge change in his life. His forehead was sweating, and with the back of one hand he started scratching at something invisible on his chin. He looked around for help but found none. It appeared as though he wanted to open the door and walk out of his life into another, safer world.

Kendrick was beginning to feel some sympathy for a friend in trouble. A doorway out? Each of them would have opened it if they could have, because finding a solution to the dilemma was not going to be easy. For example, should a lawyer be called for one of them or for both Serge and Poupon? Go to the police to report the crime, get it on record in case of legal action? After all, who was going to pay compensation to Poupon for his lost wine, and how would it be valued? If they involved the police, would there be a jail term for Sandrine in the future?

Serge finally said out loud, "She's been talking often with Franck Constanzo, and he incites her. She sees you as a threat and has grown to despise the both of you."

"How could we be a threat?" Kendrick asked. "That's ridiculous."

"It's become a poison in Franck's mind that Vieux Laurier is going to take away Domaine Constanzo's business, that it's a fight to the finish, and that you, Kendrick, are on Poupon's side. Sandrine fears that I'll be blamed for any drop in reputation, that I'll be fired, that there would be a scandal and it would be impossible to find another job. It has been a terrible time at home with her. It's all she thinks about."

"Well," Poupon said, "she found one hell of a way to avoid scandal."

Soon the three of them were getting down to the nitty-gritty. Poupon did not like the idea of sending Sandrine off to prison. Nor did he want Serge humiliated. But sixty hectoliters is a lot of wine, about six hundred and fifty twelve-bottle cases, or a hell of a bunch of money, and Serge had neither. He was a hired hand at Domaine Constanzo, and salaried French workers usually don't have money to spare. If it had been Serge's domaine, he could have found a way to sneak sixty hectos to Poupon. Poupon would have accepted that, it seemed to Kendrick, in order to resolve a nasty situation, but Serge could not go to Franck and his sister and ask them for wine to fill up Poupon's empty cask. No way. Word of this loony tune could go no further.

"So," Serge tried to conclude, "sixty hectoliters in bulk amounts to about twenty-four thousand euros at the current price. I could pay you off in a few years and pay interest as if it were a loan."

Poupon curled up his nose and snarled, "To the devil with the price in bulk. That doesn't concern me. That wine would have been sold in bottle at a much higher price, and you know it. That was my favorite cask. Most of it was from the parcel, *La Poustagno*—my oldest vines, up the hill above the Roman washhouse and fountain. I might have decided to sell it as a *cuvée speciale*, which would have meant five more euros per bottle, so you can multiply your estimate by five or six. If not, we can always let the police and attorneys take over. This is not only about wine—it is also about profit."

"What can I say? It will take years, over a decade to pay you back unless Domaine Constanzo decides to triple my pay. Maybe I can sell my wife. No, excuse me. I was trying to be funny. I could sell my house."

They kept trying to come up with a solution until Kendrick had an idea. "The vines are insured in case of hail, right? What about the wine? Fire, flood? Insured or not. What about a leak?"

Yes, Poupon was insured, but he wasn't sure about leaks . . .

"Well then, we come up with a story. There was an accident. It would be nice to be honest, but in this case, no way. If we tell the truth, insurance policies always have pages of small print. What a bunch of crooks. You pay all your life and when you finally need insurance, there's the small print."

Both winemakers agreed with that.

"Who knows if criminal activity is covered?"

"They'd find some way to avoid paying," Poupon said. "I'll bet you anything. Those insurance companies are so rich—in Bordeaux, a couple of them have so much money, they each bought a classified growth, châteaux and vineyards."

"It's happening in Burgundy, too," Serge said. "The vignerons can't afford to buy more land, but the insurance companies can."

"So," Kendrick said, "you two have to come up with a credible explanation. How could you accidentally lose a cask full of wine down the drain?"

"Someone didn't close it tight?" Poupon suggested.

"Couldn't a washer break or come loose?" Kendrick added.

Serge came up with the solution. Early in his career, he was an intern at a winery in Châteauneuf-du-Pape. With a miniature tractor, one of the employees was moving a stack of wooden pallets in the cellar and sheared the wooden spigot right off the front of an oak cask.

"Someone noticed fairly quickly," Serge said, "so they didn't lose all the wine, but if it had been close to the end of the day and no one else was there, it would have all been lost."

Problem solved, they agreed, except for one last detail. According to Poupon, the insurance company would never agree to fully reimburse him. "You can be sure they'll only reimburse me the price of the wine if it was sold in bulk."

Serge said he could come up with the difference. He had some cases of rare Bordeaux, all from 1961, that his father had left him. Petrus, Latour, like that. Some were worth thousands of euros per bottle, and he could sell them under the table for cash from the three-star sommelier he'd dined with the night before, the night that became known to the three coconspirators as "The Night of the Open Faucet."

Poupon cleared his throat while raising one hand. "Wait," he said. "There's one thing I don't get. Okay, Sandrine hates us and fears for your job, your income. But why open the faucet? How does that solve her problem?"

"It was just lashing out," Serge said, "striking a blow. With Franck full-time scaring the hell out of her . . ."

"Hey," Poupon said slyly, "your wife seems to spend an inordinate amount of time with Franck."

"You asshole!" Serge said with a smile. "Anyway, it drove her crazy, so she strikes out blindly. I'm so tired of all this, my own mind is permanently damaged."

CHAPTER NINETEEN

A couple days later, Poupon came up the hill in his white camionette with a five-liter gift jug of his own olive oil. "I'm thinking of tearing out that plot of Ugni blanc I told you about," he said. "What if I told you I'm going to plant more olive trees there instead?"

"I don't see why not," Kendrick answered. "There's a huge demand for good olive oil, and the prices are going up like crazy."

"On our drive up to the Alpilles, seeing those olive orchards—I want one of my own, even if it's not profitable."

Kendrick looked at him, surprised. "You mean just for the pleasure of seeing them?"

"Right below the house there, it's not really a terroir for wine grapes. I'd rather look out and see rows of olive trees."

They sat on the terrace with cups of steaming black coffee and listened to the *hee-haw* siren of an ambulance down on the main road. The sun was so bright it was almost too much—everything seemed to shimmer. Kali showed up with a green lizard in her mouth and started toying with it under the table.

"I can't get over that empty cask," Poupon said. "It's one of my best casks, so of course I put my best cuvée into it. That was one hell of a wine down the drain. That crazy woman. Sandrine. I'd like to throttle her, give her something to think about."

He threw his Camels on the table. Kendrick went in and came back with a green plastic ashtray. Poupon leaned over to see it better. "What's it say here? Isn't that Italian?"

"Right you are. It says *Rubato dalla Trattoria del Meriti Ubriachi.*"

"I can see that, but what's it mean?"

"Stolen from the Trattoria of Drunken Husbands."

"They sell ashtrays?"

"Not at all, but wouldn't you take that as an open invitation to steal one?"

"The world is so immoral, so rotten. *Mon dieu*, Kendrick, even you? A petty thief? You should be ashamed."

"Are you serious? Look at it. It's a crappy piece of plastic—probably cost a penny or two to make. They expect people to steal them. Why else would they have printed what they did?"

Poupon chuckled. "I can't imagine you sliding it like a sneak into your coat pocket."

"I did it right in front of the waiter when he brought the check."

"Yes, and he knew if he turned you in, you wouldn't have given him a tip." Poupon took a sip of coffee and took a good, long pull on his cigarette. "You know what I think? Sometimes I think women are from outer space."

Kendrick almost spewed out his coffee, but he managed to keep a straight face. "*Mon dieu*, Poupon, what an original thought. That is wisdom surely earned by serving nobly for decades in the battle of the sexes. Hard earned, I might add."

"Hard enough," Poupon said with a lewd chuckle. He lit another Camel with his shiny black-and-gold lighter. His expression changed. He looked keenly into Kendrick's eyes. "Hey, are you bullshitting me? Oh *merde*, then, go ahead. What do I know about anything? Stolen ashtrays, outer space. What do I know about anything, including women?"

Finally, Poupon stood up. "So Kendrick, what's up today? I'm off to Sanary, check out the port, see what the fishing boats caught this morning."

"I'm free. Yeah, sounds good to me."

"Okay, I'll head back to my place to get ready. Come on over when you're ready, and we'll take my new car to Sanary."

Kendrick was left wondering what Poupon meant by "get ready," and when he drove over, Poupon emerged from his front door in a rigidly starched bright white shirt unbuttoned to within an inch of his navel, sporting a golden chain with a shiny gold and green metal eagle flopping against the furry zone between his chest and well-fed belly. When Kendrick was still about five feet from the would-be Adonis, he couldn't help wincing as his trusty nose received a searing blast of macho aftershave lotion.

"Thank god we're not tasting," Kendrick said.

"Why's that?"

"Whatever shit you splashed on yourself is ten times stronger than Habanista. They should label it Hiroshima."

"Listen to me, Kendrick." He puffed out his chest and struck a pose, something like Lawrence of Arabia surveying his next battleground. "When I arrive in town, I want everybody to know it. There's Poupon! Poupon's arrived! And hey—wait 'til you see—I bought myself a new toy. We're taking it to Sanary." His toy was a big bruiser, an all-black SUV from BMW. And suddenly, to Kendrick, the white shirt made sense. Poupon actually had a sense of color coordination. Black with white. "Look at this beast," he continued. "I bought it cheap from a friend who couldn't afford the gas it takes to power it. Imagine how women are going to melt into pudding when I come cruising by."

They settled into the most spacious car and the most comfortable seats, beyond anything Kendrick had ever imagined. The leather smelled brand new. It was not far from Poupon's to Sanary, but a minute or two quicker by the autoroute because you could legally drive at 130 kph. Once through the toll, Poupon floored his mighty beast. Kendrick slammed back into his seat, thinking if the BMW had wings, the car would have soared. The trip to Sanary took only about two minutes because Poupon revved it up to 180 kph. "There's no radar until the tunnel at Toulon," he said, "so, nothing to worry about."

Sanary has a pretty little port where four or five fishermen still unload their catch and sell it right off the boat. Across the street are several bars and restaurants, the inevitable *tabac* and pharmacy, which in France go together like a horse and carriage.

Kendrick took a table in front of the Café du Port while Poupon ducked into the *tabac* for a refill. When he came back, the café proprietor was waiting, and he and Poupon pretended to kiss each other's cheeks. Poupon introduced Kendrick as his American importer while the proprietor, another Jules, set a bowl of black olives on the table.

"Well, Monsieur Kendrick, we're all hoping that you are going to import all of Poupon's rotgut. Won't you, please? We prefer to drink fine wines in France."

"You're lucky to have any at all," Poupon said. "Kendrick would take my entire production if I let him."

"Go ahead, sell Monsieur Kendrick all he wants. It's true, isn't it, Poupon? You and your enologist can cook up more of your pinard whenever you run out. You don't even need grapes, right?"

"Watch out, *cher ami*," Poupon said. "If you had any balls, I'd cut them off years ago." Both broke out laughing and exchanged pretend punches. "Hey, Kendrick, did you know that in French, *jules* is another word for 'toilet'? So, Monsieur Toilette, I'll have a pastis. And you, Kendrick?"

"Same here. Maybe it'll kill the smell of your aftershave." When Poupon offered him a smoke, he said, "Yeah, thanks. I'll save the smoke for the pastis. By the way, what does *pinard* mean? I know it refers to insipid wines, but the word itself, where did it come from?"

"It's the wine the soldiers were generously rationed in the war of 1914, so you can imagine the quality. But the troops needed to tranquilize themselves with something before they were commanded to stand up from their trenches to be mowed down. It's said that some of them were so drunk they bled pinard instead of blood. Nowadays, it just means any shitty wine."

Two glasses of pastis arrived with a bowl of ice cubes and a pitcher of water. Kendrick filled his glass to the top with ice, while Poupon put a sole cube into his while informing Kendrick that Americans have a reputation in France for over-icing everything.

Out came the cigarettes, and Poupon supplied the flame. When he inhaled, he coughed one, two, three times. Kendrick motioned with his cigarette, aiming it toward Poupon's chest and questioning with his eyebrows as if to suggest that the cough was the result of smoking.

"What?" Poupon asked. "You believe all that propaganda?"

Kendrick shrugged. "Just the other day I read about a doctor, a French specialist of some kind, who quit smoking, quit eating gluten, gave up lactose and alcohol, and he says now he feels secure, after all the experience he's had with his patients, that he'll live to the ripe old age of one hundred and twenty."

"Oh, he'll be ripe, all right," Poupon said. "He'll be rotting on broken bones by then. Who the hell wants to be a hundred and twenty years old? What a jerk. And anyway, here's a true story. I forget her name now, but there was an old woman who lived in Arles and even knew the painter van Gogh. She was a hundred and fourteen years old, the oldest person in France, a lifelong smoker, and she had a fondness for Cognac. Then her doctor convinced her that for her health, she'd damn well better give up smoking and drinking. Which, believe it or not, the old lady managed to do. Not easy, I'll bet. And *bang*! A year later, she's dead. Don't you agree, there's a lesson there?"

"That's quite a story," Kendrick said, lingering with extra pleasure over the latest puff drawn from his cigarette. He considered himself one of the lucky few who could enjoy an occasional cigarette without needing a follow-up soon afterward. "You mean you think she would still be alive if she'd kept on drinking and smoking?"

"No, I'm just saying, that's all. Nobody will ever know. But listen, here's my philosophy," Poupon said. He swallowed the dregs of his pastis. "There are a million ways to die. You could be driving down the highway happy as a lizard in the sun, windows down, puffing on a cig, when some truck driver on amphetamines smashes into you head on. Imagine all the ways to die that could very well happen before smoking kills you. If you'd quit smoking before the truck happened, you'd have quit for nothing. When I smoke, I know the danger. I choose the risk myself. At least if tobacco kills me, it was my choice and not some ridiculous accident out of nowhere. Like playing Russian roulette, cigarettes are a gamble. Okay? But I don't want to play Russian roulette, so I don't. However, I do like to smoke, so I choose to do so despite the gamble."

"Here's to you, Henri Poupon. That's the best excuse for cigarette addiction I've heard so far."

Kendrick picked up the bill before Poupon could, and they crossed the street to take a look at the fish on ice at fisherman's row. Kendrick bought a small slice of tuna for dinner at home, and Poupon a huge *loup de mer*. It weighed six kilos. Kendrick asked if Poupon had guests coming, but he said no, he'd just never seen such an enormous *loup*, so he couldn't stand not buying it—that he'd probably freeze it for a rainy day and invite a crowd over.

They arrived back at Vieux Laurier at eleven thirty. "Have a glass of rosé before you go, and that smoke we talked about," Poupon said.

"Bring me a red, thanks. That sounds good to me right now."

"Kendrick, *merde*, you think I haven't noticed that you don't like my rosé? So tell me, what's wrong with it?"

"Again? Tell you again? Okay. I don't like it because it tastes exactly like all the other shitty rosés out there. It's technoville, all fake, almost not wine."

Poupon reeled with the punch, and Kendrick continued. "Quit adding those yeasts your enologist sells to you. You have plenty of them in the vineyard—your vineyard, your yeasts, nature's yeasts, the yeasts from right here, a combination of yeasts that nobody else has. And quit blocking the malolactic fermentation. Let the wine finish fermenting like god intended. Yours tastes like *fermentation interruptus*. And quit filtering it. You filter out all your rosé's lusciousness. All its flash and sass. I don't get it. You're not a techno kind of guy. Your rosé doesn't even smell like wine."

Silence, a long silence during which Poupon had flinched three times as if dodging blows. "Okay, okay, I'll get you a glass of red, and listen, someday, no, next year, I'll try making my rosé your way."

"You are such a phony, Poupon. You say that every year and then turn around and let your genius enologist tell you how to make your rosé again. I'm sick of discussing it."

By the time Poupon returned, they'd both calmed down. Cigarettes fired up, they clinked their two glasses of red and settled in.

"I'll bet you're getting sick of eating mussels whenever you come over, right?"

"Not at all. Just the other day I cooked up a bunch outdoors—your recipe with rosemary and garlic—and soon I'll get around to making them *à la Provençal*."

"I've never made my mother's pot-au-feu for you, have I?"

"You know, Poupon, hard to believe after so much time in France, but no one has ever served me pot-au-feu. I feel deprived. I had it in a bistro once, but it tasted like boiled beef, period."

"Well, I started one at six this morning. If you'd like, we could enjoy it together."

"Not possible today. Will it still be good tomorrow?"

"Hmm, well, the bouillon is definitely better the first day. And I made a lot. Come see."

The kitchen was bursting with aroma, like a thick cloud of meaty deliciousness. A huge clay marmite sat on the stove above a teensy flame. Poupon lifted the lid to find the bouillon bubbling along very delicately.

Kendrick sniffed until his lungs were full. "That's maybe the best thing I've ever had the opportunity to smell in my life."

Poupon chuckled. "That's what you said about the 1947 Cheval Blanc."

"What is it? Like a beef stew, right?"

"Yes, tons of beef. I always make as much as my mother made for the whole family, because the measures are simpler that way. Plus, I'm not good at division. It takes some serious shopping, believe me, and the butcher is glad to see me coming." Poupon reeled off a long list of ingredients, including a whole chicken and a kilo of beef ribs.

Kendrick said, "It sounds like we'd better fast for a couple of days before we dive into your pot-au-feu."

"Au contraire, it's better to build up resistance by eating well."

"What's this last cut you mentioned? A *gite-gite*?"

"It's a flat, stringy piece, just below the thigh. It's full of good stuff if you cook it good and long. Very gelatinous. But younger butchers won't know what you're talking about. You'll need some vegetables: leeks, turnips, celery, tomatoes, onions, carrots, potatos, cabbage. And garbanzo beans. Oh yes, and don't forget throwing in a few cloves and bay leaves."

"What, you just boil it all together? I don't have a pot big enough."

"You'll have to learn to divide before you give the butcher your order. But listen, you can be imprecise with the quantities. That's permissible. However, there is one unbreakable rule about making a good pot-au-feu. Above all, do not cook the cabbage and chickpeas with the rest, or even together. Those must be cooked separately in a little of the bouillon. That's when you've got it!"

"Okay!" Kendrick said decisively. "An offer I can't refuse." He inhaled through his nose a big whiff of pot-au-feu. "I can come back tonight if we eat on the late side."

"Kendrick, you are the client and, *chez moi,* the client is king."

CHAPTER TWENTY

On Kendrick's terrace, he and Poupon huddled over a road map of Corsica, arguing about their upcoming trip and feeding from a bowl of ripe black cherries. "We could fly to Bastia from Marseille," Kendrick said, "rent a car, and an hour's drive across the top of the island later we'd be knocking on Baltazaru's door in Patrimonio."

"You're the type who likes to waste money," Poupon said. "You're so rich you can burn euros in your fireplace to heat your house on a cold day. Impressive. I'm jealous."

"Oh, come on, Poupon. That ferry from Marseille takes forever. They're not hovercraft like they have from Nice, so for a three-day trip, we would waste one sixth of our time on a damned slow boat to China."

"Sure, the ferry is slower, but we can take one of our cars with us on the ferry. Why pay to rent one? You Americans. Time is money, right? Well, let me assure you, time is time, and you can't deposit it into your back account."

"I know what it is. You're a cheapskate. Here's the rest of my plan—I'm not going to drive from Baltazaru's to Marchelli's and then to Santini's. That would take about twenty-four hours winding up and down those ridiculous Alpine peaks just to save some money."

"Alpine peaks? Have you lost your mind? Has Corsica moved to Switzerland?"

Kendrick wondered how to say it without sounding insufferable. "I was reading about Corsica—the island is actually part of the same chain of granite as the Alps. Corsica is where some Alps stick up out of the Mediterranean Sea."

"So, what now? We sprout wings and soar over the mountains from one end of Corsica to the other?"

"No," Kendrick said, "we sprout rotor blades—we rent a helicopter."

"You really are rich."

"No, we're going to split the price. It's a business trip, a tax deduction. We'll fly Air Corsica to Bastia as I said, see Baltazaru in Patrimonio, return to the airport, return the car rental, helicopter to Marchelli's, and when we're done there, helicopter to Carlo Santini's. There's a flight to Marseille from the Figari airport, and Carlo will be happy to drive us there when we're ready to fly home."

"You heli-hop if you want. Me, I'm driving." Poupon looked immoveable.

"Poupon, you're no longer a peasant who has to hoard every centime away for a rainy day. It's time to say *bombs away* to your family roots and act like who you really are."

"And who exactly am I?"

Kendrick told him to hush up, pay attention, and try to understand. "Money isn't really yours until you spend it. The bank has your savings, right?"

Poupon nodded. "Pretty much, yeah," he granted.

"Right now it's the bank's money. They're spending and investing it for their own good as we speak. Follow me? You don't think it's just lying in some vault, do you?

"I guess not."

"So it's only worth anything to you when *you* spend it. I'm providing a way for you to enjoy the fruits of your labor."

Poupon caved, finally, but as it happened, they ended up on the Marseille-to-Calvi flight because the timing worked better. As the little propjet descended for landing at the Calvi airport, it began to be buffeted by powerful gusts of mistral. A woman's voice, the pilot, warned the passengers to expect extreme turbulence. The plane began to feel about as solid as a sheet of paper. They were thumped by increasingly violent gusts followed by moments of weightlessness.

The plane wobbled, lifted, and sank, jerked and was jolted again and again. It flew low over the bay of Calvi, but who on board could enjoy its incredible beauty as everyone began to consider the prospect of a quick end to their time on earth? The airport is in a valley surrounded on three sides by enormous granite peaks, and a pilot has to circle inside the naturally formed amphitheater in order to approach for landing in the proper direction. The craggy mountainsides were so close to the plane, Kendrick could make out individual plants from his window seat. One wrong move, one gust too strong, and bye-bye to everyone—mere wreckage scattered in the crags.

But the worst was still to come, and a baby must have gotten the vibe, because it started screaming its lungs inside out. As the wheels were about to touch the runway, the wind seemed to float the aircraft slightly upward, then a mighty gust lifted the left-hand wing. Kendrick watched the right-hand wing dipping toward the runway. When the wing tip was about a foot away, the pilot won her struggle to regain control. The plane leveled off, and there was a gentle thump when the wheels touched tarmac. As they walked from the plane to the terminal, Kendrick saw the pilot coming down the stairway behind him. She was as white as a ghost. Nobody's heart, including Kendrick's, was beating normally.

They rented a dark blue Volkswagen Golf and headed north along the coast into the mountains and the Désert des Agriates, following a winding, twisting road that proved to be no fun at all behind a delivery truck that could barely manage the hairpin turns and steep hillsides. If you could manage to forget the narrow highway that made passing almost impossible, the scenery was lovely. A few dirt roads led off into the dry, barren landscape west toward the ocean and some marvelous white sand beaches, but you'd need four-wheel drive to manage them.

After Saint-Florent, they drove alongside an ochre-colored beach of rounded stones, then passed through what looked like a rip in the limestone hillside as if Mother Nature had picked it up, torn it in two, and put it back, leaving just enough room for a two-lane highway. And suddenly there they were, the vineyards of Patrimonio—green leaves, white chalky soil, and a slice of blue Mediterranean visible through the pass where the highway left the sea.

For both Poupon and Kendrick, seeing Baltazaru was always a treat. A heavyset guy—you could see he liked to eat well—he was built solid, with a headful of thick salt-and-pepper hair. When he was younger, he probably had the pick of any woman he wanted—and at fifty-five, maybe he still did. Yet he was as devoted to his wife—Lucia—as any husband Kendrick had ever been around.

Poupon and Kendrick were prepared for hours of wine, wine, and more wine, but Baltazaru had other ideas. It was getting close to lunchtime, so the three of them squeezed into his crowded cellar and quickly tasted six or seven unbottled wines from the most recent vintage, Kendrick scribbling into his tasting notebook almost nonstop. Then the three climbed into Baltazaru's minivan and drove farther north along the coast on an almost vertical mountainside, the narrow road carved roughly out of the rock, the gorgeous Mediterranean way down below. "I hope you're as hungry as I am," Baltazaru said, "because we're going to my favorite fish restaurant." He explained that foreigners all thought Corsicans were a maritime people who lived off the bounty of the sea, when, in fact, they were more a mountain people because, with pirates and one invader after another, they literally had to head for the hills to survive. Boar were more important to their diet than seafood. Indeed, much of the seafood offered in Corsica was imported.

Descending into Marine de Canelle—where there were a dozen homes at most—was a big deal because the road was so steep it felt like gravity would pull their car right down, splashing into the turbulent sea. The restaurant, Da Ragnola, was built on rocks just above the crashing waves and had a concrete dock for customers arriving by sea.

The proprietor saw Baltazaru enter and in mid-sentence left a table of diners. He feigned a kiss on each cheek, shook hands with Kendrick and Poupon, then guided them to a table next to the window overlooking the seascape outside.

"*Chers amis*, what will you open with? Rosé? White? Frizzante? Muscatellu?"

Baltazaru shrugged and looked at Kendrick. "What suits your thirst?" he asked.

"No, you choose. What about something new, something you've tasted and liked lately?"

Baltazaru pondered a moment, then looked up at the proud host. "Do you have Calisto's new white?"

"I have both his 2004 Bianco Gentile and the 2003 Patrimonio blanc."

Kendrick spoke up. "Let's try the Patrimonio. Personally, I haven't yet learned what there is to love about Bianco Gentile."

Baltazaru nodded his approval to the patron. "Patrimonio blanc to start. But Kendrick, you know that Bianco Gentile is a true Corsican grape variety, not one that came from Italy or France. Around here, we're all planting it, trying to bring it back."

"Yes, I'm aware of the story and the ambition to establish the wine. I'm not against it, but so far the flavor is not very interesting to me, and the shape of the wine not seductive. In fact, all of them I've tasted seemed a bit formless. Vermentino is sculpted; Bianco Gentile so far doesn't seem to have been chiseled into shape—it's like a hunk of marble, white with no contours."

"Any bright ideas how you would try to fix that?"

"Don't harvest so late, for one thing. Try making it with less fat on the bone. And maybe give it a longer maceration, see if the grape skins have anything of interest to offer. That might add some flavor interest. It's worth a try."

"I'll try a small cuvée like that next year. It's true, the instinct here has been to leave the grapes longer on the vine, hoping riper will translate into more flavor interest."

The three of them mulled that over for a few seconds, then Kendrick spoke up again. "So, Baltazaru, how is your wife, Lucia, these days? Sorry I missed her."

The Corsican brightened up, showing his big smile. "She's fine. You'll see her later today. Driving here—the road gives her vertigo. I don't see her enough lately, either. I'm telling you, I'm turning into an old grouch. My life is too crowded. My little winery under the house feels like it's shrinking. I'm suffocating down there in the middle of those vats and bottles and cartons, plus I have too many clients showing up all the time."

Poupon spread his arms open and spoke up. "Well of course everyone wants to visit you. You're on the superstar map now."

Their wine appeared alongside a platter of raw, peeled prawns with a sauce of passion fruit, ginger, and winter savory, according to the owner. Baltazaru looked at the platter for a long moment, then called for the patron to come back.

"Hey, what's this? At the prices you charge, you can't even cook the food anymore?" When he turned, laughing, back to his two guests, Baltazaru said, "I like to give him a bad time. Did you see the look on his face until he realized I was joking?"

"Pulling his leg," Kendrick said. "*Tirais sa jambe.*"

"I didn't touch his leg. Never have."

"No," Kendrick said, "it's American slang for when you're kidding someone."

After that, eight little tapas-like starters arrived along with a second bottle, a white from the Ajaccio region. There were slices of coppa, *saucisson*, tapenade toasts, whole radishes, *beignets de morue*, roasted red peppers, potato salad, and chickpeas. Then, without even ordering, a cauliflower gratin full of eggs and cheese with a thick layer of spicy tomato sauce on top appeared, steaming and smelling impossibly good.

Again, Baltazaru yelled out to the patron, who was sharing a pastis at the bar with a couple of friends.

"Hey, Yves, I like you, you like me, right?"

"*Si, si*, of course."

"Then what in the name of god are you doing? You expect us to continue drinking this beautiful white when your heavenly gratin is down on its knees begging for red wine?"

Kendrick couldn't help laughing, but admitted, "You're right, it has to be a red."

After the owner poured Patrimonio—a red Patrimonio—the three of them devoured every last bite of the cauliflower gratin.

Baltazaru said, "Remember a few years ago, Kendrick? You told me you were interested in buying a little place for yourself here in Corsica, that you'd been thinking of staying a month or so per year until you retire, then move in full time."

"Yes, and I still think about it, but you didn't seem to encourage the idea much."

"In those days, foreigners were not welcomed. On the contrary, they were discouraged from moving here. It was Corsica for Corsicans. Strictly enforced! There was no killing—don't get me wrong. But your house in Corsica? You might have come home and found a big hole where the roof used to be. Now, however, I feel like I can safely encourage you to pursue the idea, if you still wish to. Things are changing here, I'm afraid. Money is more and more what speaks loudest to people, and opening up sales of property to foreigners has resulted in drastically higher prices. Prices few Corsicans can afford. So listen, if you decide to move on it, tell me, and I can grease the wheels of the deal with the hidden powers that be."

No one had ordered, but a platter arrived smoking, exhaling one of the most wonderful smells of Kendrick's lifetime: roasted hunks of octopus tentacles served on roquette leaves and a fantastic dressing of olive oil, vinegar, sorrel, and raw, minced garlic. To conclude, they were served a press pot of coffee with chestnut cookies.

As they were leaving the restaurant, a long, sleek, all-black yacht rode the waves about forty yards from the boat dock. Even the sails were black. The three of them stopped to watch awhile as two super-chic couples climbed down into a bobbing black Zodiac and fell all over one another. A sailor drove them to the dock, but the Zodiac was bouncing around so much there was no way they could secure it to the dock. After several minutes of trying, they turned around and headed back to the mother ship.

"I thought the world was going to lose one of its great voices," Baltazaru said.

"How's that?" Poupon asked.

"Didn't you recognize him? The one with the big chest and white skipper's cap? That was Lorenzo Caldavia, the Italian tenor."

"Oh sure, *merde*, of course," Poupon said. "I was just at the opera the other day."

"And the other guy is the tire guy, one of the richest men in Italy. I delivered two cases each of red, white, and rosé to that sailboat the other day when they were docked in the port at Saint-Florent, and one case of Muscatellu. They gave me and Lucia a tour top to bottom of the yacht. And, believe it or not, they have a tender nearby in

Saint-Florent. It is much larger. In case there's no wind, you know, it has a smokestack and everything you can possibly imagine—for example a wine cellar stocked with old Barolo, Brunello, Yquem, Romanée Conti. And believe it or not, the tender is not black, it is Technicolor. As you watch it, it changes color right before your eyes. I don't know how the devil they do it. He's a guy, the tire guy, who knows how to spend a whole lot of money. He's talented, you know, at spending his riches."

When they turned back into Baltazaru's driveway, he announced that it was time for his beauty sleep. If they wanted, there were a couple of beds free, then when they all woke up, they could do some serious tastings in the cellar. And that's what they did. They tasted later and later into the evening crammed into Baltazaru's cellar full of stainless steel tanks of various sizes and shapes—a shiny metal ambience full of good wines. At one point, the three of them got into a which-was-better discussion. Baltazaru liked stainless steel for fermenting and raising his wines. Poupon had cement fermenters, then used large oak casks. Kendrick said he'd opt for wood, that stainless steel tanks, because of some magnetic or electrical impulses, could trouble the wine and make it difficult to bottle without filtration. "Metal touching wine, plastic touching wine—it doesn't sound right to me," he said with a distasteful shake of his head. "I'd stick with wood all the way, from the harvest to the bottle."

"What?" Poupon asked. "Where are you going to order your wooden bottles?"

"You know what I mean. Glass is made from melted sand. Glass is neutral. I wish I could ferment in glass tanks."

Baltazaru said he dreamed of building a new, larger winery that would allow him to experiment much more than his crowded basement allowed.

Poupon said that his father and grandfather had used wood and he wasn't about to disturb the dead by putting good grape juice into metal or plastic.

Before lunch, they'd tasted from stainless steel tanks. Now the bottled wines from the previous year's harvest appeared, were uncorked, poured out into the three glasses, and each wine was discussed more or less in detail—things like the color, the smell, the taste, the texture, the balance, the aftertaste, and so on.

Lucia brought down a platter of Corsican sausages to munch on, then later a selection of local cheeses, and finally a chestnut cake that was devoured with glasses of Muscatellu, Corsica's dessert wine. Kendrick told Poupon that if he wanted to drive women crazy, he should give up his aftershave and douse himself with Baltazaru's Muscatellu.

CHAPTER TWENTY-ONE

Heading back from Patrimonio to Saint-Florent, once a port for fishing boats and almost entirely given over to pleasure craft now, the Hôtel Casa Mare was between the highway and a maroon-colored rock beach—nary a speck of sand to be seen. Walking barefoot was pure torture. The Casa Mare didn't put on any airs—you were on the beach, and that should be enough. Who cared about the stained, trampled-half-to-death beige pile rug in the room? Or the crisp, dust-colored carnations standing in a tall, dried-out water glass?

In the morning, Kendrick examined the pathetic *petit déjeuner* on the hotel terrace facing the huge bay of Saint-Florent. The baguette was so hard it could have used a nutcracker. He gazed out upon a vast amount of water and towering mountains without much civilization to muck up the view. Far away on the south shore of the bay he made out the ruins of a round stone tower. Corsica was ringed by them—watchtowers built so guards could alert the population to danger.

Kendrick and his Provençal sidekick returned their rental car to the agency at Calvi's airport and climbed aboard their rented helicopter. They were headed to the Figari airport, close to the southern tip of the island near Bonifacio and Porto-Vecchio.

In a whirlybird, there was no conversation. The blades didn't whir; they chopped with a clatter that drowned out all other noise, so if anyone wished to speak, it had to be with hand signals—pointing down, perhaps, to some idyllic beach, or a thumbs-up for marvelous cliffs, or arms opened wide in appreciation for the immensity of the chain of towering mountains. An airplane went forward, and its wings gave it lift, but in a chopper, Kendrick had learned, you couldn't know what to expect. It tilted and swooped and jerked around in the sky. He had instructed the pilot to fly along the coastline because of the visuals, so they ascended or descended constantly depending on the terrain, climbing to get over a mountain, then swooping down the other side to get a good look at a beach or yacht or whatever. As they flew low over a long white sand beach near Ajaccio (a sizeable city with an airport), the pilot zoomed up to get over a hill, and just as he cleared it, the bottom seemed to fall out and the chopper dropped straight down like a stone—just for a heart-stopping moment—as a small, one-propeller plane swerved up over them. A collision was avoided by a matter of inches, but no one screamed. No, Kendrick's heart started to beat again, but it was practically in his throat. He glanced at Poupon and made a face as if to say *Whew*, then he squeezed his forefinger and thumb together as if to say *That was a close one*. Poupon bobbed his head up and down yes and raised his eyebrows.

"It's a dangerous métier," Kendrick shouted. "Two near-death experiences in two days." Poupon, however, couldn't hear him.

Carlo Santini, who Baltazaru once told Kendrick might be Corsica's most talented winemaker, met them at the Figari airport. Carlo carried himself with a sort of gentle power—as if he could throw his weight around to get what he wanted but would rather be a nice guy. He said he'd heard a lot about Poupon's Vieux Laurier and perhaps Poupon could be convinced to trade some bottles with him. Poupon actually blushed through his tan, probably because Santini's wines sell for twice as much as Poupon's Bandol.

They piled into a dirty white Ford Explorer. "First a little tour," Carlo said. "I want to show you what I believe will be Corsica's best white wine vineyard once the vines mature. Pure chalk-white limestone cuddled right up next to the Mediterranean waters. The grapes will be caressed by a freshening sea breeze. Freshness! Super important in the south. Then we'll go have a quick look at Bonifacio and Porto-Vecchio. Afterward, onward to lunch on a beach at a *paillotte*. The sky, the sea, the sand, the fish, the you, the me, the wine . . . Thank you, Jesus. Right?"

"You forgot to include women in your list," Poupon said.

Carlo turned to grin at Poupon in the back seat. "My wife might join us for lunch, or do you mean you'd like me to arrange a woman for you?"

"Yeah, sure, one of those black-haired, big-busted Corsican beauties. Right, Kendrick?"

"Not my style," Kendrick replied. "Not my modus operandi."

Bonifacio is perched on a bleached white promontory rising straight up from the clear, blue sea. It appeared that one wrong move— a tidal wave or earthquake—and it would all tumble and slide down into the deep. Kendrick considered it an unforgettable site and had often walked its ancient streets. Poupon had only seen it in photos.

Porto-Vecchio? Not at all a sight for sore eyes—a small but far from quaint harbor that did not merit its name. For the first time, though, Kendrick spotted a number of signs of development—new roads, streetlights, roundabouts galore, new shopping centers, a gas station with around forty pumps, and For Sale signs all over the place. It felt not at all like the Corsica he'd known and loved. Now it began to resemble beach towns everywhere. Carlo turned off the highway onto a dirt road toward Santa Nuncio Beach. As they drove past several little concrete huts, Kendrick asked Carlo to stop.

"What happened here?" he asked. "Did they raise animals in these kennels?"

"No," Carlo said, "they were for human beings, tourists."

"They look about the size of a bathroom," Poupon said.

"No, I assure you, they were to sleep in. There was a large public bathroom. It was to be almost like camping out."

"So odd," Kendrick said as he examined them more closely. "See how the roofs all have big holes open to the elements."

"For stargazing, maybe," Poupon said.

Carlo got a kick out of that. "They've been this way for decades. What you see is an early attempt to build a Club Med in Corsica. They selected one of our most beautiful beaches, received building permits, and probably paid a pretty penny under the table for them, but they neglected to obtain the approval of the locals. So, just days before their grand opening—*boom!*"

Poupon asked if the police ever caught the guy who did it.

"Oh, you know how it is. They threw a couple of problem kids in jail for a week or two—just for show. If they'd arrested the guilty party, the police might not have made it back to headquarters alive. They knew better."

"I can't believe it," Kendrick said. "It's a form of terrorism, but they didn't hurt people."

"No, they blew it all to hell in the middle of the night—no workmen, no clients. And they got what they wanted. No Club Med to despoil our pristine beaches."

"If only the French had protected the Riviera like that," Kendrick said.

Carlo laughed. "Ah, the French—they like money too much. They'll trade beauty for money at every opportunity."

"That's all very good," Poupon said, "but you can't tell me that something isn't going on around here. Somebody is cashing in—bigtime. A gas station as big as the tollbooth on the A7 at Lançon, yet the place is empty. It's eerie. Where are all the cars going to come from?"

Carlo said that indeed, land around Porto-Vecchio was being sold for vacation and retirement homes. The powers that be had given the green light.

"You mean the mafia, right?" Poupon asked.

"Some call it the mafia, yes, but the peasants are also very happy to sell their little farms for big prices nowadays. The peasant sells to what you like to refer to as the mafia, and the mafia resells it to rich mainlanders at ten times the price."

"That's going to put all you Corsican bombers out of work," Poupon said.

"You two, in the USA and France, you've entered the twenty-first century. Maybe we in Corsica are about to enter the twentieth."

On a white sand beach at a restaurant open to the air, they enjoyed yet another version of octopus salad followed by spicy Corsican-raised lamb ground into sausages and grilled over coals. After lunch, they tasted in Carlo's vast new winery building, which felt incredibly luxurious after Baltazaru's cramped cellar.

Kendrick and Poupon's final stop of the trip involved coptering back north into the mountains above Ajaccio. On a relatively flat, grassy field, the pilot gently set them back on earth near the home and winery of Yves Marchelli.

They tasted about sixty different wines—a whole lotta spitting going on, for sure. Some wines were tasted out of barrels, some from stainless steel, cement, clay, and of course, bottles. Red, white, and rosé—young, old, and in between.

Yves sported a vibrant white mustache and, what truly endeared him to Kendrick, a remarkable joviality. If anyone could sell you on the idea that the wine life ain't no bad life—no, not bad at all—it would be Yves. Even his smile as he poured you a glass of white wine could have you thinking the best thing that ever happened to you was about to happen. They ate outdoors under enormous oaks whose branches were strung with multicolored party lights. Yves had a wood cabin built with a big kitchen—his very own restaurant out in the woods for family, friends, and clients—which Kendrick considered a very cool idea. After crispy radishes on ice, black olives, and sliced salami, they were served a platter of fresh sea critters chopped finely and served raw. The radishes came from Yves's wife's garden, and the sausage from his brother, who raised pigs and goats and other livestock. The sea critters were from Ajaccio.

Yves then danced out through the cabin door with a cutting board raised over his head until he swooped it down upon the table, his eyes glowing with excitement: a leg of baby boar browned beautifully. Kendrick praised its mahogany finish, then Yves's wife brought out a thick, bubbling-hot tureen of gravy full of white pearl onions. Everyone stared at it as if somebody had just put the *Mona Lisa* on the table—all because of Yves's gift for making everyone feel like life was one miracle after another.

While all eyes gazed at the platter of boar, Yves poured everyone a red and said, "People claim that Corsican wines aren't for aging. Let's see how my father's red is doing. He only made two wines a year, this red and a sweet Muscat. I make fourteen different cuvées. I'm just that way—curious, you know?"

"And they're all good," Poupon said. "Hell, I'd even drink that rosé of yours."

"It's known that you're not much of a rosé man, so thanks for the compliment. Now this red—see the vintage?"

Kendrick saw it, and his heart beat faster. "What a great vintage all over Europe," he said.

When the chunks of meat were served with the gravy, they all attacked without a word. It was not at all like Poupon's rubbery boar. Yves didn't try for rare or even medium—his boar was well done in more ways than one. Kendrick even deigned to take seconds! He was in heaven. Poupon noticed the enthusiasm, perhaps because at his dinner party Kendrick had managed not one word of praise, while at Yves's, there he was raving about how it was the best roast meat he'd ever eaten.

"My god, Kendrick," Poupon said, "are you on drugs or something?"

"What do you mean?"

"I mean, I've never seen you like this."

"What's wrong? You don't like the boar and the 1964?"

"Of course I do. Of course. It's fabulous."

"So . . . ?"

"Well, maybe your taste is more for well-cooked boar instead of served rare," he said peevishly.

"Maybe so," Kendrick said and turned to Yves. "This is outstanding. What went into the preparation?"

"I learned it from my father, who probably learned it from his father. Both were hunters, and you know that Corsica has always been swarming with wild boar. Anyway, I always preferred the tender, young boar, the *marcassins*. I take the leg or a shoulder and marinate it in Muscat with herbs from the maquis for two days. Finally, I roast it slowly, covered, at a low temperature for six or seven hours until the meat is falling apart."

"I never imagined boar could be so delicious," Kendrick said. "That crust of honey and herbs at the same time as the juicy, falling apart, tender flesh from the interior—incomparable!"

Poupon looked like he had a piece of raw boar lodged in his windpipe. He started to say something, stopped, started to say something else, and finally almost yelled at Kendrick. "Have you ever tasted the ravioli stuffed with wild boar and blueberries from Madame Vivonne at Gonfaron?"

"No."

"Well, then, you don't know anything, do you?" And Poupon went silent, firmly silent, until it was time to say thanks and goodbye before he and Kendrick entered the helicopter. Then he let out with an enormous, "*Merde!*" But with the copter's explosive clatter, Kendrick couldn't hear a thing. He didn't need to. Seeing was enough. He was halfway disturbed by Poupon's temper tantrum, but at the same time, rather touched to see that Poupon cared so much about whatever Kendrick might think about anything. He looked back through the years. He hadn't had such a close friend since his high school days.

CHAPTER TWENTY-TWO

Kendrick had no difficulty obtaining Babette's Nice address. One day when Poupon was absent, he asked Poupon's secretary, Flo, if by any chance she had the info on file. For once, Flo managed to avoid hissing. She looked up the address in a black leather notebook, wrote it down on a pink Post-it—including Babette's phone number—and handed it over with a single word: "Voilà!" Kendrick wouldn't be surprised if Flo, too, had half a mind to become Madame Henri Poupon someday.

In order to avoid the commuter traffic jams in Toulon, Kendrick left Milles Vents at nine thirty in the morning. Once in Nice, he easily found the Place Garibaldi where Babette lived. A huge square, it was surrounded by several yellow buildings, each one four stories high. It could be that every building in the square had, by law, to be painted the same yellow color. France could be like that. In Alsace, for example, it looked like everyone was legally required to have geranium planters blossoming outside their windows. The buildings in Place Garibaldi all had arcades at street level. The ground floors were for commerce, including four restaurants with outdoor tables, and upstairs for apartments. As squares go these days in France, it was fairly classy.

Kendrick found a parking lot because cars were not allowed in the square, then located Babette's building and her name next to a doorbell. He took a table at the restaurant with the best view of Babette's front door and ordered a glass of Nice's own Bellet blanc, figuring there was nothing to do but wait for her to arrive or depart and take it from there. About one thirty, he ordered a black-truffled croque monsieur and a glass of Bandol rouge.

The hours passed uneventfully. At seven p.m., still nothing. Maybe she had a job? Babette? No way. Out of town? Possibly. He ordered a glass of the same Bellet blanc. It had a lemony edge and a crisp, dry finish that hit the spot. Once that was downed, he stood and roamed around the square, reading menus. The one that appealed to him most was at a restaurant that still offered enough of a view of the entrance into Babette's building.

A waiter, a freckle-faced redhead with a Parisian scowl, handed over the menu, but Kendrick said, "I already know what I'm having, thanks. The *friture de petite poissons* and the *soupe de poisson, s'il vous plait*."

"But you choose-ed two entrées," the waiter said in heavily accented English.

"Yes, I'm aware of that," Kendrick continued in French. "And bring me the wine list, too, please."

The waiter snapped up the menu and went to a nearby table to take the order of a starry-eyed young couple—possibly, Kendrick imagined, on their honeymoon. He was seated at a table for four under a large forest-green parasol. A young man arrived with a basket of bread and filled up Kendrick's water glass.

"May I see the wine list please?"

"I'll call your waiter, sir." He looked panicked all of a sudden, out of his depth.

"Can't you simply hand me the wine list? I'd like to look it over and order a bottle." But no, fifteen long, dry minutes more passed with Kendrick twiddling his thumbs. The young lovers, however, were on their second glasses of Champagne. The first waiter appeared with a platter of deep-fried fishes, each about an inch long, but before he could set it on the table, Kendrick raised a hand to block him. He said politely but firmly, "Please, monsieur, I have asked twice, and this makes the third time—may I see your wine list? I don't like to start my meal without some wine with it."

"I going get it," the waiter said, and started to set the plate down again. Again Kendrick blocked him. "By the time you bring me the list, I choose a wine, and you go off to find it and uncork it, my *friture* will no longer be hot."

The waiter spun away, muttering loud enough to attract attention. Certain words carried, like, *un Americain* and *il est con*, which meant "he's a jerk" or "an asshole."

Kendrick did, however, finally succeed and ordered a Cassis rosé. His *friture*, certainly reheated, arrived at the same time. The waiter splashed a taste of rosé into Kendrick's wine glass. Kendrick took a sniff, raised his eyebrows as if to say *What next?*, and shook his head no. "This won't do at all. Unfortunately it's badly corked."

The waiter blew a breath out between gritted, nicotine-stained teeth. He grabbed Kendrick's glass and stabbed his nose into it. "Wine is good. Not cork-ed."

"Good enough for you, perhaps, but too cork-ed for me. You can drink it yourself—after you get me a decent bottle. Oh, and heat up those poor fish one more time while you're at it."

The waiter revved up his pace as he stormed away with the rosé. After a couple of minutes, he returned. "The cook say is good. Is perfect!" he shouted. Kendrick stood and kicked back his chair, more to be ready to defend himself than anything else.

"What's going on here?" It was a woman's voice. A strong-willed woman's voice. Kendrick and the waiter turned toward it, and there stood Babette.

"Branislav! What's going on here? Tell me right now."

Out went the lousy English as he answered in French. "This American fool is ordering us around like we were his servants."

She looked at Kendrick with questioning eyes.

"Nothing serious. The wine is corked and the service is dreadful here, that's all."

"This American idiot says the wine is corked because maybe he doesn't like it."

"Go, now!" she said. "Bring him another bottle. He's an American who knows more about wine than you or any hundred waiters put together. Go!"

Kendrick imagined the top of Branislav's head exploding and volcanic rocks and lava spewing out of the cone in an angry shower of sparks and flames. Instead, the waiter stomped off, and Kendrick didn't see him again. Another waiter brought a new bottle of Cassis, uncorked it, and poured. Kendrick sniffed it and nodded approval.

Kendrick invited Babette to have a seat and a glass of rosé, and asked, "Do you work here?"

"No, just passing by. But I live nearby, and I know a lot of people who work the square. What are you doing here?"

"Oh, I met one of my wine producers for a Côte-de-Provence tasting at a wine bar. I saw the menu here and thought I'd have a bite to eat before driving back home."

The new waiter then set a wine glass in front of Babette and, with the flourish of a toreador, poured her some rosé.

"The service certainly has improved since you joined me," Kendrick said. "Are you sure you're not part owner?"

"Just a neighbor and a longtime client."

"It's not often I'm victim of anti-Americanism."

"Is that what it was? I'll admit it exists, but some of your countrymen earn it."

"Give me an example—something that really happened."

"Well, French people who visit the United States are always impressed by the contortions required to rinse off at the end of a shower. You practically have to stand on your head to get the soap out from between your legs and all that stuff down there."

"Okay, I'm with you. I love how French showers have a fixed showerhead and the handheld kind, too."

Babette nodded. "We like to soap under the fixed and rinse with one on a flexible hose so you can aim it where you need it. Okay, your turn now. What do we do to bug you?"

"Easy. You don't have the manners to wait your turn in lines. Your own sweet grandmother will try to squeeze in and steal your place. Americans like first come, first served."

"You're right. It's a national sickness. Have you noticed when we French are in line to board a flight, we'll crowd like crazy to get to the head of the line, even when everyone has a reserved seat and the plane won't leave until everyone is seated? In other words, when it is totally useless. So, touché, good point."

"Now, back to you," Kendrick said.

Babette smiled, enjoying the game. "You Yanks are an egotistical breed. You act like everyone in France and around the world should understand English. And another thing. This time I can't claim to be an eyewitness, but all French know that American men think our bidets are for making wee-wee."

Kendrick took that as a moment to pounce. "And in France, in airports, for example, even hospitals, for some reason all the toilet seats have been removed. Where did they all go? And what, you're a nation that prefers to sit on cold enamel? How comfy. And in your public toilets, there is never any toilet paper. Do you all travel with your own?"

"Monsieur Kendrick, you are even more handsome when aroused, defending your motherland. However, you cannot deny that in the States, you don't even *have* public toilets. How do you hold it all in, for heaven's sake?"

Kendrick paused and considered while holding up his wine glass and gazing into the pale rosé. There wasn't much left in the bottle. They were both appreciating their give-and-take, and were almost laughing out loud.

"Madame, as long as you insist on keeping our discussion in the WC, answer me this satisfactorily, and I will concede defeat. Why does every bathroom in France have a brush next to the toilet?"

"Over here, we like clean toilets. Did you never think of that?"

"Ours are designed to do the job, flush everything away, but yours are not. A brush is mandatory. Strange thing is, French toilet manufacturers could simply steal our designs, and voilà, no more mess."

"I'll be your first customer," Babette said.

Kendrick had the advertising jingle in mind for French television: "Just flush, you won't need to brush." But no, the French wouldn't get it. It had to be in French. He searched his mind and came up with, "*Tire la chasse, efface les traces.*"

"Why don't you do it?" Babette asked. "You'll make millions, and the French will give you a medal."

"Aromatically, I prefer the wine business. But you said 'we French' earlier. What part of France? I mean, where are you from?"

"Around here. Maybe you notice a little accent. My mother was from Trieste, and any accent you discern when I speak French, I caught from her."

After his fish soup, Babette invited him up to her apartment for a cup of coffee. "I have an espresso machine that makes much better coffee than here," she said.

Just what he was hoping for. He would keep his eyes open, and who knows what might turn up?

Her building and apartment were at least a couple centuries old. The parquet floor had a lovely pattern and didn't squeak at all, indicating it was designed with a moneyed clientele in mind. The big view over the square gazed out upon the rooftops of old Nice and out to sea. Only the furnishings were humdrum—Kendrick was adding things up—IKEA quality in a luxury apartment. *Hmm.*

"How long have you rented here?" he asked.

"Oh, I don't rent. This view is expensive. I wouldn't be able to afford it." She smiled hopefully as if maybe Kendrick might be about to solve her financial problems.

"You borrow the apartment?"

She gazed at him a couple of beats as if deciding whether he was being nosy or making conversation.

"No. It's all mine. Part of a divorce settlement."

She stood and shook out her hair, blonded again this time, and said she was going to make the coffee. "Shot of Armagnac in the cup, too?" she called, but he declined.

"I've still got about two hours of road ahead of me," he said. While he waited, he ruminated. During his youth, blondes were rare, but now most French women were blonde, and the younger women seemed to be going for two layers—obvious brunette roots with a blonde exterior. Brunette lashes and smoky lids. It was definitely fashionable.

When she returned and placed the coffee cups on the table, Kendrick noticed that she sat on the sofa a little closer to him this time. When she crossed her legs—slowly, elegantly—he noticed how tan and shapely they were. She knew how to use those legs, in Kendrick's opinion, and it was not as a long-distance runner.

"I have a guest bed if you prefer," she said.

From down a hallway, her phone rang. She excused herself. "There's more coffee in the kitchen if you want. I promise I won't be long."

"Take your time," Kendrick told her.

She turned into a hallway, and a few steps farther he heard a door click shut. He followed after her—luckily the hallway was carpeted—and, cupping an ear to the door, heard her well enough. She spoke in a bossy, whispery tone, nothing like her earlier manner. "No, you can't." Pause. "He's still here." Pause. "Who knows?" Pause. "Just let me see where it leads." Pause. "I'll call you when he leaves . . . I mean, *if* he leaves. But don't you dare come up until you hear from me again." Pause. "Hush, I'll be fine."

Kendrick tiptoed back to the sofa. About five minutes later, Babette returned.

Kendrick's eyes widened. "It appears you've changed into something more comfortable," he said.

It was tasteful—somewhere between a dress and a slip, eggplant colored with turquoise trim to frame her cleavage, making it more 3D. She offered a generous view, and as he gazed at them, he could not help trying to ascertain, true or false? Easy—there was not a squiggle of natural to them. And yet, while in his mind, he was critical and disapproving, concurrently the room seemed to be warming up. His mind raced through a flurry of axioms, not always word-by-word quotations:

Judge not, lest ye be judged.
Walk a mile in my shoes.
Let he without sin cast the first stone.
Empathy engenders wisdom. And vice versa.
Search not the splinter in someone else's eye when there is a giant Sequoia in your own.
Point your finger at someone, three of them are pointing back at you.
You're right from your side, I'm right from mine.

He had enjoyed their verbal jousting, and physically he began to see what attracted Poupon to her. He began to question himself. If he lived long enough, Mother Nature would probably offer him a choice: Viagra or bust? He had to admit, faced with such adversity, he would stand tall, even if it meant chemical intervention. And that liver spot on his forehead—he'd given his assent at the dermatologist's when she offered to burn it off with her liquid nitrogen. *So*, Kendrick thought, *you are a hypocritical, sexist pig. You have no right to judge a woman because she tries to remain youthful looking.* Still, all that self-reflection did nothing to change his opinion of Babette d'Orsini. There was something crooked about her, something that raised SOS signals.

Babette asked how Poupon was doing.

"Fine," he answered. "He's still the Poupon we know and love."

"Good to hear." She leaned closer, and he was struck by her confidence that she could reel him in. "Tell me the truth. Do you get the impression he is hopelessly in love with me?"

"If you think Poupon confides in me," Kendrick said, "you're mistaken. We talk about wine, and that's about it. You've seen us together."

"Oh, I haven't seen the two of you together at length, but I know enough about men to know that their conversation is very different when no women are present."

"Wine, wine, and more wine. Sorry, but that's me and Poupon. The extent of our discourse."

"I've grown very fond of him. But I'm at a point where a little encouragement in terms of his intentions is quite important to me. My future plans, you know?" Her hand glided to Kendrick's nearest knee. She tightened her grip to demonstrate how emotional she was about Poupon, and, just possibly, he thought, to excite him into some kind of reaction. "I can make a man very happy. I'd like you to understand that. And you're Poupon's best friend. You must want to see him satisfied, happy, aglow. You and I really should be in cahoots together, you know? To please the guy."

Kendrick felt enveloped by the humid warmth of her voice. "Yeah, but how exactly do you intend to 'be in cahoots'?" he asked.

"I need to learn about wine. I might very well be the wife of a vigneron someday. And on the subject of wine, you know everything I need to know. You teach, I learn, and after each lesson I make it worth your while, as you Americans say."

She leaned closer until he felt her lips pressed against his. For a moment, Kendrick closed his eyes. His mind reeled with the speed of her attempted seduction. What was he doing? He cursed and pushed straight up out of her clutches, unable to keep a look of disgust from his face.

Babette was momentarily astonished before her own eyes turned furious, then ferocious. She snarled like a wounded dog and raised her hands ready to claw his eyes, but he shoved her back onto the sofa as he fled, racing for the front door while she shouted most unduchess-like slander at his scrambling retreat.

Wow, he thought as the elevator delivered him to the ground floor, *did I ever touch a nerve.* Was it a reaction to being scorned, or the realization that Kendrick was her opponent when it came to her plans for Poupon? Both, he decided as he hurried to the parking lot in case Babette or her sidekick decided to give chase. Wheezing slightly from the run, he found his car, put it in gear, and zoomed off as fast as his un-Mighty Modus could go.

On the autoroute back home, Kendrick wondered if all he had witnessed could mean anything other than the fact that Babette was conniving to add another divorce settlement to her collection, namely Poupon's Domaine du Vieux Laurier. He suspected that it was Branislav's voice on the phone that Poupon had mentioned hearing when he rang Babette's apartment a couple months earlier. Was the guy her friend, brother, lover, accomplice? And of course, how to tell Poupon? And even whether to tell him anything at all, because it could all blow up in Kendrick's face and lose him a pal. He looked forward to his two-hour drive—the road was almost empty—and to ordering his thoughts.

CHAPTER TWENTY-THREE

The next morning, Poupon telephoned while Kendrick sipped his morning coffee. "Kendrick, bonjour. How do you like this wind? It's so strong it could blow the horns off old man Litchov."

"Glad you called, Poupon. But who's this Litchov?"

"He was from here, from l'Estournel. Everyone knew Achille Litchov because he ran the city water supply. In his mid-sixties, he up and married for the first time—a twenty-nine-year-old sex bomb. When she walked by, I swear, all us young bucks would moan like a bunch of hyenas. The cool thing was, she'd jump in the hay with just about anyone."

"Even you? My god."

"I granted her the favor a few times, yes, out of the goodness of my heart. But don't get me wrong. We respected her. It was fun to do it with a woman who enjoyed sex as much as we did. She had no complex about it at all. Birds and the bees. Right as rain. Pour it on. Right?"

"Great. Very happy for you both, but no pornographic details before my second cup of coffee, please. Just try to explain what all this has to do with Litchov and the mistral."

"Kendrick, don't they teach you anything in your schools in the USA? Litchov was a cuckold, as I just explained. Everybody was buzzing around his wife's honeycomb. And a cuckold grows horns. Don't ask me why, but here in France, everybody knows—a cuckold grows horns."

"Really? I'll bet you anything Litchov did not have horns sticking out of his head."

"Stop trying to be funny. It never works. Look, if you're not from Provence, not from right around here, you might not say it like that. You could also say that the mistral was so strong it blew the tires off your car or the tail off your mule. But here, because Litchov's wife was so unfaithful, he had such a solid set of horns that it would take an unusually massive mistral to blow them off."

"Well, it was literally screaming here at Milles Vents last night. Scared the hell out of me."

"Hey, why don't you come on over, have a glass? The stone wall by the fountain will shield us."

"I can't right now. I'm finishing an article explaining what a Saint-Véran is, and I have to send it off tonight."

"So, in two words, what is a Saint-Véran?"

"A Chardonnay from southern Burgundy."

"Hey, Kendrick, see if you can smell this all the way over at your place." And there followed over the phone the blast of a rather mighty fart, followed by laughter. "You won't believe this, Kendrick, but I did that with my voice and not my rear end."

"Who wouldn't be impressed by that?"

"You know," Poupon said, "that time you made the sound of a Champagne cork popping? You used your tongue, snapping it off the roof of your mouth. And I couldn't do it no matter how many times I tried. Only a feeble *click-tock*. But I'd like to hear you make a farting sound like I just did."

"Let's maintain our differences. Opposites attract, we say in English. You be the guy who sounds like a fart, and I'm the Champagne guy."

"All I know is, when you make that *tock* sound with your tongue, it's so real I expect you to hand me a glass of Champagne."

"I do need to talk to you soon, though," Kendrick said. "Are you free any time this week?"

"Take your pick: Wednesday lunch or Thursday dinner."

"Let's make it dinner. The wind should have shut down by then, and we can eat outside next to your fishpond now that the sun is setting so late."

"I've been wanting to make my favorite chicken dish for you, and it is so loaded with garlic, your schnoz will never stop thanking me."

Kendrick had guessed at the start what Poupon meant by "blow the horns off old man Litchov." He acted clueless just to see what would come out of Poupon's mouth next. Interacting with Poupon, he felt a direct connection with the Provence of prior centuries.

CHAPTER TWENTY-FOUR

Overhead, Thursday turned out to be a triumphant day. The mistral had performed one of its two positive roles: it had blown away every imperfection the sky might have contained, leaving a heroic, intense blue azure above and off into the distance. The other positive effect was reserved for wine lovers. During harvest, if there is rain, a mistral is likely to roar to life and blow-dry the grapes, to the great joy of the wine world. Wet grapes in hot sunshine? A recipe for disaster. Rot begins to multiply quickly on the grape skins, and rotten grapes make rotten wine. With certain exceptions—Château d'Yquem and the Sauterness, for example.

When Kendrick drove up, Poupon strolled out of his kitchen with a spatula in one hand. Zarina followed him out, bearing little resemblance to her usually cheerful self. She gave Kendrick a peck on each cheek, said she had to pick up her daughter at her sister's, and *boom*, she was gone. Kendrick thought she looked ready to burst into tears.

Poupon took a seat on the edge of his fishpond and peeked up guiltily at Kendrick, then put on his bravado. "*Merde*, these women! How can you know how they want us to act?"

"Who's 'us'?" Kendrick asked. He was on the verge of getting pissed off because he sensed that Zarina had been hurt by something Poupon had said or done.

"Us. Us men. You know what I'm saying?" He chuckled, trying to nudge Kendrick into a jocular mood.

"What just happened between you two?"

"Oh, nothing. Just Zarina being Zarina. Too sensitive. You know how she is."

"Just fill me in on exactly what you said to hurt her feelings."

"Hurt Zarina? Are you crazy? She's just in one of her moods."

"Can't you quit dancing around the question and tell me what happened?"

They were still outside the kitchen door. It was not a great start to the evening.

"I won't say another word about it without a glass of rosé in my hands," Poupon said. He left quickly, then came back outdoors with a bottle and two wine glasses. He motioned Kendrick to follow him to the table and sat down. "I swear, this new bottling just gets better and better." He poured each of them a glass. "Doesn't that smell good? It's fresh, isn't it?"

"To me," Kendrick said, "it smells like the men's room at the *Gare de Toulon*." He stared coldly into Poupon's sheepish eyes. "And I'm sick of discussing your lousy rosé."

"But this year, people really like it. It's a wine that pleases. I'm almost sold out already."

"Great. If that's all you care about, I'm sure you're proud as can be."

"Zarina loves it."

"Oh yes, she's the perfect judge, right? And if your mother were still alive, I'll bet she'd love it, too. Zarina loves it? What absolute bullshit." Kendrick pronounced it bull*sheet* because Poupon somehow understood that.

Poupon stared off into space while Kendrick took a slug of rosé and loudly spit it out onto the ground. He threw what was left in his glass after it. "At least offer me some real wine. Hell is to be stuck on a desert island with nothing but this crap to drink."

"I'm not drinking it, either," Poupon declared. "I hate rosé." He started trudging off toward the house and his wine cellar again. "But I'll be damned if I'm going to open a bottle of my own red tonight. The mood you're in, you won't like my red, either."

He came back with a decanter of a well-colored mystery red.

"Last chance," Kendrick said. "What happened between you and Zarina?"

"Wait!" Poupon stopped pouring the wine into Kendrick's glass and raised his hand. "Try to concentrate on the taste of this red. Maybe it's corked. Who knows?"

Kendrick sniffed, trying to dislike it, but his nose was magnetically attracted deeper into the glass. On the outside, he still wore a frown, but on the inside, his willpower was failing him. It did not smell like Bandol. After a few moments and a long, slow swallow, he smacked his lips as he concentrated on the aftertaste. He looked over at Poupon.

"Châteauneuf-du-Pape?" he asked.

"Yes!"

"1985 or 1989?"

"Maybe."

"The perfume shows a lot of elegance for a Châteauneuf-du-Pape."

"You want to know who made it or keep guessing?"

Kendrick stood up and grimaced as if he were stuck in a tight situation. "Oh what the hell, if it's not from Clos des Papes, I give up."

"You got it!" Poupon was excited mainly because his pal was finally getting distracted.

Both took a sip and sucked air over it into their mouths to release the wine's perfume. The two swallowed almost in tandem.

"There's good presence to it," Kendrick said. "I love the way it sinks into the palate. The tannin, you know? It has more grip to it than most 1989s, so, without a lot of confidence, I'll guess it's the 1985."

"Hey, super, Kendrick," Poupon said. "Hold on a minute." He ran to the kitchen and came back with the bottle. He held it up, and on the vintage strip, Kendrick read the date, 1989.

"Don't feel bad," Poupon said. "I never would have known it was a Châteauneuf-du-Pape. It is red, that's all I would have known for sure. I bought it from Eric, the sommelier up at the Circuit du Castellet," Poupon said. "We traded. One magnum of 2001 Vieux Laurier for a bottle of the well-aged 1989 Clos de Papes."

"You got a sweet deal," Kendrick said.

They sat mesmerized by the old classic, swirling, sniffing, sipping, oohing, aahing—no more spitting for them!

"You know, Poupon, wine? Sometimes it can be more than wine."

"What's that, a riddle or something? What do you mean?"

"That it can take you beyond what you'd always believed the limits of wine could be. That some wines have depths to be explored. Like people, they each have their own personality."

"Do you remember the greatest red wine you ever tasted?"

"My god, what a question. Do you?"

"Not really," Poupon said. "I haven't had much experience outside the Bandol appellation."

"It's strange, because number one is very clear to me, but there are around a hundred different wines tied for second place."

"So, tell me," Poupon said, "what was the best? And don't tell me it was my 1993, because I won't believe you."

"It was a 1961 Romanée Conti from the Domaine de la Romanée Conti."

"And it was really that good?" Poupon asked. "Why that one? What was so good about it?"

"Poupon, have you ever heard Bach's second cello suite?"

"Hmm, sounds familiar. But no. However, I do know how to sing 'La Marseillaise,' 'Jingle Bells,' and 'Joyeuse Anniversaire.'"

Kendrick realized that wine had played one of its roles and calmed tensions between the two men. He forgot about telling his story about Bach and Romanée Conti. A few minutes later, without being asked again, Poupon finally offered that Zarina had asked him if he was in love with her. "Now," he wondered, "why would she ask something like that?"

"Maybe in order to know if there's any possibility of a future with you," Kendrick answered. "Have you ever told her you love her?"

"Are you kidding? Listen, my older brother has a lot of success with women. He could charge them admission. And he tells me to keep them guessing. See? You don't want them to know how much you care, or they'll lose interest in you."

Kendrick thought that one over. He sniffed the 1989 again and continued. "Maybe. Maybe that could be true if you're talking about a woman you're just playing around with. But if there's love, it would be more loving of you to let her know. So, do you love her or not?"

"Zarina? I guess you could say that. But then, Babette, you know? That's a woman with class. I imagine her here when I'm receiving important people for dinner, and she's the hostess. It would change everything. By the way, she still calls me all the time. *Ooh la la.* Don't pretend I don't understand the opposite sex."

"So, you're telling me you love both of them?"

"Oh, all of that is such, I don't know, such movie stuff. Okay, love them in different ways or for different reasons. *Merde.* This is scrambling up my brain. I guess I do something that does resemble loving them both." Poupon poured another glass of Clos des Papes for both of them.

"And did you tell Zarina that you love her when she asked?"

"Like I said, keep 'em guessing. So, I said 'No,' and she said 'Are you sure?' and I told her she was getting too personal. You should have seen the look on her face."

Kendrick felt like he was watching a Chinese movie without subtitles.

Poupon laughed. "You wait and see. She'll be back. I have something she won't want to go without."

Kendrick said he'd never seen Zarina so wounded and angry. "I'm not so sure she'll come back for more of the same. And as for your Babette, we need to talk about that."

"Glad to, but I can smell dinner from here, and it smells ready. And even if it's not ready, I am."

The feast opened with chard ribs sauced with an *anchoïade.* Kendrick said, "Seems like everybody I know throws away the ribs. They cook the leafy part as if it's the meat, and the ribs are bones to discard."

"Here in Provence," Poupon said, "we don't waste. Up to recently, Provence was a dirt-poor region. We figured out how to make use of the ribs. If they're delicious, no one's going to throw them away."

"Like *ris de veau,* or sea urchins, or especially *vioulets.*" Kendrick remembered the first time he had tried the shocking little neon yellow sea creature, a local delicacy forced out of its very hard shell and always eaten raw despite its potent iodine taste and downright rubbery texture.

"You don't cook them. Never. You eat them raw or not at all," Poupon said.

"Right, I know, but just the fact that a human being one fine day figured out that inside that rocklike shell there was something edible hidden away—they're not easy to open, even with modern knives."

"Strange," Poupon said, "I have never thought about the first time a human being ate a *violet*. And their taste is so unusual, after the first one, I'm amazed they went to the trouble of opening a second one."

"And pig ears," Kendrick continued. "I never see them in the States, but over here, don't you have a variety of pig ear preparations?"

"The best is the way my father cooked them. My mother didn't like the cartilage, you know, so when she was sick or away, my father cooked pig ears for the rest of us."

They were eating outdoors at the big table. Just Poupon and Kendrick. Chard ribs *à la* Poupon. The sky in the west was a regal pink just beginning to take on some flaming red at the horizon. Kendrick was occupied by the chard, the old Châteauneuf in his glass, the idea of pigs' ears, and trying out ways to bring up Babette and Branislav. Instead, he asked him how his father cooked up the pig ears.

"It's so simple. You put the ears in a pot with carrots, onions, parsley, and thyme. Simmer them about four hours or so, cut them into strips, toss them in beaten eggs, coat them with breadcrumbs, then fry them crisp. I like them better than french fries."

"No sauce?"

"Oh, salt and pepper is all you need, but some people like lemon juice. Some like mayonnaise. My brother likes them with ketchup. My father drank beer with them, but I serve rosé—that is, unless I'm with someone who has a super delicate palate."

"Let's make a deal. You cook the ears," Kendrick said, "and I'll supply the rosé. You know, this sauce on the chard tastes a lot like the *anchoïade* I had on the beach the other day near La Londe."

"Not Chez Robert? Pecheurs du Golfe?"

"That's the place."

Poupon seemed to drop into reverie for a moment. "I've known him forever. He's the only one left around here who still serves a true *friture* from the Mediterranean. *Putain!* Everyone else uses frozen fish from up around Norway. Or his grilled sardines served without silverware. You eat them off the bones with your hands. We call them *brûle-moustache* or *brûle-doights* depending on whether you have a mustache or not. Robert taught me that an *anchoïade* has to have winter savory or it's a waste of time. Up in the hills above Signe—where I usually go to hunt—winter savory grows wild all around there."

"Bring me some next time, will you? An entire plant, roots and all. I'd like to see if I can transplant it at Milles Vents."

"Of course," Poupon replied, "but why be foolish?"

"What's foolish about that?" Kendrick asked.

"Ha, and you're supposed to be the great terroir preacher. At your place, the *sarriete* won't have the same altitude, sunshine, or soil, so of course it won't taste the same."

"And who made you the expert? I'll plant some and see."

"If it was meant to grow at Milles Vents, it would already grow there. Look at all the thyme and rosemary you've got. You didn't need to plant those, did you?"

Kendrick started to respond with an edge, but instead he smiled and said, "Chef Poupon, the earthy flavor of boiled chard ribs is exquisite with your *anchoïade*. And someday maybe you'll take me up to where the good *sarriete* grows. Hell, it's not that far. Instead of transplanting it, I'll go collect some once in a while."

"I'll drink to that, and then I'll bring out the bird."

Kendrick downed the last gulp of Châteauneuf and pondered the Babette dilemma. He couldn't stop wondering if he shouldn't sic a detective on her trail and get more proof of her fishy conduct. Poupon should realize that the woman he might someday wed is living with another man. But how do you tell a pal something like that?

Poupon returned carrying a heavy cast iron pot, then opened the lid on a well-browned roast chicken. There were thirty or forty whole cloves of garlic floating in the sauce. Poupon left again and returned with a bottle of 1975 Bandol from Domaine Tempier. As he pulled out the cork, he said it was one of several bottles given to his father by Lucien Peyraud, probably in return for some kind of favor.

The roast chicken with carrots and potatoes was followed by a soft, ripe, grassy Saint-Nectaire. Once they were both satiated, Kendrick accepted a smoke, and Poupon himself solved Kendrick's dilemma of how to bring the subject back around to Babette. He asked, "And what's this you have to tell me about Babette? I hope you haven't fallen under her spell, too."

"No, but I can tell she's after my body," he said, imitating Poupon. He wanted to toss a little hilarity into the conversation, but Poupon didn't hear it that way.

"Ho, hey, wha . . ." he mumbled until Kendrick started laughing and told him he'd been kidding.

"Well," Poupon said, "congratulations—you manage to be funny and not at all funny all at the same time."

"Calm down. I was just being you."

"You couldn't be me without undergoing a penis transplant," Poupon said and fell out of his chair laughing. Kendrick couldn't help roaring with laughter, too, above all at the sight of Poupon on the ground.

When Poupon was back in his seat, Kendrick said, "I'll never forget this evening, the time I drank mighty Poupon literally under the table. Okay, now listen. Here's what happened. I had business in Nice recently and was having dinner in the Place Garibaldi—you know, with the arcades."

"Sure, I've been there. That's where Babette lives. She's invited me up to her apartment a couple times, and I don't care whether it's more than you want to know or not—I did rise . . ."

"Aw, shut up about it. Isn't there a school around here that could teach you some class? Anyway, so Babette lives there? I see. Well, a car pulled up and parked nearby, and she got out on the passenger side, and some guy, pretty solid, a young-looking guy, got out on the driver's side. They walked into one of the arcades, and I didn't see them again. When I finished dinner, the car was still there. I went to a movie and hit a couple of night clubs. When I got back to the square, the car was still there, and it was quite late. I thought about you and figured you'd be curious, so I rented a hotel room right down the street. Sorry to say, but the next morning the car was still there."

"*Merde! Putain de merde!*" Poupon leapt up from his chair and started pacing around the table, sat down again, lit up another smoke, and exhaled a mighty cloud. "Well of course! What do you expect? Woman like her . . . Doesn't have to sleep alone . . . She loves me,

Kendrick, I'm sure of it. This is what I get for letting her dangle out there in front of every guy in the universe. I'm a dope! Stupid! Too stupid! *Putain.* I don't deserve her, you know? I'm just a dumb farmer. What do you expect? We have an old saying, 'When the cat's away, the mice will dance.'"

That was not the reaction Kendrick had expected. He asked himself why he hadn't simply told the truth about his trip to Nice. It wasn't at all like him to make up lies. But he felt like he was walking through a minefield and he risked losing one of his best friends.

They moved on to a dessert wine, and Poupon continued to berate himself. When Kendrick asked what he would do about Zarina if he ended up married to Babette, Poupon broke into a smile. He giggled coyly, his eyes blurred from all the wine. "Remember the saying? You know, cat and mouse? You better believe, Henri Poupon can dance as well as any mouse in town."

As Kendrick was climbing into his Modus, he remembered the other subject he'd meant to discuss with Poupon.

"In the next couple of weeks, is there a day or two when you'd want to fly with me to Bastia? I've got something to discuss with Baltazaru."

"Fly? What the hell, can't you discuss it with him by phone?"

"Rather not."

"How many days did you say?"

"Oh, just one night, I imagine."

"Go ahead, choose the date yourself. I'm free. It's always a treat to see Baltazaru."

CHAPTER TWENTY-FIVE

The next morning Kendrick brewed coffee and toasted a slice of *levain*, which he gave a light scrape with a clove of raw garlic, dribbled olive oil on it, and topped with a layer of lavender honey. Then he phoned Baltazaru and told him he wanted to fly down to see him about something again but was already scheduled to go to Burgundy for a few days of tastings.

"I can be free whenever," the Corsican said. "I have nothing to do here but avoid the tourists."

Kendrick arrived in Burgundy on a hot gray day and began his tasting at a wine domaine in the outskirts of Meursault. The winemaker kept glancing at the huge, charcoal cloud in the sky above. "It could mean hail," he said, "and hail combined with this heat is the devil's recipe for the worst thing weather can do to a grapevine. The hail tatters the vines—the branches, the leaves, the fruit. If any grapes are left, the hail will have torn open the grape skin. Rot makes itself at home and thrives, the juice dripping from open wounds, the sun beating down—it's a bacchanal, an orgy for botrytis. You can see the rot growing like black fuzz on the grapes."

"A day or two before the 1983 harvest," Kendrick said, "I was a young man visiting Nuits-Saint-Georges when a memorable hailstorm attacked the vineyards. There was a thick black cloud very low to the ground. I pulled over to the side of the road because I couldn't see to drive. Suddenly, there was a ferocious clatter. Like a bombardment.

My rental car had craters all over it, and the landscape was like the middle of winter—not a leaf left on the branches."

"So, you remember the 1983s here in Côte d'Or?"

"An unforgettable vintage, for sure," Kendrick answered. The two of them agreed that what reds were made in 1983 turned out to be pretty tough—hard wines with a grainy, dry tannin—but that some spectacular whites were produced. "Opulent white Burgundies," Kendrick said, "with an unusual perfume—Chardonnay with noble rot."

"If you're going to have rot, noble is the best kind," the winemaker said with a smile, "because the rot in Burgundy is usually far from noble compared to the Sauternes region, the Loire, or Alsace." Changing the subject, he mentioned the Domaine Gardon-Lepré in nearby Saint-Aubin. He said that the current winemaker, Alain Lepré, would love it if Kendrick paid him a visit, and indeed, Kendrick was up for it, because early in his career he'd imported three or four vintages of Saint-Aubin whites from Auguste Lepré, Alain's grandfather. Kendrick gave them a call and learned that the only time he and Lepré were both free was that very evening at six thirty, after his other scheduled tastings. Kendrick had always been impressed by the white Burgundies from Saint-Aubin, the only problem being that the village lacked a winemaker who could realize the potential there. To him, that specific terroir was capable of producing Chardonnays that offered a lot of charm, and charm occupied an important place in his esthetic universe.

After Alain's grandfather Auguste retired, his son, Adam, took over, and the quality changed—not for the better—so Kendrick stopped importing their wines. Hopefully, the current generation was again making remarkable wines.

A long, narrow village almost never visited by tourists, Saint-Aubin is right up there in back of the Puligny-Montrachet and Chassagne-Montrachet vineyards. Domaine Gardon-Lepré's gate was open, and as Kendrick slid out from the driver's seat, a German shepherd raced up and stopped about two feet from him. Kendrick froze, his heart pounding as if it wanted to scream and be heard. The dog snarled wickedly, ready to pounce, before being interrupted by a man's voice speaking heavily accented English.

"Pardon me, monsieur. Sit! Sit! My wife forgot to put her dog away. Sit, Thatcher! Sit!"

Thatcher sat down, slobbering and grumbling. Meanwhile, Kendrick told himself to calm down. In his career, he'd so far been twice bitten, once by a Doberman, once by a German shepherd, and his view of people who don't control their dogs was not filled with love and forgiveness. Anyway, bad start. Alain Lepré, however, turned out to be an unusually sweet guy, who somehow ended up married to an Austrian woman who could not keep her dog on a chain, even when the gates to the winery were wide open.

On the upside of forty, a rounded fellow with a scrubbed look, clean-shaven face and scalp, clean clothes—and who knew, maybe also a clean mind—to Kendrick he appeared to be a totally harmless wine man. In fact, he radiated innocence. Whatever might happen, it wasn't really going to be Alain's fault.

Alain led the way into his winery, which was in a large rectangular cement building constructed with thrift in mind. It sat above ground—at least, that is, the winemaking part. As Kendrick learned later, there was a bottle-aging cellar underground. The winery installation was filled with gleaming stainless steel tanks, all with refrigeration units, all computer controlled. Kendrick looked at his reflection on one of the silvery tanks. He was stretched ten feet tall and very thin in the middle, yet the hair on his head bloomed out about ten times larger than in real life.

They tasted several—what were, for Kendrick—fairly pathetic white Burgundies, while Alain discussed the different Saint-Aubin terroirs, and how, geologically, the various soils had been created. Plates and volcanos and limestone formations—Alain was knowledgeable, passionate, and entertaining. "Why is one *premier cru* vineyard's wine leaner and another's fleshy—a difference that remains true from vintage to vintage? That," he answered himself, "can only be explained geologically." Then Alain disclosed that he now blended all the domaine's terroirs into one bottling labeled Saint-Aubin *premier cru*.

So, this passion for terroir on one hand and the generic bottling on the other—Kendrick considered all that intriguing and bizarre. "I remember your grandfather's bottling of Les Murgers des Dents du Chien. That seemed to be his pride and joy," Kendrick said.

"Not only my grandfather. Any vigneron in Burgundy would love to own a few rows of Dents du Chien. If the yields were proper, I think I could come up with a pretty good wine there, too."

"Why don't you?"

"Way back when, there was a marriage in the family, and the father-in-law invested in our domaine. Those were difficult days in Burgundy. Saint-Aubin had a hard time attracting buyers. Later, we took on the Gardon family and their vineyards as partners, too. Anyway, when my father took over, they all voted, and the decision was made to change the direction of the domaine. There were years and years of cutting costs, increasing quantity, lowering prices—a list of decisions, you see? And the result was and still is a successful winery in terms of profitability, facility, and stability, but not much personal satisfaction, at least not in my case."

"How very sad," Kendrick said.

"Sometimes I think of selling my shares, packing up, and moving to the Languedoc—buy a few hectares, you know, make my own wine."

"Why move?" Kendrick asked. "You were born here. Your blood is Burgundian. Why not turn back the clock? Make wines according to your own esthetic. I'll be first in line for an allocation."

"You didn't understand. I'm only one of six voting shareholders. I'm hired and paid to make the wines, and they are all quite happy to keep things the way they are—decent profit, good distribution, low prices that protect us from difficult times. No worries. Don't kick the ant hill, as we say."

"Yes, don't rock the boat."

At that point there was a knock on the open cellar door. "I hope you don't mind," Alain said to Kendrick, "I permitted myself to invite a couple friends, both vignerons, and neither of them has ever seen an American importer, not to mention one named to the Forum Bacchus de France.

"How'd you know about that?" Kendrick asked, surprised.

"I've followed your career. Aren't you the only foreigner to win the award? My grandfather spoke of you. He was very upset when you suddenly stopped buying our wines after my father took over. Anyway, let me introduce Pierre Gaillard from Pernand-Vergelesses and Jean-Christophe Planchet from Santenay."

They were a couple of old-timers. Relics of another era. Even their clothes looked antique. Hands were shaken all around. Pierre was a heavyset fellow who still had all his hair. Impeccably trimmed, it was a handsome head of hair. His mustache was salt and pepper—a big old Burgundian bristle that, if he chose to, could be used to clean his boots or scrub a burnt skillet. He handed Alain a folded blue-and-white-checkered cloth napkin that turned out to contain little puff biscuits.

Alain spoke up. "Ah, Pierre, thank your wife. She makes the best *gougères* in Burgundy."

Jean-Christophe was taller and thinner with an austere, skin-pulled-tight face. Something about his appearance prompted Kendrick to check to see if he wore a priest's collar, but no. From his coat pocket, Jean-Christophe pulled out a *saucisson* and handed it to Alain. A quick look told Kendrick it was homemade and promising.

The four of them went down a stone staircase into the bottle cellar. Alain began pulling wines from mold-covered bins. "I checked my grandfather's archives for your orders. You were a buyer here for four vintages." He uncorked four bottles and from one poured a generous taste into each of the waiting glasses. He looked at Kendrick. "See if you can remember which is which."

Kendrick swirled the wine around in the glass, and before sticking his nose in to take a sniff, he said, "Well, there is no mistaking that color. It's a giveaway. Deep gold with green tints." The other three took to swirling and sniffing. Then each took a taste and slurped and sucked in air and smacked their lips after swallowing.

"Has to be 1983," Kendrick said. "There's only one 1983—no other vintage had such a deep, beautiful, golden color."

"1971s had good color," Jean-Christophe said, "but not nearly as golden as 1983."

"Another year with hail," Pierre said.

"He's right," Alain announced, "this is the 1983 Murgers des Dents du Chien."

"Only a schmuck would spit out this one," Pierre said.

They tasted through the other bottles, discussing them and the vintage character of each while they snacked on sliced *saucisson* and *gougères*. The last of the four bottles lit them all up—a 1979. Jean-Christophe said it was one hell of a vintage. "Beaugravières 1979 is one of the best reds in my cellar in Santenay. Everyone in the world wanted to talk about 1978, but 1979 was better for whites. They tasted great right out of the barrel, in their youth. And look how well they've aged. What more can you ask?"

"The 1978 white Burgundies never really came around, did they?" Kendrick asked.

"They were always a little bit squarish and unyielding," Pierre said. "Like my first wife. I'd go to kiss her, but her lips were hard. Very unsettling. They had no give to them. It was like kissing the lips of a statue."

"The 1979 is a perfection," Jean-Christophe said, "but that 1983, I wouldn't kick her out of bed."

"Voluptuous. Ample. Fleshy," Pierre said. "Way too much woman for a skinny fart like you. You'd be better off with the 1980, which is too old and tired to resist your shrinking charms."

Alain repoured the 1979. "If you ask me, this is one of the best vintages my grandfather ever made."

Jean-Christophe said, "Everyone insists we have to reduce yields, reduce yields, but 1979 was an abundant year. So was 1982. Great whites and fat bank accounts."

"All four are from the vineyard Dents du Chien. Do you know where that is on the hill?" Alain asked Kendrick, and he went on without waiting for an answer. His cheeks had reddened, probably from the wine. No one was spitting. "It is just barely a St. Aubin, barely over the cusp of the hill from white Burgundy's grandest *cru*, Le Montrachet. Well, Dents du Chien's vines go up the hill on the Saint-Aubin side, and Le Montrachet's vines down the hill on the Puligny side."

"Ah." Pierre nodded. "You're saying that proximity counts."

"You know as well as I do. Aren't I right? And Dents du Chien, a lovely Saint-Aubin—right?—practically touches Le Montrachet, the grandest of the *grand cru* whites."

"I agree with you that the two are close to each other," Pierre said, "but have you forgotten the old saying? A woman's pussy almost touches her you-know-what, but the perfume is not at all the same."

Jean-Christophe burst into laughter, almost choking on the mouthful of wine he'd been swallowing. "And, Alain," he finally said, "the price of a bottle of Les Murgers des Dents du Chien is a long, long way from the price of a bottle of Le Montrachet. Several kilometers away. That might tell us more about how the two wines compare than their geographic location."

"You're not laughing," Pierre said to Alain, then he turned to Kendrick and Jean-Christophe. "Maybe he understands terroir better than he does a woman's anatomy."

Alain seemed to try to laugh, but it came out slightly strangled. Kendrick got his breath back and said, "Pierre, I hope someday you'll write a book about terroir. We need one from your point of view, although the wine authorities would probably censor it."

"We French are now becoming more like you Americans," Pierre said. "Can you believe it? It is now illegal to show a sexy woman in advertising if she is holding a glass of wine. If there is alcohol involved, you cannot use sex to get people's attention. But listen to this—you can show a topless man, nipples and all, drinking wine or even vodka. But not even a half-dressed woman would be permitted. And that's called equality? *Vive la France!*"

Alain announced that he had one more wine to taste to celebrate Kendrick's visit. He brought out a green-colored bottle almost covered with mold. He pulled a handkerchief out of his back pocket and brushed the mold off the top of the bottle before twisting in his corkscrew. The wine poured pale ochre into the four glasses. "It's from my grandfather's first vintage, 1947."

"What's that?" Pierre asked. "*Merde*, I've never seen a 1947 with a robe like that."

All four found the color odd. What the hell could it be? A white that had taken a bad turn? A red that had dropped all its color? When they sniffed it, wow, excitement in sleepy Saint-Aubin. What a nose! The bouquet showed that the wine still had plenty of life to it, at more than half a century old. They were taking turns finding compliments, but no one could guess what it was.

Finally, Alain explained. "My grandfather always made one barrel of rosé. He didn't sell any of it. It was just for the family, and the 1947 was so good, he hid away a few bottles. So this is a rosé made from Pinot Noir."

Pierre said, "No one is going to believe us when we say we had a 1947 Saint-Aubin rosé and it was still alive and kicking. This is no pretty little piece of fluff that you forget as soon as you've had a taste. This is like a guy, an old guy, sure, but a guy who's still got something in his pants."

"True," Kendrick said. "I'm sure you mean its structure and depth."

Indeed, it had aged so well, they stood eating and drinking until the bottle was empty.

Kendrick finally shook their hands, said his goodbyes, and then drove straight to his hotel in Beaune, where he went to bed without officially eating dinner. The snack had been enough. He wasn't hungry, and he didn't want anything to interfere with the beautiful flavors still hanging around on his palate.

CHAPTER TWENTY-SIX

Without a single gust of mistral, Kendrick's landing in Bastia was many times less harrowing than it had been at the box canyon airport outside Calvi. Poupon had finally decided to skip the trip—four hundred baby olive trees had arrived and needed to go into the ground—which, after all, pleased Kendrick, because it would be better to have Baltazaru all to himself given the nature of the conversation he envisioned.

And there stood the Corsican vintner, waiting as cool as a five a.m. cucumber when Kendrick walked out the glass doors of the airport terminal. They gave each other a little French hug and pretend smack on each cheek before climbing into Baltazaru's white camionette. "We're going to lunch here in Bastia," he said. "I know a place. They'll put us in a side room with a view of the sea where we can talk alone, like you wanted."

According to Kendrick, you can't make good wine without a good palate, so you can trust talented winemakers to know where the local dining gems are hidden, places tourists would never think of entering. In Corsica, it might be best they don't, because they might not be totally welcome. Baltazaru took an exit off the highway and turned toward the sea. In a grove of trees at the edge of a sandy beach, he pulled into the dirt parking lot of a thatched-roof little joint called Sans Chemise. The owner met them at the open bar.

"Kendrick, this is Antoine, but we all call him Toin-Toin for some reason."

"Yeah, my father was named Antoine, too, so my mother started calling me Toin. That way, the right Antoine would know which one she was talking to. Then, I don't know why, at school my classmates turned it into Toin-Toin." He seated them, handed both a one-page wine list, and said, "In case you're thirsty."

"Of course we're thirsty. Whenever we get together, it seems to make us thirsty, right, Kendrick? This is Kendrick Thomas, my American importer."

"Oh, so that's why you never have any wine for your old friends. Ah, who cares? Who can afford it anymore except for rich Americans?"

"Hey, shut your skinny little ass. You get more of my wine than you deserve. Let's put it that way. And why do I sell you more? Because I feel sorry for you." He and Kendrick studied the short *carte de vin*. "What's this?" Baltazaru asked. "You've got Abbatucci's rosé? Isn't that kinda ritzy for Sans Chemise?"

"Not all my customers are as cheap as you are, you old whore. Some of them even show a little class," Toin-Toin said.

"Class? I'll bet the bums who eat here never spent a day of their life in class. Now, get us our rosé—in an ice bucket—and leave us alone. *Merde!* A couple of guys just want some wine and have to put up with all this bullshit."

Toin-Toin looked down at Baltazaru and broke into a victorious smile.

"How are you going to eat if I don't return to take your order?"

"I wouldn't eat here even if my beloved wife begged me to bring her here. We just want some wine. We intend going back to the highway to eat at McDonald's. At least the food is consistent there."

Toin-Toin left and returned with two glasses and the rosé in an ice bucket. Out came the cork and out poured a glass for each of them. "I'll be right back with the menu," he said. "We'll see if there's anything to tempt you two to stick around for lunch."

Kendrick clinked glasses with Baltazaru. "*Santé,*" he said.

"*Salut,* Kendrick."

Toin-Toin came right back, holding the menu with both hands, because his menu was, in fact, an enormous wooden cutting board filled with goodies: a couple of quail, de-plumed, still wearing their heads; a few unusually small rougets; a good-sized, well-marbled *Côte-de-boeuf*; two bright-eyed whole fish that looked to have been just plucked from the sea; two raw sausages that had never touched an assembly line; and a stack of inviting lamb chops with the long rib bones intact so all the good meat and fat was there for nibbling— "*Avec l'os noncassé*," as Kendrick said to French butchers.

A discussion followed as the three of them worked out how this and that might be prepared and whatever might serve as an accompaniment.

Kendrick wondered aloud if there might be a *figatellu* around. *Figatellu* is an inimitably flavored Corsican sausage that contains a good bit of pork liver in it. "I haven't had one in quite a while, and I have a weakness for them."

Baltazaru made a tsking sound and shook his head hopelessly. "Kendrick, this is not at all the season. Come back next winter, and we'll tour the best *figatellu* producers and dine on their favorite ways to eat them."

"Cooked outside over coals with some decent bread and wine," Kendrick said, "that's good enough for me."

Baltazaru continued shaking his head and looked up at Toin-Toin. "This guy"—he jerked a thumb toward Kendrick—"he's American, so it's natural he wants to eat *figatellu* out of season. Americans want everything you can possibly imagine, and they want it all the time. Their supermarkets are full of tomatoes year-round. So, *merde*, why not *figatellu* in the summer? And listen to this: They label their crappy cheap whites Chablis. What are you going to do with people like that?"

"Okay, okay," Kendrick began, "but you go a little too far. French supermarkets are full of tomatoes all winter nowadays, too."

"We copy your bad habits," Toin-Toin said.

"And for years," Kendrick said, "it's been illegal to label an American wine Chablis, Burgundy, or Rhine, for example, like they used to."

"Good! Finally! It's only common sense. But tomatoes, you won't catch me or Toin-Toin buying tomatoes until it's their season."

Toin-Toin said, "We don't need to. Here at the restaurant, we put enough away in jars to get us through the winter."

Kendrick ordered barbecued lamb chops with french fries and *tomates provençales*—it's the season! Baltazaru opted for quail roasted with pancetta and garlic cloves.

"And," he said, "for both of us, some of that chickpea salad to start. The one with chopped raw fennel and those baby shrimp, right?"

Toin-Toin nodded, then waited. And waited.

Finally Baltazaru asked, "What is it—you paralyzed or something?"

"Both of you are going to ignore this beauty? Look it in the eye. It has barely had time to realize that it is out of the water."

"A beauty?" Kendrick asked. "A monster's more like it. Look at those spikes, and the body. My god, it looks armored."

"You don't eat the spikes or the armor," Toin-Toin said. "I'd hate for you to miss it. And, with a good Patrimonio blanc . . ."

"Here's the solution," Baltazaru said, "salad to start, we split the fish in two for the second course, then proceed as planned after that. You do stock at least one red for the quail and chops, I hope."

"Wait," Kendrick said. "Is that fish called *chapon de mer*?"

"No, monsieur. Do you see the beard?" Gingerly, he picked up the colorful fish and held it closer so Kendrick could see it better. "A *chapon* doesn't have a beard, but, in fact, it is almost the same fish. My mother calls it a *scorpina*. That's the Corsican name for it. I'm going to roast it for you, then debone it, then place the filets on a bed of diced raw cucumber, shallots, and cherry tomatoes. I'll deglaze the baking pan with a little splash of lemon juice and white wine and pour it on top. It is not poisonous, and you won't get spiked. Sound good?"

Baltazaru raised his glass, and Kendrick followed with his. "Here's to Toin-Toin," Kendrick said, and they each downed a slug of rosé. Once they were alone, Baltazaru got right down to business.

"Okay, now, what's the big secret? Is this about buying you some property over here?"

"I wish," Kendrick said, "but it seems like the more time passes, the less interest I have. The roads here are so narrow, with so many curves and cutbacks and steep grades—and always more and more tourists. More buses, more campers, trailers, trucks . . ."

"Right, the roads don't change, but the traffic does."

"I'm afraid that before long, Corsica will be one very mountainous traffic jam."

Toin-Toin knocked and, when invited, came in and set down a bowl of chickpea salad and a basket of steaming rolls or biscuits. Kendrick's expression lit up.

"What the hell? I smell *figatellu*. But they look like *gougères*." He picked one up and had a bite. "My god, taste that," he said to Baltazaru. "It's like I've died and gone to heaven."

Toin-Toin said, "I'm like you, monsieur. I hate to go for months without *figatellu*, so I created *gougères* flavored with *figatellu* instead of cheese. I freeze the dough and use it whenever the mood strikes."

"That's genius," Kendrick said. "Baltazaru, you know some very cool places to fill your belly."

Toin-Toin left again, and they downed some food to join the rosé that had been sloshing around in their empty stomachs.

Kendrick recalled that he had not come only for fun and games. He looked Baltazaru directly in the eye. "I want to discuss the bombings here in Corsica. I remember seeing construction projects in progress and roofs blown wide open to the sky. I heard there were bombings for independence, too, but never bombings that resulted in fatalities."

"Corsica has a long history of violence," Baltazaru said, "invasions, civil wars, world wars, and of course mafia assassinations. But then we had the bombings meant to prevent the destruction of beauty, the natural beauty of our island, to preserve Corsica for Corsicans. Look what happened to France's Riviera. It's a crime against nature and against future generations, lost forever. Or Honolulu in your Hawaiian Islands. Without the bombings, it would have happened here in Corsica. And you are correct—people were not targeted. On the contrary."

"But now, you don't think things here are changing? Down around Porto-Vecchio, I noticed a lot of new construction covering a huge surface."

"Yes, the machinery is in place and shifting into high gear. A decision has been made."

"Will it happen here in the north, too?"

"A few families bought up land from the peasants over the years, and now they are developing it and also selling it off parcel by parcel. Vast fortunes are being made."

"You mean mafia families?"

"They don't need a name. People say *mafia* because Corsicans have Italian names, but after all, isn't it simply capitalism?"

"Rob the poor to feed the rich?"

Toin-Toin knocked and placed the platter of fish on the table. He deftly divided the ocean beast in two, placed a filet on the vegetables and spooned his sauce all over it. He left and an instant later returned with a bottle of Patrimonio blanc, which he poured, bowed an inch or two, and disappeared out the door.

Once alone again, Baltazaru continued. "We did live some really violent years, so-called mafia wars, but that had nothing to do with protecting our island, protecting it from turning Corsica into another Riviera. We had more assassinations per year than Sicily, yet Corsica has a much smaller population. Sicily has about five million inhabitants, and we are barely three hundred thousand. For example, maybe a mayor wouldn't approve building apartments somewhere, or a supermarket—he'd be gunned down for his refusal, after a kindly warning, of course. I remember when Toussaint Fraticelli was hit. He was leaving a café, and someone shot him not once, not twice, but eight times in the back. After his death, the city voted his daughter, Marcella, mayor even though it was known that she ran a whorehouse. She's not a bad mayor, by the way."

"Here's to Marcella," Kendrick said, "who had the proper background for getting into politics." After the toast, he leaned toward Baltazaru. "Tell me," he said softly, leaning in closer, "do you personally know any people who actually pulled off bombings? Built them and set them off?"

"Kendrick, what in the world are you getting at? *Merde*, you could get into big trouble asking questions like that. Problems with the police, or with people involved. Why do you want to know?"

After a discreet tap on the door, Toin-Toin and a waiter appeared to clear the table and serve the main courses. "And to drink?" he asked.

"Bring my cuvée Colluciu' rouge," Baltazaru said. When the door closed again, he asked Kendrick if he was researching an article about Corsica.

"Not at all. But I think maybe I shouldn't tell you everything. The less the better, in fact."

Baltazaru slammed his fist down on the table and shook his head violently. "Hey, my friend. Stop! On such a sensitive, dangerous subject, it is better I know every detail in order to keep you from doing something stupid. You love Corsica, and you understand its wines, but you don't know how its people think. This is not a comic strip we are in, you know, all full of laughs. You risk getting into trouble. Big trouble. You don't want a bomb going off in your face, do you?"

A tap on the door, and the red wine made its entrance. Toin-Toin poured a taste for Baltazaru, who sniffed and nodded approval. It was poured, and they were alone again.

"Smell that blueberry?" Baltazaru asked. "It is the first time I've picked up any blueberry in one of my wines. In the reds, it's usually raspberry or cherry. I like it a lot. I hope it's not just a passing phase."

"Blueberry with that perfume of the maquis? Sign me up."

"So, Kendrick, why the interest in Corsican bombings? As I've said, they're history."

Between bites and sniffs, chewing, sips, and swallowing, the conversation proceeded.

"Where I live near Bandol, a neighbor built a horrible home on his property. A real eyesore. And now he's rented a little piece of his property to a cell phone company. They built a cell phone antenna there, and it has destroyed my calm and my lovely view. Now the asshole is planning two or three more antennas even taller than the first one. There is no way to block it off with a wall or with trees because he's across a small valley from me. To wall him off, I'd have to wall off a large part of my view. See what I mean? In effect, his ugly house and the antennas will be my view."

Baltazaru put down his silverware and ran his big paw through his silvery hair. He looked like he'd eaten a rotten egg. He picked up his wine glass but paid no attention to it.

"I have only one rule about life," he said. "You cannot allow an asshole to ruin it for you."

After a heartbeat or two, Kendrick cracked up. Baltazaru joined in.

"I see where you're going," Baltazaru said.

"Yes, in the dead of the night, a toppled tower, no one hurt, but the phone companies would think long and hard before investing more money in the same location."

Baltazaru's eyebrows shot up. "You mean you don't want to blow up the house?"

"Love to, but no. It might be . . ."

"No, no. No need to explain. I know you, and what you tell me fits your character. I agree to think this through. We'll see if this can be one hundred percent safe. And I'll speak to Rafale and the Tractor about it."

"The Tractor?"

"Yeah, a nickname. Something to do with disposing of evidence, you follow me? The guy's real name is Nino, but everyone refers to him as the Tractor."

"And Rafale?"

"It's a French word for a squall at sea. But tell me the truth now, this red, wouldn't it have been better if I'd given it a good dose of new oak?"

"Change one thing about this beauty, you'll answer to the Tractor."

CHAPTER TWENTY-SEVEN

Cruising along in his automobile, Kendrick again approached the rather large—fifth largest in France—city of Nice. Road signs announced the glamorous names of one village after another: Cannes, Antibes, Juan-les-Pins, Saint-Paul-de-Vence—legendary sites where the likes of Matisse and Picasso, D. H. Lawrence and F. Scott Fitzgerald are only four on the long list of luminaries who had thrived there and added to the Riviera's luster. Undeniably, artistic temperaments were inspired there. Visually, however, few reminders of that former glory have survived. Kendrick stared out his car windows and saw litter—architectural litter, that is what the surrounding cityscapes resembled—as if some pissed-off deity had strewn garbage all over the once-gorgeous coastline. Towering construction cranes were scattered everywhere in the skyline, the expansion continuing and the litter spreading upward and outward. He wondered if humans are the only species to commit suicide in their own garbage, and how could the powers that be have authorized this all-consuming ugliness. Whatever happened to governance?

The first private detective he visited, Philippe Merlot, had his cubicle of an office in the *zone industrielle* near the Nice airport. When Kendrick walked in, a fairly young French dandy in a tight-fitting chartreuse suit catapulted out of his chair so suddenly—well, it might have been months since his last client. His pants were short enough to show off the glittery silver stars on his dark blue socks. His head was shaved, shiny, and pink, but his chin and upper lip looked black-and-bluish with three or four days' growth of bristle. He wore a flimsy mask of self-confidence, and when he spoke, his voice changed constantly as if he were trying to find the right register. When Kendrick asked what experience he had, he said he'd had beaucoup and never lost a case. *Lost a case?* Kendrick wondered. *Aren't cases for lawyers?* No, Sherlock Holmes either solved case or didn't. He didn't lose it. Where would he lose it? Kendrick realized that he was looking for reasons to criticize Monsieur Merlot, so he quickly thanked him, shook his hand goodbye, and set out to find his second address, which Madame Martignac had provided. Kendrick found the sign, DETECTIVE PRIVÉ: RECHERCHE ET INVESTIGATIONS, on rue Eric Satie, a spacious, palm-lined street with boutiques and restaurants in no danger of being mobbed by bargain-seeking tourists. In France, when you see *confit de canard* on a menu, you could be at the Ritz or in a truck stop, but when you see *ris de veau* with black truffles, you know the clientele is not there to pinch centimes.

Kendrick entered the front door. A young man sat behind a desk, finishing a phone conversation. "Yes, ma'am," he said in American English, "we'll take care of that without delay, and yes, you are down for Wednesday next, ten a.m." He was casually dressed and well groomed. He looked up at Kendrick with a friendly expression and asked politely, "*Est-ce que vous souhaiteriez parler anglais ou français?*"

Kendrick thought for a moment. "How about English? It'll be relaxing to speak my native tongue for a change. I have an appointment to speak with a detective."

"Yes, Mr. Thomas, you're expected. I'll let her know you're here."

The young man picked up the phone again, tapped a button, and said, "Your appointment is here." He led Kendrick in to a comfortably sized office. The parquet floor squeaked elegantly as Kendrick walked toward three green leather chairs arranged in front of a large, piano-shaped desk. Its surface was lustrous black like a concert grand. Kendrick thought it was clever in just the right way. He was definitely not in Philip Marlowe's Los Angeles office, and if one of the desk drawers had a bottle in it, it wouldn't be rye.

The assistant made the introduction even though the detective's name was written right there on the desk in front of Kendrick's eyes:

LORNA DARLINGTON, PHD. When she stood, the top of her head reached the level of Kendrick's eyes, so she was about five feet eight. He was taller, but she won the hair contest easily. Hers was dense enough to dive into—thick, sandy blonde, swept back over her ears—and if someone organized an ear contest, she'd win that prize, too. Oh yes, and a lovely, white, short-sleeve silk blouse that accompanied—in perfect harmony—her lightly tanned skin. Kendrick was at a loss for words. She walked around her piano desk to shake his hand and revealed long, well-dressed legs in beige slacks.

The two of them took their seats as her assistant excused himself.

"I'm curious," Kendrick said. "The sign says PhD. In what subject?"

"I wrote a thesis on the French Revolution and Mozart's *The Marriage of Figaro*." Her voice was a cool, well-pitched alto.

"Well, what a combination. One was bloody and the other a bloody good opera. My favorite opera, in fact, if I had to choose."

"You might not be aware of it, but the opera's libretto was much less revolutionary than the original version."

"Version?" Kendrick asked. "Wasn't Da Ponte's the original?"

"Da Ponte's libretto was based on a play by Pierre-Augustin Caron de Beaumarchais. The text of the play was a hundred times more revolutionary than the libretto. In fact, the play was banned in Austria, while Mozart's opera was permitted."

"Thank you, madame," Kendrick said, standing and heading for the door. "That's exactly the information I needed. Send me your bill, please." He stopped and turned back, saying with a smile, "Just kidding. Now how did you . . ."

"Get from Robespierre and Cherubino to being Nice's best private eye?" she finished.

"I'd love to hear it, Dr. Darlington."

"Please, call me Lorna," she said. "Now it's my turn to ask a question."

"Go ahead."

"Why do you need a private detective?"

A sexy smile lingered as her hazel eyes tightened to better focus on her prospective client.

"It's about a friend of mine, a winemaker in the Bandol appellation."

Lorna raised a hand to stop him. "Excuse me, but fully half the people who come in here tell me it's for a friend, a relative, or a business partner. We'll progress more quickly and successfully if you give me the facts right from the start. I'm on your side. Remember that."

Kendrick laughed easily. "Oh my, that scenario hadn't occurred to me. I believe you, but here and now I don't have a way to prove that this really is a question of protecting a pal. If we end up working together, I'm sure your investigation will prove quickly that I'm not the subject of this inquiry."

He went on to tell her what he knew about Babette and Branislav.

"So you fear they're taking Monsieur Henri Poupon for a ride, and you want to protect him."

"That's it, without losing him as a friend."

"And all you have is her name and address and the strong belief that she and Branislav are more than friends. Well, after all, it's not such a bad start. We know how to find her, and that often saves quite a bit of time. And therefore money."

Kendrick's eyes still had found nothing to complain about. "Speaking of money," he said, "what can you tell me about the cost of this investigation?"

"Two thousand euros deposit, then you'll be billed by the hour."

"Like a lawyer? I mean, if we're on the phone and I ask how's life treating you, your timer is ticking?"

"I suppose so. Anyway, when my assistant works your case, he's seventy-five euros an hour, and I'm two hundred and fifty."

"Ouch! Any predictions?"

"About how long? No, but I should know more once I've done some research about Babette's possible aliases."

"Okay, it's a deal, but if ever I ask how you are, just skip it. Give me the facts and nothing but the facts."

She smiled, which for Kendrick was like seeing the sun come up after a long, dark winter. "And expenses, too, which are, by the way, entirely unpredictable." She pulled out a contract, dated it, and pushed it across her Baldwin desk to Kendrick, who signed it without reading it.

"I'm surprised," he said, "that you haven't asked me anything about me. Or about Henri Poupon."

"We learn that in Detective A1. Get the contract signed and the timer going *before* gathering details. Now we're official, so yes, please, tell me about you and your winemaker friend."

Kendrick explained his line of work and that Poupon was one of his wine suppliers. "Henri Poupon has humble origins, but I'm sure his domaine near the coast is worth enough to interest money-grubbing, over-the-hill blonde bombshells."

"Well," Lorna said, "let's hope it's not like that. Let's hope it's true love and that they live happily ever after."

"I'll give you good odds if you'd like to bet on it."

"Not a good idea. I might doctor the results of my investigation in order to win the bet."

"Oh, I have no worries about that."

"Now I have a question for you," Lorna said, "and the meter is unplugged for the time we spend on it. Since you know wine, maybe you'll know why, when Don Giovanni dines before meeting the Commendatore and the flames of hell that will soon engulf him—his very last supper—why would he be drinking Marzemino? Have you ever heard of Marzemino?"

"Ah, what a good question. And you came to the right person. As you know, Da Ponte was from northern Italy. Venice, Verona, around there, and Marzemino is a local red wine grape. It makes an everyday wine, nothing grandiose, but a quaffer that back then was surely *frizzante*. However, the opera takes place in Spain, in Seville, and even today, believe me, no way anybody would run across a bottle of Marzemino in Seville. So Da Ponte probably liked his glass of Marzemino and wasn't familiar with Spanish wine, or maybe the name of the wine fit the rhythm of the music."

"No, first Da Ponte wrote the text, then Mozart came up with the music," Lorna said. "But I do like the way the word *Marzemino* rolls off the Don's tongue."

They stared at each other for a couple of beats. Lorna reached out and took back the contract. "Here's your copy, and this is my cell phone number in case you think of anything else."

"I'm sure I will," he said, his head full of risqué ideas.

"Now, let's seal the deal with an aperitif." She opened the bottom drawer on the right side of her desk and pulled out two glasses and a chilled bottle of Bienvenues-Bâtard Montrachet. Then she opened her black alligator purse and threw a pack of Sobranie Black Russian cigarettes onto the black patent desktop. She flicked a hidden switch, and Sade began to moan in her soulful nymphomaniac voice.

"It's warm in here," Lorna said in a breathy whisper. Her lips turned up into a sly smile, a devilishness to her suddenly. With one hand she reached up and began to unbutton her . . .

Or so it was in Kendrick's fantasy as he cruised back to Milles Vents. "Wow, wow, *wow*," he said. "Zowie." *Wow*, he'd said many times during his life, but that was his first *zowie*.

CHAPTER TWENTY-EIGHT

I'm thirsty enough to drain Lake Annecy and all the fish in it," Poupon said. It had been a dry, sizzling hot day, and by seven p.m., it hadn't grown much cooler.

"Let's check out that new wine bar up in l'Estournel," Kendrick said. "I could use a change of scene."

"So, my cooking is no longer good enough for you? *Merde, alors.* And order what?"

"Whatever strikes our fancy. I haven't been there yet."

"Well, let's see. They have shitty wine that'll be hot to the touch. Salt-flavored sausages. Their hard-boiled eggs are cooked to death, their aioli is made with rancid oil, and their . . ."

"Okay, okay, I get it. You must have been there already. You want to go someplace good?"

"You want to go someplace shitty? I feel like thirst has me in its clutches, but I don't enjoy hot wine. And you?"

"I'm getting thirsty, but I really need something to eat—no hurry, but there's no reason to delay thinking about it."

"Let's get outta here. It's too hot to cook."

For some reason, Poupon took his little white camionette instead of the BMW. They left the domaine, and at the entry to the autoroute, he pulled over to the side of the road. "I'm thinking a fresh, simple grilled fish and cold wine," he said. He turned and looked Kendrick in the eye. "Come on. Give me some help."

"I'm not picky, but I'm developing a good appetite. I ate about two spoonfuls of I-forget-what for lunch, and I put up with a day without wine—so far."

"Hey!" Poupon slapped Kendrick's knee. "What about daube? *Daube à la Provençale*. Ravioli stuffed with daube. Do you know the road to Méounes-lès-Montrieux from Signes?"

Before Kendrick could answer, Poupon ground the camionette into gear, and off they rattled and roared. The air coming in through the floorboard and the open windows felt good. Avoiding the autoroute, they circled Le Caniveau and wound their way up the hillside toward the Camp Castello and the Philippe Cornu racetrack, then over the plateau and down into Tignes, where they stopped and enjoyed a short break at a café next to the village fountain.

"Strange what a glass of pastis in the shade of a plane tree and a gurgling fountain can do to mitigate the heat," Kendrick said.

"My ancestors weren't total blockheads," Poupon said. "They knew how to deal with the heat without air conditioners. Without electricity."

"I just hope wherever we're headed has a table for us. We didn't reserve, and my belly is beginning to wonder what's going on."

Poupon laughed as he stood up. "Reservations. Worry, worry, worry." He drained his glass, and off they went again.

From the narrow, winding *route départementale*, a few hundred meters before the city limits sign for Méounes, a dirt road led down into a clearing and stopped at the Auberge du Gros Cerf, where everything was under the shade of some kind of tree or another. They entered the restaurant—plastic tablecloths, neon Paul Ricard sign, fabulous aromas—and were seated by a young woman around fifteen or sixteen.

"Henri!" she screamed with big brown eyes open wide. "You haven't been to see us in months."

At the precise moment that Kendrick's and Poupon's rear ends hit their chairs, a bottle of white wine arrived and landed on the table with a thud, held in the grasp of a paw easily the size of Poupon's. The tough, hard-nosed waiter wasn't even looking at them. He was staring across to the other side of the room where six lads all clad in

Olympique de Marseille soccer shirts were having beers and paper cones filled with deep-fried fresh anchovies. They were not paying attention to the waiter, who also turned out to be the proprietor of the place and father to the teenage cutie-pie, but he was certainly giving them the evil eye. He turned back mumbling, "What a bunch of punks," then he noticed Poupon.

"Hey, look at what the tide brought in," he said. "Marie, do you see what I see, or is it a mirage?"

"It's really him, Papa," she said. "Our favorite winemaker."

"Bonsoir to you both," Poupon said. "I brought along a wine importer from the USA—picked him up hitchhiking in Signes. Let's fill him up to the brim and see if he explodes. Kendrick, meet Marie and her father, Clarius, although when you compare his mug with her pretty face, you have to wonder how much he really had to do with her conception."

The meal began with slices of toast, one topped with tapenade, the other with brandade. The bottle of white was empty when Marie showed up to clear the plates.

"Not bad," Kendrick said, "but there's no label to tell us what it is or who made it."

Marie explained that it was a Côtes-de-Provence from a small domaine near Cuers, purchased in demijohns and bottled by Clarius as needed. As she walked toward the kitchen, Kendrick started to say something about how the little white wine was so good because, obviously, it hadn't been filtered to death, when they heard a yelp from Marie, and she dropped the dirty dishes she was carrying onto the floor as she passed the table of young predators across the room.

Clarius stormed out of the kitchen and demanded to know what had happened, but it was obvious without asking because Marie was rubbing her left rear jean pocket and had tears in her eyes. Clarius picked up the nearest guy out of his chair, turned him around, and kicked him in the ass hard enough to send him rolling over another table. Clarius turned back to the other five—two were standing, thinking too long about launching an attack, and three remained seated, frozen.

Poupon walked over to stand beside Clarius and said, "You stupid jerks, you're not from around here, are you? Or you'd know not to fuck around with my pal Clarius."

The unfortunate lad that Clarius had booted in the rear end suddenly came charging back across the room. Poupon turned at the sound, tucked back his arm boxer-style, and unleashed a wicked right jab straight into the kid's face. Kendrick cringed when he heard the cracking sound of a broken nose and saw the blood that went with it. The kid fell, out for the count before he hit the floor. His face would wear a souvenir of his bêtise for the rest of his life.

That seemed to de-punk the rest of the gang. They were ordered to pay up and clear out, which they did, carrying their fallen warrior. Poupon escorted them outside while Marie convinced her father that she was fine. The pinch had surprised and embarrassed her more than anything.

Poupon returned carrying a soccer ball and put thirty euros on the table. "It's the tip they forgot to leave. I reminded them."

Kendrick asked what the ball was for.

"Not bad, right? They didn't have any more cash on them to pay for damages—I mean, look at the mess they left—so they gave me this brand-new professional World Cup soccer ball for Marie. They claimed it sells for over a hundred euros."

A couple minutes later, Clarius showed up with a dusty bottle of Cornas. The vintage strip said 198_, the final digit worn off. Clarius poured it, purplish black, into Kendrick's glass. "We'll let our importer judge if it's fit to drink," he said.

Kendrick sniffed, nodded as to its fitness, then tasted it. His mind turned back through the vintages of the eighties. 1981? No, 1981 was thinner, more wiry. 1982? More diluted. 1983? No, that was a magnificent wine, but wild and rambunctious. 1984? Nope, totally forgettable. 1985? *Ah yeah, gotcha*, he thought.

"Is it a 1985?"

Clarius shook his head. "No idea, sorry. Might be. For years, it's been down there mixed in a bin of this and that."

"The vintage is not on the cork?"

"Nope, they didn't do that very often back then."

"That's true," Kendrick said, reading the label. "This Noël Verset—now there's a vigneron who knew what he was doing. It's as fresh as can be and much more velvety than Cornas usually is."

"Velvet," Poupon said. "The tannin is there, but it's a velvety tannin. How the hell did he do that?"

Kendrick thought it over and asked, "Why don't we pop up and see him one of these days? He's only about two and a half hours from Bandol."

"I know you," Poupon said. "You think I've got something to learn, that I should pick up some tricks from the guy, right?"

"I'm just trying to file down your rough edges. No major surgery required."

"That's how you see me? A rusty old saw?"

When the first glasses of Cornas were emptied, a platter of steaming ravioli arrived. The heady aroma had Kendrick and Poupon ready to gobble them up with their fingers. When the first platter was empty, a new one appeared.

Poupon exhaled from deep down and said, "This daube Clarius prepares for his ravioli, you taste it once, all the others seem canned."

Clarius heard him and walked over to their table again. "This daube cooked two full days in a clay pot next to the coals in the wood oven. Barely at a simmer. Who does that anymore?"

Kendrick said that every time he'd eaten ravioli with a meat filling, it had tomato sauce.

"*Putain*," Clarius roared. "All that does is cover up the taste of the daube you work so hard to make."

"Don't exaggerate," Poupon said. "And what work are you talking about? All it does is cook for two days. What's the big deal? You put it in the fireplace, and you lift it out two days later. Wow, you must be totally exhausted."

Clarius ignored the dig. "This sauce is nothing but juices from the daube, some parmesan, plus a little olive oil and red wine vinegar. The vinegar—a cook has to be super careful. Add it drop by drop. Too much and you'll eat with a grimace. You want just enough to energize the daube. You don't want to be conscious of its presence."

Another platter of steaming ravioli came out of the kitchen, then another and another. Finally, Poupon pulled out his smokes. Kendrick refused the offer.

When Poupon's cigarette was nothing but a butt, Marie served a beautiful green salad with yellow, orange, and red nasturtiums scattered on top. "Clarius picked it leaf by leaf while you were smoking," she said. When the salad was gone, Clarius himself emerged carrying an oozing reblochon on a wooden cutting board. "I'm glad you enjoyed your main course," he said. "I was afraid, you know, in this heat . . ."

Poupon nodded. "When your stomach is growling for ravioli, you don't listen to the weather report."

"How about some cheese?"

"Are you kidding? In this heat?"

"None for me either, thank you," Kendrick said.

"The Cornas was top," Poupon said, "but I thought the bottle was too small. What was it, fifty centiliters?"

"Are you joking?" Clarius said with real indignation. "I'm worried about you."

"Maybe the bottle shrank in your cellar. Maybe the rats down there have straws, and they drank some of it. You don't expect us to pay for a full bottle, do you? It barely lasted through the ravioli."

"Still thirsty? Is that it? You must have hollow legs. If you want more red, tell me. I'll bring more. On the house!"

Poupon acted offended. "To drink with our coffee? Great timing, Chef. And you call this joint a restaurant?"

After Clarius returned to the kitchen, Kendrick said, "*Mon dieu*, four dozen? Doesn't seem possible."

"That's nothing," Poupon said. "When Madame Brulat, Clarius's aunt, had this place, the actor Raimu—you know, from Bandol?"

"Marcel Pagnol's favorite actor," Kendrick said.

"Right. Well, he and Blavette ate here way back when Madame Brulat was still in the kitchen. Raimu and Blavette downed twelve dozen each! Two dozen dozen."

"That's heroic," Kendrick said. "Epic. And obviously impossible. I'll bet they ate six dozen each, and as the years race by, the number of dozens somehow grows."

"*Merde.* What would an American know about Raimu? We have it from Blavette himself. It is written. Twelve dozen each! And Raimu, remember? He was a storage facility of a man. A giant. Not a barrel of a man, no, he was shaped like an enormous cask: tall, little feet, little head, but swollen out plump in the middle."

They headed back toward the coast well after dark. Kendrick hadn't mentioned anything about Lorna and Babette. He popped a Tums into his mouth and, despite the car's rattle and roar, fell asleep sucking on it.

CHAPTER TWENTY-NINE

Their slender waiter stood, pencil poised, awaiting Lorna's order, hoping that if he looked her over, goggle-eyed, and gaga enough, she would not be able to resist his charms. Meanwhile, Kendrick was surveying her, too. He could not get over how her mouth might be considered on the small side, yet her lips were so lusciously . . . he searched for the word—suggestive. He was also still basking in the afterglow of their Mozart/Marzemino conversation. He hoped that a meeting of the minds would be a fine overture to further meetings. They were at Domaine Terre Noble near Sanary-sur-Mer, a winery with its own restaurant. Kendrick chose it because it had outdoor tables, plenty of surrounding vegetation, seafood from local waters, and artisanal wines. They were together there for lunch and Lorna's progress report.

She looked up at the waiter and started to order when a well-tanned, middle-aged man in khaki shorts and a Beethoven's bust T-shirt stopped at the table and interrupted her. "Kendrick, bonjour. I saw your name on the reservation list. Good to see you. I simply want you to know that we are rich in seafood today. We can bring out a series of little dishes of this and that, or you can order from the menu."

Kendrick looked to Lorna and raised his eyebrows. "Sound good?"

"Perfect," she said. "I never know what I'm in the mood for."

The host waved the waiter away and said with a subtle bow, "Madame, I'm sure wherever you are, you will always be surrounded by people who are anxious to satisfy whatever mood you choose to be in. Welcome to Terre Noble. And you, Kendrick, I just purchased some interesting older Burgundies from a client whose doctor won't allow him to drink anymore."

"Not even wine?" Kendrick said in a shocked tone. "The poor sap should change doctors. Hasn't he read the Bible, Jesus turning water into wine? He wants us to think that Jesus Christ would change water into something unhealthy? That's blasphemy. My doctor knows that his job is to keep me healthy enough to finish everything in my wine cellar before I kick the bucket." Given that Kendrick had around sixty thousand bottles in his two cellars, and that he kept adding new vintages, he might live long enough to set a new wine consumption record. "When it's my time to go, I'm going out on an overdose of old Yquem and heroin," he said.

"Kendrick, I like the way you think. I see the logic," the host said.

"Have you ever tried heroin?" Lorna asked.

"No, but I'm told you become super receptive to music. It's like being inside the music, you become the music. So, put on Dinu Lipatti's final recital at Besançon, a transcendental performance, one of the most beautiful goodbyes in existence . . ."

The proprietor motioned for the waiter and told him they would not be ordering from the menu and to bring Kendrick a copy of the newly printed reserve wine list. "But—quick—pour each of them a glass of our rosé to get their juices flowing," he added.

Kendrick looked over the old Burgundies on the list. "Does white Burgundy sound good?" he asked Lorna.

"I'll be your disciple. Lay it on, fill 'er up to the brim. I mean, of my wine glass, bien sûr." The waiter arrived with a platter of six large, flat, circular, local wild oysters on ice.

Kendrick ordered a 1986 Morey Saint Denis blanc from Jean-Marie Ponsot. As the waiter turned away, Kendrick told Lorna, "Business before pleasure. Let's hear about Babette before the Burgundy goes to our heads."

With an elegant movement, Lorna brushed back her hair, revealing dime-sized gold and emerald earrings. "Well, the plot does thicken," she said. "Babette owns her apartment—inherited it three years ago when her husband died. He was a count. The Count Leopold Flavinius d'Orsini."

"There's a moniker for you. Cause of death?" Kendrick asked.

"Very much like Grace Kelly. Almost a copycat. His noble head was bashed in when his car ran off a road winding down into San Remo, where he had a small bungalow."

"You saw the police report?"

"But of course, boss, and it was noted: 'Victim and car were too damaged to draw conclusions about possibly suspicious indications.'"

"So he might have been run off the road purposefully?"

"Oh, Kendrick, you'll never run out of coulda-beens. Yes, it could have been murder. The murderer could have been Babette. Or, the count could have been dead drunk, or someone whacked him with a maltese falcon and put him in his car before rolling it down the hillside. Or, as far as the evidence shows, he could have driven off the road on purpose. Goodbye, cruel world."

The waiter returned, appreciating Lorna as long as he could while picking up the two rosé glasses and the platter of oyster shells and putting down another platter—this one covered with spiny purple and orange sea urchins, *oursins* in French. He also poured the nineteen-year-old white Burgundy.

Kendrick sniffed and nodded approval. "It's in great shape," he said. He felt the same way about Lorna.

She sniffed her wine and asked, "Does the year really matter?"

"You mean the year the Count died?"

"No," she said. "I mean the year of a wine."

Kendrick laughed at himself. "Sorry. My god. I was still with Count d'Orsini, rolling down the hillside, dead or alive."

"Easy to do. We've got *oursins* and Orsini."

"What more do we know about him?"

"His family was wealthy enough leading up to the First World War. They had a good bit of land and investments in France, Italy, and Serbia. His middle name was Slav."

"I see what you mean about the plot thickening. It's so thick it's sticking to the spoon. And by the way, yes, the year, the vintage—very important to the style and quality of a wine. More about that later."

The waiter brought another platter, this time with six bizarre-looking shellfish called *vioulets*, in an array of yellow-, orange-, and ochre-colored flesh, new to Lorna. Kendrick explained, "They're found offshore from Toulon to Greece. Quite rare these days and getting more so. They're also known as sea potatoes, but they look more like rocks. Once sliced in half, like these are, you thumb out the flesh and eat it raw, like this."

Lorna wasn't crazy about the rubbery texture and said they were too saline for her.

"Yes, they taste strongly of the sea," Kendrick said, who happened to like them. "They are a shocking sight—brightly colored, an odd creature inside a rocklike shell."

The waiter asked if Lorna and Kendrick preferred their mussels raw, *marinières*, or fried and served with a saffron-flavored aioli. They both opted for deep-fried.

Lorna continued, "By the time the count earned his just rewards, the family fortune had been squandered, and what was left was divided between his two kids from a previous marriage and Babette. She got the Nice apartment, but after all the debts were paid, no income. And by the way, I had the apartment staked out. Branislav is there all night every night. He lives with her."

"Not the handsomest couple in the world," Kendrick said. "From what I saw of him, he's capable of murder simply to round off a pleasant day."

"But from what you saw of them," Lorna said, "she gives the orders, right?"

Two local prawns grilled over coals finished off the shellfish parade, then they were offered either grilled swordfish ("just salt and pepper and a dollop of fresh butter") or *blanquette de veau* for their main course.

"Had enough from the sea?" Kendrick asked.

"I love *blanquette de veau*, but I'm so full."

The waiter, ready to do anything to make her happy, assured her the servings were modest.

"Make it two," Kendrick said, "but just a sec. We'll need a red with the veal." He looked down the list quickly. "This Mercurey, it says several vintages available."

"We haven't had time to itemize them," the waiter said. He called his boss over.

"The seller," he explained, "must have purchased Mercurey Rouge each and every vintage from the man who owns Romanée Conti. I bought everything he had from 1991 to 2003. A pal ordered the 1997 the other day. He said it was good."

"Red or white, I'm not much of a fan of 1997," Kendrick said. "The grapes were ripe enough, but the wines have never shown me much. No pizzazz. Let's give the 1993 a chance. And when you uncork it, have a taste with us. That way, if anyone asks, you'll know what's in the bottle. Great price, by the way—not much more than the most recent vintage."

"The poor guy just wanted to move them out of his sight so he wouldn't be tempted."

After he came back with the 1993 and exchanged appreciations with Kendrick, Lorna continued. "To conclude with my investigation so far, I'm afraid we're going to need some help from Serbia. If I were to go myself, I'd get nowhere. Well, maybe dead from prying."

"Why Serbia?" Kendrick asked.

"Because I've got a hunch that Babette's story begins there. For one thing, Branislav is Serbian."

"A hunch? How much would one of your lovely hunches set me back?"

"I'd hire a detective there in Smederevo, where there were a couple of d'Orsini properties, or hire one from Belgrade, if necessary. I'm sure you'll have to pay over a grand, maybe two. It will mean looking at documents at city hall and the police station, checking archives and newspapers, maybe interviewing family members. Serbia is pretty cheap, as I understand it."

"How much have I spent so far?"

Lorna pulled an envelope out of her purse. She handed her invoice to him. "We're up to twenty-three hundred euros," she said.

"I can't drop the case now," Kendrick said. "It would be like leaving Poupon in the middle of the Mediterranean without a life vest. What I mean is, what you've dug up so far tells me we have to keep digging."

"To help you," Lorna said, "I won't take a commission on the Serbian investigator. I'll bill you only what he or she bills me."

Kendrick raised his glass toward her. They clinked, sealing the deal. They stared into each other's eyes a beat longer than needed before raising their glasses to their lips and downing a swallow.

Lorna asked what he thought of the 1993 Mercurey.

"It's flawless," he said. "It's so good, if you weren't as beautiful as you are, I'd be raving about how beautiful the wine is."

"How does it compare with the year you didn't want to order?" she asked.

"Smell the '93. When I smell it, I think of it as complex and possessing energy. It's fairly old, but it has the energy of a much younger wine. A 1997 is likely to be monotone instead of complex. And it certainly wouldn't show the same energy. It would just sit there on your palate, calm as a grave."

"What if I like calm, gentle wines?"

"Good point. To each his own. Then you'd prefer the 1997, which is not a bad thing at all. Why don't I order a 1997, too? That way you'll taste the difference for yourself instead of trying to imagine it."

"No, Kendrick. No, I'm simply not that dying to know. I believe you."

"The only way to know for sure is to taste and compare. Otherwise, you just happen to think or believe something without a true taste test."

Lorna took another sip of Mercurey and asked, "What was my birth year like?"

"You mean you're going to divulge your true age on our first date? I'll bet you five euros Babette wouldn't do that."

"Watch out who you're dealing with here," Lorna said. "Remember my métier? Anyway, I checked you out, checked into your background, and apparently you aren't much of a sexist, racist, or ageist pig. I trust you, so, 1985 is my vintage."

Kendrick did not for a moment believe that she was twenty-one years old, but he played along with it. What could he say? That she looked older than that? Instead, he said, "Let's keep the discussion to Burgundy, okay? So, 1985 in Burgundy, red and white." He looked her over in what, for Kendrick, was an almost brazen manner. "Yes, 1985. I remember it well, because I was in Burgundy right after the grapes had been harvested." And once more, he looked her up and down with a critical eye. "The guy who made this Mercurey told me he'd never seen such beautiful grapes. On the vine, they were picture perfect."

Lorna was delighted. "So I come from an excellent year?" she asked.

"All the critics thought so. One idiot called it 'a vintage of the century,' as if there can be several of them, but grammatically, nope, sorry. It doesn't work. I thought 1985s were good, not great."

"Why doesn't it make your 'great' list?"

"On the surface," he said, "it seems to have everything." He aimed his glass at Lorna and said, "Here's looking at you, kid."

Lorna laughed. "What does *Casablanca* have to do with it?"

"Well, I'm looking at you, and you're picture perfect. But we're just getting to know each other, I hope. So, the point is, superficially the 1985s looked great, but as I got to know them, when you get down into the very depths of them, they can seem sort of boring."

Lorna laughed. "Kendrick, I imagine you in a bathing suit and goggles swimming around in the depths of a 1985 Burgundy and being so disappointed by what you see."

"And I imagine you out of your bathing suit, and I'm the one wearing the goggles as you zip around underwater. You are truly and by far the best 1985 I've ever seen."

"What about the year I was conceived?" she asked.

"1984? Less ripe, less fruity. After the aroma, there wasn't much on the palate. Most of them were short and austere. But I had a weakness for their aromas. Very terroir sensitive."

They continued talking on through their coffees. More importantly, when they walked to their cars and said goodbye, Kendrick ignored the cheeks and went straight for her lips. He gave her a good, quick kiss, then smacked his lips together. "Yum," he said.

CHAPTER THIRTY

No phones, no emails, no letters—nothing in print," Baltazaru said. "Nothing that can be traced. We'll talk where there are no walls, no ceilings, no hidden microphones."

So Kendrick flew from Marseille to the Bastia airport again. He ordered a Volkswagen Golf, but all they had was a flaming red Renault Clio. Very stealth! The rental agent proudly told him he was lucky to have that. This time our conniving wine specialist turned south on the *route nationale*—to his right, mountain after mountain rose steeply into a cloudless blue sky, and to his left, to the east, an endless—and, for Corsica—relatively charmless beach. The highway was asphalt and the beach sand, and both were flat and straight and about the same width as far south as he could see. On both sides of him, frontage roads were filled with the ugliest commercial strips imaginable, everything built with one goal in mind: cheapness! How low could you go? Corrugated metal, converted shipping containers, plastic cubicles, a chaos of tacky signs fighting for attention, all of which bugged Kendrick because he considered Corsica an impossibly beautiful island, excepting the man-made crap.

Following Baltazaru's detailed directions, Kendrick navigated the heavy traffic. After exactly 14.3 kilometers, he turned right between a vegetable stand and an entrepreneur selling plastic toilet seats at "low warehouse prices," which reminded him of his conversation with Babette. A road sign indicated nine kilometers to Suffagio, where the rendezvous was scheduled, and then it was up, up, up, and away until Kendrick thought he could feel the oxygen supply diminishing. He and his Clio never experienced another straightaway, never reached over forty kilometers an hour as the road coiled and climbed up into the mountains.

Suffagio is a strange little hamlet atop Mount Garaban. The road ends at a parking lot. You either enter it, or you turn around and head back down, because Suffagio has no streets—nothing but paths, stairways, and tunnels between the ancient dwellings, every bit of it made of rust-colored stones, medieval and rustic as can be. However, all the homes have bright white television antennas. As Kendrick looked it all over, he understood that yes, they had to have TV. What else was there to do? It was, however, still a cool place to be, for a while—unless you suffer from vertigo.

He pulled up to the ticket machine at the entrance to the parking lot, threw some coins in, then realized that the metal bar was missing, so paying was unnecessary. He'd been too busy checking out the environs to notice. Within the unpaved parking lot stood several plane trees and a Romanesque church with a tall, skinny belfry, the highest building around. There were only four other cars and a little buvette, Chez Danelu, site of the clandestine meeting. It looked mobile. If you wanted to, you could probably hook up Chez Danelu and tow it away. It was as funky a restaurant as one can find, with mismatching tables and chairs made of wood, plastic, canvas, metal, and straw. It featured open-air dining with a few closed parasols here and there, ready for action in case the sun or rain got to be too much. The menu was in chartreuse chalk on a big blackboard. Another blackboard had sayings on it, for example: "The role of nouvelle cuisine is to empty the wallet without filling the stomach."

Baltazaru casually rose from his chair to shake hands with Kendrick. With him were a couple of characters the likes of which Kendrick never, ever thought he would be associating. The one who turned out to be the Tractor was massive, dressed in a square-shouldered blue suede suit with no shirt under his coat, paired with sandals. One look at his huge, sockless feet and only a masochist would take a second look. But then he showed Kendrick the sweetest smile, featuring perfectly straight, bright white teeth. *Dirty feet, clean teeth? How unusual.* When the Tractor took Kendrick's hand for shaking, he said, "*Santé, santé,*" as if Champagne had been poured.

For a few seconds, Kendrick froze up and flubbed his greeting. "*Enchanté, Monsieur Tracteur,*" he said.

Baltazaru almost bent in half laughing. "Oh Kendrick, all of Corsica will hear about that one. When we talk about him, he's *Le Tracteur*, but when we talk *to* him, he's Nino."

Next came Rafale. When it was his turn, he jumped up from the chair with such agility, Kendrick thought of a gymnast. He was a young man, mid-twenties, and dressed in black shorts and a green and orange Hawaiian shirt with palm trees, ukuleles, and hula dancers. Instead of shaking hands, he raised one hand in the air for a slap as if he were an American basketballer.

A young woman in jogging shorts and an unlikely T-shirt saying in English, BUSH-WHACKED, came out with a smile and asked about aperitifs. When the three Corsicans ordered Corsican Muscatellu, Kendrick did, too.

While they downed their aperitifs, Baltazaru said, "Don't let appearances here fool you. Her husband, Danelu, has good ingredients and knows how to put them to use. People who know, they'll travel to eat here."

Studying the blackboard, Kendrick shook his head in disbelief. "A swordfish-burger with homemade fries. Made in Corsica? Great. I know what I'm going to order."

Madame toured the table taking orders, and when Kendrick gave his, she asked, "Tomato?"

"Yes."

"Red onion?"

"Yes."

"Bacon?"

"Yes."

"Mustard, ketchup, or aioli?"

"Yes," Kendrick said again, which got a laugh.

But Madame wondered aloud, "Seriously?"

"Aioli on the burger, the other two for fries," he said.

"So be it." And off she went.

"Danelu, what a pal," the Tractor said, "salt of the earth."

Then Rafale said, "And his wife, a beautiful woman, inside and out."

The Tractor frowned and leaned toward Rafale like a tiger about to spring into action. "What's that supposed to mean?"

"That she's a raving beauty, sexy, sexy, and she wasn't always married to Danelu."

"You'd be wise to shut your filthy garbage can of a mouth. That's Danelu's wife you're talking about."

"What, you think she was a virgin when she married him? Listen, Nino, sex is good, clean fun. You got a dirty mind, my friend. I love ya. I'd die for you, but you got a dirty mind."

The Tractor searched for a comeback. "Well, if I've got a dirty mind, I wouldn't trade it for your clean one."

That seemed to be all they could manage to wring out of that subject, so Baltazaru turned their attention to the reason for the meeting. Kendrick was a dear friend who had helped make the world pay attention to Corsican wines. Now he needed their expertise to solve a big problem that had absolutely no other solution. And so on.

The conversation continued while they ate. Baltazaru had a large salad with all kinds of lettuces and tomatoes in it, flecks of anchovy and little hunks of grilled swordfish. Kendrick's swordfish burger was a treat, and the fries! The previous best french fry he'd ever had was back in his twenties when he lived on the Lower East Side in Manhattan, at a joint called The Old Reliable near E. 4th Street and Avenue C. Here, finally, he'd found fries as good as The Old Reliable's.

As they were finishing, Danelu came out. He brushed off all the compliments with a wave of his hand. "Listen, I just got a call from Gianni. Yes, that Gianni. He's almost here and wants to be sure you'll wait for him."

The three Corsicans practically ran their words into each other assuring Danelu that of course they'd wait, were ecstatically happy to wait for Gianni, wouldn't miss him for the world.

When Danelu returned to his kitchen, the Tractor rubbed his forefinger back and forth under his nose and asked no one in particular, "I wonder how Gianni knows we're here?"

"Danelu, probably," Rafale said.

"No, no, don't worry," Baltazaru said. "I told Gianni. Of course I did. If he doesn't like the plans we've made, it doesn't happen. And he had to hear about it from us. That's all. Us and no one but us. Of course I told Gianni."

Gianni's driver pulled the beige Ford sedan right up to Chez Danelu. No black Maserati limo for Gianni, who turned out to be about seventy years old with a hairline crazy old baldheads would kill to acquire. That, however, was the most youthful thing about him. He didn't move easily as he walked around the car, and up close his complexion was splotchy—red splotches on a pale face. He wore blue jeans, a black T-shirt, black espadrilles with no socks, and an ankle chain.

Kendrick, meanwhile, wore a what-the-hell-is-going-on expression.

Everyone stood to greet Gianni. He cheeked Baltazaru, gave Rafale a smile and an endearing slap on the face. He and Kendrick shook hands.

"He's my importer in the US," Baltazaru explained.

"Aha, the guy who's pushing up prices so high I can't afford to drink your stuff anymore."

"Hey, my friend, my adopted brother, Gianni, I'll have Alexandre deliver a couple of cases to you tomorrow. You can tip him if you want to, but the wine's on me."

Gianni and the Tractor cheeked, then Gianni said, "Two cases? That's a lot for me these days. My doc allows me two glasses of wine per day, one with lunch, one with dinner, and not even a watered-down pastis in between."

"Hey, Kendrick, tell Gianni what you told me about your doctor," Baltazaru said.

"If your doctor tells you no more wine, you drop him and find another. And to the new one you say, 'Your job is to keep me healthy enough to drink wine.'"

Gianni liked that. Danelu walked up, and the two men cheeked. "What are you having, Gianni? Your usual?"

"Yeah, yeah, don't waste time on me. Make me one of your charcuterie platters, some of those tomatoes you got—don't touch 'em except to slice 'em, salt 'em, and pepper 'em."

"A glass of the usual?"

"One glass is better than none."

"I'll check each tomato and select the best," Danelu said.

"Okay, boys," Gianni said as they all sat down. "Fill in your old pal. Why this summit meeting?"

Kendrick wondered if that had been a joke. The meeting was indeed taking place on a summit.

Baltazaru began explaining Kendrick's dilemma at Milles Vents. Gianni didn't say anything—just nodded his head once in a while to show he was following the story. No one paid any mind as Danelu came out again and began serving Gianni's lunch. Something caught Kendrick's eye, something that didn't seem quite right. It turned out to be the wine glass Danelu placed next to Gianni's plate. It was a large one. Enormous. He pulled the cork from a bottle of red. The label said *Sélection Danelu*. All eyes were now on him as he poured Gianni a glass—and poured and poured until there was no more to pour.

"Thanks," Gianni said. He lifted the giant wine glass and with both hands guided it to his lips. He took a damned long pull on it, then let out a sigh full of satisfaction.

"I hate not being able to enjoy an aperitif like normal human beings do, like normal people all over this silly globe do, but this condition I have, I promised Marie I'd follow doctor's orders: one glass with meals. So, an aperitif? No, that would require two different glasses."

"Everyone knows you're a man of your word," the Tractor said.

"An iron will!" Baltazaru affirmed.

"A model for the next generation," Kendrick added.

"*Va bene, va bene, va bene,*" Gianni said, calling the meeting to order with his tone of voice. It was clear they were there for Gianni's authorization. He had questions, good questions. He wanted to know, for example, how close the antenna was to the nearest school. An injury to a youngster, that would be a catastrophe—the worst thing that could happen. He wanted a detailed map of the vicinity. Which neighbors had dogs? Stuff like that. At one point, Gianni asked Rafale and the Tractor if their skills were still honed. Could they successfully carry out such an operation?

They claimed they could pull it off blindfolded and that they were glad to do it, even eager, because they both hated mobile phones. The Tractor spoke up. "You see these fucking idiots driving, or trying to drive, while they're yapping away to somebody on their cell phones. *Putain!* I almost plugged some asshole the other day. I'm behind him at a red light, and when it turns green, he sits there lost in his phone—can't even put his foot down on the gas pedal. I got out and kicked his motherfucking door as hard as I could. He practically croaked, it scared him so bad. So, yeah, I dig this job. Righteous fucking work, if you ask me."

"Yeah," Rafale said, "me too, and I'm against all those brain tumors they cause."

Gianni said that Kendrick should immediately fill out an application at a telecom company as if he wanted to rent space for an antenna at Milles Vents—a good way to divert suspicion. He also said the deal had to go off in the middle of the night during the winter, while Kendrick was in the US.

"And now we settle the cost," Gianni said.

"Leave me out of the calculation," Baltazaru said. "I owe Kendrick a favor."

"Understood. Rafale, Nino, you'll receive twelve thousand euros each, top. We can settle between us later, depending on how it goes. But, monsieur," Gianni said to Kendrick, "you will pay in advance. None of this half now, half later bullshit. Baltazaru will vouch for me—your antenna problem will be solved, and you are going to receive a lot of peace of mind for your money. As for my own peace of mind, you will understand, I trust, when I warn you—never tell anyone that any of us were involved, even if you are arrested, tried, and convicted. You rat on us, and I'll see to it you need a new set of balls to replace the originals. *Capito?*"

Gianni looked into each man's eyes, including Kendrick's, until each nodded agreement. Then he lifted his fishbowl-on-a-stem wine glass, sniffed it nostalgically, and finished it off.

CHAPTER THIRTY-ONE

It was a cool, windy day at Milles Vents while the sky continually changed from gray to blue as thick clouds swept past overhead. Kendrick was in his bedroom showing the busted zipper on his favorite cardigan to Zarina, his advisor about such matters from way back. At the same time, how could he help admiring the fit of her summer shorts and how fetching her satiny dark skin looked against the snow-white cotton? Her expression told him she could use some tenderness, some comforting. He felt the urge to reach over and pull her into his arms like he used to do when—*bang!*—he suffered a bout of moral turmoil, which supposedly leads to civilized, let's call it governable, human behavior. Would collapsing on the bed with Zarina be wrong or right or a harmless blend of the two? Instead of a hug and a kiss and so on, he stood frozen, puzzling out where he was with Lorna, and where Zarina was with Poupon. And Poupon with her. Well, as far as he could tell, those two weren't seeing each other at all, and Poupon seemed more interested in landing Babette. And now it came back to him that Zarina had mentioned having a couple of dates coming up, so she clearly considered herself free of Poupon.

As for Lorna? Nothing new to report, so far, but Kendrick had high hopes. Then it occurred to him, he and Lorna weren't married, engaged, or going steady, weren't even seeing each other enough to suit him. Maybe she was dating others. Yes, probably.

It came down to, if he jumped in the sack with Zarina, would he feel guilty when he saw Poupon? *Not very,* he thought. And when he next saw Lorna? *Not really. Not solidly guilty.* A minor pang, perhaps. Nevertheless, he would be her steady if he had the chance. And didn't he have to consider how Poupon and Lorna might react if word about their encounter got around? That's when it dawned on him that moral turmoil had extinguished his urge for an X-rated cuddle with an ex-lover on a perfect day for one. He cared very much for her. Their affair had been short and sweet, and they managed to get out of it with their friendship intact. *Not bad,* Kendrick thought, *how often does that happen?*

"I was just remembering our hotel in Florence," Zarina said, "the frescoes on the walls, those gorgeous carved beams. I'm not sure if you realize how incredible that was—leaving my life and stepping into another.

"Excuse me for differing," Kendrick said, "but what sticks in my mind was before we ordered room service . . ."

"And you ordered a bottle of Chianti older than I was. I loved it, even if I usually only like whites."

"I've forgotten the name of the wine," Kendrick said, "but I'll never forget that we made love all afternoon until the streetlamps came on outside our window."

"Yes, I was wondering if you were ever going to climax. Wondered if you knew how. Not really, Kendrick. Just teasing. Anyway, it was also a treat to see the kind of world you work in—all the restaurants, the cellars, so many wines to taste, people to meet."

"Speaking of wine," Kendrick said, "it is entirely legal to have a glass right now if we want to."

"Why not? Then I have to pick up my daughter from school."

Kendrick decided on a nice bottle of plump Meursault from a sunny vintage because he knew Zarina's taste. Too much acidity, and she wouldn't touch the stuff—seemed almost insulted by it, as if the winemaker had done it on purpose.

Once Kendrick had poured the wine and they'd clinked glasses, he asked if she'd seen Poupon recently.

"Not since you saw me leaving him that day. He treats me like I mean nothing to him. I don't need that."

"Do you love him? You've never said."

"Sometimes we're very good together. You could say that when he loves me, yes, I do love him. It's as if he really does love me, but something inside him won't let it get out."

"Aren't a lot of men like that?"

Tears came to Zarina's eyes. "I'm so tired of it all," she said. "If someone can't treat me right, I'm gone. It's just not worth it. Yes, he's called, said he's sorry, asked forgiveness, but I told him it's over. That last time I left, when you were there, I needed to know does he love me or are we just fooling around."

Kendrick raised the bottle of Meursault to pour another glass, but she said she had to hurry off so her daughter wouldn't have to wait on the street outside school.

"And you know, Kendrick, he would tell me that Babette, that glorified whore from Nice, he would tell me that she is the love of his life. He says it as if I am his best friend, not his girlfriend, not his lover, and when he sees that he's wounded me, he laughs as if he's only joking."

"He thinks he's teasing you. Poupon can be such a horse's ass. But men are strange that way—they tease someone they love because they love them. Even their own kids. They really do think it's fun for some unknown reason. I assure you, he believes both of you are enjoying the teasing, both playing a game, and when he sees that, uh-oh, perhaps he has said something he shouldn't have said, he laughs to try to let you know he's only kidding."

"Maybe Babette will enjoy his teasing, but I've removed myself from his menu."

She gave Kendrick a peck on the lips goodbye, walked down to her wreck of a car—a French jalopy that showed how she barely had enough money to live on—and off she went, bouncing down the hill with springs squeaking.

Kendrick vowed to himself to buy her a new car before he returned to Seattle. Then he telephoned Poupon. "Monsieur Poupon, bonsoir. Does the Mighty Poupon have dinner plans?"

"Sort of," Poupon answered. "I just put a rabbit to cook on top of the stove with some thyme branches and garlic. It's a rabbit that's been devouring the leaves of young Mourvèdre I planted this year up by the fig tree. After a diet of that, you know it should be tasty. Oh *merde*, I forgot bay leaves. Rabbit without bay? That's like trying to jump rope with one leg."

"Well, bring the pot over and let's eat here. I found some good-looking sardines in Sanary. We can grill them outside, enjoy the end of the day. The clouds are gone, and it feels like it's warming up."

"Anything else I can bring?"

"No, nothing. I found a well-aged Comté—forty months old. And Poupon, I need to make space in my cellar—you can help me empty it out tonight, so don't bring any of your homemade plonk."

"Hey, watch your tongue. You're not making me feel very welcome."

"Well, aren't you turning sensitive in your old age? I'm just teasing, Poupon. Ha ha, get it?"

Poupon chuckled. "You're sure I can't bring along anything? Maybe a magnum of rosé? I made it myself."

"Bring along a smoke. No, two. One for outdoors with the aperitif, and another for after dinner."

"Well, at least I'm good for something, but only because you're too cheap to buy your own cigarettes."

"If I kept some around, I might end up sucking them to death like you do."

"Touché," Poupon said. "See you soon."

About an hour later, Poupon arrived with his rabbit still hot in the casserole and a straw basket of red and orange mushrooms.

"Beautiful," Kendrick said. "They look so fresh, like you hunted them on your way over."

"They're for the grill," Poupon said.

"How did you think I'd cook them? Boiled?"

"No, of course not, but everyone knows you Americans like everything fried. That's how we French see Americans. You drink your liquids almost frozen. Ice cubes in everything. Even tea. And food crispy-fried."

"Jesus, Poupon, America is the barbecue capital of the world. Where do you frogs get all your weird ideas?"

"Frogs?"

Outdoors, Kendrick crumpled up some newspapers on the ground and put a bundle of dried grapevine branches on top. Poupon stepped forward with his lighter and put the flame to paper. While the branches blazed brightly, Kendrick chopped garlic and parsley and added them to a bowl with some olive oil, salt, and the orange-colored mushrooms.

"Aren't you feeling well?" Poupon inquired. He looked at Kendrick with concern.

"Feeling fine."

"You seem out of sorts. No psychological trauma, concussion, stroke, death in the family?"

"Not at all. I'm the same old me. Why do you ask?"

"Well, I've been here ten minutes and I'm still parched with thirst, so I figure you must be fucked up some way or another."

"You're right. What a lamentable lack of hospitality. Do you need to lie down while I prepare a cure for what ails you?"

"You run and prepare my cure while I toss the mushrooms on the grill. The coals look about right."

"See the sardine grill propped up there? Put them on, too."

Kendrick returned with a bottle, two wine glasses, and a corkscrew. While he pulled out the cork, he told Poupon that he'd seen Zarina earlier in the day.

"How'd she seem?"

"Bright-eyed, bushy-tailed."

"That sounds like our main course."

"She laughed at all my jokes."

"Ha, she must really like you because you're about as funny as a dead cat."

It was time for the two wine professionals to sniff and sip.

Poupon did so and said, "*Merde!*" He then took a longer sniff and a larger sip. He sloshed it around in his mouth a few times and swallowed. "*Putain,* but that's good. For a white. I've never had anything quite like it before. Where's it from?"

Kendrick slid the sardines onto a platter, then with prongs he took off the mushrooms one by one and placed them alongside the fish. "It's Italian, from the hills above Lake Garda."

"It makes my white seem like horse piss."

"No comment."

They ate with their hands and threw the sardine skeletons onto the dying embers.

"I should have served these as separate courses," Kendrick said. "They don't exactly go together, mushrooms and sardines."

"Hey, what's your problem? We're not painting the Vatican ceiling. It's just Poupon and Kendrick, remember?" He gazed around quickly. "And what a perfect evening. We're just a couple of dumb fucks lucky to be eating at all. And this wine! *Merde*. I should sell my winery and look for another job."

They clinked glasses, and Kendrick changed the subject. "Anything new in the Poupon-Zarina drama?"

Poupon's mouth twitched. He raised a paw to still it. He blinked three or four times. Kendrick almost choked on his Quintarelli bianco when he saw a teardrop make its way down Poupon's craggy cheek.

"I've been trying to write her a letter," he said. "It never turns out how I want it to."

"Which is how?"

"It's hard to say it, but I'm not happy when she's not around. That's all. I think about it, you know, but when I've got the pencil and paper in front of me, it comes out all twisted."

"Have you called her to tell her you want to see her?"

"Oh yeah. You know what she said? She said, 'Why me? Is Queen Babette busy?' *Putain!* I've gotten myself into a real fix. Why can't I just love one of them? Or, even better, have them both? That could have been so beautiful."

Kendrick wondered again if he should tell Poupon about Babette's husband's suspicious death, but he decided to wait for more of the story from Lorna.

As they moved into the kitchen to continue dinner, Kendrick asked Poupon if he'd noticed how well the white wine went with the mushrooms.

"Sure, sure it did, I guess, but by then my mind was on Zarina. Why the hell did you have to mention her?"

"I only said that I'd seen her today."

Poupon shook his head. "Oh, I know it's not your fault. It's me. I'm going to mail her this letter, tell her I love her, and once I say goodbye to Babette, Zarina and I can get married. I could take care of her and her daughters, you know? Offer them a real home."

At table with Poupon's rabbit, they ate Kendrick's potato gratin, which he'd thrown together and put in the oven about an hour earlier. He lined the bottom of the gratin dish with bay leaves, sliced the potatoes fairly thin, and layered them. Over each layer he sprinkled salt, pepper, slivers of fresh garlic, and olive oil. Lots of olive oil. Then he added enough water to almost cover the potatoes and placed the gratin into a hot oven. When Kendrick lifted it out, only olive oil remained because the water had evaporated. Olive oil flavored with bay and garlic. The toughest part of the recipe, if you asked him, was finding potatoes decent enough to bother with.

He poured a twenty-year-old Morgon from the Beaujolais as Poupon continued.

"My first two marriages didn't work out so well," he said.

"You found two women willing to marry you? They must have been either super courageous or really dumb."

"You jerk," Poupon said, laughing. "You know deep down why women are more attracted to me than to you, and it's not only my wonderful personality."

"I'm sure you're right about what it isn't, not so sure you're as good in bed as you think you are."

"You'll be the last to know. Anyway, I'm serious, so listen. My first wife was from Alsace, and she . . ."

Kendrick, astonished, interrupted him. "Alsace? You've got to be joking. Are you making this up?"

"What's wrong? What's wrong with Alsace?"

"Poupon, I know Alsace. I've been going there for years. Mixing you with an Alsatian woman is the least likely matchup I can imagine. It's like trying to mix an iceberg with a forest fire. Something's got to give."

"Well, I couldn't understand why she always seemed to be mad, always pissed off at me, you know? Finally, she simply quit speaking to me. Then she wouldn't even look at me. It was like I'd disappeared.

And, one day, she disappeared. No note, nothing. I think she moved back to Wiedergestucken."

"Your rabbit is sensational," Kendrick said.

"And here"—Poupon gestured broadly as if taking in the whole kitchen—"you and me, did we ever create a perfect marriage. The rabbit, the gratin, and then there's this delicious wine, it's nothing but perfume and flavor."

"Yeah," Kendrick said. "You don't even notice the body."

"But you know," Poupon said, "that wasn't true of wife number two. Even a saint like you would have noticed her body." Poupon turned up both hands in front of his chest as if he were carrying something weighty in each one. "*Abbondanza!*" he yelled and let out a cock-a-doodle-doo. "Oh Kendrick, I wish you could have been there, or at least that I'd taken some photos. There's no way I can put into words the magnificence, the way they sloped downward and outward at the same time, the slow-motion way they swayed back and forth—they were masterpieces!"

Kendrick searched for a play on words: masterpiece, master piece of ass, but no, in French it wouldn't work, and Poupon would wrinkle up his forehead, not understanding. He also realized that it didn't work in English, either. Or at least not very well.

"Oh lord, Kendrick, did I ever have fun."

Kendrick was enjoying the show. "However," he said, "obviously two breasts were not enough to keep the marriage together. What happened?"

"Sure, but first give me a refill—more potatoes, please, and pass that bottle to me. So, one day she up and announces that if I don't stop drinking, she'll divorce me. Can you imagine? I'm a vigneron. Drinking is almost my métier."

"It was a choice, then?" Kendrick said. "You had to choose between her and wine?"

"Well, wine, sure, and pastis. An occasional beer during soccer matches. Anyway, then she went gaga over yoga and meditation, and there was some quack in Toulon who she saw every week whether she was sick or not. Biorhythms or something like that, controlled by acupuncture. I'll bet I know what he was puncturing. First, she quit smoking. Then everything we ate had to be organic. Suddenly, even a smidgeon of smoke bugged her all to hell. So I found myself with two ex-wives and missing terribly my second wife's finer qualities."

"Well said, *mon ami*. Her 'qualities.' How gallant. I like that." Kendrick refilled both glasses until he saw the sediment start pouring out of the bottle. "And now you're going to write to Zarina and ask her to marry you?"

"Well, to move in with me, yes, just like being married. But then, every time I think I'm going to ask her, I think of how I might have a chance for something I never thought I could possess—a woman of class, of higher station. It shows what I've made of myself. I mean, if it does happen."

"You mean Babette d'Orsini, right? And you're playing the Cinderella role."

Poupon's expression turned dreamy. He giggled. "I just never thought a farmer like me, peasant stock and all, might land a woman so sophisticated, almost an aristocrat."

"Let's go outside and have that after-dinner smoke," Kendrick said. He'd had enough of Poupon's Babette fixation for one day and was ready for the evening to be over.

Poupon continued to lament his dilemma until Kendrick pulled a euro coin out of his pants pocket.

"See the head? That's Zarina. The other side is Babette." He flipped it, caught it, and slapped it down upon his left wrist. "There! Problem solved. It's heads. Now shut up and let me enjoy my smoke."

CHAPTER THIRTY-TWO

Kendrick had to leave at ten a.m. for the Bandol train station and an eight-hour trip to Bordeaux and its roughly six thousand wine châteaux. Once out from between his sheets and fully dressed, he decided he was in the mood for a *petit déjeuner du vigneron*, or, a wine grower's breakfast.

Not so long ago, when vignerons set out at sunrise to work their vines, each took along a snack and a bottle of wine. Around nine a.m., they'd take a break and meet in little groups throughout the vineyards to snack and exchange news. Usually the snack was handy trio: a *saucisson*, half a baguette, and a hunk of cheese. Kendrick wasn't crazy about today's baguettes, so he toasted a slice of *levain*, sliced a few rounds of *saucisson*, plus half a round of goat cheese. He raided his cellar and brought up a half bottle of Gigondas. In the old days, vignerons each showed up with a bottle to taste and discuss. It was a great exchange of information and learning from one another's experiences. Kendrick was thinking how sad it was that with today's tractors, there weren't many breakfasts in the vines like there used to be. Today, who can eat and share experiences when a tractor is belching exhaust fumes and noise pollution all over the place? On the other hand, not many would volunteer to trade their tractor and go back to a horse and plow.

He was packed and ready to leave for his train when the phone rang. He wasn't in the mood and almost didn't answer, but when he did, after seven rings, it was Lorna Darlington, private detective.

"Listen," she said, "I'm in my car. I have some work to do in Marseille for another client, but I was wondering if by any chance you might be free afterward."

"Oh no. Damn it. I'm just leaving for Bordeaux. I have five days of tasting scheduled. Why, do you have some news about Babette?"

"Not yet. I'll finish in Marseille this afternoon around five—just thought maybe you and I could grab something to eat, and either I'd drive home afterward or find a hotel room somewhere near Bandol and head home tomorrow morning."

"My god, you're breaking my heart. I would have loved to see you."

"I'm expecting news from Serbia any day now," she said. "I'll let you know, and we'll get together then."

"Over lunch or dinner," he said. "Promise?"

"Love to. Happy wine tasting."

Kendrick headed to the Bandol train station. As soon as he found his seat on the train, he pulled out a book. He was in the very middle of the first-class railway car where two rows of seats faced each other, which is typical on France's TGV. Luckily, the occupant across from him was not very tall, so tangled legs were not a problem. The fellow looked to be about seventy or so, his head ringed by wispy white hair. He had high, puffy cheeks, chipmunk-like, and glasses with thick magnifying lenses that made his eyes twice their actual size. As he peered at the cover of the book Kendrick was settling in to read, he looked ever ready to open his mouth about something. About halfway to La Ciotat, Kendrick sensed that the old fellow could no longer control himself. He was right.

"Excuse me, monsieur. The last thing I wish to do is interrupt anyone lost in concentration with a good book, but are you by any chance a connoisseur of fine wines?"

As a matter of fact, Kendrick detested train and airline conversations, because once begun, how do you put an end to it without appearing snotty? He raised his eyes and winced when he found two immense, beady black eyes intently staring back at him with an expression tingling with exhilaration.

"I'm in the business," Kendrick said and looked quickly down to take up the text again. He groaned inside, regretting not having said just the opposite. Something like *Never touch the stuff,* but no, even that wouldn't have stopped Monsieur Beady Eyes.

"Hmm," the fellow said, "*Cepages et Terroirs du Languedoc,* by Pierre Lagravière." He chuckled humbly. "What would you say if I told you—oh, this is too much, ho ho, quite a coincidence—that I once served on a committee with Professor Lagravière and that we coauthored the pamphlet *A Socio-Economic History of the Languedoc Region Between 1914 and 1945*? Sometimes—I am compelled to say it—Lagravière had his point of view, and I mine. For example, he concluded that safer drinking water led the French nation to slowly but surely reduce their wine consumption, while I argued that better schooling alerted the citizenry to the dangers of drunkenness. The two World Wars were rather sobering as well, in my opinion."

The train was passing through the vine-covered hills of Cassis by then, so it was about halfway to Marseille, where they would have to change trains. Unfortunately, Languedoc and Bordeaux were in the same direction, and Kendrick realized that he might be face-to-face with his new acquaintance for hours.

"Very interesting, but I must finish this book by evening," Kendrick lied, "and really don't have the time for conversation—even about wine."

Monsieur Beady Eyes clapped his hands emphatically. "Ha! Understood. Really, sir, I know the feeling. Yes, when one has to have information for a speech—or maybe you are writing a thesis of sorts? Do I detect an accent, by the way? Just curious."

"Yes, American." Downward went Kendrick's eyes again.

"Ah, an English speaker but not an Englishman—I've hit ze nail on ze head," he said and then continued to pester Kendrick in English.

"You say you are a member of ze wine profession," he said. "If so, I can alert you to certain, how do you say, inexactitudes in the work you are reading. I'm afraid our Professor Lagravière, the author of your text— You are not of his acquaintance, are you?"

Kendrick looked up, shook his head, and relentlessly looked down. Yet again.

"I'm afraid he relies on his own advices and not of experts more knowledgeable than he. Even in ze first *chapitre,* ze very first *chapitre . . .*"

On and on he droned until Kendrick's brain was ready to explode into a million particles. The train squealed loudly to a stop in Aubagne. Kendrick stood up abruptly and took his suitcase down from the rack.

"Sorry, monsieur, but I forgot my pocket flask of whiskey, and I need a drink. A strong one." He jumped down off the train seven and a half hours from Bordeaux, hurried out the station door to the hot, asphalt parking lot, and finally into the first taxi in line.

"Le Caniveau," Kendrick said to the driver. "I'll explain how to find the house once we get there." He pulled out his phone and called Lorna. "Hey, it's Kendrick. I hope you're still free later because my plans have changed for the better. Why don't you come over to my place, and we'll decide what to do about dinner over a glass of wine? Great! From Marseille, you take the autoroute A50 along the coast toward Toulon, but you'll exit one exit before Bandol. Yes, it's indicated. The sign says L'Estournel and Le Caniveau. When you get to Le Caniveau, pull over and call me. I'll drive down to lead you back up the hill to my place. It's too hard to explain."

Then he called his office in Paris. He pinched his nose closed with his free hand and said, nasally, "Hello, Rachel, it's me, Kendrick. Listen, I've developed a sinus infection. It's horrid. Yes, Dr. Mardon filled me up with a five-day course of antibiotics, but I can't smell a damned thing, can't even tell whether a wine is young, old, or in between. You'll have to cancel all my appointments in Bordeaux. No, not sure about next week yet. We'll see how the pills work. Talk to you later." He leaned back, quite satisfied with himself because he'd found a fabulous way to use the sinus infection he'd suffered not so long ago.

CHAPTER THIRTY-THREE

From the taxi as it navigated the narrow driveway, Kendrick thought Milles Vents was looking good, certainly much better than the inside of a train where they might seat you face-to-face for several hours dealing with the most boring example of humankind you could possibly imagine. You boarded the train sane, then they carted you off a blithering idiot. Yes, Milles Vents—idyllic, rustic, timeless, the sun baking down, a hint of breeze to temper the heat, the sky overhead clear except way out at sea where a cloudbank was discernible. It felt like the power of the sun would have no trouble keeping those clouds at bay.

Kendrick paid the taxi driver and quickly got to work. First he called Poupon with a proposition: "I'll trade you a couple bottles of that Italian white you liked so much for some game birds or a rabbit or something."

"You mean bottles of that sweet white from Lake Garda?"

"Sweet? What are you talking about?"

"I mean, it's a sweet wine. Everyone knows Americans have a sweet tooth. They talk dry, sure, but they drink sweet. I had it explained to me, and by a real connoisseur. Leave some sugar in to thicken a wine, and Americans will call it luscious."

"You are measurably cuckoo."

Poupon laughed. "Don't be so defensive. Me, I make dry wine. No wonder you like the Italian wine better."

"You go screw yourself. You really think I can't tell the difference between . . ."

"Ha. You jerk. Can't you take a joke? You fell for that one—admit it."

"Okay, you got me," Kendrick said and halfheartedly joined the laughter coming from the other end of the line. "Now, do you want to trade or waste more of my time?"

"Oh, excuse me, monsieur, but I believe you called me."

"Sorry, Poupon. You're right again. But I do have a lot to do."

"It must be a woman. I've never heard this side of you. All business. How about a couple of pigeons? Would that work?"

"Sure, great."

"Or a guinea hen? I pulled the trigger on it yesterday—haven't even had time to put it in the freezer yet."

"Even better. I can see it now, roasted slowly until it falls apart, with black olives and red peppers in the pot. Maybe a couple of anchovies in there, too."

"Whatever," Poupon said, "but tell me, your hot date, what are you going to do if she tries to get in your pants?"

"No problem. I'll call you and ask you to take care of it for me."

"Anything for a pal. But seriously now, for the bird, if I'm not home, just go into the winery door next to the garage. I'll plume the hen and get it ready for you. It'll be in the fridge just to the left of the door."

"Poupon, are you crazy? You're still leaving things unlocked?"

"Calm down. Save your energy for tonight. And don't forget my two bottles of bianco. Above all, don't do anything I wouldn't do."

Kendrick ate the sack lunch he had prepared for the train, then put on the Larghetto of Mozart's Clarinet Quintet for mood music while he napped. Afterward, he went up to the top of the property to clean the swimming pool and brought the towels down for washing. Then he headed off here and there, shopping for dinner and beyond, because, given his planned departure to Bordeaux, his fridge was nearly empty.

Lorna called from the parking lot of Le Caniveau's soccer field, and Kendrick succeeded in talking her up the road. He laughed at himself when he realized how excited he was, standing on the terrace, looking down the hill, stretching his neck waiting for her. A yellow convertible came into view. Her hair blew gently behind her, and her car kicked up dust from the dirt road. She beeped her horn in greeting when she saw him.

She wore an almost simple green skirt. Almost. He wondered how to describe it. Green on green? Slightly darker green stripes, or possibly pleats on the green background—and when she moved, there was a subtle action of color and form to hold your attention. Or was it some kind of optical illusion? Top it with a short-sleeved pink blouse, and you have a classic color combo that reminded Kendrick of the cover of Elvis's first LP and the Clash's *London Calling*. It looked cool, daring, and punk, all at once. She leaned in to cheek him, but he said, "Hey, wait. We're not French." And he proceeded to give her a good old American smack on the lips.

It was warm out, so, right off the bat, Kendrick invited her up to the pool for a swim. She said she didn't pack a bathing suit, which caused Kendrick to wonder if she neglected to bring one on purpose. After all, they were on the Mediterranean coast. Didn't she keep a suit handy in her car the way Kendrick did? He almost allowed a lecherous grin to sneak out when he told her not to worry, that undies would be fine (which, *ooh la la*, turned out to be true) and that, anyway, he could barely see without his glasses (which wasn't true). They swam, and it was difficult for him to concentrate on where he was as he basked in the glistening marvelousness of her fanny rising up above the wavelets. Diaphanous undies? He approved, but it wasn't enough. No, he wanted them off. It was the most important thing in the world. And damned if he didn't talk her out of them. First, he removed his Calvin Klein's and threw them up poolside, then said something about how if she was like him, she enjoyed the freedom you feel when skinny-dipping.

"How very right you are," she said after swimming a few strokes top- and bottomless. "Undies don't weigh anything, but once you shed them, what a difference."

After a couple of laps, she stood against the edge of the pool and leaned back on her elbows, which just happened to lift up and out of the water two deliciously formed parts of her anatomy. Lorna pushed back her hair and shook her head like a cocker spaniel, flinging drops of water all over the place and instigating one of the favorite motions of many a man.

Kendrick's pool wasn't heated, but it was heating up. He patiently swam several more laps so as to not appear too eager, then waded over to stand facing Lorna. "What a day, isn't it?" he said, gesturing at the vast blue sky, the sea, the mountains. Then the two of them seemed to fall together into a kiss, which inspired a second, and then a third which went on and on, on and on. Meanwhile, underwater, a certain part of Kendrick went knocking at a certain part of Lorna, which responded by welcoming him into something that prompted him to think of liquid velvet. Yes, easy as pie, he was inside. After a while he pulled his lips away from hers to suggest they move onto one of the poolside recliners. Which they did, and which offered more freedom of movement.

"Don't worry," Kendrick said, "only the birds and the bees can see us up here." He forgot to mention the miniature red squirrel who lived in the pines above the pool.

Kendrick makes love the way he drinks wine. No chugalugger, he likes to linger, savor the details. He appreciated lovemaking with a long aftertaste, what he called sharing the afterglow.

Then, what could be better than a dive back into the hillside pool after a cold glass of the local rosé? So, Kendrick barefooted it to the stone pool house, opened the fridge, and came back to Lorna with two glasses of just that.

CHAPTER THIRTY-FOUR

Together on the terrace where Kendrick had already set the table, Lorna looked it over and said, "So, I take it we're eating in."

"A masterful deduction, Holmes, but the truth is, if you prefer eating out, it's fine by me. Poupon blessed us with a wild guinea hen, but it'll taste almost as good tomorrow. Would you like a glass of anything?"

"If it's up to me, I'd say that the occasion, which is far from everyday, at least for me, calls for Champagne."

Once he'd carefully twisted out the cork, in order to avoid creating too much foam, he tilted her Champagne glass as he poured, stopping when it was only about half full.

"Why do you do that?" she asked. "Don't you like the foam?"

"Well, it's actually better if the tiny bubbles stay inside the Champagne and don't vanish into thin air. The Champagne-maker, hopefully, put a lot of effort into the quality of those bubbles, so it would be a shame to allow them to dissipate uselessly."

It was still daylight. A warm, quiet, windless evening, late enough that the swallows were showing up to begin their nightly skyborn feeding frenzy. From the Pageot house, they heard a child cry, the mother screamed something, then a second time, and very quickly one slammed door followed another.

"Neighbors," Lorna said and held up her glass of Champagne.

"Here's not to them," Kendrick said and raised his to clink against hers.

"I wondered if you poured our glasses only half full so the Champagne wouldn't heat up?"

"Hmm. Too warm. Never thought of that. If you hold it by the stem, your hand won't warm it up. But no, I do it so I can swirl it better, which helps release a wine's aroma. Champagne is wine. The aroma is important." He raised his glass. "Here's to you," he said, gazing into her hazel-colored eyes. "You look ravishing, even with your clothes on."

"Actually, I'm feeling rather ravished, inside and out."

They each managed to down a sip in the midst of their self-satisfied grins.

"Yum," Kendrick said, "you look good enough to eat."

She took another sip and licked her ruby red lips. "Don't make promises you don't intend to keep. Oh my god! Two sips of bubbly and listen to me."

"Happy to," Kendrick said. "All night long if you want."

"Don't tell me you think I'm going to drink Champagne and then who-knows-what kind of wine you're going to serve with the bird, and then I'm going to say au revoir and drive all the way back to Nice? Oh no. If you don't want me in your bed, a couch will do."

"I want you in my bed. Is that understood?" he asked sternly. Everything seemed to give them a good reason to laugh.

The Champagne bottle was still more than half full when Kendrick uncorked a white Hermitage. He retired the Champagne flutes and poured the Hermitage into standard wine glasses. It was not really white—more of a golden hue. That's when Lorna asked Kendrick to teach her how to taste wine.

"You're a pro. Pretend you're teaching a class of rookies. In the future, if we have one, of whatever kind, I'll bet you'll enjoy my company more if I'm not always saying dumb things about your area of expertise."

"Okay, but first . . ." He took the Champagne bottle out of the ice bucket, poured the ice and water into a flowerpot, and set the bucket at their feet.

"Why in the world did you do that?" Lorna asked.

"If you're a pro, you have to learn how to spit. That's lesson number one. Wine kindergarden." Kendrick gave the Hermitage a sniff, took a sip, sucked air into his mouth, chewed around for a moment, then spit the sip into the bucket. *Kerplunk!*

"If the wine is good, do I have to spit it out? I mean, we're just pretending, right?"

"Lorna. Did you get your PhD by arguing with your professors?"

"God no. I kissed ass. That's how I did it."

"I can attest, it's taken you far, but now let's see what kind of spitter you are."

She tried to copy him. Part of her wine dribbled into the bucket, part onto the floor, and the rest down her chin.

"Okay, don't feel bad. Your aim could show a little more precision. It's like target practice with a gun—practice makes bull's-eyes."

"Or bull something-or-other," mumbled Lorna.

"Listen, kiddo, let's say I take you tasting with me. No student of mine is going to graduate and embarrass me by spitting onto some winemaker's white sneakers."

"That really happens?"

"Especially if there's no spittoon and you're underground spitting wine onto a dirt floor. And don't think people won't notice. There is one English wine critic, every time he spits, you would swear the wine splatters all over his shirt and tie. It's hard not to laugh when you see him take aim, trying to spit accurately, and the wine burbles all over every which way."

"The poor man," Lorna said. "He must be courageous to spend a good part of his time looking ridiculous."

Kendrick did a double take, as if considering Lorna anew. "Yes," he said, nodding with a mix of agreement and admiration. "Never thought of it like that. He must know what he looks like when he spits, poor chap, must hear the snickering. In professional wine tastings, in a way, you're in the spotlight. Not a big spotlight, but people are observing. The absolute worst for me is when I suck air in over the wine in my mouth, and some of it gets sucked down the wrong pipe. Result? A grotesque coughing and wheezing for air at the same time—no way to hide it, and it can go on for what seems to be forever while your face grows redder and redder. Or, when I swirl my wine around in the glass and end up with a streak of it across my chest. So, lesson number two—never go wine tasting in a white shirt."

He had Lorna take ten straight spit-shots at the bucket. She did, and her increased precision was obvious.

"See," Kendrick said, "you just had a glass of rosé at the pool and a couple of glasses of Champagne. If you hadn't spit out this Hermitage, you'd really be feeling the alcohol right now. If you go tasting with me someday when I'm working, you might have to taste up to two or three hundred different wines or cuvées."

"I still prefer to swallow," she answered.

"Just the kind of woman I've been looking for," he said. "Anyway, you'll do fine at spitting. Now, on to the actual tasting experience. First, use your eyes. Look at the wine in your glass. A white background is handy. Here, this napkin will serve, but first, hold your glass up like this."

They held their glasses up to eye level.

"What color is the wine?" he asked.

"It's gold with greenish glints," she said.

"Perfect. Now hold it over this white napkin."

"Strange. Now it's just golden."

"Hold it up again. There they are—the green glints. Now lower the glass without lowering your eyes. What do you see?"

"Oh my. Of course. The vineyard and the cypress trees along the driveway, which explains the green glints in my glass."

"And that's why it's best to have a colorless background. I usually carry a notebook with white pages in my left hand, and the glass and a pen in my right hand. Listen, is that enough for your first lesson?" Kendrick asked. "Are you starting to feel hungry?"

"Absolutely, and what I smell coming from the kitchen must be the *pintade*. But first, why spend time looking at a wine?"

"It's usually just a quick glance, but it is important. As a professional, I'm looking for flaws. If the Hermitage looked brownish instead of golden, I'd be afraid it had been badly stored or was too old. Don't forget, though, part of the pleasure of a wine can be visual, so you want to be looking at the wine's color, hoping simply to be dazzled by the beauty of it. But watch out. A lot of people are impressed when they see a black, inky wine, as if opaque is some kind of achievement, a sign of a remarkable wine."

Kendrick told her he'd be right back, then went into the house and returned with a book. He leafed through and found what he was looking for. "This is what Henri Jayer said about red Burgundy. He was one of the twentieth century's best winemakers.

Black is not the color of Burgundy wine. You must be able to see through a glass of it. The Pinot Noir has a pretty robe, glistening and shimmering like a cat's eyes, sparkling like a diamond.

"To make a wine with a color like that takes talent," Kendrick continued. "Anyone can do black. Black wines can be found as close as the nearest supermarket. And sorry to have to say it, but these days a winemaker can easily add color—you know, dye a wine as dark as he or she wants."

To accompany the Hermitage, Kendrick slowly scrambled some of his chicken's eggs with sea urchin roe. He decided it was not the time to inform Lorna that what is called roe from a sea urchin is, in fact, the creature's gonads.

Lorna took a bite and closed her eyes. "When the flavor of the eggs meets up with the flavor of the Hermitage, it's like a starburst. It's intense. A happening."

Kendrick clinked glasses with her and said, "Here's to us and many momentous moments."

"Wait, what's that lewd smile mean? Oh, like up at the pool?"

For the *pintade*, or guinea hen, he decanted a 1983 Châteauneuf-du-Pape from Henri Brunier. He poured two glasses half full and watched Lorna look into her glass, then swirl and take a sniff.

"No way I'm spitting this one," she said.

Kendrick took a sniff and left his nose in the glass. "It is a wine that has a lot to say." He took a sip and closed his eyes, exhaling a sigh of pleasure.

"What does it say to you?" she asked.

"I think it's a great bottle at every stage of the tasting experience—robe, aroma, palate, and don't miss that gloriously stony aftertaste.

Three of your senses are engaged—sight, smell, and taste. The wine says harmony, and you see that power and finesse can coexist. But I must say, that lingering finesse wasn't there twenty-two years ago. When it was a youngster, it was a rambunctious powerhouse."

"Aren't I supposed to smell berries or roses or something like that? Do you?"

"No, but I smell Provençal herbs, and there is definitely a stony quality in there. Speaking of stones, do you like the Rolling Stones?"

"I can't say that any of them are exactly my cup of tea sexually, but I do like to jump in the sack with some of their songs."

"Well, this red is like "Stray Cat Blues" in a bottle—tough and sexy, but beware, it'll leave claw marks on your back."

Later, they crawled into bed with sugar plum fairies all in their heads and woke up the next morning in a playful mood. When Lorna had to hit the road and return to Nice, it felt like tearing something apart.

CHAPTER THIRTY-FIVE

Kendrick's metal mailbox was stacked with sixteen others down on the main road seven or eight hundred yards from the house. It had been arranged so the mailwoman wouldn't have to bounce all over those bumpy hillside dirt roads delivering to each home. Being bounced to smithereens was not part of her job description. In the early years, Kendrick enjoyed the walk for his mail with its scenic view down and back, but lately it had become necessary to try and avoid some of his neighbors. Running into Madame Bonacieux, for example, meant at least half an hour without getting a word in edgewise, hearing again and again about her dead husband, her two incredibly gifted grandchildren, and her horrid neighbor from Alsace, Herr Kintzler. An encounter with Kintzler himself entailed hearing the latest examples of how lazy southerners cannot compare to the master race. And the two housemates with the mad dog? Kendrick couldn't bear them on principle, the principle being those with snarling, mentally deranged dogs do not have the right to be recognized as fellow human beings. And, finally, on Kendrick's to-avoid list, the decrepit, saddest sack of Le Caniveau, Bertrand Iliac. Fired from a managerial position in the nearby munitions factory, he fell from his rather low heights and proceeded to lose his wife to their idiot son's best friend, the driver of one of Le Caniveau's three taxis. Kendrick was astonished how quickly Bertrand's physical appearance had become racked by the emotional blows he suffered. His arms, legs, and back were shriveled and bent, and he caned slowly here and there, half ghost. Even his hair had turned into melancholy gray wisps. He was always searching for someone to stop and complain to, tell them that life is the shits, and with the passing years, it stinks more and more. *Thanks, Bertrand, always a pleasure.*

Kendrick's mailbox contained a good half-pound of useless publicity. Yet again, he mentally kicked himself for never remembering to buy a *Pas de Pub* sticker. He sorted through to make sure nothing important was hidden in all the junk and found his phone bill and a folded sheet of cheap notepad paper. No envelope, no return address. Unfolded, it read *Stay home Tuesday for the Adventures of Toin-Toin.* Kendrick hadn't checked his mail in the last two or three days, and today was, in fact, Tuesday. To Kendrick that could only mean one of three things: there would be a television program about Corsica, a visit from Toin-Toin or somebody else from Corsica, or that the dread antenna would be blown up during the night—no more eyesore, no more microwaves, no more brain cancers.

He walked down into Le Caniveau and bought a television schedule and a sticker for his mailbox but couldn't find anything about Corsica in Tuesday's television schedule. So, one possibility eliminated. It was not an easy morning for Kendrick because he kept thinking of possible scenarios. If a Corsican were to visit, in his judgment that would happen before eleven or noon, while a bomb blast at the base of the antenna would take place in the dead of night. At ten thirty, suffering from nervous energy, he began arranging salad makings on the kitchen counter. He had green- and red-leaf batavias from his garden, cilantro leaves, avocado, four seven-minute eggs, and a can of tuna belly. He rinsed the salt off some caper berries—pity the poor green salad, according to Kendrick, that didn't have salt-cured caper berries— and rinsed the salt off a few of his own home-cured anchovies. Both were chopped into little specks that went into a wooden salad bowl, a large one for easy mixing. For the vinaigrette, he chopped up a shallot, threw in some salt and dried thyme, and added a little of Poupon's very own red wine vinegar. After a minute or two for the shallots to absorb some of the vinegar and the salt to dissolve, he added a squeeze or so of lemon juice—to give it all a little thrill—and finished with several glugs of olive oil.

He poured himself a second glass of Baltazaru's Patrimonio blanc. That's when he heard the *crunch-crunch* of footsteps in his parking lot. Kendrick separated the cork fly curtain and stepped from the kitchen out onto the terrace just in time to greet Baltazaru walking up the curved stone staircase. He was dressed like a hiker with a green felt cap pulled low over his forehead and a pack on his back. He and Kendrick laughed upon seeing each other.

"*Mon dieu*, Baltazaru, you look like an Austrian mountain climber in that hat, and what are those pants? Lederhosen?"

"*Ja, mein Freund*," Baltazaru said and pushed through the strands of cork into the kitchen.

Kendrick grabbed another wine glass. "Did you parachute in? Where's your car?"

They clinked glasses and downed a sip.

"Ah, that's better," Baltazaru said, letting out a deep breath. "I left the car up on top of the hill in the old chapel's parking lot. Then I hiked down through the woods."

"That's quite a hike," Kendrick said. "It's totally wild, no paths left."

"You don't need to tell me. My ankles and calfs are lacerated. And do you know, you have a sizeable boar population up there above your property?"

"Unfortunately, yes. I had to put an electric fence around my vegetable garden. They don't eat the vegetables, but they tear up the irrigation lines, looking for water, I presume. Poupon wants to loan me a gun so I can thin out the herd."

Baltazaru looked around the kitchen. "Hey, good! Looks like you're about to eat. But what is this crap wine we're drinking? Surely you can afford better."

"See the label? It's yours."

"Kendrick, *mon dieu*, you must be desperate. Or were you expecting me? All those great bottles in your cellar, and, well, I'm quite moved to find you drinking one of my own. But that's handy because I brought you some goodies from the island. We can dine Corsican."

He opened up his well-worn backpack and began pulling out hand-wrapped packages of food. "All truly made in Corsica. You can be sure of that." There were cheeses, cured meats, and sausages to unwrap and prepare for serving.

"We'll need another bottle," Kendrick said. "Maybe another white for the charcuterie, then some red for those beautiful cheeses. What's this one called?"

"That's *Tomette de Brebis* from Ajaccio. But don't serve me another Corsican wine. Show me something you like from the mainland."

Kendrick brought up a Saint-Joseph blanc from the northern Rhône, a red Burgundy, and a bottle of California wine.

Baltazaru raised his thick, graying eyebrows. "Zinfandel? Where's that?"

"It's not a where," Kendrick answered. "It's a grape variety. You don't have any Zinfandel vines in France or Corsica, but there's a lot of it in California."

Lunch was served. "So, what's up?" Kendrick asked. "You park on top of the hill and fight your way down through the forest. You're wearing a disguise. The handwritten note in my mailbox . . ."

"It's about our project. I took the ferry to Marseille with my van full of wine to deliver to customers up in Paris—restaurants, wine shops. I do that six times a year, so no one thinks anything about it. We don't want any traces of my visit—even telephone records. And we don't want a neighbor to notice a car on your property with Corsican plates. *Incognito* is the word! I'll sleep on your couch and hike back up to my van at sunrise. Then I'll hit the autoroute to Paris."

"Okay," Kendrick said with a big smile. "Just in case we're being recorded, I'll call you Wolfgang. Here's a white Saint-Joseph."

They looked into the wine, sniffed, and knocked back a slug of it.

"Nothing is floating around in it," Baltazaru said, "but it's not ultra limpid. It smells like a beehive. Wax and honey. Hey, nice—there's stones in the hive, too. I love the fleshiness. It's ample, but not at all flabby."

"No, it hasn't been screwed up," Kendrick said. "Indigenous yeasts, complete malo, and, almost unheard of these days, a white that hasn't been filtered."

They gabbed about the white Saint-Joseph's grape variety and terroir until Baltazaru changed the subject. "Listen, my friend, have you looked into renting a piece of your property for the installation of an antenna?"

"It's done. I spoke to an SFR salesman, had email exchanges, and received a contract for a six-meter antenna, which, of course, I won't sign, so there's a good trail to prove that I am not anti-antennas."

"Think back. Have you ever signed a petition against cell phone antennas or donated money to any organizations?"

"No, I thought about doing so—joining the neighborhood collective, for example—but unfortunately never got around to it."

"Very good. It is no longer unfortunate. Donating money would have achieved nothing concerning that dreadful plastic cypress, but it might have cast suspicion on you if we get the job done."

Once they'd finished the salad and charcuterie, Kendrick pulled the cork from the bottle of red Burgundy. Baltazaru stretched over to take a look at the label. "I like to know what the hell I'm putting in my mouth," he said. "Mazis-Chambertin. Kendrick, what's this? My god, we're going to celebrate *before* the antenna falls? Isn't that bad luck in your part of the world? Come on, let's not tempt fate."

"We're celebrating your visit. Two wine guys like us, what's abnormal about sharing a good bottle?"

"Yes, but a Mazis? And 1990! That was a big vintage, wasn't it? Even in Côte d'Or?"

"Well, we'll just pour it and give it a taste, see what kind of vintage it was."

"It is dense," Baltazaru said, looking into his glass. He took a sniff, then looked up at Kendrick with wide eyes. "Are you pulling one of your tricks on me? I won't fall for it. This is not Pinot Noir from Burgundy. Either that, or it's not pure Pinot Noir."

The Corsican took a taste, sloshed it around, opened his mouth slightly, and sucked air over it, then chewed on it a bit, and swallowed. He stared off into the distance, studying the wine's aftertaste.

"It's grandiose," he said. "To say it is good doesn't begin to describe it. But there is some trick here. It doesn't taste like other red Burgundies."

"I like the word *grandiose*," Kendrick said. "It fits this wine perfectly. And Mazis is, in fact, a *grand cru*. One expects a *grand cru* to be grandiose, but to experience one worthy of that description is too rare."

"He's a rugged fellow, our Mazis," Baltazaru said. "The density on the palate and the depth are not typical of red Burgundy. No, it is suggestive of a red from the south. It could be a blend of Cornas and Burgundy."

"I see what you mean, but some southern notes might be due to the vintage—1990 was a warm year all across France. The grapes were ripe, and this wine tastes ripe. However, you were right in the sense that it is not typical Pinot Noir. It is from a plot of very old vines. According to Bernard Maume, who made this Mazis, it is from pre-clonal Pinot Noir. He says the grape bunches are smaller and tighter than today's clonal selections. And the individual grapes, too—very small and thick-skinned."

Baltazaru had another taste. Every bit of him was concentrated on what the Mazis had to say. "That might explain the exceptional tannin," he said. "I've never had a Burgundian red with such beautiful tannins. One could say that by comparison, the wines from modern clonal selections are dilute, that there is not at all the same textural interest, the same sappy intensity, the same grip—yet, with all that, try to imagine a more perfect finesse. The iron fist in the velvet glove, as the Burgundians used to say."

"Right. Today's clones don't have much of a fist and not much velvet, either."

"Feel how it stains the palate, how it penetrates. Like a symphony from Herr Beethoven," Baltazaru said. He stood and held his arm out as if inviting the heavenly choir down to sing hosannas to a miracle. "This is one great bottle of wine."

"There are a couple more points of interest," Kendrick said. "When Maume inherited them, the vines were already old. He told me that in the vineyard there were Pinot Gris vines mixed in with

Pinot Noir—much like the presence of Viognier in the Côte-Rôtie appellation. When his ancestors planted a vineyard, they planted a Pinot Gris vine every now and then, so, in fact, it is indeed as you suggested, Pinot Noir blended with another grape variety, but, strangely enough, a white grape variety."

"Viognier must have been planted to add perfume to Côte-Rôtie's Syrah, but in Burgundy the Pinot Gris might have been added to eliminate the need to chaptalize."

"Makes sense," Kendrick said. "If only everybody had taken that path instead of clonal planting." He arranged the four Corsican cheeses on a cutting board and took the corkscrew to the bottle of Zinfandel.

"I'll never forget this Mazis-Chambertin," Baltazaru said. "At least in the world of fine wine, France still has its kings. Try to imagine what we would have if all the reds of the Côte d'Or were planted with this Pinot Noir variety—think of the Pommards, the Volnays we'd be drinking. The Cortons. I've never had a Corton that sings anything like this beauty, His Royal Majesty King Mazis. But now, Kendrick, how is your Zinfandel going to follow our experience with the *grand cru* Mazis? Aren't you worried it will be overshadowed?"

"I always go from young to old to older in any progression of wines. That's just me, perhaps, but it almost always works out. Once, however, I followed a grand old Échezeaux with a Beaujolais Nouveau, and somehow it wasn't at all jarring—maybe because they were both impeccable and totally different, so it was not a competition."

"But I haven't seen the vintage of your California wine. Is it a nouveau?"

"Like I said, younger to older." Kendrick turned the bottle so Baltazaru could see the vintage.

"Are you serious!" he cried. "A 1969—twenty-one years older than the Mazis?"

"I'm not saying another word," Kendrick said.

"By the way," Baltazaru said, finally taking his seat at the table again, "when do you return to California?"

"In about five weeks."

"And you'll be back here when?"

"Not sure yet. I met a woman who has me where I hope she wants me. I'm hers for the asking, you know? But I will have to be gone at least four weeks. I'm going to try to convince her to visit me in Seattle."

Baltazaru mulled it over. "In terms of daylight, that's good timing. Sundown will be early by then. People tend to stay indoors after dark when it's cold out."

"And it can get horribly cold here on this side of the hill," Kendrick said. "After dark, only boar and foxes venture out."

"I brought a camera. At sunrise tomorrow, I'll snap some shots of the antenna. That way, the boys will know what to expect. And you, again I have to insist, not a word to anyone—not to your best friend, not to your girlfriend. If the police were to find out about us, they'd make it a national scandal. My god, Corsica and the United States committing a terrorist act on French soil. Remember, behind bars you'll find no Mazis Chambertin, plus that new girlfriend of yours might not get enough loving on visitors' days to stick it out several years, waiting for your release."

"I'll cut my tongue off before I spill the beans," Kendrick said.

"Spill what beans?" Baltazaru asked.

Kendrick ignored the question—he didn't want to explain what *spill the beans* meant in English and preferred to concentrate on decanting the old Zinfandel. He poured the two glasses half full.

"That color," Baltazaru said, "you can't tell me that the wine has not been refreshed with a younger wine. It looks as young as the Mazis."

"It has been in my cellar since 1971," Kendrick said. "I swear, it has not been refreshed or recorked."

Baltazaru took a good long sniff and declared, "Impossible! It even smells younger than the Mazis. A California wine? Who made it?"

"Joseph Swan," Kendrick said. "No one knows how he produced such great *vins de garde*. Regrettably, he was struck down by cancer before he himself had a chance to observe his wines' superb evolution."

Baltazaru leaned back, shoulders slouched, a crestfallen look on his face.

"I'll never make wines this . . . this majestic."

"Listen to you. Thirty years ago, Corsican reds were cooked before they went into the bottle. And look at yours today. That 1999 red of yours will put the fear into many Bandols or the finest from Tuscany. And you're not finished yet, I hope."

And so it went, hour upon hour, never lacking something to discuss. The next morning, when Kendrick woke up, Baltazaru was gone.

CHAPTER THIRTY-SIX

J udging wine is not the only thing your nose is good for," Lorna said. "That rotten aroma you noticed trailing in Babette's wake? Congratulations. Your suspicions are justified, to put it mildly."

"Do we have to talk about Babette d'Orsini?" Kendrick asked. He was lying on a deck chair on the beach at Le Lavandou, gazing at his sweetie pie, who was spilling splendidly out of her bikini top. A large turquoise umbrella shaded them, about ten feet from where the little wavelets ran out of gas and the white sand beach began. "Here I am," he continued, "looking you over and thinking how fabulous that bikini is for you. Canary yellow becomes you. It makes your skin look uncommonly healthy. Wholesome, you know? Especially right there where your breasts duck for cover under the bikini top."

She watched as his gaze left her eyes and dropped slow-motion downward. His eyes seemed to be trying to will her breasts out of their harness. "Ah," he said, "this is better than talking about Babette any day."

A waitress in a T-shirt and short shorts arrived and asked if they'd like an aperitif and a look at the sandwich menu.

"What do you think?" Lorna asked.

"I think we'll do better across the street at l'Etoile de Mer," he answered. "It's a rule of mine—never order Champagne or wine by the glass from a restaurant right on the beach. It's bound to be a health hazard. I already reserved for us at l'Etoile, but we can lunch where and whenever you wish."

"Let's jump in once more," Lorna said, "then tend to that insatiable appetite of yours."

"Are you implying that I eat too much?"

"Not at all. I was talking about your sexual appetite. But I do have one question. When eating or drinking, is there ever a moment when your mind is not at work, judging?"

"I suppose not," he said. "I guess I'm someone who is always measuring wine and food against the way it should or could be."

"You're given a glass of water. What happens in your mind?"

Kendrick imagined it. He tried to be objective. "I raise the glass to my lips while my nose registers the chemicals, the amount of chlorine, for example. My hand on the glass registers the temperature, and, as the water tilts toward my lips, I've decided whether I really want to drink it or not. Then come the finer points of texture and balance and minerality, depending, of course, on how urgent my thirst happens to be."

"And when you look at me," Lorna continued, "are you forever silently judging me esthetically?"

My god, he thought, *what have I gotten myself into?* He looked her up and down. *If I swear to her that she is absolute perfection, would that put an end to this perilous interrogation?* Something told him it would be difficult to defend either a yes or no answer, so he leapt up without a word, ran into the water, and dove into a wave. He stayed swimming underwater for at least sixty seconds before surfacing and turning to look back toward the beach. Her lounge chair was empty, but he saw the top of her head and her arms as she plowed out through the surf to meet him.

"You're evading the question," she sputtered.

"Very perceptive, Sherlock, but I refuse to answer on the grounds that, yeah, I might get myself into hot water." He figured the splash of seawater she delivered him full in the face was a small price to pay.

Once they were seated for lunch and their table decorated by two glasses of Cassis blanc, Kendrick felt safer, more in his element. They were dining outdoors in an enclosed patio under the shade of a parasol.

As they studied the menu, a couple businessmen took a table behind Lorna. They were both in suits and ties while everyone else was dressed for the beach. The waiter took the order from Kendrick: two *moules marinières* and a *loup de mer* (or sea bass) grilled for two. Kendrick knew the restaurant, so he told the waiter to ask that the cook hold off on the sauce he uses at the barbecue—"Just lemon slices on the plates will do."—and to take the fish off the grill right *before* it was done.

Lorna asked, "Why's that?"

"The fish are as fresh as anybody could ask, but the cook always bastes the fish while it's cooking. I've been back there with him and seen how he does it. And it is systematic. He has a big paintbrush and dips it into a pot of sauce that seems to neutralize or at least hide the taste of the fish. Plus, he always leaves the fish on the grill just long enough to dry it out a bit."

Their glasses of Cassis were refilled (or "refreshed" as they say in the fancy joints) when the black iron pot of mussels was lowered onto the table. The waiter lifted off the heavy lid and the garlicky, winey perfume spread through the air. With a large dipper, he scooped out some mussels and broth into two soup bowls. At the same time, one of the two businessmen behind Lorna pulled from his inside suit pocket two sausage-sized cigars. As Kendrick and Lorna smiled and proceeded to dig into their mussels, a match flamed, and the two cigars were sucked and coaxed into life. A thick, gray smoke rose into the businessmen's parasol, hit its underside, and the sea breeze caught it and swirled it down right onto Lorna and her soup bowl. The stench was gruesome. Kendrick saw what was happening, jumped up out of his chair, and sped over, looking for a waiter. The only one he saw was a young woman serving water and bussing tables. When Kendrick—yes, pissed off about the experience—told her what was happening, she looked around for the waiter, too, who quickly noticed them and hurried over. Once he realized what was happening, he apologized profusely but said there was nothing he could do, that on the patio, under French law, it was perfectly legal to smoke. Lorna walked up to join them wearing a disgusted grimace, her nose all scrunched up.

"Doesn't the restaurant have rules against noxious fumes?" Kendrick asked the waiter.

Lorna added her two cents. "Listen, no one can eat in the middle of a tobacco cloud like that."

"Sorry," the waiter said again. "If it were up to me, I'd have a rule. It's obnoxious. There's no excuse for it. But I'm afraid all the outdoor tables are full now. Maybe you'd prefer to be seated inside where smoking is prohibited. No one is in there so far. You'd have it to yourselves."

Kendrick considered his choices. The food wasn't bad, there were some decent wines on the list, and he'd never found anything else acceptable in Le Lavandou. *And* it was time to eat!

The waiter reseated them inside and said, "The bottle of Cassis is on the house. Dreadfully sorry about all this. We'll start you all over again with a fresh pot of mussels."

Lorna raised her glass for Kendrick to clink. He did so, but he still wore half a snarl on his face. "Come on," Lorna said, "let's enjoy ourselves. Don't you care about Babette and Branislav?"

"You'd think it would be easy to make the restaurant experience a pleasure, wouldn't you?"

"Oh god, no, Kendrick. Are you serious? There are a million big and little details that can go wrong. Stick to wine, if you ask me." She smiled and leaned her pretty head to one side. Her expression said *Can't we go back to having fun yet?*

The wine importer melted into pudding. *Ain't love grand?* As they wined and dined, Lorna told him about Babette. She had prepared a complete dossier but wanted to sum it up in person. The trail led from France to Italy to Serbia. Luckily, Babette and Branislav had angered a few family members who were quite excited by the opportunity to tell all.

"Babette was born Snežana Trbovich in Guča, Serbia, where her father was a prison guard. Her mother died when she was ten. Two years later, her father remarried and, with his new wife, had a son, Branislav."

She stopped, seeing that Kendrick's mind was trailing just a little behind. Finally he looked up at her. "Branislav?"

"Yes."

"The same, um, Branislav?"

"The one, the only, Branislav Trbovich."

"But wait. If the prison guard . . ."

"Simo Trbovich."

"If Simo fathered Babette *and* Branislav, that makes them . . ."

"Hip hip hooray," Lorna cheered. "Branislav is Babette's half brother."

Kendrick continued to swirl his wine glass absent-mindedly while computing the various possibilities. "Well," he said finally, "they could just be rooming together."

"It gets juicier. At sixteen, she married a guy named Nadir Jankovich. That lasted through an abortion and Nadir's losing a leg in a tree-cutting accident. Maybe Babette didn't like being married to an amputee, because she quickly divorced him. Three years later, she was jailed in Belgrade for prostitution."

"That's great! How cool? There is no way Poupon is going to marry a whore. That's his favorite swear word. I can just hear him. *Putain de merde! My princess, my Babette, a hooker.*"

The fish arrived and was deboned by their waiter. Alongside it were crisp fries and on each plate a little bowl of aioli. Lorna squeezed lemon onto her sea bass while Kendrick tried a fry. "Not bad," he decided out loud.

"The fish is perfect," Lorna said. "Better than I can do, anyway. I'm not much of a cook."

"Prove it," Kendrick said.

"Cook for you? Do you really want me to suffer a nervous breakdown?"

They concentrated on eating for a while before Kendrick said, "Then we'll cook together."

"What if I don't chop the onions fine enough or the aioli falls apart or I cook the pigeons too long? Will you freak out?"

"Not if we cook naked," Kendrick said.

Lorna laughed.

"What's so funny about that?" he asked.

"Nothing, dear, in fact, it's good to hear that something is more important to you than the quality of food and wine."

After the fish, they each had a green salad and ordered coffee.

"Back to Babette?" Lorna asked.

"There's more? Great! The more the merrier."

"Get ready! When Babette was thirty-one years old and named Snežana Jankovich, she married again . . . Wait a minute, let me find the name of the town . . . She married a nineteen-year-old boy in Vukovar, Croatia, and again became Snežana Trbovich."

"You mean she changed her name back to her maiden name? Well, what's so unusual about that? My mother did the same when she left my father."

"No, her name changed back to her maiden name when she married Branislav Trbovich—her brother."

Kendrick was overwhelmed trying to add it all up in his mind, when Lorna said, "Yes, so far we've got her on charges of prostitution, incest—or at least half incest—suspicion of murder, and Kendrick, I ain't finished yet!"

Lorna sat back and exulted over a job well done.

"Unbelievable," Kendrick said. He signaled the waiter for a little more coffee. "It is all beyond anything I'd imagined. But how will I tell Poupon? And, my god, you say there's more?"

"Blackmail in Torino," she said.

CHAPTER THIRTY-SEVEN

For almost a month, Kendrick had been agonizing, trying to come up with the right way to inform Poupon of the facts of life pertaining to his girlfriend, Babette d'Orsini. One chilly evening after dinner, the inspiration came to him while he and Lorna were snuggled up in bed in front of the fireplace, watching a movie, *Babette's Feast*, from 1987. In the film, the austere, pious, puritanical villagers on a remote coast of northern Denmark turn somewhat euphoric during a feast of French wine and cuisine, which gave Kendrick an idea. Why not prepare a special meal for Poupon with some great bottles, try to overwhelm him with deliciousness, and then reveal the odious truth Lorna's investigation had unearthed? Feasting had to be better than simply handing over the dossier or mailing it to Poupon anonymously. In fact, Kendrick doubted the big lug would read it, wondered if Poupon ever read anything.

But upon what, exactly, would they feast? Lorna was no help because she still hadn't met Poupon. He looked through some cookbooks. Richard Olney's *Ten Vineyard Lunches* proposed French regional menus to be accompanied by local wines. *Lulu's Provençale Table* had some great ideas, dishes that would really bring out the best in any Provençal wines he might choose to serve. He revisited M. F. K. Fisher's wonderful tale, *Define This Word*, from 1936, which recounted a blissful meal she ate all alone, the sole client in a remote Burgundian auberge. Burgundian wines, however, were not going to send Poupon and his Provençal palate off into blissful consciousness, but Kendrick was committed to filling Poupon with the same kind of awe M. F. K. Fisher experienced in that auberge. It had to be magical!

Inspiration arrived in a mundane fashion. He was approaching Nice on his way to dinner with Lorna when he saw for probably the two hundredth time in his life the road sign for Monaco, Menton, and Vintimiglia, the first Italian town across the border. He thought back to the first time he had decided to leave the autoroute behind and headed due north from Vintimiglia, up, over, and down into Cuneo and the Piemonte by way of the Col de Tende—a breathtaking drive full of steep zigzagging climbs up giant mountains—climbs worthy of Corsica, and, in fact, part of the same Alpine chain. Near the top at 6,135 feet was a two-mile tunnel built in 1882.

Piedmont? Hmm. Drinking Barbera, Barolo and Barbaresco. And Piedmont in November? Nothing less than the season for magnificent white truffles!

From Lorna's he telephoned Aldo Lignetti, one of his producers in Monforte d'Alba, and found out that the truffle season was only a day or two away from opening and that freezing weather and cold ground were assuring a top-quality crop. Then Kendrick invited Lorna to go to Monforte with him. When? Next weekend, and be sure to take the following Monday off so she could be at the feast for Poupon. That afternoon, he drove back home and dropped by Poupon's place at aperitif time to invite him to Milles Vents for dinner Monday next, which would be the day after his return with the white truffles.

"There's someone I want you to meet," Kendrick said to Poupon.

"Ah, your special someone? The one you've been hiding from me? Aren't you afraid of what she'll do when she meets a real man?"

"Just promise you won't wear aftershave or make any farting sounds. I'll have some older wines to taste with you."

"Taste? Don't we get to swallow?"

"Of course we'll swallow."

"Then why didn't you say it? You said 'taste with you.' You Americans are such puritans."

Friday afternoon, Kendrick took off for Lorna's and spent the night again. Early Saturday morning, they hit the road for Italy. Autumn had settled in, and the morning was close to freezing. A mist hovered close to the ground, but not a blinding mist—more like a vapor. Right after crossing the border into Italy, they left the autostrada, turned north, and followed the course of the Roia River up into the mountains. The road kept going from Italy into France and back into Italy again. At each crossing, there were old customs stations, thoroughly deserted these days of the European Union.

Kendrick was proud of himself because he'd remembered to bring along the perfect CD for their trip. Years before, he'd pulled out his favorite Christmas album, *Noëls*, composed by Claude-Bénigne Balbastre, and noticed the songs had been recorded in Tende, performed on an 1807 pipe organ in the village's remarkable cathedral. The pieces were delicate, full of charm and lightness. That it was not yet December did not matter at all—the *Noëls* created a perfect ambience in his little Modus. Kendrick also explained to Lorna that the route via the Col de Tende tunnel took at least an hour and a half longer than the autoroute, but the scenery was something she'd probably never forget. When they exited the long, dripping tunnel, they stopped, and the two of them had a stretch.

"Imagine," Kendrick said, "our third president took this same route over two hundred years ago, before there were cars, before there was a tunnel. Can you imagine such a ridiculous climb? And, as I understand it, he was on a mule!"

"It must have taken days," Lorna said. "I wish we had him back. He apparently played a pretty good violin, by the way, in addition to all his other accomplishments."

"I'll bet it would have been more fun if he'd had you along for the ride," Kendrick said, followed by the most heartfelt kiss he could come up with.

They broke for lunch about half a mile off the main road in an Alpine flavored rock and timber lodge. There was no à la carte menu. Lunch simply began. Thin pink slices of veal with tuna sauce arrived first, then two bite-sized focaccia sandwiches for each, one containing tapenade and the other prosciutto. The main course was a couple barely fried eggs topped with white truffle shavings.

"First of the season," the waiter said, glowing with pride.

The exotic aroma seemed thick and almost psychedelic up in the summit's thin air. Lorna loved the pitcher of white wine—there was no wine list, only pitchers of red or white. Kendrick told her the white smelled like Arneis, a Piemontese grape varietal. Then came a little hunk of Parmigiano-Reggiano for each of them, topped with a few drops of aged balsamic vinegar. Panna cotta. Espresso. In Kendrick's view, all quite civilized.

Once they'd arrived in Contorto d'Alba, he drove up to the top of it to his favorite local hotel, Villa Belmondo. Off in the distance, half the horizon was filled with snow-covered Alps. Around six in the evening, it was already dark out with a starry sky above as they drove down the hill. A few hundred yards outside the city limits, they parked in front of Aldo Lignetti's home and winery. Lorna tasted wine alongside Kendrick and Aldo and hit the spittoon unfailingly, which put a smile on her face. Aldo was an unusual-looking man—his black hair shockingly kinky, and his hairline had not receded one centimeter with age. Above his eyes lay densely packed eyebrows, a little bit of forehead, and then, suddenly, the thick, inky, twisted hair. His face, however was a different story. He was one of those who wrinkled earlier than most. Kendrick figured it must be genetic, because there was a photo of Aldo's father in the same tasting room—super kinky hair, wrinkly face, young hairline, old face—all on the same head.

Around eight they sat down to dinner. The first wine, served with sliced salami, was a cool, slightly sparkling Freisa—a red. After tasting it, Kendrick said, "This is not the Freisa you send to me in the States, is it?"

"No, of course not," Aldo answered. "We can no longer commercialize this kind of Freisa. My father made this one. He's retired, as you know, however, he makes a little Freisa every year for friends and family. I thought you'd like it because you're always asking about the way wine used to be made."

"Why can't it be commercialized?" Lorna asked. "It tastes fine to me. Sign me up. I'll take a case."

Aldo said, "The old-timers ate a lot of salami and always drank Freisa with it. It was a bit *frizzante,* but back then the sparkle was difficult to control. Sometimes it sparkled a little, sometimes a lot.

Nobody cared, but then it was consumed right around here and everyone understood. It was a living being, like a family, no two bottles identical."

"You could say the wine was less tamed. Less civilized, less predictable," Kendrick said. "In the Loire Valley in France, Vouvray Petillant was like that. Each bottle had its own sparkle, its own personality, and the locals understood that. Nowadays, the public doesn't accept deviations from bottle to bottle, but the fact is, deviations can be good or bad."

"Yes," Aldo said, "those wines had a certain charm, but especially with red wines that sparkle, you send them to the US or to a restaurant for tourists in Rome, people say it must be a flaw, so now we make sure there is no fizz at all before it goes into bottle."

"And the name," Kendrick asked, "why the name Freisa? Does it mean anything?"

"It's made from the Freisa grape," Aldo said. "And the name goes back centuries. It is a grape native to the Piedmont. DNA research, however, shows that it is very close in profile to the Viognier, which of course is a white grape from the other side of the Alps, in France."

"It must have turned white crossing the Alps to get to France," Lorna said.

Aldo laughed. "I imagine it was a scary journey before the automobile was invented."

"Strange," Kendrick said, "because Viognier has nothing in common with Freisa."

"*Freisa* sounds like it could be Italian for 'strawberry,'" Lorna said.

Aldo said no. "In Italian we say *fragola* for 'strawberry,' and the Latin is *fragom*."

"Well, there's the *F, R* and the *A* at least," Lorna said. "I wonder where the French *fraise* comes from, if not Latin."

"Do you ever notice a strawberry-like fragrance in Freisa?" Kendrick asked.

"Maybe," Aldo said, "but no more than cherry or raspberry."

"*Freisa* could mean 'fresh,'" Kendrick said. "It is drunk young and fresh, never aged a long time."

"We drink it up during its first year in bottle," Aldo said.

"*Fresh* is '*frais*' in French," Lorna said.

"Or the feminine *fraiche*," Kendrick added. "And *fresco* in Italian, words not far from *freisa*."

Finally Lorna changed the subject by pointing to a bowl in the center of the table. "What are those weird-looking things?" she asked.

"White truffles," Aldo answered.

"Like we had on the eggs at lunch," Kendrick said to Lorna, "but, wow, a whole bowl of them?"

"We dug some up from our vineyard this morning," Aldo said.

"There must be a small fortune in that bowl." Kendrick picked one up and held it up for Lorna to smell.

"My god!" she said. She seemed to search her mind but couldn't find anything to add.

"Almost all wineries here have truffles growing in their vineyards and nearby woods," Aldo said. "We've always had them on the table like this during the season. So to us, we don't pay a cent for them."

"But if you sold them," Kendrick said, "you'd make a good bit of money."

"We don't look at it like that."

"Everyone should be so lucky," Kendrick said.

"Really, when you think about it, it is only during my generation that they've been shipped all over the world and become so valuable. It is simply a part of our year—like the fruit from our trees."

"So it's sort of like when I put a bowl of apples on my kitchen table," Lorna said.

"Very much like that," Aldo said. "We don't take them for granted, but they are a normal part of our year. The nice thing is, I'm not going to weigh the truffles before and after grating one like they do in restaurants, so each of us can put as much as we want on our pasta."

Bowls of steaming *tajarin,* the egg-rich pasta of the Piedmont, arrived. The three each had their own truffle to grate, and so they did, and as the truffle slices floated down onto the hot pasta, there was an explosion of perfume enveloping the table. Next came plates of chopped raw veal. Each took a turn with the grater. Kendrick swore it was the best tartare he'd ever eaten. Lorna made wordless sounds of appreciation. Aldo explained that the veal was from a special race of beef raised on Alpine slopes: *vitello di fassone*. Then came slices of roast pheasant on a steaming hot puddle of white polenta.

"I know tomorrow is Sunday," Kendrick said as he and Aldo enjoyed an after-dinner smoke with the dregs of a twenty-six-year-old Barolo, "but do you think it could somehow be arranged? I'd love to buy some white truffles and *vitello di fassone* to take back to France with me for a special occasion."

Aldo said he could easily arrange it. His sister has a restaurant in Monforte, so, no problem.

"Enough for four or five people will do," Kendrick said.

"Then stop in around eleven. Delizie di Sonio di Gemma, on the road to Serralunga."

"That's your sister's place? I've been there. Always good, always full of locals instead of tourists. All these years, and I never knew it was your sister's. One of the waitresses looks like Anna Magnani, right?"

"Yes, that's the one. That's Irani, the redheaded Anna Magnani, an aspiring jazz singer. The restaurant is unpretentious, no frills, so the tourists avoid it. Why don't you and Lorna meet my wife and me for lunch tomorrow? I'm sorry she couldn't be here tonight, and so is she. She has the late shift at the hospital."

"So, who made this wonderful meal for us?"

"My mother, but she's so shy, I couldn't talk her into joining us for dinner."

"Well, sorry to have to miss lunch with you, but I have some work to do, so Lorna and I will have to eat on the run on our way back to France."

The following day, once they'd picked up the veal and truffles, they set out southwest toward Dogliani d'Alba. The fog was so thick, Kendrick could only see about ten feet ahead. They chugged along at under ten miles an hour. The fog, however, seemed not to exist for the locals, who knew exactly what lay ahead and zoomed around the Modus with an impatience Kendrick sensed intensely. On the outskirts of Dogliani the fog lifted, and he took the narrow paved road up to Cissone, an nondescript village with a population of two hundred, a church, a post office, and three restaurants. Kendrick parked near the restaurant Trattoria di Colma. At noon, the bells began to ring, sounding cracked and senile. In the cozy restaurant bar, Kendrick and Lorna ordered glasses of Arneis and sat down on a sofa near the fireplace. Suddenly, the chill in the air outdoors, the dense fog, all of it seemed fun and exciting. Kendrick asked for the restaurant's wine list. He wasn't there for the food—he wanted to study the collection of older Piemontese wines. When they were seated at a table, Kendrick ordered a 1995 Barbera d'Alba from Cantina Porro.

The waiter asked in English, "You're American, aren't you?" He was a fresh-faced young man in Levi's and a purple Milano soccer shirt.

"Both of us, yes," Kendrick said.

"Congratulations—you're the first American who has ever ordered an old Barbera from us."

"How old is ever?" Kendrick asked.

"What do you mean?"

"I meant, how long have you been working here?"

"Oh, yeah, got it. I'm the chef's son, so I've been in the restaurant, working or not, since I can remember."

"Your English is great," Lorna said.

"I spent a year in New York at Babbo," he said. "Anyway, the only Piemontese wine Americans want to drink is Barolo, Barolo, Barolo."

"It's the most expensive," Kendrick said, "so they think it must be the best." He explained that he was in the wine business, imported several Piemontese domaines, and along the way had learned to appreciate aged Barbera.

After lunch, Kendrick asked to speak to the chef, the boy's father. "I just have a moment," he said when he arrived at their table. "Still plenty of diners to feed, you see?" He gestured toward the ten or so tables, which had all filled up.

Kendrick quickly explained that he was an importer, shipping Italian and French wines to the US, and that this was his fifth or sixth meal in Cissone. "I'm making a special Piemontese meal for a French winemaker tomorrow. I have white truffles and *vitello di fassone* in the trunk of my car, but in France, I can't find the best Italian wines. Nothing but cheap, badly stored plonk. Would you consider selling me three or four older Barberas and Barolos?"

The chef looked off in the distance, thinking about it, then jerked himself back to attention. "Yes, but too busy now. Come back at three thirty or four."

The two had time for a brisk hour's walk around the hills of Cissone. A strong breeze had appeared while they were inside eating and was responsible for the shower of autumn leaves. When they returned, they ordered coffee at the bar and sat again in front of the fire. Once the other customers were gone, the chef turned out to be totally agreeable. Kendrick had to promise to say nothing to anyone about their transaction because it was not quite legal, especially as payment was required in cash. Kendrick selected four older bottles and paid the same price that appeared on the wine list. He considered himself lucky. The wines went into the trunk, each bottle rolled up in a good bit of newspaper to protect it. They drove away with another hour of sunlight left in the day. Kendrick knew the route—get on the autostrada to Savona, then onward west to Nice and Le Caniveau—around four hours, with the raw veal safely on ice.

CHAPTER THIRTY-EIGHT

Kendrick and Lorna woke up around eight a.m., groping sleepily under the sheet, Kendrick on his right side, Lorna almost flat on her back with her legs bent over his hips. That way, lifting the sheet, he could see a lot of her, and her lips were within reach for some tender kisses. The culmination was long, slow, and still showed a proportion of drowsiness. When Kendrick could manage, he cleared his throat. "Wow, that one came all the way from my toes."

"How romantic," Lorna said, wearing a playful, sexy grin that made him wonder about spending the rest of the day in bed. "So erogenous, aren't they, toes?"

In order to perfect the dishes planned for Poupon's feast, Kendrick decided to prepare a test run for lunch. In Monforte d'Alba, he'd purchased a package of *tajarin* pasta. They cooked some and ate it with one of their truffles, but they did not ooh and aah as much as he'd expected, even though the truffles alone supplied an emphatic sensation of bliss.

He told Lorna, "White truffles like to be served with eggs and egg things, and this brand of pasta isn't eggy enough. It's like putting truffles on flour."

"Your chickens do such a good job—shame to waste their eggs. I'll throw together some tagliatelli, because I don't know how to make *tajarin*. I'd never even heard of it before we went to Contorto d'Alba."

Kendrick liked her idea and grabbed a couple books about Italian cuisine. As far as he could tell, *tajarin* was a flat pasta like tagliatelle, but made without egg whites—yolks only, and plenty of them. So that's how they decided to proceed for Poupon's dinner. Then he called Aldo's sister at her restaurant and asked if she added anything to her chopped raw veal before it left her restaurant's kitchen for the table and the final crowning dose of fresh truffle shavings.

She kindly explained, "I gave you the rump, the best cut for tartare. Our family chops it finely with a good, heavy, super-sharp knife, then adds some olive oil—on the delicate side, if you have a choice—salt, pepper, a drop or two of lemon juice, and a tiny bit of anchovy paste. Be sure to mix it with your hands, not a fork or spoon."

Kendrick sharpened a large knife with a curved blade that was made for chopping and mincing. First he cut the veal into little hunks and then began rocking the knife up and down to mince the meat even more finely. The meat was easy to work with, and he quit mincing before the veal could turn mushy. At the same time, he was wondering if the *Fassone* veal would make a good hamburger patty. His quest for a gastronomically remarkable hamburger kept him entertained.

Earlier, he'd taken a gift from Poupon out of the freezer, a frozen rabbit that Kendrick intended to braise slowly in Barbera. However, that would be for their dinner's main course—no need for a practice run—so, after lunch he and Lorna took her convertible and drove to Bandol. He guided her to the harbor and told her to park in what looked like an illegal parking space, but he'd never been ticketed there. It was convenient for catching the little ferry, which went back and forth to Bendor, a tiny island a mere five minutes away. The ferry wasn't cheap, and since Bandol didn't attract big spenders, Bendor was always relatively deserted. They toured the island on foot—taking only about thirty minutes—and he showed her where he liked to dive off the rocks into the Med when weather permitted. They waited ten minutes for the ferry back, then returned to Milles Vents for a nap. Before getting out of bed, they discussed the chores before them, and Kendrick revealed an offbeat idea for the wine he'd be serving.

"We're going to tell Poupon all about Babette, but at first we won't tell him who we're talking about. We'll begin with the prostitution charges when she was just getting started. Do you know how to draw at all? How much of a calligrapher are you?"

"I'm possibly above average," she answered, "but not a pro. More of a dabbler."

"Great, because I want to make fake labels for the wines I'm uncorking tonight. They'll be chapter headings in the story of Babette d'Orsini."

"Meaning?"

"The first wine, we'll label it Whore, but in French, of course, for Poupon. Then on to the other juicy titles."

"Incest, for example?"

"I have a wine to start with that would actually work well labeled Whore, but how would I do Incest? Oh well, maybe it's all right if the name on the label is not really relevant to the wine in the bottle. You follow me?"

"Oh yes, but I think it'll be better if it's relevant. You're saying that the first wine has something whorish about it."

"That's it," Kendrick said. "Cheap thrills, too much makeup, a vulgar exhibitionist. See what I mean? Lacking discretion."

"All that in a wine? I would never have imagined."

"You'll taste it tonight with Poupon and see for yourself."

"Do you have any reason to be anti-whore?" she asked.

"No, I'm not anti-whore. However, given the choice, I'd rather be with you."

"Oh, Kendrick, you say the nicest things. And I'll bet I'm cheaper, too. Hmm, we'd better move this conversation forward. So, Babette and Branislav are half sister and half brother. Maybe you could fill a bottle with half Barbera and half Barolo and label it Incest."

Kendrick found that hilarious, but he wondered if Poupon would get the joke. "Well, anyway, we have to cook *and* design four labels today."

"I'll get dressed," Lorna said.

"Oh no you won't."

"What, you think we have time to play around again before work begins?"

"No, dear. We're going to work without getting dressed."

"Are you crazy? What if a neighbor comes up to the door to the kitchen? It's a window door. See-through."

"I'll hang up the cork curtains again. It only takes a minute."

"We'll freeze to death."

"I turned up the heat in there before our nap. We'll be fine. And besides, you owe me."

"I owe you? What are you talking about? I owe you prancing around in the kitchen naked all afternoon?"

"I won the bet, remember?"

She didn't remember any bet, but in time, she gave in. Kendrick had a blast. He told her she was a sight for sore eyes and that work in the kitchen was no longer work. Then they ended up putting bits and pieces of white truffle—a little bit here, a little bit there—and back to bed they went to lick the crumbs off one another. One thing led to another . . . What a world.

They got dressed again and attacked the label-making chores, which they didn't take at all seriously. Finally, they ended up with four of them, and Lorna pasted them on the chosen bottles while Kendrick prepared the rabbit for the oven—white wine instead of Barbera, lots of thyme branches, unpeeled cloves of garlic, salt, and pepper.

At eight, the Mighty Hunter himself drove up in his camionette. He looked freshly shaved and showered but was not in his macho pussy-wagon attire. He looked presentable and eager to have a good time.

"Here's the woman I told you about," Kendrick said. "Lorna Darlington, meet the one, the only, Henri Poupon."

They cheeked, and Poupon leaned back to take her in. "As usual, Kendrick, your taste is impeccable. Leave it to you to pick the most beautiful woman on the Riviera."

Lorna smiled and blushed just right.

"Lorna. Is that correct? Lorna. We don't have that name in France. At least not in Provence. But I like it. We *should* have it in Provence."

"Poupon," Kendrick said, and finally Poupon turned toward him. They shook hands. "Let's move into the living room by the fire. I apologize because I'm going to force you to at least taste one white wine. You don't have to drink it, though."

Kendrick brought out three glasses, poured the white, and put the bottle on the mantel of the fireplace so Poupon couldn't quite see it clearly.

The three of them sniffed. Poupon had a nose-jerk reaction, actually backing his head away from the glass.

"*Mon dieu*, that one's not shy, is it?"

"It has a lot of perfume," Kendrick said.

"What did they do," Poupon asked, daring to manage another sniff, "add perfume?"

"Probably not. No, it's from a winemaker I know well. Not the type to dress up his wines."

"Dress up is well said. Dressed to kill, red dress, high heels and all," Poupon said.

They each had a sip.

"*Putain!*" Poupon blurted, almost in anger. "What's in here, syrup?"

"It's a sweet wine. A lot of good wines are sweet. Baltazaru's Muscato is sweet. Château d'Yquem is sweet."

"Fine, but this is what we call a whore, *un vin putain*."

"What's wrong with that?" Kendrick asked.

"Well, you know, a whore sells her body."

"What's wrong with that?"

"You know what I mean. Nothing is real. It's all faked to get your money. What is this? A fruit cocktail?" Kendrick handed the bottle to Poupon, who said, "What the hell? The name of the wine is *Putain*? Is that legal?"

Lorna spoke up. "I like it a lot. That aroma is sexy. If she's a whore, she's a real temptress. And the sweetness—after that huge, fruity perfume, wouldn't it seem weird if it was austere on the palate?"

"Here's the truth," Kendrick said. "This is a Gewurztraminer from Alsace, and, in my opinion, a good one. Too sweet to drink with dinner, but as an aperitif or a dessert wine, well, that bouquet is amazing."

"It's all show," Poupon said. "It glitters like gold, but it's fool's gold. And that label. You can't tell me that it is your winemaker friend's real label. It looks like it was made in nursery school."

Kendrick explained that the wine was part of a story, that Lorna was a private investigator and had been working on an unusual case that could be of interest to Poupon. Lorna took over and explained about Snežana Trbovich in Croatia, and how she had been arrested at a young age for prostitution. Poor Poupon looked swamped. He couldn't figure out what the hell the two loonies were up to. From Gewurztraminer to Snežana, he was in foreign territory. At table, right before the truffled egg pasta appeared, Kendrick set down a bottle of red wine. Of course the label did not say half Barbera half Barolo, but that's what it was. Poupon looked at it as if his mind had just absorbed another foreign object that threatened to lobotomize him. He raised both eyes and read the label out loud. "L'Incest." After a pause, he continued, "We are going to drink incest?"

Kendrick poured the wine. They enjoyed a glass, then he put the hot bowls of pasta on the table and grated a third of a baseball-sized truffle over each bowl.

Boom! The ravishing perfume filled the room. Forks in hand, they chowed down with an almost manic glee—Jack Nicholson in *The Shining!* Poupon opened his large, beige, cloth napkin, draped it over his head so the perfume from the steaming bowl could not escape, then leaned over his pasta and continued eating.

Throughout the first course, Poupon said nothing. However, odd noises did emerge as he chewed and tried to mentally cope with what he was experiencing. Once the bowls were empty, he took the napkin off his head and let out a long sigh of contentment.

"Remarkable," he said. "The best pasta in my entire life."

"Lorna's handmade pasta," Kendrick said, "made with eggs from the chicken coop behind the house."

"No more fox attacks?"

"No, but I had to dig a ditch almost half a meter deep and fill it with cement. That's how they got in that time—they dug under the coop's foundation."

Kendrick poured more l'Incest, and Poupon looked at Lorna and winked. "You're some catch," he said, "but so is Kendrick. It seems that at least for the moment, you've chosen him to receive your love. I can tell by the way you two act. And you've chosen well. He's become one of my true friends, and knowing him has changed me, changed the way I taste, the way I make my wine. He has uncorked so many bottles for me. An education, really. Before meeting him, I knew only our local wines. He's given me his advice much more like a friend than a client. Now I have an idea of how big the world of wine is, and that the wines I had been making were of fair quality. For here. But a long way from making ripples anywhere else. And you can trust Kendrick for sure. He's not the kind of guy to have a girlfriend in every appellation."

Poupon took another sniff and sip of the red. "I have no idea what kind of red this is or why you labeled it l'Incest."

Lorna explained the family history of Snežana and Branislav, ending with their marriage.

"Do either of you know," Poupon asked upon hearing it, "when, exactly, relations become incest? The Catholic Fathers didn't go into detail. Cousins marry. Is that a sin? Uncle and niece? Half brother and half sister—does that add up to a whole sin or just half an incest? And this woman, Snežanova . . ."

"Snežana," corrected Lorna.

"She marries her half brother, and yeah, she's twelve years older. But the guy is no longer in diapers. He's nineteen, so you can't serve me a bottle of Pedophilia."

"And we won't," Kendrick said. He'd already cleared the table and prepared the veal tartare. Out came a bottle labeled Le Chantage, which in English meant "blackmail." He decanted the wine and poured some into each glass. Poupon sniffed and asked if it was from the same grape variety.

"Same terroir, different vintage and winemaker, but this one is pure Barolo. Barolo is the place, Nebbiolo, the grape."

Back and forth they went describing the difference between Chantage and l'Incest, the conclusion being that the Barolo/Barbera blend still contained much more aging potential and was the larger, deeper wine. Poupon turned one gnarly hand into a fist and said that the Barolo packed more wallop. Eating the tartare, Poupon announced that it was the best of his life, forgetting his identical compliment for the pasta. It was proof to Kendrick that his friend shared a weakness for white truffles, because he'd topped the veal tartare with them, too.

Kendrick thought the recipe from Aldo's sister was ingenious. The taste and texture of the few assembled ingredients seemed inevitable, definitive, the platonic ideal of steak tartare.

It was altogether too delicious to talk through, so Lorna waited 'til the plates were empty. "Snežana and her half brother–husband left Croatia for Italy, and the first evidence of their presence I could find there was in Torino, where they left a boatload of resentful victims and a warrant for their arrests. They were wanted for blackmail. Their modus operandi? Snežana seduced wealthy businessmen or politicians, and Branislav took photos of them in action. It was more like 'coitus operandi.' The old story: 'Pay up, and we won't release the photos to the press or your family.' When one victim refused and went to the police, two others gathered the courage to appear and offer evidence."

It slowly dawned on Lorna and Kendrick that Poupon was losing his concentration, so they brought out the rabbit along with the final bottle, labeled L'Assassin. Poupon picked it up and read from the label. "It says *Domaine de la Femme Fatale, Mise en bouteille au Croquemort.*"

"Before you continue," Kendrick said to Lorna, "let's pay attention and appreciate our final red, a thirty-year-old Barolo from Alfredo Currado." The fact was, Kendrick did not want Babette's name to come out into the open until Poupon was through chewing and swallowing. He didn't want to kill Poupon's appetite. Finally, they moved to chairs in front of the fireplace, each with a glass of the old Barolo.

"That's class," Poupon said of the Barolo. "I know I can make a Bandol like that. There's no reason why not. That's a wine with character."

"Okay, back to Snežana," Kendrick said. "Lorna, let's hear the last chapter before my friend falls asleep."

"Don't worry about me. *Merde*, I'm ready to match you bottle for bottle. We'll see who falls asleep."

"I'm not worried about that. I've seen you in action plenty of times. You're a rock, but I'm afraid Snežana might have you yawning."

"This Snežana sounds like dynamite," Poupon said. "She had men falling all over. And it appears that they all had a pretty rough landing."

"A rough landing," Lorna said. "That's a good title to our final chapter. So, she and Branislav next appeared in Alghero, in Sardinia. She succeeded obtaining papers with her first husband's family name, so she was traveling as Snežana Jankovich to elude the arrest warrants. In Alghero, she attracted the eye of a nobleman. He had a vacation home in the Catalan section of Alghero, one in Varigotti on the Ligurian coast of Italy, and an apartment in Nice. He was twenty years older than Snežana, and he fell for her. His wife had been dead for a couple years, and he was ripe for the taking. Snežana married Count Leopold Flavinius d'Orsini, chose herself a new first name, and became Babette d'Orsini."

Silence. It became obvious that Poupon's mind had been wandering through a maze. Slowly, he seemed to regain some concentration. "*Merde*," he said, as if angry at himself. "I'm not asleep. But how did Babette get into this story? I missed that part."

Kendrick jumped in. "It's cold outside, I know, but let's get our coats on and have a smoke on the terrace. That should feel good after the food, the wine, and the fireplace."

"Poupon, I'm sorry," Lorna said. "My voice must have hypnotized you."

"Ha, I agree. So now, in the future, your will is my command. Anything you ever need—anything!—you call on me. I'll be there for you, just like I am for your boyfriend here. But let's back up a bit. How did Babette get into the story?"

Poupon pulled out a pack of cigarettes. Kendrick slid one from the pack and lit up. Lorna passed. It was a bright night, the stars were thick in the sky, and the cold freshened them up.

Kendrick got back to the business at hand. "Lorna was explaining how Snežana Trbovich became Babette d'Orsini by marrying Count Leopold d'Orsini. Oh my god! I just realized we could have had a fifth bottle and labeled it La Bigamie because she was still married to Branislav."

Poupon raised a hand. "Wait, wait, wait. So Babette married a count?"

"That's right. Not the richest, but Count d'Orsini all the same."

"Aha, so I was right all along. My Babette is an aristocrat, a countess!"

Kendrick peered up into the starry night and took a long drag on his smoke. *What in god's name do we have to do to get through to this guy?*

Lorna tried backing it up a bit. "So, you heard the part where Snežana changed her name to escape charges of blackmail and moved to Sardinia? Then she married the count and changed her first name to Babette. And you understood the part about bigamy?"

"Yes! That I got. She changed her name back to her first husband's name and therefore when she married the count it was bigamy?"

"Poupon! No!" Kendrick said emphatically, trying to wake him up. "Remember her second husband? She had three, right?"

"And that's bigamy?"

"Her second husband is her half brother, Branislav. When she married the count, she was still married to Branislav. That's bigamy. Two husbands at a time."

"So," Poupon said, "you're saying that all this time, Babette and Snežanovich are the same person."

Lorna and Kendrick answered at the same time, but she said *Correct* and he said *Yes*.

"It's too cold out here," Kendrick said. "Let's go back inside."

Poupon was visibly trying as hard as he could to add it all up, and couldn't, but it was beginning to dawn on him that Babette was more complicated than he'd thought.

He picked up his wine glass as he contemplated. "The empty glass smells like tramping through the woods with my hunting dogs in winter. Hats off to whoever made it."

Kendrick went to the kitchen and came back with the bottle. "Don't forget this label," he said.

Poupon took a look. "L'Assassin," he read aloud. "*Mon dieu*, who murdered who?"

Lorna explained. "The wine wears that label because the marriage was ended by a rather convenient automobile accident. The count—Babette's husband, remember?—rolled and tumbled to his death. He was driving down a winding hillside above San Remo when his car went out of control. There were some questions raised in the police report, but they were never really pursued. Babette ended up with the apartment in Nice where she lives with her half brother and second husband, Branislav."

"However," Kendrick said, "she did not come away with enough to live on. She's a hungry femme fatale looking for a fourth husband."

"Ha, Kendrick," Poupon said, laughing. "Don't you two worry about me. Femme fatale? You think I can't defend myself?"

"Surveillance shows," Lorna said, "that she is not involved with any prospective victims other than you."

"Only you," Kendrick said.

Poupon stood up and flexed his biceps like a weight lifter. "Well, we'll talk later. I'll leave you two lovebirds, and I'll think about everything you told me tonight. Thank you for a dinner I'll never forget."

Lorna handed him her Babette report and advised him to read it later to refresh his memory.

Poupon didn't meet her eye. "I have an idea. One of my biggest fans is a lawyer in Toulon. I'll invite him over, get him drunk, and ask him to explain your dossier."

As his camionette disappeared down the hill from Milles Vents, Kendrick said, "I'll bet he's right. He'll never, ever forget tonight."

"Are you sure?" Lorna asked.

"Are you kidding me? He'll always be able to bring the memory of it back because he'll never forget those funky labels. Wine people are like that!"

CHAPTER THIRTY-NINE

Kendrick finally returned to his native Seattle for the first time in several months. Jet lag and missing Lorna meant lack of sleep, even though she was booked on the same flight to Seattle three weeks later when they would welcome the New Year together. Their goodbye scene at the Marseille-Provence airport was rough on him. They had a last juicy kiss and a long, searching look into each other's eyes before he joined the security line. She walked away and stepped onto the escalator descending to the parking lot. She waved a wilted hand and flashed an insincerely courageous smile as she glided silently downward, disappearing from view—her legs, waist, torso, finally just her head turned back toward him. Then she was gone.

Once in Seattle, the poor sap suffered terribly from jealousy—at his age! He imagined his sweetheart driving her convertible down the autoroute and some handsome trucker signaling her to exit for a rest stop tryst. Her acupuncturist was finding it beneficial to concentrate his treatments on her most private, titillating parts. She went to night clubs filled with handsome Frenchmen—each one debonair in his own lousy way—and she had the pick of the bunch! What was there to stop her?

Finally, she flew into Seattle on December twenty-ninth. They spent a lot of time under the covers helping her adjust to the nine-hour time change. Kendrick, of course, was sitting on top of the world. He loved having her around. They took a late afternoon walk up and down the streets of Seattle, Lorna amazed by the salmon flying through the air at Pike Place Market. The same evening they had a good pizza at Chez Nono, a Chez Panisse graduate. None of those California hippy-dippy toppings, he told Lorna, just tomato, cheese, anchovies, and salt-cured capers, like the good lord intended.

"What's a hippy-dippy pizza?" she asked.

"You know, with pineapple slices, grapefruit and salmon eggs on a crust."

On New Year's Eve, they discussed what they should do to celebrate and voted for a cozy celebration at home—set up a little table in front of the fireplace and throw something on the grill. Around eleven that evening, the phone rang. It was Poupon, which surprised the hell out of Kendrick, because in the years he'd known him, Poupon had never called him from France. Long distance to the US? Have you lost your marbles? Poupon would be feeling each centime like the crack of a whip.

"Bonjour, Poupon," Kendrick said. "Let's see, it must already be New Year's Day for you."

"It's eight o'clock in the morning here, January one, 2007. Where are you? I asked Chantal in your Paris office where you might be reached."

"You called my home number here in Seattle. I'm in my living room with Lorna. We're in front of the fireplace, waiting one more hour before the clock strikes midnight and we uncork a good Champagne to toast you and Zarina and all our friends a happy New Year."

"Zarina is here in bed with me. I won't bother you with details, but we welcomed in the New Year with a big bang."

"Atomic or hydrogen?" Kendrick asked.

"She says I'm learning to be a more nuanced lover, *mon ami*. More finesse! Hey, just like my new reds."

"That's great news, you big lug. I wish you both a happy New Year, and all the best from me and Lorna."

"Kendrick, I'm curious. What's happening with you and cigarettes?"

"Haven't had one since I saw you."

"Oh. Honest? I figured in the USA, without me around, you'd buy your own."

"No, I really only smoke once in a while. Special occasions. What about you?"

"Since you left, zero. I only smoke so you can bum them from me. But listen, I am now going to instantly make your cozy little tête-à-tête even better. You will be amazed. We saw it on the morning news about an hour ago. Pictures of Pageot's property. I even caught a glimpse of Milles Vents. Anyway, someone blew up Pageot's antenna. Toppled it. Nothing left but melted green plastic and pieces of metal that look like bicycle spokes."

"Oh my god!" Kendrick turned to Lorna and said, "Poupon says someone blew up the cell phone antenna down below my house."

"Maybe your neighbor needs a private investigator," Lorna said, which, for a moment, confused the hell out of Kendrick, our pacifistic terrorist.

Poupon continued, "For now, the police don't know who did it. It's good you're far away. You'd probably be one of the first to be interrogated. Tell the truth, are you happy it happened?"

"Better than happy. Ecstatic! I'm going to pull out the oldest, finest Champagne in my cellar and raise a glass to whoever blew it up. This is the happiest New Year's Eve of my life. Lorna right here next to me, for one thing, and no more plastic cypress."

"I can't wait for you to see it. I'll airmail you any newspaper articles I see about it. Zarina says she'll snap some photos."

"And, Poupon, whatever happened with your countess?"

"Ah, yes, la belle Babette. Well, I suppose I finally got it through my thick skull that you and Lorna were only trying to save my life. I realized what kind of scam Babette was trying to pull, so I had to come up with a revenge to fit her crime. That's because I'm Provençal. Remember The Count of Monte Cristo? We never forget, never let bygones be bygones. Ha! You'll never believe what I dreamed up for Babette. That witch! She is one big gob of shit, right?"

"That's one way to put it," Kendrick said.

"Well, now her apartment is, too—chicken, horse, dog, and yours truly. I got into her apartment and left her quite a present. It'll be months before anyone can live in there without a gas mask. And she might have trouble finding someone to clean and repaint the walls.

Whoever does it is going to have to be truly hard up for work. I rigged up a sort of splatter gun. Use your imagination. I wish I'd seen her expression when she walked in."

"Bravo, Poupon. You really lived up to your name."

"What are you saying?"

"I'm saying that by splattering poop all over the place, you're living up to your name."

"Kendrick, you're trying to be funny. I can tell. But what you say has no meaning."

"Well, in English it does."

"I don't speak English. Remember? You should sign up for joke lessons."

Lorna shook her head in disbelief. "*Poop on?* Really, my love? How could you ever have thought he would understand that?"

After Lorna returned to Nice, Kendrick had to spend six more lonely weeks in Seattle. They were still at the can't-keep-their-hands-off-each-other stage, but fifty-five hundred miles apart.

The gendarmes showed no sign of suspecting Kendrick as the culprit in the antenna bombing case. However, according to Zarina, they did arrest the leader of an environmental group that actively opposed cell phones and their antennas but then released him after three days of interrogation. Those were rough days for Kendrick. He feared he might have to confess if they charged the wrong guy with the crime—even though Gianni had warned Kendrick that he'd need a new pair of balls if ever he ratted on the bombers. And if he confessed, then refused to divulge to investigators the names of his accomplices? That could have meant a stiff sentence.

Six days before Kendrick's flight back to France, Poupon called again and claimed that eating mussels is known to be the best cure for jet lag. And, according to him, other cell phone companies had given up the idea of erecting any new antennas on Kendrick's hillside. Too risky. He also mentioned that he'd purchased a Fiat for Zarina. "She told me you offered to buy her a car, but forget it, no problem. I took care of it. From now on, you can keep your lousy car out of my garage," he said, laughing. "Trust me. I am capable of taking care of Zarina all by myself. And get your sorry ass over here, my friend. I don't know what to do with myself, and I worry I don't drink enough without you."

"Believe me, Poupon, I'm ready to get out of here. I had lunch at a fine French restaurant down in San Francisco last week, and only two other tables in the whole place were having wine with lunch. I felt like I was in Bakersfield."

"What's a bakersfield?"

ACKNOWLEDGMENTS

To John and Fran Freeman, a couple of UC Berkeley grads who married and moved in next door to me during my San Luis Obispo High School days. They turned me on to music, largely Beethoven (but I branched out), and to wine at table with meals. Yes, folks, meals. Plural. Lunch and dinner. Very civilized behavior. Thank you, Freemans. And what a coincidence. Kermit just happens to mean Free Man in the Irish language.

To Sharon Bowers, my literary agent who has become much more: pals, cohorts, passionate editors. With Sharon along for the editing of *Poupon*, it was a gas, gas, gas, punctuated frequently by peels of laughter. "Uh, Kermit, don't you mean peals? And isn't peals of laughter—don't take this badly—a mite cliché?"

And with thanks to the hard-working team at Podium for their confidence and enthusiastic support—in other words, excellent working conditions—including Stephanie Beard, Laura Vorhees, Erin McClary, Mindy Fichter, Taylor Vaca, Elizabeth Yaffe, Taylor Bryon, Daniel Wikey, and Nicole Antos.

ABOUT THE AUTHOR

Kermit Lynch is a world-renowned wine merchant as well as an author and singer-songwriter, having published three books, including the award-winning *Adventures on the Wine Route*, and recorded five albums. Although his hometown of Berkeley, California, is only one hour away from the prized vineyards of Napa Valley, Lynch felt called to the other side of the globe to specialize in French wines. Today, bottles bearing his import strip are sought by the most discerning wine lovers. His many accolades include having been knighted by the French government with the Légion d'Honneur, France's highest civilian award, and winning two James Beard awards. Lynch divides his time between Provence and Berkeley, where his distinguished wine store is located.